FEAR ITSELF
NICK WALLACE

DOCTOR WHO:
FEAR ITSELF

Published by BBC Books, BBC Worldwide Ltd,
Woodlands, 80 Wood Lane, London W12 0TT

First published 2005
Copyright © Nick Wallace 2005
The moral right of the author has been asserted.

Original series broadcast on BBC television
Format © BBC 1963
'Doctor Who' and 'TARDIS' are trademarks
of the British Broadcasting Corporation

All rights reserved. No part of this book may be reproduced in any form
or by any means without prior written permission from the publisher,
except by a reviewer who may quote brief passages in a review.

ISBN 0 563 48634 1

Commissioning editors: Shirley Patton and Stuart Cooper
Editor and creative consultant: Justin Richards
Project editor: Christopher Tinker

This book is a work of fiction. Names, characters, places
and incidents are either a product of the author's imagination
or are used fictitiously. Any resemblance to actual people living
or dead, events or locales is entirely coincidental.

Cover imaging by Black Sheep © BBC 2005
Printed and bound in Great Britain by Clays Ltd, St Ives plc

For more information about this and other BBC books,
please visit our website at www.bbcshop.com

For my wife, for my daughter, for always

It was the first lesson we learnt when we reached for the stars: for everything, there is a limit.

No matter how far we had come, how hard we had struggled, there would always be things out there beyond the comprehension of man.

This is inherited knowledge, the lessons of history. It was decades ago that humanity broke free of its chains, leaving Earth behind to venture out into the dark and the cold. And in that time, before I was born, those first hostile encounters took place.

We had left behind our old playground, but didn't yet understand the rules of this new one. A misunderstanding could lead to war in a moment. And with war, that simple lesson to be applied to all our achievements: for everything, there is a limit.

Beings beyond understanding, weapons that could not be matched, forces that were all but unstoppable. The terror must have swept across our race like an ever breaking storm. One minute we stood among the stars, tall and proud; the next, we were beaten back by nightmares manifest. You can see those moments even now, replayed in miniature every time we step into battle. Fear on the faces of the young and the innocent.

Decades since those first moments of terror and so little has changed.

Beings beyond understanding, weapons that cannot be matched, forces that are all but unstoppable. Presented with such obstacles, we find ourselves with the only option we have ever had. To fight.

Such a fight is, of course, no job for an amateur.

MARS

It wasn't that long ago that Anji had sat in her brother's bedroom on a cold winter's night. A cardigan wrapped around her shoulders to ward off the chill, leaning out of the window to smoke a cigarette, a brief first-term habit. Her parents were downstairs, oblivious, watching *Stars in Their Eyes*. Rezaul was next to her at the window, complaining about light pollution as he focused his telescope.

Home for the holiday, astronomy with her brother made a change from long days in the library and long nights in the union.

There'd been a burst of triumph from Rezaul, who'd blindly waved a hand at her, eye fixed on the lens. Anji had stubbed the cigarette out on the underside of the sill, blown the last smoke into the night and pulled back into the room. When Rezaul stepped away, she bent over the telescope herself. Blackness filled her vision. Then, with a blink, she found the orange disc.

Rezaul flicked through an astronomy book, calling out the major features. The Valles Marineris. The polar ice caps. And the biggest mountain in the solar system: an extinct volcano, he'd explained, so tall it pressed the roof of the planet's atmosphere.

Olympus Mons on Mars.

Two hundred years later and they'd built a town there.

It was set on the lip of the caldera, and the view was stunning. On one side of the town, the mountain sloped away to red soil miles below; on the other, a hard drop to the dead heart of the volcano, its far side lost over the horizon.

Looking out through the bubble shell that protected the town, Anji Kapoor watched the sun set over Mars.

'Spectacular, isn't it?' The man was tall, with chestnut hair and an easy smile. 'Sorry,' he said, 'Didn't mean to disturb.'

'That's all right,' Anji replied. 'And, yes, it is spectacular.' She shrugged. 'You're probably used to it.'

'A little,' he answered, leaning up against the rail next to her. 'Sometimes you forget where you are. And then you see something like that and remember.'

'You're not in Docklands any more.' Anji looked past him to where the TV crew were finishing their set-up. 'You're the cameraman, right?'

He nodded. 'Michael.'

'Anji Kapoor.'

They moved away from the blister wall, back towards the crew. 'Why did they pick here for the shoot?' Anji asked, making conversation.

'As good a place as any,' Michael shrugged. 'The foundation work was done by Wal-Mart, supposed to be Mars' first commercial trading post. They sold it on to the government when Sheffield got established here first.'

'No point being second to the market.'

He nodded at her head. 'What happened there?'

Anji fingered the spray-on bandage covering one corner of her forehead. 'A fight of all things.'

He laughed. 'A fight? How does a historian get into a fight?'

'Economist,' Anji corrected. 'Couple of squaddies turned nasty in a café. In Sheffield, as it happens. I didn't do a lot of the fighting.'

'Sounds nasty.'

'I had...' Anji paused. 'I had friends who helped out.'

The director waved. Anji gave Michael a pat on the shoulder. 'Duty calls.'

While Michael returned to his camera, Anji talked the presenter through the on-screen graphics. The woman was bright, but her grasp of old-fashioned capitalist models was slim. Which, Anji supposed, was fair enough. If anyone ever asked her about the trading routes of the eighteenth century she'd be able to murmur some half-remembered history and comment on their economic legacy, but no more than that. She worked in futures, not histories. And that was what her knowledge was to these people: history.

It was weird. Dislocating. But the Doctor had promised to get her home and, bit by bit, he seemed to be getting there.

That was Fitz's spin, anyway: Mars was closer to Earth than Earthworld, even if it was the twenty-second century. Anji wasn't sure who he'd been trying to reassure most: her or the Doctor.

It was as they were preparing the day's final shots that Anji heard it.

The broadcast unit had a small TV showing the network feed. It was just background noise to Anji; there was nothing in the headlines she knew or could easily reference. It was probably why the name leapt out at her. A quiet voice talking of news just in and unconfirmed reports.

'Turn it up,' Anji whispered, but nobody heard. She started pushing through the crew. 'Turn it up!'

And finally somebody did.

– corporation ship reported the signal at ten to four this morning. Military spokesmen are currently refusing to confirm or deny the reports, but long-range scans from civilian arrays can find no trace of the Station –

'Oh, God,' Anji said.

– while little information is publicly available about the research undertaken at Farside Station, the general understanding is that this is one of the key components in Earth Forces' science programme. If, as reports suggest, the Station has been lost with all hands, it's a major blow to –

The world started to spin, her breath roaring in her ears.

'Oh, God,' Anji repeated.

She grabbed at a table for support, sending a jug of water crashing down on to the floor. Someone was at her side then, holding her arm, keeping her upright, but it didn't matter.

It was too late. Two hundred years and millions of miles from home.

'Not this,' Anji whispered. 'This isn't my life.' She fell then, knees hitting hard on the red concrete surface of a Martian town. Someone was calling for an ambulance. Anji wanted to tell them not to bother. There was nothing an ambulance could do.

She wasn't supposed to be here. This wasn't her life.

JUPITER SPACE
Now

It's the eyes that worry O'Connell.

He's been studying the Professional for days now; it's a long flight from Mars' orbit and O'Connell's had little else to occupy his time. He's watched the Professional hustle and tweak the parameters of his suit's AI; fill and seal every scar on his body armour; strip his plasma rifle time and again, cleaning every interface and greasing every moving part.

But for all this, O'Connell can almost believe the Professional might be passed in the street as an unexceptional man.

Medium height and medium build; hair cropped so close to the scalp its colour is all but lost; the long midline of his nose distorted by a break to make a boxer proud. Deep creases around the mouth mean he looks older than he might otherwise seem, while the fat-free jawline just adds to the impression of a face honed by long years in space. In itself it's not exceptional. O'Connell could walk down any street in any one of a hundred towns on the system colonies and see two dozen faces like that.

Except none would have eyes like the Professional's. Cold eyes that have seen too much and speak of things a mouth would never tell.

More than once O'Connell has wondered what a man has to do to get eyes as cold as that. And now, despite himself, staring at the Professional through a flickering viewscreen, he has another thought: if he had seen those eyes beforehand, orders or not, would he ever have agreed to this job?

The shuttle rocks and O'Connell is thrown back in his seat and out of his reverie.

O'Connell's an old-fashioned pilot; a man who, a hundred years back, would have been said to fly by the seat of his pants. He's good at his job – so good his superiors keep throwing him into situations like this one – and likes to think he's sharp enough to ride any storm, just trusting to skill. But part of that skill is knowing enough's enough. And if a sudden wave of atmospheric pressure throws him from his chair and he breaks an arm or a rib, it's all over.

So O'Connell pulls at the harness he never uses. Magnetic catches snap shut and he hauls the straps one notch tighter, just to be sure. He toggles a switch, opening the intercom, and says: 'Buckle up. It's going to be a rough five minutes.'

He's not expecting his passenger to take the advice but feels honour bound to give it anyway. Jupiter's trying to kill them and if a man's going to die, he deserves to know the cause.

'What's happening?' The Professional's crisp tones distort over the speaker.

'Turbulence,' O'Connell says, activating another previously redundant system. The cockpit is normally a tight, dark space; just the bare minimum of flight systems online. For the past half-hour it's been lit up like the Mars Orbital. 'I'm trying to compensate.'

The Professional checks the AI screen on his wrist, then says, 'The correct atmospheric current is 1500 metres below, Lieutenant.'

'I'm aware of that.' A warning flashes red over O'Connell's shoulder. He punches an override and makes another course correction. 'You handle your end of the business, I'll handle mine.'

This time the Professional nods, then turns his back to the camera, checking the seals on his suit one more time.

O'Connell's worked with plenty of soldiers over the years, flown some generals, even carried a government minister one time. He's also worked with other Professionals. Most never take off their armour, never reveal the faces beneath the helmets. But none has been as focused as this man. Not deviating from his own course by a single word or action.

O'Connell checks the intercom is off, mutters that two can play at that game. Then he tilts the shuttle's nose forward and they push on down into hell.

Until now, the orange and red of Jupiter's atmosphere has flared only briefly above the cockpit. It's been comforting to O'Connell to look up and see the stars appear in those gaps, tiny glimpses of what he best calls home. Now there's one last flash of dark and then it's gone.

They're enveloped by gas and tiny particles and God alone knows what else. Just like space, it's as if there's no horizon, no up and down, just some featureless void. Unlike in space, in Jupiter's anonymous atmosphere there is an up and down and it's pretty damn important to get that distinction right. As a crosswind catches the shuttle and throws it at forty-five degrees to the invisible horizon, O'Connell decides – orders or not – it's the last time he's ever doing a job like this. Atmosphere is now, officially, a bigger bitch than O'Connell's ex.

Redlining the engines drops the Professional's 1500 metres to fifteen. Now ten. The crosswind eases. Five. O'Connell gets the shuttle flying almost level. Zero. They're in the right place, and even if the navcom wasn't telling him, the feedback from the controls would. It's not plain sailing, but it's better than it has been for some time.

The Professional is statuesque on the viewscreen, helmet tucked under one arm, plasma rifle locked across his suit back.

O'Connell checks his instruments, reactivates the intercom. 'This is as good as it gets. The signal from the Station's pretty weak. We're in position for now, but that could change in a second and we might not know until it's too late.'

The Professional checks his AI again. 'It's within tolerance. We proceed.'

'Hey,' O'Connell says, 'I'm just playing the percentages, OK?'

The Professional slips the sheer metal helmet over his head. Bad as the intercom is, O'Connell can still hear the seals hiss tight as the suit pressurises. The camera lens is reflected in the helmet, all that is visible where the Professional's face used to be. But, damn, if O'Connell can't still feel those eyes.

'Start the cycle.'

O'Connell almost asks whether the Professional's sure. Instead, he slips a cover back, turns a key and watches a series of lights blink from green to red.

On screen, the airlock doors creep open. There's a moment of stillness as the atmosphere sweeps out of the compartment, the Professional braced against its pull. Then the room gets foggy as Jupiter rushes in to fill the void, O'Connell's passenger a hazy silhouette against billowing clouds.

And despite all his study of the man, part of O'Connell still can't quite believe he's going to go through with it. Until the silhouette steps up to the edge of the airlock, steadies itself and jumps.

O'Connell is sick and impressed at the same time. He's never seen anyone leap to near-certain death before, and having witnessed it once he's almost sure to see it again.

He checks the atmospheric tolerances, then – against everything he's ever held dear – activates the autopilot and releases his harness. Praying nothing bad happens, O'Connell pulls himself back into the shuttle's interior. Slipping one arm around a pipe for support, he powers up a screwdriver and starts undoing the access panel for one of the fuel tanks.

O'Connell's shuttle is old and it shows all the signs of age. Here and there shiny metal shows where broken parts have been replaced or modified to bring them up to date. But it's mostly battered and bruised; surfaces caked with years of blood and grease and dirt. Every screw on every bulkhead is so old and worn you couldn't get a bit to hold on them if you tried.

Except for the screws on this panel. Neat, shiny screws, with a crisp, sharp cross ingrained on their heads. O'Connell has worried about these screws every day since Mars. Worried that the Professional's eyes might settle on them and not move. When the panel falls away, O'Connell's worry is already anonymous within a spacesuit.

He sighs. 'Dammit, lady, I was hoping you'd come to your senses.'

His face dances on the helmet as the stowaway shakes her head. He takes hold of a gloved hand, pulls her back along the shuttle.

'You heard the intercom, you know the signal's weak.' O'Connell glances at her. 'The Station could shift, crosswinds could change, any number of things could go wrong. Be prepared.'

They've reached the airlock now. O'Connell reverses the cycle, lights shifting back to green as filters push Jupiter's atmosphere back out where it belongs.

'First thing to remember is this: you make it down there and he finds you, you were never on board this ship. You were on an independent charter; you shadowed us from the perimeter. You were never here.'

O'Connell hauls the interior door open, catches the stowaway's arm as she steps into the airlock. He raises a wafer-thin circuit in front of her.

'This is the code for his AI. It'll let your suit tap into his, access his data, copy his movements. He makes it, you make it. But before I give you this…'

She doesn't need prompting. A small glass slide is placed in his hand; plugged into the shuttle's comms system, it will authorise a very substantial contribution to O'Connell's retirement fund.

He slips the circuit into the slot on the stowaway's suit, then seals the door behind her.

O'Connell starts the cycle one more time, leans into the intercom panel: 'You've got until I reach my seat to jump clear. I get to the controls and this ship is gone.'

If Anji Kapoor answers, he does not hear it.

The Station is shifting.

Six weeks ago the *Charing Cross* was dispatched to Jupiter to study a shift in the planetary weather systems. It found more than anyone expected.

For six weeks, a guide signal has been beamed from a satellite. A pulse goes out, an echo comes back. For six weeks, that echo has been constant, waiting to draw the Professional down into this maelstrom. And now the moment has arrived there is the tiniest change in the pitch of that echo. The Station is shifting.

Mission insertion, plus 190 seconds. Time enough to compensate. The situation is recoverable.

Since he jumped the AI has been projecting a stream of figures on to the interior of his helmet, scrolling upwards as the length of each line decreases. It's the narrowing list of probabilities affecting the Professional's course through Jupiter's atmosphere. The AI absorbs every detail the sensors can feed it, factoring a thousand options for a thousand possibilities, formulating responses to every one of the million possible outcomes.

Now, another column appears to the right of this first one. A new set of variables to be brought into line with the first: the movement of the Station.

The Professional focuses the AI on the task – which direction has the Station moved in? What will it take to get the first column of numbers to mesh with the second?

The Station has shifted at the precise moment it might most jeopardise his mission. Sceptical though the Professional is, it's most likely accidental; the sudden drift any object this deep in a volatile suspension of gas and dust will experience. A bubble of air pressure breaks, the Station drops ten metres. Without further evidence, the movement is best attributed to bad luck.

The AI suggests course corrections – pushing him into a marginally different windstream – to compensate for the Station's movement. There's a slight pressure in the small of the Professional's back as the suit's thrusters fire. The two columns of numbers stutter. There's a pause as the calculations catch up, a split second when the numbers grow larger. Then both sets of figures start falling into line with each other.

Back on course. Mission insertion, plus 237 seconds.

Jupiter flows around him. There is something odd, almost familiar, about this experience. He does not know his family, cannot remember his mother, but wonders if this is what it felt like to be in the womb.

He blinks, refocuses.

Mission insertion, plus 253 seconds.

The Professional should reach the Station in the next forty seconds. He could take charge of the touchdown, but has an AI program prepared for the purpose. This could be his only chance to get a good look at the Station's exterior. Any detail missed because he's doing his AI's work might cost dear.

The streams of numbers continue to roll upwards, line lengths dropping from six figures to five.

Mission insertion, plus 274 seconds.

Something huge snaps out of the fog as the AI routine comes online. The shape gains clarity as it explodes in his vision: a spherical hub, surrounded by a web of circles and spokes. The Professional lets the AI take hold of the suit's mechanisms, pushing him around, manipulating his limbs. A tower flashes past and the suit angles his torso, the arms fling forward, explosive bolts release, more systems come alive and two lines fire out into the mist.

There is no sudden jerk as the grapples take hold of the Station's surface; that kind of stop would pull the cables free of their anchoring points on each forearm. Instead, the lines unravel and only slowly do the motors begin to bite. Once a quiet equilibrium is reached, they begin to reel him in.

The rows of five-figure numbers drop to four.

The surface of the Station is battered: hull plating hangs loose in some places, in others it is pitted by meteorites and the sundry debris Jupiter has thrown at it. A blister of scarred metal and a small hole mark an overload and hull breach.

The suit pulls the Professional in towards a tower, one of the spokes that dissects the entire structure. The Station is big enough for him to make out the central hub only dimly through Jupiter's atmosphere; sight of anything beyond is subject to the elements. The arc lights on the exterior are dim, some cracked, some missing altogether, leaving cables trailing in the wind. Proud painted letters are worn away to ghost writing: FARSIDE STATION.

The four-figure numbers slip to three.

Though it's difficult to tell through the haze, the central hub looks bright.

Four years. Could people have survived down here?

Three to two.

The AI magnetises the suit's extremities – the boots and the gloves – and as the Professional's feet touch down, it retracts the grapples and powers down other systems, instead charging servomotors to compensate for the wind shear and weight of Jupiter. Allowing him to move in something approximating a normal fashion.

Mission insertion, plus 380 seconds.

The numbers on his helmet have been reduced to blinking zeros. The Professional replaces them with a schematic of the Station.

He's standing on what is labelled as the North Tower. He pauses, slowly taking his bearings, then heads south towards the central hub. Just before the tower meets one of the rings there is an access hatch.

Anji Kapoor watches the Professional move away. Part of her curses her own stupidity; a larger part curses O'Connell's.

This is the code for his AI. It'll let your suit tap into his, access his data, copy his movements. He makes it, you make it.

When O'Connell said 'copy his movements', Anji hadn't assumed he meant this so precisely. Natural forces have created a slight variance – her grapples are lodged twenty feet from the Professional's – but ideally she would have doubled that, maybe hauled herself in on another one of the tower's faces. As it is, if the margin of error had differed in another direction by another degree she'd have stapled herself to his head.

The Professional vanishes into the fog, and Anji lifts her head from the artificial horizon of the tower and looks up into Jupiter's maw.

In this instant she is sucked back into the nightmarish descent: the suit pushing her this way and that, her mind, torn by circumstance, unable to take a proper hold on the situation. Anji Kapoor. In free fall above Jupiter. One part of her mind wondering what she's doing there, because this must be suicide; another part telling her she's been dead for four years and this is her one chance at feeling alive again. And in that context, it all makes sense.

She's not going to make it through this by panicking.

That was then – a dizzying nightmare of violent forces, whirling colour, lost perspectives. It's what the streaming vapours above and around remind her of. But it's not the same. Ever since those grappling hooks sunk into the Station's hull the purpose that brought her here has returned. Four years of not quite knowing how the universe changed around her are about to end.

Anji is guessing the Professional's mission is twofold: locate any survivors and find out what happened here. The most obvious place to achieve those aims is the central hub. From her helmet schematic Anji assumes the Professional is heading towards an access hatch to the environmental systems. From there he'll work his way into the maintenance ducts – just like a soldier – and deeper into the structure.

Anji is not a soldier. She never has been and most likely never will be. She sees no reason to crawl around in maintenance ducts – just like a soldier – when corridors are available. Take things steady, keep an eye out for danger, and there's no reason why one route should be any less safe than the other.

So she moves north to where the more conventional access of an airlock is situated. It takes thirty seconds to transfer power from her suit to the locking mechanism but, that accomplished, the door grinds open with surprising ease. As other systems come online and pump air into the chamber Anji notes an odd residue on the interior surfaces; not quite a moss or lichen, not quite rust. Her suit's database can't find a match, just declares it non-toxic.

One final hiss of pressurised air and the automatic locks on the inner door click off. Anji releases her helmet catches and tucks the metallic fishbowl under one arm. The room has a reassuring scent. She pulls open the inner door to reveal the Professional directly beyond it, the grate from a maintenance duct at his feet.

Anji drops the helmet.

There are a number of things her body tells her to do in this moment. She wants to reach for the side arm she brought with her and fight; she wants to keep still and not provoke him; she wants to slam the door shut and depressurise the airlock and flee. But most of all, despite all this, she cannot help but look at his face.

From the muffled conversations on the shuttle, Anji knows the Professional unnerved O'Connell. She suspects O'Connell didn't realise what panicked him, but Anji's life has given her a different perspective.

She knows straight away there's something wrong with the Professional's face. It's the face of a dead man.

There's no emotion in that face, no life or soul. Set flat against the world, its lines speak of hardship not joy. It's a face that hides mental processes and adds nothing of its own. It speaks of unerring determination, of the kind of man who doubles back through sixty feet of maintenance duct just to check whether he's being followed.

A cold face with a cold voice: 'Of course. The fuel tank.'

Which is when Anji realises how his kind have got their name. Every trace of personality is subsumed by the job he does. Professional.

Something inside her breaks and she reaches for her side arm. The Professional kicks it from her grasp, then grabs her wrist and twists her arm about. Anji rolls with the movement, hits the floor and – as the Professional releases his hold – pushes up on to her feet. Her energy and speed surprise herself as much as they do the Professional and it's a slightly narrower margin of victory this time when he catches the fist she's swinging at him.

As she attempts to pull free, he places the tip of the plasma rifle against her neck. Anji freezes.

'I recognise you.'

'Yes.'

'You're a reporter. For one of the Martian news networks. Anji Kapoor.'

She hesitates, confirms. 'I present a programme. On the antique stocks market. I'm not really a –'

The basics established, the Professional tightens his trigger finger. The rifle's batteries whine, anticipating the energy release. It is, Anji realises, his way of showing that all their exchanges to date have been non-consequential. It's the answers she gives from now on that are going to count.

'Why are you here, Miss Kapoor?'

'I came looking for my friends.'

'What friends?'

Anji knows her story doesn't sound convincing, but it's the only one she's got. 'The Doctor and Fitz.'

A brief pause, then the Professional pushes her up against the wall before taking a couple of steps back.

Giving himself space, Anji thinks, and giving himself time to react. Because he's going to have to take his eyes off you. Because he's going to check something. Because he can't afford simply to dismiss you.

And, in those terms, his reaction seems obvious enough.

She can't be certain how much the Professional knows about her, but their conversation suggests a train of thought that's not dismissive of her plausibility. The only facts he has mentioned are public knowledge. She reviews antique stocks; she's not a gung-ho reporter looking to make a name for herself; she clearly has no camera or recording equipment with her. There's no – for want of a better word – professional reason for her presence. So, unless she has a personal stake, why come here?

'Full names and titles.' The Professional is looking at his AI screen. Anji can guess what it's showing. It's had a few euphemisms over the last four years: the 228; the list; the missing. The names of those presumed dead ever since this Station fell from orbit. Swallowed by Jupiter, never to be seen again. Until now.

'Dr John Smith, Mr Fitzgerald Kreiner.' Anji can tell from a flash across his eyes that the list is scrolling up and down, searching. 'But you won't –'

The flashing stops. 'How do you know those names?'

'I don't understand,' Anji says.

Except, as she thinks about it, she does. The Doctor and Fitz were never included among the 228; she'd always assumed some query about their status meant they were logged with the classified personnel whose presence was never disclosed. 'That's the full list, isn't it?' she asks.

'On the passenger manifest from the PSV *Pegasus* four years ago.'

'They were here?' Anji says, 'They were here when – ?'

'If you are their friend, their presence on this list should be no cause for celebration.'

'What do you mean?'

'Despite the evidence supplied by your following me down here, Miss Kapoor, I'm going to give you the benefit of the doubt and say you're not stupid.' For the first time the Professional lets the barrel of the gun drop away from Anji. 'Look around you. If they are here, they've been dead four years already.'

Four Years Earlier

Fitz had long ago decided the Doctor's most annoying habit was turning a pleasant, everyday activity into a life-threatening crisis.

Case in point: today's activities. Seven days out from Mars on an Earth Forces' personnel carrier. As transportation went, the *Pegasus* was better than most. They had a cabin and hot food. Recreational facilities were minimal – it was a military vessel, after all – but there was an observation lounge where you could quietly stargaze.

They'd been seated there a few minutes earlier: the Doctor studying one of the holographic slides that had replaced paper in this time period, Fitz watching Jupiter swallow space in front of them.

Final approach to Farside Station. It made a neat contrast to one of the least appealing things about travel by TARDIS: that you never got the impression of travelling anywhere, you just arrived.

Then the ship's pilot had walked past. He'd paused at the steps down into the ship, looked up at the view, then walked on.

And when the Doctor turned to Fitz at that moment, Fitz had somehow known he was about to have a very bad day.

'There's something wrong with his eyes. Like that trooper on Mars.'

And then he was off, chasing towards the steps and Fitz was trailing in his wake. By the time he'd caught up, the Doctor was at work in the corridor outside the cockpit. It was one of the few areas off-limits to passengers; something a female mess officer was trying to make clear at pretty much the exact moment the Doctor's most annoying habit came to the fore once more.

The ship had gone crazy around them, with the ninety seconds following living up to all Fitz's expectations of life with the Doctor.

'If I die pretending to be an accountant,' Fitz said, 'I'll never forgive myself, I swear.'

The Doctor looked at Fitz. A deeply unhappy look that impressively conveyed the message that self-pitying wit was not the order of the day; what was really impressive was the way he continued to pull wires from the bulkhead and splice them together as he looked.

'Here.' The Doctor handed him a long strip of cable. 'Hold this.'

Fitz and the mess officer looked dubiously at the lead. For some reason she remained unhappy with their involvement; muttered, 'I'm really not sure you should be doing this.'

'Don't worry,' the Doctor answered. 'I'm sure Earth Forces' insurance is pretty comprehensive. If anyone asks, I'll tell them you weren't in a position to stop me.'

The floor lurched beneath them and Fitz grabbed the mess officer to stop her falling over.

'Besides,' the Doctor continued, 'if I don't do this, there's a very good chance we'll be dead in five minutes.'

The mess officer looked at him, then pulled free of Fitz's grasp and stumbled back towards the passenger compartments.

'She may be going to get help,' Fitz said.

'Yes,' the Doctor murmured, 'we could do with another set of hands.'

'The critical thing being, of course,' Fitz continued, 'whether the help she brings –'

'Thinks we're the solution or part of the problem.' The Doctor nodded, connecting his wiring to a nearby computer terminal. 'With any luck we'll have it all sorted by the time she gets back.'

Fitz frowned.

'There!' the Doctor exclaimed triumphantly.

During the exchange from orbital lander to personnel carrier Fitz had only glimpsed the craft they would be travelling on; he'd devoted most of his time to the Martian landscape beneath them. However, that glimpse was enough for him to place the diagram on the terminal as representative of the *Pegasus*. The fact that huge sections were covered in red warning symbols didn't bode well.

'I repeat,' Fitz said, 'if I die pretending to be an accountant, I'll never forgive myself. Or you.'

'We'll have to see what we can do about that then.' The Doctor looked at the cockpit door. 'The lock's jammed from the inside, but the flight systems all seem to be operating efficiently.'

They were jerked from their feet as the personnel carrier dived.

'It's just that the pilot has misplaced all his flying skills.'

'You're not reassuring me, Doctor.'

'Sorry.' The Doctor pulled himself over to the cockpit entrance. 'Any sign of our stewardess?'

'They're military,' Fitz replied. 'I think they like to be called mess officers. And no, no one's in sight.'

'Good, because strictly speaking, as an accountant I shouldn't have a device like this on my person –' The Doctor produced the sonic screwdriver from his jacket pocket and thrust his arm into the open bulkhead. '– Or use it to do something like that.'

'What?'

There was a brief hum and a flash. Then the cockpit door slid open. 'That,' the Doctor smiled.

The first thing Fitz noticed was the blood on the military-clean floor. The second thing was the source of the blood: a series of wounds on the pilot's leg. This led to a whole series of realisations.

The thing causing the wounds was the tip of a miniature harpoon, still sitting in a high-tech harpoon gun. The gun was in the possession of the pilot, who was stabbing himself with one hand while crazily manipulating the ship's controls with the other. And crazily really was the word. Because the pilot was a bug-eyed lunatic, and the odds on Fitz actually dying while pretending to be an accountant had suddenly reached evens.

Then the Doctor stepped into the doorway, blocking the view. Fitz knew the routine. The Doctor was making good eye contact, keeping his body language non-threatening, speaking with that contradictory voice of his. Old, but young; strong, but calm; peaceful, but determined. A voice to ease any trouble, right any wrong.

The corridor was filled with an explosion of noise and movement.

The door to the cockpit crashed shut, but Fitz didn't really notice. The Doctor was sitting on the floor a couple of feet away, one hand tight around the harpoon embedded in his abdomen.

Which was when Fitz realised 'bad day' wasn't about to cover what was happening.

The Doctor blinked twice. 'That,' he said, 'was far too close.' And with a jerk he pulled the shaft free.

'Wha–' Fitz managed.

The Doctor climbed to his feet, blood staining his shirt. 'Handkerchief?' he asked Fitz.

Fitz produced one, which the Doctor pressed tight against the wound. He glanced at Fitz. 'Are you all right?'

'You caught it,' Fitz said. 'Took the worst of the momentum out, twisted your body so it missed any vital organs.'

The Doctor frowned. 'I do this kind of thing a lot?'

Before Fitz could reply they were thrown against the wall. The Doctor hissed, pressing Fitz's handkerchief harder against his side. 'What does the console say?'

Fitz peered at the terminal, 'Nose down, engines overheated. Exterior conditions and windspeed.' He paused. 'You don't get windspeed in space, do you?'

'He's taking us into the atmosphere,' a voice said.

A tall man, muscular, with close-cropped hair, was coming down the corridor towards them, the mess officer following behind. Dressed in civilian clothes, the way he braced himself against the ship's movement told another story. A soldier.

As the Doctor turned, Fitz noticed he'd buttoned his jacket to hide the wound. 'And you are?'

'John McCray, 101st Airborne.'

'Currahee,' the Doctor muttered obscurely.

Before McCray could answer there was a gasp of air from the cockpit door, followed by a burst of sparks.

'Now what?' Fitz asked.

'The pilot's engaged the pressure door and fused the lock.'

McCray checked the terminal. 'We don't have a lot of time: this ship isn't rigged for atmospheric entry.' He glanced at the wiring running between the terminal and the wall. 'Did you do this?'

'Yes,' the Doctor replied.

'Could you rig access to the flight systems?'

The Doctor's eyes narrowed as he considered the wires. 'I could access the flight routines,' he said, 'but without rewriting the command structure, protocol is always going to defer to the cockpit.'

'Not a problem,' McCray answered. 'Get to work.'

As McCray turned to a separate wall panel, the Doctor knelt by the terminal again. 'This won't do any good,' he said.

'Will someone please explain what's going on,' Fitz demanded.

'I can wire this computer into the flight systems, but control has to be released by the cockpit before we can use it to fly the ship. Which still leaves us with the problem of getting through that door. With that pressure door locked in place, we don't –'

'The pressure door,' McCray interrupted, 'makes it possible. C-grade personnel support vehicle; in emergencies, the pilot engages the pressure door and the cockpit section is jettisoned as an escape capsule.'

He finally released the wall panel, revealing a heavy red unit complete with warning stickers.

The Doctor frowned at the sight. 'Explosive bolt?'

McCray nodded. 'Just because the ejection control is in the cockpit, it doesn't mean we can't use the mechanism.' He slid a pistol from his jacket, pointed it at the unit. 'Trigger one bolt and the rest fire in sequence. Lose the cockpit, gain flight control.'

'What about the pilot?' Fitz asked.

The Doctor and McCray looked at each other. 'The cockpit has an independent air supply,' the Doctor told Fitz. 'If we jettison it, the pilot has a chance of survival.'

The ship rocked again, and the hull began to creak.

'More of a chance than he's giving us.' He nodded at McCray. 'Do it.'

There was no worse sound than the 'message waiting' tone before seven in the morning, not for Jennifer Valletti. The hour didn't bother her; twenty years' service had left her capable of handling a late night, an early start, or – more often than not – both together.

It was what the tone signified: trouble.

Valletti's command was a research station sitting in Jupiter's orbit, far from prying eyes, two days from the nearest help. Trouble was never welcome.

Now, thirty-five minutes after being woken by that sound, Valletti was in uniform, watching the docking-bay doors open as heavy power drones hauled the *Pegasus* in. Twenty years and she'd never got used to that sight: the vacuum of space before her, only an invisible mix of magnetics and force fields keeping the air in her lungs. An uncomfortable reminder of how fragile life still was out here. She trusted the technology but was always happier once the doors were shut.

The atmospheric shield fizzed as the ships nosed through it. A fizz that was lost to a deafening scream: engines running silent in the vacuum suddenly given voice by the Station's atmosphere. There was a thump as the *Pegasus* was released on to the floor, then the engine noise geared down as the drones edged away to their landing zone.

Valletti recognised the acrid smell coming from the *Pegasus*: burnt-out engine coils. Although the emergency crews were on standby, it looked like the worst was over.

She trusted her crew to get on with their jobs, and as they ran their checks she waited. Only when they were done did she approach. Battered by their flight, passengers and crew filtered down the off-ramp. There was a slight break in the flow of personnel, then the final three passengers disembarked.

As soon as she'd checked the manifest, Valletti had an idea who'd pulled the *Pegasus* out of its suicide dive. Sure enough, McCray was there, complete with two civilians. She checked their faces against the passenger list, finding the accountancy team she'd requested six months earlier.

McCray was dedicated, smart and approachable. Even so, number-crunchers were odd bedfellows for a paratrooper.

The lead accountant was Smith: bright-eyed with thick floppy hair and an easy and elegant movement that reminded her of the men back home. Even though his assistant, Kreiner, was wearing an identical designer suit – House of McCartney, charcoal grey, fashionable half-lapels – he somehow looked shabbier in comparison.

McCray straightened as he saw Valletti, snapped a salute.

'At ease.'

'Ma'am.'

The lead accountant offered his hand. 'Dr John Smith, my assistant Fitzgerald Kreiner.' He smiled. 'You can call me Doctor.'

Valletti nodded at the ship. 'I hope you're not planning to put this mess on my budget.'

McCray answered: 'The Doctor was instrumental in regaining control of the *Pegasus*, ma'am.'

'Reconfiguring military-grade computer systems,' the Doctor shrugged. 'Everyone needs a hobby.'

The easy manner extended beyond his walk; not what Valletti expected from an accountant. 'I requested a business team to clear the paperwork, not create more of it. I want statements from all three of you by tomorrow morning at the latest.'

'Oh, good,' Kreiner said, 'homework.'

Back when he was a kid, Fitz had met some soldiers while playing in a bombed-out house: American GIs who didn't know his surname. They'd laughed and played and handed him a chocolate bar. While it was a military image more recently supplanted by frogmarching guards who'd shoot first with no promise of questions later, Fitz still remembered them.

Both McCray and Valletti had a business-first attitude, but standing there watching Valletti lay out her credentials Fitz could see more than a hint of those GIs. Making sure he and the Doctor knew who was in charge, yes, but a hint of a smile and something in her eyes assured Fitz that giving orders was her least favourite part of the job. Authoritative, but kind.

He put Valletti in her early forties, slim and attractive – green eyes and auburn hair set off by the crisp white of her uniform jacket – but just a little too worldly-wise for the Kreiner charm.

She was telling the Doctor something about the audit she wanted when Fitz noticed a change in McCray. Like Fitz he'd drifted away during the finance talk, but had suddenly come back to life, turning to the massive doors leading into the Station.

Fitz looked and saw a swarm of troops entering, one of them calling out: 'Captain!'

He turned to McCray. 'Yours, I take it?'

'For better or worse,' McCray answered. 'Commander?'

'You're excused, Captain.'

'Ma'am.' He saluted, then strode towards his comrades. In the moment before McCray was enveloped by their cheers he turned, nodding a smile at a janitor. The man's hands were still on his mop, and only when McCray and his squad had gone did he start cleaning again.

The Doctor tugged on Fitz's arm. 'Grab the cases, will you?'

Twenty minutes later they were alone in their quarters.

It wasn't a huge space but there was room enough for them both, plus a bunk bed, washbasin and small window on to the stars. Thankfully, the toilets were positioned down the corridor: there were still some things Fitz didn't want the Doctor privy to.

The Doctor handed him a small disc. 'Slip that in the comms unit, will you?'

'Comms unit?' Fitz asked.

'The TV set in the wall over there.'

'Right,' Fitz said, finding the slot beneath the screen. As he slipped the disc inside the unit came to life: a middle-aged man behind a desk, gravely intoning headlines. Two hundred years and the news hadn't changed that much since Richard Baker.

'Was it meant to do that?' Fitz asked.

The Doctor settled back on his bunk, slowly unbuttoning his jacket. 'I'm piggybacking a signal across the commercial networks.'

Fitz was about to ask what kind of signal, but the question died on his lips as the Doctor opened his jacket.

'Bloody hell,' Fitz said.

'It looks worse than it is,' the Doctor answered. The strain in his voice said otherwise.

'That,' Fitz replied, 'is a lot of blood.'

'Most of it's dry,' the Doctor gasped, peeling the handkerchief away. It was true; although bruised and puckered, the puncture wound itself had started healing. Fitz dampened a towel and began to wipe away the blood.

'You should get this looked at.'

The Doctor shook his head, 'I can't.'

'You just saved a ship full of people. They're not going to begrudge you a bandage, Doctor. Besides, I thought you'd squared away your physique for their security stuff?'

'A faked medical record referencing a bicardial mutation wouldn't account for my blood work. It's probably never a good time to be an alien infiltrator, but this definitely isn't the right period for it.' He caught Fitz's look and smiled. 'I'll let you figure out why.'

'Oh, God,' Fitz groaned, 'I've heard about your initiative tests.'

With a burst of static, the news report was replaced by a grainy image of Anji Kapoor. The swelling had gone from her face, the only remnant of the attack a large sticking plaster on her forehead. She was looking away from the camera when the signal came through, eyes focused further down the hospital ward. Then she turned and saw them; there was a moment of indecision on her face before she finally broke into a laugh.

'Is this a good time for you both, or would you like to be left alone?'

Fitz looked at the Doctor's naked torso, the damp towel in his own hand and the way he'd been bathing his friend. He dropped the towel, pushing himself back along the bunk. 'Now's fine, thank you.'

'How are you feeling?' the Doctor asked.

'Much better.' Anji put a hand to her face. 'I don't know what they're using in the twenty-second century, but when I get home I'm buying shares. I still would have preferred to go with you.'

'That was quite a fracture,' the Doctor said sternly. 'Halfway between Mars and Jupiter would not have been the place to discover any complications. You were better off staying in hospital.'

There was a pause, then Anji nodded, any jollity fading as she asked, 'Any idea what happened?'

'We've only just got here,' Fitz protested.

Anji tucked a strand of hair behind her ear. 'You said you were good at this kind of thing.'

The Doctor interrupted before Fitz could respond. 'Anything more from the authorities your end?'

Anji shook her head. 'Two squaddies on leave from Farside Station run amok in a Sheffield mezzanine. Authorities reassure the time-travelling futures trader unfortunate enough to get in their way that the parties involved are simply suffering from stress. Quote one officer, they've gone space happy, unquote.'

'Nothing we didn't already know.' Fitz turned to the Doctor. 'I told you this was a wild-goose chase.'

The Doctor shook his head, 'I don't think so. One person might snap like that, but two? Within seconds of each other?'

'There is something you don't know,' Anji said. 'They're still in custody, but no charges are being brought. Rumour has it they're being shipped back to Earth for specialist treatment.'

The Doctor leant forward, steepling his fingers. 'Interesting. Did they say what they were treating them for?'

'I don't know.'

'Couldn't you have asked? It might be important.'

Anji shook her head. 'I didn't get that from the military. It's secondhand information from a source; that's all they knew.'

'You've only been on Mars ten days,' Fitz protested. 'How do you get to have a source?'

'I...' Anji paused before continuing, 'I've been watching a lot of TV. One of the news networks has a series on economic history.' She looked away bashfully. 'I may have phoned in to complain about some inaccuracies.'

'I do hope you're not drawing attention to yourself,' the Doctor said.

'Relax. I used the ID you created; they bought it and, well, they offered me some consulting work on the last couple of episodes. The researcher asked about the cut on my head; she's the one who told me about the squaddies.'

'Almost thirty years living on Earth,' Fitz said, 'and the best I could manage was a job in a garden centre.' He threw up his hands. 'Ten days on another planet and you land a gig in television.'

Anji smiled. 'It helps to have some kind of work ethic to begin with.'

Fitz opened his mouth to reply but the Doctor raised a hand, silencing him. 'That'll do, thank you.'

He turned to Anji. 'They're releasing you?'

'Tomorrow,' she nodded.

'Take care,' the Doctor said, 'keep a low profile, and we'll be in touch.'

'See you in a week or so,' Fitz said.

As the screen clicked off the Doctor said, 'A week might be optimistic, don't you think?'

'I thought that was the point of our cover.'

'Posing as Earth Forces' accountants gets us here, provides good access to this station's files, and isn't so high-powered a job that security will take more than a cursory look at our credentials.'

'Which is good, because they're fakes.'

'Exactly.' The Doctor glanced at Fitz, curious and uncertain. 'We've done this a lot, haven't we? That's why you think we'll be back on Mars in a week.'

'This?' Fitz said. 'Infiltrating research stations around Jupiter? No. But we've done enough similar stuff the last couple of years.'

The Doctor nodded, taking this on board. 'There's something wrong here,' he said. 'The way those two suddenly turned, the way they attacked Anji...' He looked to the window and the stars beyond, his voice dropping to a whisper: 'She didn't ask to be out here. She's my responsibility, and if she's been hurt I want to know why.'

'I know this is a daft question, given we just travelled halfway across the galaxy –'

The Doctor sighed. 'Solar system, Fitz. Not galaxy. Different things altogether.'

'Solar system, then. But... You are sure, aren't you? That whatever the problem is, it's here?'

'We checked every lead on Mars and found nothing. Those soldiers were on the planet less than twelve hours.' The Doctor shrugged. 'I'm taking it one step at a time, tracing back along their path. Before Mars they were here. If there was any doubt, the pilot's behaviour on our flight in clinched it. That's three people now, all with one common link. This station.'

'So, what do you think happened to them?' Fitz asked.

'I don't know,' the Doctor said. 'This is a weapons research facility. They could have been exposed to a nerve gas or neurological disruptor. Either containment procedures aren't up to scratch...'

'Or?' Fitz prompted.

'Or someone's testing their work outside of the laboratory. Whatever happened, something needs to be done.'

As Fitz slept the Doctor worked on their statements, keeping the grammar loose to non-existent on the one Fitz would sign. For some reason, that seemed appropriate.

Fitz was confident this would all be over soon; a confidence the Doctor wished he shared. It had taken a lot of work just to trace the two soldiers this far.

It had been nearing five o'clock and they'd spent the day exploring Sheffield. Wandering into a mezzanine, Fitz had spotted the New

Jupiter Café; the irony of their last port of call demanded a visit, apparently.

Anji had found a table while he and Fitz went to fetch drinks. In the mirror behind the counter the Doctor saw the two soldiers – one dark, one blond – approaching the New Jupiter. The first was agitated, his friend trying to calm him. Then the dark-haired soldier had stiffened, pushing his way into the café, screaming.

The Doctor went to intervene, but was stopped by the blond soldier who looked straight into his eyes and told him he wasn't needed.

The first soldier began to throw over tables, and punched his hand through a glass counter, shards lodging in his knuckles.

As the Doctor stepped forward the blond trooper stopped him once more, only this time his expression had changed. His eyes lost focus. A moment later he was swinging a fist. A second after that, Fitz had smashed a bottle over the soldier's head and he'd sunk unconscious to the floor.

By the time the Doctor reached the first soldier, the man had already landed five hard blows on Anji. A concussion she was still clearing almost ten days later.

When they reached the hospital the soldiers were placed under military guard. There was no response when the Doctor asked what was going to happen to them; more importantly, he wanted to know why the incident had happened.

As Fitz sat with Anji he'd found the troopers' names on the hospital register. A starting point from which the Doctor had worked backwards. The hotel rooms they'd checked into, the restaurant they'd had lunch in. Looking for similar symptoms across Sheffield, widening the search to all of Mars.

He'd found nothing. The last search was a hack into the Mars Orbital's database, finding out where the soldiers had come from. Farside Station meant nothing on its own but a cursory search of public records had told him enough.

People didn't just snap. Not like those two had.

There had to be an answer, and that answer was most likely here.

Despite its specialist requirements the Station was a standard design. A central, spherical hub housed reactors, administration and research labs; concentric rings and spokes surrounded it, holding docking facilities, positioning thrusters and storage bays. That standard design placed the commander's office at the Station's highest elevation, on top of the spire rising out of the central hub.

The first thing Valletti had done was move her office down into Command and Control. The previous location had obvious psychological inferences which she'd never cared for. Leadership wasn't the same as demanding people look up to you. Respect was earned. Symbolism aside, the move placed her at the heart of the Station, able to judge its mood just by looking up and seeing the faces of her staff.

This meant that when the Doctor and Kreiner walked in the next morning she could watch as they made their way through the control boards and technicians. Both quite comfortable; the Doctor obviously taking more in with every glance made.

She picked up a slide as they approached, and scrolled through their statements. 'You're quite adaptable, aren't you, Doctor?'

He smiled. 'Lucky more than anything.'

'That's good,' Valletti answered. 'I think I like lucky more than adaptable. Did you find your office?'

'Yes, thank you. It's not as impressive as this one.'

She shrugged. 'The best I could do under the circumstances. I've been waiting for an accounts staff for six months, then you arrive with a week's notice.' Valletti picked up a pair of blank cards from her desk: 'Just add your biometrics to these.'

'Our what?' Kreiner sad.

The Doctor turned the card over in his hand, then glanced at Kreiner and said, 'Look at the dot in the centre.' He held his pass at arm's length and smiled. As his face appeared on the front he showed it to his colleague. 'What do you think? Good likeness?'

Kreiner frowned suspiciously at his own card, then blinked, horrified. 'Oh, balls, I wasn't ready.' As his confused portrait faded into view he hurriedly tucked the card into the breast pocket of his suit.

'Those passes give you access to most departments,' Valletti explained. 'Try not to lose them.' She smiled, guiding them towards the main lift. 'Time for the tour.'

As the doors opened she tugged the card from Kreiner's pocket. 'Sorry, but you do need to keep your pass in sight at all times.' She ushered them into the lift. 'It helps the security systems keep track.'

'Do I have to?' he answered, glancing down at his frowning face. 'I really wasn't ready.' He smiled. 'And it's Fitz, by the way. We don't stand on ceremony in accounts.'

There was a whisper of air as the lift swept upwards.

'I don't care for ceremony, either,' Valletti explained. 'But you need to remember, you're here for one reason. When this facility opened it offered a secure locale for a half-dozen research projects. We've grown since then. You're here to keep things running smoothly.'

The first stop was the sight Valletti liked to show everyone when they arrived. An illustration of the scale of their task.

The doors opened and the Doctor let out a brief whistle. 'Nice reactors,' he said.

A dozen fusion engines formed the Station's heart: pulsating towers, eight storeys high, held in a latticework of cables. Technicians clambered over and around the towers, while a long catwalk ran around the edge of the enormous spherical chamber that held them all.

'A station this size,' Valletti said, 'would normally use half this number of reactors. At any one time there are over forty projects under way on Farside Station.'

The Doctor stopped, studying the main control console as he said, 'Takes some managing, I suppose. The Station, I mean, not the reactors.'

Valletti shrugged. 'I can deal with people.'

'But not budgets.'

'Bookkeeping.' She smiled. 'That kind of fight I'm not trained for.'

They reached the opposite side of the chamber and boarded another lift. Fitz watched Valletti watching the Doctor. Then he looked at the map next to him, trying to get a bearing on where the massive reactors had been. As the lift slowed he pursed his lips, thinking about the Doctor's initiative test.

The next level was more conventional. A central corridor led on to a mix of open lab space and enclosed test facilities, some empty, others filled with oversized machinery. There were a few bearded, science types, but mostly it was just regular people, hard at work.

A deep throb sounded as a glare filled one compartment. As they passed a mannequin stood burning on one side of the room, a smoking cannon on the other. A six-inch slab of metal was untouched between them.

Reaching a convenient stopping point, Valletti turned to them. 'I've shown you this and the reactors for one reason. You're cleared for access to all these areas, but if things were left to you, you might sit in your office and never venture down here.'

She gestured at the corridor they'd just come down. 'I said I wanted this station running smoothly. But this place is not just columns and numbers on a page. You're both old enough to remember the occupation. Well, this is the cutting edge, where the work is done to stop that ever happening again, to keep our families safe for the next hundred years. Don't let me down,' she entreated. 'Don't let them down.'

'I understand,' the Doctor said solemnly.

While Fitz had taken in the emotion behind the speech, he'd struggled with the context. Either the Doctor's background reading was paying off or he'd just demonstrated how good a liar he could be. Regardless, Valletti seemed satisfied the message was received and understood.

Heading back to the lift, the Doctor nodded at an empty room. One corner of the floor and wall was missing; sliced clean away to reveal the electrics beneath.

'Experiments go awry,' Valletti explained. 'This is what happens when you create an artificial singularity and it goes wrong.'

'No more than ten feet across,' the Doctor mused. 'You're lucky it didn't swallow half this station.' He checked the nameplate on the door. 'Professor Deschamps.' He frowned at Valletti. 'Artificial singularity? For some kind of bomb?'

'Testing moves out into space in the next few months,' Valletti said, then smiled. 'If Deschamps hears you're running finance, you'll have plenty of opportunity to ask him about it.'

Installed in their office, Fitz started rearranging the pot plants as the Doctor got on with the business of accountancy.

'Did you notice?' the Doctor said.

'You only ask things like that when you think I haven't. So,' Fitz said, 'let me surprise you.'

The Doctor raised an eyebrow.

'Commander Valletti is big on the whole team thing,' Fitz continued. 'One of the lads, works with all the personnel, and they all get along famously, fighting the good fight.'

'Except?'

'Except, not everyone is in on the team thing. The reactor room, chock-full of dirty hands and sweaty overalls, right?'

The Doctor nodded.

'And those labs had lots of nice white coats. It takes thirty seconds to get from one to the other, but you didn't see any white coats near the reactors or overalls near the labs. That's the most extreme example' – Fitz tapped the Station layout mounted on the wall – 'but it's all over the design of this place. This ball bit is where the important people live.'

'Research and administration.' The Doctor nodded.

'Whereas out here –' Fitz pointed to the Station's rings '– is where you find your minions. And never the twain shall meet.'

The Doctor smiled. 'That's very astute.'

'Not really,' Fitz said, settling down to light a cigarette. 'I'm not that smart, but I'm good with people.'

'It wasn't what I was talking about,' the Doctor said, 'but it was very astute.'

'Oh. What were you talking about?'.

'The control panel in the reactor room. There's no power being drawn to level six.'

'So?'

'There must be something on level six. And if there's something, then it's got to be using some power.'

Fitz shrugged. 'This is a military base, Doctor. There's bound to be classified stuff.'

'Maybe.' The Doctor tapped his pen against his teeth. 'Commander Valletti seems quite welcoming; there's no hint of deception or malice about her. Either she's very good at lying or –'

'She's got the hots for you,' Fitz said, matter of fact.

There was an uncomfortable silence. Fitz looked up to find the Doctor staring at him. 'Oh, come on,' he said, 'a hundred years stuck on Earth. You must have learnt something about women.'

The Doctor continued to stare at him.

'Maybe not,' Fitz muttered.

The Doctor turned to the computer built into his desk – another one of the glass slides – and mused, 'Whatever's on level six must be funded somehow.'

'"Funded"? You're not going through with this accountancy stuff, are you?' Fitz said, suddenly nervous. 'Because the thing is, I was never very good at maths.'

'Don't worry,' the Doctor answered, producing a glass chip from his jacket pocket. 'While you were watching the world go by on the *Pegasus*, I was writing an AI program to take care of the bookkeeping.' He tapped the chip triumphantly. 'If you want an audit, get yourself an AuDoc.'

He slipped the chip into the computer and a new graphic blossomed on the desk screen. 'It's capable of adaptive thought, so if I ask AuDoc to locate black-money projects, it'll figure out how to do that itself. We just have to sit back and wait for the results.'

Fitz looked around the office glumly. 'I've got to be honest with you, I think I've done all the waiting I can in this room.'

'Is there something else you'd prefer to be doing?'

Fitz smiled.

That something else was the standard Kreiner mooching around. It wasn't the structured approach the Doctor would have taken, but Fitz felt his record spoke for itself. Mooching delivered results.

He left the Doctor playing with his computer program. Which in itself wasn't right.

About a month ago, by Fitz's reckoning, the Doctor had saved the universe for the umpteenth time. Only he hadn't escaped unharmed. The victory had come at a huge personal cost, leaving him and his TARDIS badly damaged. The only solution had been for Fitz to leave his friend and the time ship on Earth to recover, rendezvousing with him later on. And while all that was just a few weeks ago for Fitz, the Doctor had spent more than a hundred years recovering.

Fitz's problem had started when they'd met up again: the Doctor said he couldn't remember anything from before he'd woken up on Earth.

And Fitz believed him.

But then they'd arrived on Mars and he'd seemed quite at home in the future. Not as off-the-cuff blasé as he would once have been, but quite capable of hot-wiring spaceships, writing accountancy programs or expertly forging Earth Forces' credentials.

Something Fitz could only explain as being flashes of the old Doctor breaking through.

While reluctant ever to look a gift horse in the mouth, those flashes of memory left Fitz worried. Only a couple of weeks earlier the Doctor had taken a risk to try and get those memories back. He'd failed, and while Fitz had been relieved at his failure at the time, now he wasn't so sure.

Leaving administration behind, Fitz paused at a junction.

A right turn led back to the central hub. If those soldiers' rampage had been the result of research gone awry, the answer would be found there. Only, while Fitz could bluff his way through most situations with a bit of authentic future slang, deciphering space-age weapons programmes was beyond him. So he turned left towards the outer rings, where the white coats and dataslides were replaced by overalls and tool boxes.

As he walked, Fitz realised his problem was not what the Doctor could remember but what he couldn't.

They were friends; at least, they had been.

Fitz's life had been one of continual underachievement until he'd met the Doctor. Since that day, he'd seen things beyond imagination. True, he'd faced death more often than he'd have thought possible, but he also felt alive. And the Doctor had been the best of travelling companions. Brave and intelligent, caring and funny. He and Fitz had a history.

Only now the Doctor was still there, still doing Doctor-ish things, but that history was gone. And Fitz didn't know how to react.

Did the Doctor want to know the how and why of his lost memory? Fitz had assumed not, but could he be sure? And if the Doctor couldn't remember Fitz, if they didn't have that history, what was it that made them friends?

The next junction led Fitz to the docking bay. A sign was flashing over the main doors: NO ENTRY – DOCKING IN PROGRESS.

Fitz was looking for a viewing point; somewhere with a comfy chair where he could sit with a cigarette and watch whatever was going on. Quiet observation was, after all, just as instructive as casual mooching.

In the end, he settled for trying a smaller set of doors away to the left. These led on to a small cargo hold and a scene of organised chaos. Crewmen worked on small platforms, rising and falling between tall shelves, hefting boxes on their shoulders, racking up canisters. The main docking bay had been clean like the central hub, and while the corridors of the outer rings hadn't been quite so pristine they were nothing compared to this. Even if he hadn't been able to see the stained overalls, dented bulkheads or puddles on the floor, Fitz would have recognised the smell: oil and dirt and sweat.

This was the factory floor.

'Hey, you!' a thick voice called.

Fitz turned to see a huge black man in overalls. Fitz pointed at his own chest, mouthed: Me?

'Yes, you. Move. People are working.'

'Sorry,' Fitz said, stepping out of the way of one crewman and into the path of another. The collision sent the box he was carrying tumbling from his shoulder; Fitz winced as it split open, small parts sweeping across the floor.

'Oh, bollocks,' Fitz said. The crewman gave a scowl that made Fitz worry about what was going to follow it up. Then the guy who'd shouted at him intervened, thrusting a slide into the crewman's hand.

'Bay sixteen, medical equipment to the infirmary. C'mon, Archer, move.' He glanced at Fitz. 'I'll clean this up.'

As Fitz dropped to his knees next to the man, he began to realise the enormity of his mistake. The box was compartmentalised and all the parts needed to be sorted and returned to the right section.

'Oh, bollocks,' Fitz repeated. 'I really am sorry. I was looking for a viewing platform.'

The man snorted. 'You're one of the accountants, right?'

'That's right,' Fitz said. The man was studying the parts, dropping them back into place. Fitz held his hand out. 'Fitz Kreiner.'

The man looked at Fitz's proffered hand, then raised his own. It was covered in oil. Fitz kept his hand where it was and after a moment's pause the man shook it: the strong grip of manual labour. 'My name's Robertson.'

As Robertson continued sorting the parts, Fitz realised there was a schematic on each appropriate box. He picked up a piece, compared it to the diagrams and slotted it home.

'That's a nice suit,' Robertson said. 'You hang around Greenwich, it's going to get dirty.'

'Place like this must have a laundry somewhere.'

Robertson chuckled; a deep timbre, warm and comforting.

'Besides,' Fitz said, 'what's Greenwich?'

'This is,' Robertson grinned. 'This is Greenwich.'

'Still lost,' Fitz said.

'Everything that comes into this station comes through here. People, supplies, even accountants. This is zero longitude, where life on this station begins and ends. Turn right outside and it's Greenwich East, turn left –'

'– and it's Greenwich West.'

'Strictly speaking, we're in Greenwich East here. The systems access hatch in the docking bay marks the meridian.'

'And you're in charge?'

Robertson nodded. 'Ships and cargo. I sign it in, I sign it out.'

'Big job,' Fitz said.

'Big enough.' The man's tone gained an edge not present a moment earlier. 'Doesn't mean I can't cope, or that I like it when people muscle in on my territory.'

Fitz looked at the part in his hand. 'Sorry, I was only trying to help.'

Robertson smiled. 'Not you, Mr Kreiner.' He nodded his head towards a set of doors. The hold they were in sat adjacent to the docking bay; the same sign that was over the main doors outside was flashing above this smaller set.

'Hang on,' Fitz said. 'If you're in charge of ships and cargo and the sign says docking in progress then –'

'– what am I doing in here? Good question.' Robertson tossed the last component into the box as a chime sounded. 'You helped pull the *Pegasus* out of that dive?'

'More my boss than me.'

'Either way, you might be interested.' Robertson hoisted the box up on to a shelf, then crossed to check a control panel. 'Exterior doors secure.' He released the lock, and the doors into the docking bay hummed, sliding back on well-oiled runners.

The shuttles and drones had been eased over to one side, leaving an open space in the middle of the bay. A half-dozen men in spacesuits hovered around a pair of grapples, holding a familiar shape: the cockpit section of the *Pegasus*.

'What the – ?'

Robertson nodded. 'McCray and the boys. Went in this morning to retrieve it.'

Fitz looked again. 'That's McCray?'

Robertson nodded.

'So what's the problem?'

'Basic training doesn't qualify me to run combat missions, so why are they doing cargo and salvage?'

Explosive bolts fired and the canopy flew across the docking bay. Before it even hit the ground, the pilot was climbing from the cockpit. Twenty-four hours tumbling around Jupiter's atmosphere hadn't improved his mood. But before he could get any further, the spacesuits touched down in a circle around him. The pilot flailed wildly at one, only to be grabbed by the wrist and flicked over on to his back. As the pilot landed the other suits moved in, holding him down.

A tall woman, dressed in white, slipped into the circle and sunk a needle deep into the pilot's leg. A few moments later he was still.

'That,' Fitz said, 'is how to hold your nerve.'

The soldier who'd flipped the pilot stepped back, raising the visor on his helmet. McCray. He gave Fitz a curt nod, then the man was loaded on to a stretcher. McCray and the others formed a procession out of the docking bay, the woman in white in the lead.

'Maybe that's why they were doing the salvage?' Fitz offered.

'I can handle myself,' Robertson snorted.

The docking bay was already grinding back into life. The janitor had started cleaning the grubby exterior of the *Pegasus*, while Robertson took hold of a trolley and began to haul it back towards the cargo bay.

'I never trained at Marineris,' Robertson continued, 'but I can take one guy with a rush on. Besides, if all they did was salvage I wouldn't mind. But they do cargo and they break stuff.' He looked at Fitz. 'Anyone who breaks things on my team doesn't stay on it.'

Fitz struggled not to laugh. In Robertson's world, breaking stuff was clearly a capital offence.

The muscles stretched across Robertson's back as he lifted one of the crates from the trolley. He seemed like a nice guy, but Fitz was sure his firm shake could translate into a stone fist if required.

He glanced at his watch. The Doctor would be ironing the tweaks out of AuDoc for another couple of hours and, when all was said and done, Fitz didn't suit office work. He hung his jacket over the door handle and – as Robertson chuckled – began to roll up his sleeves.

'Right,' Fitz said, 'where do you want that lot?'

MARS

This isn't my life.

That's what she'd said one year ago. How quickly things changed.

It had taken a few weeks for her situation to really sink in. The Station was gone, the Doctor and Fitz weren't coming back. Every day the probability of their death inched closer to certainty and, with that, so did the need to plan. It finally came home to her when she left their hotel and returned to the warehouse where the TARDIS waited. As she stood in front of the police box, Anji realised the Doctor had taken his key with him and she didn't have a spare.

Fitz had implied the ship was somehow sentient. If that were true then maybe, she thought, it would recognise her and let her in. She took hold of the handle, the metal cold in the Martian night, and pushed at the door. It refused to give.

And that was when Anji started to plan.

She talked her way into a research job and a flat-share at the TV network; one of the producers was documenting the success of the antique stocks market. The ASM was an alternative investment market, based on twentieth-century economic models; like fantasy football league, if you were allowed to pick Jimmy Greaves and Bobby Moore and Jimmy and Bobby were actually Microsoft and Coca-Cola.

Her plan was to save as much money as possible and buy a ticket back to Earth. She wanted to go home.

Three weeks later she realised home didn't exist any more.

Anji had been walking across Boone Plaza in front of the network building. He'd come in the opposite direction, holding a bulky camera unit. She didn't recognise him at first – her memories of the day the Station fell were hazy. Then she remembered. The man from the bubble town's wall.

They'd smiled, had met for a drink that night. He talked about his holiday on Earth. Michael was Mars-born, so he'd done all the tourist traps: the Paris crater, the New York waterways. Anji had nodded and smiled, and quietly realised she didn't recognise the world he was talking about.

She could never go home again.

One year since the Station fell, ten months since that evening, and his hand was warm in hers now.

She'd insisted they sit in the back row, slipping into the cathedral at the last minute. The Doctor and Fitz were never listed among the Station's crew and Anji had never questioned this, fearful of the attention she might attract. Partly because of that, she felt like a fraud gatecrashing the ceremony.

When Michael had suggested they go, she'd said she hadn't known them well enough. You couldn't grieve for people you'd only known two weeks.

The memorial itself was an ebony block, the 228 listed in gold.

Hymns were sung, the marines outside offered a twenty-one-gun salute, a brief speech was made. In front of them people were crying. It was only when Michael squeezed her hand that Anji realised she was crying too. He'd think she was weeping for her friends. And while the ceremony reminded her of her loss, that wasn't it. It wasn't a goodbye to them, but to her old life.

They were getting up to leave when the shouting started.

A lone woman rushed to the stage. The soldiers caught her in time, but she was focused on one of the officers on the podium. Screaming and spitting, straining to break free. He sat there, stone-faced, staring the woman down.

It was only as she was dragged past that Anji could make out what she was saying: *What about the body, Colonel?*

As the cathedral doors shut, the words echoed around the nave.

What about the body?

As they left Anji heard a trio of women, dressed in black, talking about the protester. The crowd was drawing her and Michael on like a tide and Anji slipped her hand from his, called out to him: 'I'll see you back at the flat. I'm fine.'

Then she tucked into the cathedral's shadow, making her way back to the women. One carried medals tight in her hand. War widows.

'Excuse me,' Anji said, 'I was wondering if you knew what that woman was talking about?'

They exchanged glances, one checking over her shoulder. 'Conspiracy theory,' she said, 'that's all.'

'I'd like to know,' Anji replied.

Another cluster of glances. But, Anji noted, both times the first look had been between two of the women, who then turned to the third member of the group. It was this third one, a short blonde, who was just opening her mouth when the woman holding the medals said, 'I'm sorry, but we can't help you.'

Anji was waiting for the subway when there was a tap on her shoulder. The blonde widow.

'Hi,' Anji said.

The blonde glanced around. 'They mean well. Everyone's lost someone and...' She paused. 'Nothing was ever confirmed, but some of the relatives, the ones in the military, we heard stories.'

'What stories?' Anji asked.

The subway train rolled into the station, the crowd jostling along the platform as the doors opened.

'Officially, the Station was lost without a trace. No wreckage, nothing. Like space opened up and swallowed it whole.'

'I know,' Anji said.

The train doors closed and it pulled out.

The woman looked down the tunnel. 'The stories say that's not quite the whole truth.'

Anji felt a chill. 'They found someone.'

'No one alive,' the woman said. 'They found an escape capsule and a body, badly burnt.'

'Did they identify it?'

'DNA only.' She laughed, bitter. 'A janitor.' A pause, then a shake of the head. 'That's the story anyway.'

'You don't believe it,' Anji said.

Something was building inside the woman. Her hands started to tremble, her voice breaking. 'I don't know, I don't know. I just... All those people, all those people they were so well trained. My husband was a veteran, he was with the *Icarus* when it lost power out past the rim, but he made it home, they all made it home and –'

She stopped, suddenly glaring at Anji.

'A janitor,' she spat. 'My husband was a colonel, decorated five times over and a janitor got out and he didn't.' And she turned away, into the crowd.

The noise of the next train made the woman's last words inaudible, caught by wind roaring down the tunnel. Anji didn't need to hear them. *It's just a story*, the woman said. *Just a story.*

When Anji got back to the apartment Michael was in the kitchen, pasta just coming to the boil. She pressed up behind him, wrapped her arms around his waist, her head against his shoulder.

'You OK?' he asked.

'You were right,' Anji said. 'It was good to go.'

He turned around, taking her face in his hands, gently kissing her forehead. 'Dinner's in twenty minutes. If you want a shower, now is the time.'

Anji went on tiptoes to kiss him properly. They held each other for a minute, then she slipped from his grasp. 'Thank you,' she said. He smiled and turned back to the stove.

Anji padded into the bathroom, quickly undressing and stepping into the shower cubicle. A year ago she'd never have expected to be here. Not just on Mars, but with another man. Back on Earth she'd had a fiancé. But Dave had died soon after she'd met the Doctor, the first severed tie to her old life.

Mars had helped with that grief, she thought. If she'd got back to Earth there would have been reminders everywhere. Not here.

As she towelled herself off in the bedroom, Anji could hear the clink of dishes and cutlery as Michael set the table. She turned the TV on, checking the network news: a science piece about a comet passing through the Jovian system. The orange and red of Jupiter filled the screen.

It's just a story.

JUPITER SPACE
Now

Anji wakes disoriented.

The last thing she remembers is the airlock and this isn't it. The Professional had stripped Anji of her gun, sealed her inside, and – for good measure – taken away her helmet to prevent escape across the hull. She had banged on the door for a minute, examined the airlock for any other exit, then sat down and waited.

Now she is here.

'Here' is a cage. Although the light is dim, she can make out more cages all around her. Her spacesuit is gone, leaving her in cotton underwear. It's not cold, but there's a chill on her skin. Something about this place just feels wrong.

As her eyes adjust she begins to make out her surroundings. The cages are about six-foot square. While the crisscross of crudely welded bars makes it difficult to see far, the noise tells her she's not alone: whimpering, laboured breathing, creaking metal, a faint scratching. Underlying all that, exterior bulkheads groaning under pressure.

Wherever Anji is, she's still on the Station.

The smell of stale urine and faeces fills the air. An animal hand snaps through the bars on her left, grabbing her hair. She screams, throws her body weight against the creature, trapping it against the bars. There's a howl and the hand releases her. Anji backs away to the rear of her cell, making sure nothing reaches up from below to trip her. Her stomach churns with the sick feeling this place gives her. She steadies herself against the wall, making an effort to control herself. There's a cold sweat on her brow.

And then, just as she thinks she is about to panic, the wall in front of the cages cracks open. Once upon a time it was probably automated. Now the motors are abandoned and, as the door is hauled back on twisted rails, the animals howl and throw themselves against the bars drowning out the screech of metal.

The air that comes through the door is stale and old, but it helps clear some of the smell. That alone is enough to calm Anji as the woman steps into the room.

'Hello?' Anji calls nervously.

The woman ignores her. She drags a gantry across the floor until it's positioned in front of Anji's cage, then starts to climb. All sight is lost as a flashlight shines straight into Anji's eyes. The animals begin to howl again.

'Please,' Anji says, 'I don't know where I am.'

The woman's hand slams against the front of the cage. 'Shut up. One wrong move and I swear I'll –'

'I don't understand what –'

'Shut up!' the woman barks.

'That's enough.' A male voice now, coming from the doorway. 'She's not wounded and we need answers.'

There's something about the stress he places on the word *wounded*. Not an adjective, but a noun. *She's not Wounded and we need answers.*

'We don't know anything about her,' the woman snaps.

'Which is why we need to ask.'

A moment's silence, then the flashlight clicks off. Anji blinks her eyes clear, sees the woman shouldering past the man on her way out. The man watches her go, then turns on an overhead light. As he begins climbing the gantry Anji gets some sense of her surroundings.

The first thing she sees is what's in the cage to her left. Anji had thought it was an animal. She was wrong.

It's another woman: naked, nursing a gash where Anji smashed her arm against the bars. This prisoner is startled by the light and whimpers, scrambling towards a dark corner. The room is filled with similar noises, the metal bars rattling with movement.

'What is this place?' Anji whispers.

As the man draws back the bolt holding her cage shut, she gets her first real look at his face.

It should be a boy's. The curly hair belongs to the Renaissance, but light catches the grey running through it. The eyes are shadowed and heavy, the mouth expressionless. Someone tired of living.

The door swings open and he extends a hand. 'You're not Wounded, you're free to go.'

Anji blinks. 'What's going on? What is this place?'

'Quarantine. Or prison. Take your pick.' He holds his hands up, showing he means no harm. 'A patrol found you. In one of the airlocks.'

Anji shakes her head. 'I don't remember any patrol.'

'They vented some oxygen; put you to sleep before opening the door.' The man shrugs. 'They weren't sure what you were.'

'Weren't sure –?' Anji stammers. 'I'm human, for Christ's sake!'

The man smiles then. A long, sad smile, and says, 'Yes. Yes, you are. I'm Joshua Easter.' He pauses. 'There are others.'

Neither of them moves. The cages creak around them.

'You're free to leave.' Easter begins to retreat down the steps. 'I'm assuming you do want to leave.'

The darkness, the cramped space and the stale smell flash in Anji's mind. 'Yes,' she whispers. 'Please, get me out of here.'

Rummaging through a locker near the door, Easter finds Anji some clothes.

'Can't I have my suit back?' Anji asks. 'The spacesuit?'

'Maybe later,' Easter says. He hands her trousers and an old T-shirt, both torn and grubby. He nods at the cages behind them. 'In the end they just tear them off and...' He pauses, shrugs again. 'It doesn't leave them much dignity, but it's a waste of resources.'

Twelve cells to a row and ten rows that she can see. Most occupants invisible, keeping to the shadows. But Anji's seen enough to know a majority of those cells are occupied.

The past couple of years have seen Anji do the occasional piece of off-world reporting. Everyone tells her space travel is getting better; it's not as utilitarian as it was, but the departure points on the Mars Orbital still aren't the first-class lounge at Heathrow. Now that she's free and has some perspective, Anji can recognise her place of captivity for what it is. A cargo bay that's been ripped apart and put back together in hellish fashion: row upon row of cages fashioned from cargo pallets and scrap metal, occupants huddling in fear. Like news reports on battery farming.

Anji gets dressed, but there must be a look on her face because Easter says, 'They're Wounded. It's the best we can do.' There's real strain in his voice, and when he ushers Anji out of the cargo bay she sees how his hand trembles.

As Easter pulls the door closed behind them, Anji looks at the sight beyond. 'Oh, God,' she whispers.

It used to be a docking bay, Anji can still see that, but it hasn't fulfilled that purpose for a very long time. Bare bulbs hang from cables strung across the space. The skeletons of shuttlecraft line the far wall, each one flayed open to form a ramshackle habitat. A patchwork water tower weeps in one corner. Towards the rear of the bay four tents have been erected as greenhouses, their plastic hides damp with condensation, interiors glowing with ultraviolet light. Elsewhere the hard, electric light is replaced by the dull warmth of flames; near by, sparks fly as metal connects with a grindstone. And everywhere are the people. The tired, haunted look on Easter's face repeated over and over as they pass back and forth. Repairing the habitats, firing generators, hammering metal, carrying sacks, lifting buckets.

'Oh, God,' Anji repeats. 'What happened here?'

Easter looks at her, his tone as expressionless as his face as he explains: 'We survived.'

The Professional moves through the Station. The corridors are dark, illuminated only by the flash of distant electrics.

After leaving Kapoor, the Professional accessed the main Station systems. The central computer registered as undamaged and online, but it was impossible to access. Many systems have overloaded; carbon scorches scar the walls. His suit's diagnostics suggest an unhealthy percentage of the Station's engineering resources are shut down, all available power redirected to positioning thrusters. Jupiter is a hostile environment and the Station's continued existence suggests someone must have survived the initial disaster. By virtue of ripping half its systems apart and adapting most of the rest, that someone has done just enough to stop it sinking any further into the planet's grasp.

The flares that roll down the corridors are, the Professional surmises, the result of overloads from this continual struggle to maintain position. Whatever their cause, the bursts are not enough to really see by.

Every hundredth of a second the Professional's suit runs a sensor sweep across the EM spectrum, projecting the results on to the helmet interior and showing him far more than his eyes could ever hope to see. This sensor sweep also filters the noise around him, screening out the Station's pressure aches and the gouts of steam and the groan of ill-repaired hydraulics.

And, as the Professional moves onwards, in sweeping clean all this aural debris his suit leaves one sound that he hears over all others: careful footsteps, shadowing his every movement.

'I don't believe you.'

It's the woman who confronted Anji in quarantine. Her name is Caroline Arquette and something about her has put Anji on edge. It's taken a few minutes, but Anji's figured it out: it's the way Arquette moves.

She isn't any better fed than the rest of the survivors. Her body has the same hallmarks of borderline malnutrition; dark shadows on sallow skin speak of the same lack of sleep, and four years without sunlight. But whereas the others are tired and worn down, Arquette isn't. There's a hardness beneath the surface. Running through that body, powering its exertions, is an energy that Anji is only just recognising: blind, unrelenting hate.

'She's a spy,' Arquette barks, a statement she's made several times in the past few minutes.

Easter has brought Anji into the *de facto* headquarters of the survivors' camp. A circle of crates for chairs, around a pair of jury-rigged computer terminals that feed through an access hatch into the systems beneath the docking bay.

While some survivors carry on with their daily routine, others have come to this spot, looking at Anji with shock and suspicion. One – a thin man with patchy red hair – had moved in close when she left the Wounded, whispered, 'Have you come for me?', his eyes desperate.

Easter had drawn her away and to this place. At his prompting, Anji has been trying to explain who she is and how she came to be here. At every opportunity, Arquette has called Anji a liar.

'It's preposterous,' Arquette says.

'Why?' It's another one of the survivors. A thin man introduced as Gould.

'Four years,' Arquette snaps. 'And the only person who comes to find us is a reporter? No evac ships, no medical aid, no weapons, no support. Just a reporter.'

Anji shakes her head. 'That isn't what I –'

Arquette delivers a backhanded blow that snaps Anji's head around, leaves her sprawled on the floor. Anji tries to pick herself up, but Arquette's hand is at her throat. Anji doesn't see what happens next, but there's shouting, Easter's voice in among the cacophony, then the pressure on her windpipe vanishes.

Coughing, Anji gets pulled to her feet. Arquette is being kept at bay by two of the survivors, her eyes locked on Anji.

'Enough!' Easter shouts. 'That's enough!'

'If Earth Forces could drop on to the Station like that, don't you think they'd have done it before now?' Arquette spits. 'If she got through the blockade, then she must have been allowed through. She's working for them.'

Anji is about to protest her innocence again, but she is given a more immediate cause for concern.

'We'll find out,' another survivor says. 'Once we've caught her friend, anyways.'

'Oh, no,' Anji says.

Arquette turns, scenting vindication. 'Worried we're on to you?'

'You're tracking him,' Anji says. 'You've got men out tracking him?'

'They're going to do more than track him.'

Anji looks at Easter. 'Call them off.'

Easter frowns. Wondering if Arquette was right, Anji thinks.

'He'll kill them,' Anji says. 'That's not a bloody amateur, that's a Professional out there, and if you don't call off your men he's going to kill them all.'

Arquette snorts. 'What the hell is a Professional when it's –'

But she's cut off by a burst of sound from one of the computer terminals. Static and screams, cut through by distorted explosions and gunfire. A voice deep and desperate.

'– *trap. Sonofabitch had laser mines. Easter, do you hear? We're trapped on the secondary drag. We need help, we* –'

Arquette looks at the computer screen: the voiceprint is rising and falling. 'Robbie?' she whispers.

'Give me my suit,' Anji says.

Arquette reaches for a knife at her side. 'You shut up.'

Anji ignores her, looks at Easter. 'If you want to save them, give me my suit and give it to me now.'

The Vickers Class III Pulse Mine is less than three centimetres in diameter, attachable to any surface and remote-activated. The thirty miniature laser emitters that coat its surface deliver quarter-second bursts in a random sequence. Unlikely to score an immediate kill, the mine incapacitates without being so indiscriminate as to punch through a vital bulkhead. Standard issue for a close-quarters ambush in a confined space.

Most of the Professional's pursuers have fallen back.

One of the smarter ones has deployed some kind of smoke bomb to cover their retreat. It only makes the Professional's job easier. The head-up display cuts through the smoke, which is only masking his advance up the corridor. He takes aim at one of the hostiles – prone, clutching his leg, oblivious. Then one of the periodic overloads explodes behind the Professional, offering up his shadow amidst the smoke. The hostile sees him, raises a weapon and the Professional squeezes off a single round. A clean hit in the centre of the hostile's chest.

As he turns to the next target, feedback screams in the Professional's helmet. Then Kapoor's voice: '– *human. Can you hear me? They're the Station personnel. You're killing the* –'

The Professional cuts the signal, switches the laser mine to protective fire mode, turns back to the hostile. A young man, mid-twenties, oriental. Neither clothing nor armaments are Earth Forces' issue, placing the hostile firmly within the rules of engagement. The Professional runs his AI's scanner over the man's face. A name blinks among the 228: David Verger, electrical engineer.

The Professional activates his suit's external speakers: 'Cease firing. This is your one chance. Lower your weapons and no one else dies.'

Robertson saw a face once and it will haunt him for the rest of his days. He only saw it once, for less than a moment, but he will never be able to forget.

The stranger hasn't said much since they ceased firing. Some of the others – Fletcher and Alonso most of all – wanted to carry on the fight; you could see it in their eyes. But Robertson gives the orders and when he told them, they shouldered their weapons. When word came through from the Village, it was simple: return home, bring the stranger with you.

By the time they reach the barricades sweat is soaking the back of Robertson's shirt. In theory, he's one of the lucky ones: covering the rear when the laser mine erupted, quick enough to find cover, not taking a single hit. A couple of others were that lucky, though most have a burn on the face or a hole in an arm or something. The only serious casualty is the one weighing across Robertson's shoulders.

Robertson was one of the lucky ones, but Caroline is going to kill him if she sees him like this. The survivors don't have much in the way of body armour – crude pads hammered from the research shuttles' protective plates – and Robertson has stripped his off in order to carry David. Worse, he's had to hand his weapon to someone else.

He remembers a time before the Fall and other men like the stranger. Dangerous men. You could drink and laugh together, could gamble and cheer, but you always knew just how dangerous they were. It was the way they walked, the way they sat, the way they watched. An awareness of their surroundings; observation; anticipation.

McCray was like that.

The stranger has the same look. Silent as they move through the Village's barricades. Not asking questions but observing: electrified barriers of twisted metal, the uneven grind of automated gunpoints. His head constantly on the move as his body takes long, smooth steps.

Dangerous.

Past the final barrier and there's a hum as the power is switched back on. The stranger pauses at that, raises a hand over one of the metal shapes, doesn't flinch as electricity that keeps the enemy out arcs against his fingers. He nods and they walk on.

Weir and Carvacchio are on sentry duty. They know what's happened, are looking for the stranger as Robertson and the others pass by. Archer is watching, eyes fixed on the stranger; he looks terrified. He shouts the refrain he's been shouting for years – 'It wasn't me!' – then withdraws.

Easter is waiting, counting them in. His face falls as he sees Robertson's cargo and points to a cot-bed set near the Meridian's computers. With a final groan, Robertson sinks to his knees and rolls David from his shoulders on to the bed. Easter gets to work, tearing David's shirt open.

'What happened?'

Robertson nods back across the compound. Framed by Weir and Carvacchio, the stranger is looking up at the main entrance to the docking bay, studying the makeshift sign that reads GREENWICH VILLAGE.

'He happened,' Robertson explains. 'One shot, close range.'

'You!' Easter shouts. 'What are you carrying?'

The stranger walks towards them, studying their surroundings.

'What did you shoot him with?' Easter demands.

'Grade-seven plasma rifle.' The stranger nods at David. 'He moved at the last second. The spinal column is severed, but I missed the heart.'

Easter shakes his head, begins plugging David's wound. 'I'm supposed to be grateful it isn't worse, am I?'

'I need to speak to your commanding officer.'

Easter pulls a patch of cloth from his pocket, slapping it down for the Professional to see. The stripes they took from Captain Stokes' uniform.

'I'm the commanding officer,' Easter says. 'And you'll have to wait until this man is either stable or dead.'

Robertson is watching this exchange from the floor. As Easter works on David, packing the hole with swabs, the stranger continues to study the Village. People aren't approaching, just shooting nervous glances as they pass by. They know what the stranger has done; they don't want to attract his attention. Robertson realises they're also looking curiously at him. Fingering his T-shirt he finds it slick with David's blood.

Today was too close.

Without a word to Easter or the stranger, Robertson gets to his feet and walks away. The other members of the patrol are scattered near by, but he shrugs them off, heading for the showers beneath the water tank. The water is never hot or cold, always the same lukewarm temperature as the docking bay. The dim light is not enough to disguise the red pooling at his feet. The shower still feels good, though.

'Robbie.'

He turns, blinks the water clear. Caroline is there, fully dressed, standing on the edge of the grate that marks the shower area. The drainage pump is out, water laps at her boots. Her voice is tight.

'Are you...?'

'Not a scratch,' he whispers.

'What happened?'

'There was an alarm from one of the airlocks. We checked it out, found the woman. Howerd and Bluth brought her back here. We followed him and...' He stops, whispers. 'It was too close.'

He looks at Caroline, but her eyes are in shadow. Robertson turns his face back into the falling water. When he brings it out again, she has gone.

By the time Robertson has found himself fresh clothes, curiosity has overcome suspicion and a small crowd has gathered at the Meridian.

Caroline is there, casting hard looks at the stranger and the woman. Robertson tries to squeeze her hand, but her fingers keep slipping free to brush the handle of the knife strapped against her thigh.

David is still on the cot, its fabric soaked black with blood. There's an ugly bandage on the chest wound and Easter is programming one of the terminals to regulate pain control. He says, 'He's stable now.'

Robertson reads the look on Easter's face. What he means is David's just going to take longer dying.

Caroline's hand slips free of his again and Robertson's fingers clench into a fist. He glares at the stranger: 'You're Earth Forces?'

'Yes.'

'This is what we do in wartime now? We kill our own?'

'You were tracking me, without recognisable uniform or equipment. That made your –'

'Shut up,' Caroline says.

Robertson blinks. There's a tension across her shoulders, the hand firmly closed on the knife now.

'I want to know what's going on,' she says.

'That makes a refreshing change.' It's the woman they found, speaking for the first time.

'You're nobody,' Caroline says. 'Stuck in an airlock, no weapon, untrained. You're not a soldier, we can't use you.'

'All right,' Easter says, trying to impose himself on the group. 'If everyone finds themselves a seat, then we can start hearing explanations.'

There's a pause, then – to Robertson's surprise – Caroline breaks first, pulling up a crate. Within moments, everyone except the stranger has followed suit. Easter looks like he's about to ask the man to sit down, but changes his mind.

Easter nods at the woman. 'Miss Kapoor, I think we've got the basic of how you're here.' Robertson frowns: there's something in his memory, something about that name. 'I'd like to know the why.'

'Fitz.' Robertson whispers the name, but somehow everyone hears it. And the woman, Kapoor, turns to him, her eyes shining. 'The accountant,' Robertson continues, 'the scruffy one. He said he was here for a friend. Her name was Kapoor.'

'Anji,' the woman says. She extends a hand. Robertson blinks at it. The gesture belongs to another life. He reaches out and grips her hand.

'I'm Robertson.'

'Fitz and the Doctor were here,' Anji says. 'You saw them?'

It should be a simple question, but it's been four years. If they were any other names Robertson might not remember. But Fitz and the Doctor have come up in conversation more than once over the years; always in relation to the Fall.

Robertson picks his words carefully. 'I got to know Fitz a little. Nice guy. Your other friend, the Doctor?' Anji nods. 'I don't remember him much. Only spoke to him the one time, I think.' He pauses, 'They were stuck in a holding cell.'

Anji smiles. 'That sounds like them.' There's a pause and they can all see the hope in that smile on Anji's face.

The stranger looks at Easter. 'She came for her friends. She has no authority here.'

'And you do?' Weir calls out.

The stranger finds him in the crowd, says, 'I'm a Professional.'

'What's your name?' Easter asks.

'He doesn't have a name,' Anji says. 'None of them does.' A pause. 'He's Earth Forces Special Ops.' She laughs. 'He's here to rescue you.'

'One man?' Robertson says. 'Four years down here and they send one man?'

'There are casualties, aren't there?' It's Caroline, speaking for the first time since they sat down. She nods her head upwards, towards unseen stars, 'We're in trouble, aren't we? We're losing the war.'

A sudden quiet descends on the group.

Anji opens her mouth, but the Professional speaks over her: 'What do you know about the war?'

'Only what we've been able to figure out,' Caroline answers. 'We were attacked, the Station fell, we were boarded. We've been trying to keep the enemy at bay, but...' She shrugs. 'Look around. There's only so much we can do.'

Other voices cut in. 'We figured there must be a blockade,' Bluth calls.

'This station was a valuable resource.' A woman's voice, Lin.

'That's right.' Alonso now. 'Earth wouldn't let it fall into enemy hands without a fight.'

And then more voices, talking over each other, demanding answers. Like on so many occasions, Robertson can see Easter lose control of the meeting. Easter gets to his feet to try and calm everyone down, but it only prompts others to stand in turn.

In the end, it's the Professional who restores order. 'There was a blockade,' he says. And in a moment the silence returns. 'A rescue mission was impossible.'

'Until now,' Caroline answers. 'And if they sent you to run the blockade, then they must have needed something from this station. They must be desperate.'

It's Robertson who voices the question she's skirting around: 'We're losing, aren't we?'

Anji looks at the Professional. Both stay silent.

'Tell us,' Robertson says. 'It can't be worse than this.'

'I need to know what happened on this station,' the Professional replies. 'Start with the first attack and take it from there.'

The Professional watches. The schism in the group is clear to see. Whether by accident or design, this place – with its computer access and medical supplies – has become the default meeting point for the makeshift compound. Circular in shape, it should be an inclusive space. But when Easter sat down, he positioned himself directly opposite Arquette, leaving everyone else caught between them.

Kapoor caught the look he gave her when they began talking about a war and she's stayed silent ever since.

There are facts to be gained here that will only be uncovered if events run their course. But these people's tensions are barely held beneath the surface, every one of them carries ticks and nervous mannerisms. Easter is in charge: a doctor, young, comparatively low-ranking among the 228, always pulling at those stripes in his pocket.

The Professional looks at the small blonde-haired woman, sitting taut opposite Easter.

Her hand resting on the knife she carries.

The considered way Robertson reacts around her suggests a relationship between them; an undercurrent of need and respect absent in their peers. But even here there's tension. Need, respect, but uncertainty too.

Others contribute, random voices interrupting, but – for the most part – they let Easter do the talking.

– The alert sounded. It was that simple.

There'd been an accident and I was running triage. It's what saved me. The Defcon had been rising for a few days. None of us had access to any intelligence reports, but the stuff on the civilian channels was worrying enough. So when the alarm sounded... It wasn't a shock. Everyone had been waiting for it.

– You're forgetting the commander.

– Yes, yes, of course. Commander Valletti was on comms,

announcing the Defcon alert. But... She was panicked, afraid. You could hear it in her voice. Then she was cut off. Atmospheric control was lost and people started screaming. It was the air pressure.

- The enemy hacked the environmental system. They were trying to kill us before we could defend ourselves. Kill the personnel, leave the Station intact.

- We never found out what stopped them. The best guess is that someone in the central hub was able to interfere, to stop the worst of it. The atmospheric pressure had ramped up in a couple of seconds. Enough for nosebleeds and burst eardrums. There were conduits blowing out and hydraulics failing.

When the pressure dropped people picked themselves up, looking for orders that didn't come. None of the protocols was implemented. There was nothing coming out of the central hub.

- That's when we found the body.
- Jason. Four years of this and our only casualty.
- Until today!
- David's not dead yet.
- No, but he's going to be.
- He could still –
- Jason was killed by the enemy. Robbie and Easter don't believe that, but I do.

- When the central hub went quiet, Captain Stokes sent a few of us to make direct contact. That's when we found Jason. He was just a cleaner, but... We found him on one of the main drags, near the bottom of an elevator shaft. Burnt like he'd been caught in a plasma fire or something. I mean, really burnt. It took a DNA reading to make an identification. Except...

- He'd been poisoned.

- No. We don't know that. His DNA had been distorted and that's all we know. Medics keep things simple: patch up the wounded, move them on. In the event of biological attack, we have orders to exercise containment. The Station was falling apart, we couldn't access the sickbay... So we loaded his corpse into an escape capsule and jettisoned it.

Ten minutes after that the defence batteries opened up, then the Station's thrusters fired and our orbit destabilised. We were falling.

* * *

Anji has been listening to the words, trying to piece the story together. While they're all talking about how the Station fell, what comes over in the voices is the life they've lived since.

The more Anji hears, the more she looks around, the worse it seems to get. It's no surprise that these people look tired. Everything here – from the air they breathe to the food they eat – is the result of struggle. It shows in their faces; it echoes through their voices.

Arquette is talking now, addressing the Professional: 'Six months after the Fall, six months of jury-rigging Station systems, then the enemy showed themselves. Stokes was the first one to be Wounded.'

'The cages,' Anji explains. 'He's in one of the cages.'

And as bad as Anji had thought their life was, it suddenly gets worse as a small voice sounds.

'Don't let the monsters touch you. It's the law.'

It's a boy, dark-haired with big eyes. No more than three years old, his voice rising with a toddler's disregard for audience and surroundings. He's slipped between the legs of the adults, finally making it to the front. Arquette gives the child a hard look and he runs, the crowd parting before him.

Anji opens her mouth to ask the obvious question, but Easter catches her eye, shakes his head.

'When the enemy touch you,' Easter explains, 'you're infected with something. Some toxin and it –'

'It drives you insane,' Anji says. 'The people in the cages. That's how they were hurt, isn't it?'

'Wounded,' Easter nods.

The Professional interrupts, staring at Arquette: 'Why jury-rig the controls?'

'What?'

'"Six months of jury-rigging the Station systems." Why not hack the central computers? Why locate here rather than the hub?'

A silence falls over the group, then Easter clears his throat, explains: 'The central hub is off-limits.'

'There's an energy barrier.' It's the big man, Robertson, explaining. 'A force field or something. You touch it, it burns. You can't penetrate more than a couple of millimetres.'

That's when the pieces fall into place for Anji. 'The hub,' she says. 'That's where the Doctor and Fitz were, isn't it? When all this happened.'

Robertson nods. 'I'm sorry,' he whispers.

The Professional barely registers this information. Like he has no interest in Anji's friends at all. 'I'll want to see any records. Sensor logs, telemetry, schematics.'

'We don't have much,' Easter replies, 'and it'll take a while to gather the information.' He gestures to the terminals. 'The computers function, but they're not that reliable. Caroline?'

Arquette shrugs. 'I can set it running overnight, give you the results in the morning.'

'I want it by 06:00,' the Professional states.

'Is that it?' Arquette asks. 'Is that all the explanation we get?'

The Professional could let it go. But, as he turns to Arquette, Anji realises this isn't going to happen.

'I'm the spearhead,' the Professional says flatly. 'Sent to judge the viability of a rescue mission. You answer to my authority now.'

It's a deliberate challenge. Since she woke in the cell Anji's only ever seen Arquette pushing against her superiors. It's not something the Professional will have failed to pick up on: it's not a position he'll let Arquette take with him. Easter is reluctant to face her down; the Professional wants to see how far Arquette's attitude will take her.

As Anji watches, she can see Arquette's grip tighten on that knife. She's sure the Professional must see it too, only he gives no hint of what awaits the woman if she attacks.

Then Robertson places a hand on Arquette's shoulder, making her flinch. 'We've work to do,' he tells her.

Arquette looks at the Professional, shakes her head. 'You'll get your report,' she says. Then she shrugs off Robertson's touch and stalks away.

As the meeting breaks up Kapoor looks around, unsure what to do. She moves to follow Robertson and Easter, but the Professional takes hold of her wrist. Kapoor looks at him. He gives a very subtle shake of his head, then walks away.

The Professional walks through the camp, ignoring the looks from the survivors. One of them reaches out to touch him, pilgrim to saviour, but the Professional just brushes past. A brief glance backwards reveals Kapoor trailing in his wake. Whether it's her lack of authority or a reaction to his own dismissal of them, no one grabs her.

Approaching the rear of the compound – Greenwich Village according to the sign he saw – the Professional passes by the first greenhouse tent; silhouettes show people working inside. He opens the flap on the second – empty – and slips inside, moving down the aisle. The survivors have pieced together some hydroponics equipment. The tent has a rich, loamy scent; echoes with the slow creak of air in the pipework hanging above. The beds hold fruits and some root vegetables. Not much, but enough to help supplement their rations. Four tents, the Professional thinks, suggesting conditions are staggered across the seasons to ensure a constant harvest.

When he reaches the middle of the tent he stops and waits for Kapoor to catch up. As she approaches he turns a stiff and rusted tap. The pipes cough, then shower heads come to life and rain begins to fall. The rattling pipework and the hiss and patter of water should render conversation inaudible to anyone outside the tent's walls.

The sprinkler isn't that sophisticated and the aisle where they are standing offers no protection. Kapoor shivers as the water strikes her, soaking the dirty clothes she is in, slicking her hair.

'Don't make friends,' the Professional says.

'What?' Kapoor replies.

'You were going to sit down with Easter and Robertson. You were going to help them, to speak to them, to forge a connection with them. I have one instruction for you. Don't.'

A few minutes later, Anji steps from the tent, T-shirt and trousers sopping wet. She sees a pressure vent set into one of the docking-bay walls. Slipping behind the remaining tents, keeping out of sight, Anji makes her way over to it. The vent blows stale and pungent air, but it's hot and as Anji leans against it she can feel her clothes tighten against her skin.

As she waits, she watches.

Don't get close. Because you know what I know. You know about the past four years. There's no war. There's no enemy.

She sees Easter at a computer terminal, tugging at his hair as he works. Robertson sits near by, next to the camp bed holding the man the Professional shot. Robertson's head is sunk into his hands. His shoulders should be heaving with tears, Anji thinks, but he doesn't move.

They've been fighting a rearguard action against alien intruders for almost four years, but there are no fatalities, no evidence of sustained fighting.

Anji thinks about the red-headed man whispering, 'Have you come for me?' He'd screamed at the Professional when he walked in. She finds him now, tucked down by a habitat, checking something beneath it, his head twitching, trying to make sure no one's watching him.

Their story makes no sense.

The boy flashes across the periphery of her vision, screaming at adults who jump at the sound. In the distance she can see Arquette standing under one of the showers. Stripped of her clothes and her attitude, a marionette with its strings cut. Her head bobs up and down, gasping for breath to clear the tears from her throat. She still holds the knife, the blade brushing back and forth against her bare thigh.

Look around you, look at these people and the life they're living. What would this life do to you if you had to live it for four years?

And Anji looks across the compound to where the door to the cargo bay is firmly shut. There's a noise that undercuts all the other activity. The brain filters the sound out most of the time, but it's there. Anji has heard it every minute since she woke in this place.

It would leave you mad.

A low keening, occasionally punctuated by a wordless shout of anger and frustration.

Just like it's left all of them.

The song of the Wounded.

Four years earlier

Accounts, the Doctor decided, were amazing things.

He'd hoped he would be able to manipulate his security clearance enough to gain access to anything on file. Unfortunately, the Station's security systems were tighter than he'd thought. He could access biographies for the civilians on board, but records for all the military – including the troopers he'd followed here – remained sealed behind firewalls.

Which meant he'd have to do things the hard way. Investigation. Means, motive and opportunity.

And for that, he needed leads. Which was where accountancy came in.

On Earth he'd hardly ever seen accounts viewed in anything but a negative light: grim tales of tax returns, missed deadlines, penalties, confusion and boredom. But that was only half the story. If you divorced the trail of money from capitalist philosophy, then the numbers offered a fascinating viewpoint all of their own. Page after page of accounts was a dull sight, true, but it was the translation of those figures that gave insight. Like time-lapse photography, each line was a still moment transformed as part of a bigger picture. You could, he thought, trace the activity of a whole city just by looking at its accounts. A city or even a space station.

So when a skeletal man entered his office without knocking, the Doctor already had a good idea who he was.

'Professor Deschamps?'

The man frowned, then pulled himself up straight. 'You were expecting me, of course.'

The Doctor tapped his desk screen. 'Real-time finance. You blew out a quantum generator this morning and want to requisition another.'

'No, no,' Deschamps said. 'I have requisitioned another. Bad enough we're days away from the nearest supply centre, now

Valletti tells me I need your signature for the order to be processed.'

The Doctor looked at him. Deschamps was keeping his tone civil, but there was something about how his eyes darted around the room, the way he kept his hands wedged in his pockets. An energy just below the surface, straining to get out. Dedication to his work, maybe.

The Doctor smiled and decided to give Deschamps a push. Just to see. 'Standard procedure. With an audit in progress, all spending needs to be approved by this office.'

One hand snapped from the trouser pocket, clenched tight. 'Just sign the damn order, will you?'

'It would help if I knew what you needed it for.'

The tension was starting to show in Deschamps voice. 'You wouldn't understand. Sign the order.'

'I really would like –'

Deschamps' body was tightening, his shoulders squaring. 'Every moment you keep me here is a moment you are taking away from my work.'

The Doctor made a show of consulting his records. 'Deschamps? It's the singularity bomb, isn't it?'

'Yes, it's the singularity bomb! Do you treat all the staff here like this, or are you just making an exception for me?'

'I don't –'

'It's Mukabi, isn't it? What's he been saying? Dripping poison in your ear, is that it?'

'I haven't –'

The clenched hand slammed down on the desk. 'Sign the order!'

There was a pause, then the Doctor hit a control and smiled. 'Done.'

Deschamps snapped round, pushing past Fitz on his way out of the door. Fitz looked after Deschamps for a moment, then turned to the Doctor. 'Satisfied customer?'

'I think we both got what we wanted.'

'Which was?'

'A quantum generator for him; insight for me. That was a very angry man.'

'I could tell.'

'Struggling to keep his anger under control.'

'I'd never have guessed,' Fitz said, slumping back in a chair. The Doctor looked at his companion. Fitz had been gone a couple of hours now, and had returned red in the face, jacket over his shoulder, sweat on his brow. There was an oily stain on his shirt.

'That's no way to treat designer fashions,' the Doctor said.

'I was working,' Fitz said. 'Lending a hand in the cargo bay.'

'Useful?'

'Among other things, I think I've solved your initiative test.'

'Really?' the Doctor said. 'What exactly did you learn in the cargo bay?'

'What that occupation Valletti mentioned was, that the atmosphere on Mars used to be breathable,' Fitz said. 'A couple of decades ago there was some sort of invasion. Earth was under alien control, with alien ships blockading Mars. These aliens tried to land on Mars, but got their arses handed to them by some sort of biological weapon. They got their own back; released a virus from orbit that ate through all the oxygen.' Fitz paused. 'It's taken them years to reverse the damage.'

The Doctor watched Fitz think things through.

'When I played guitar in the clubs, I had a stage name. I was never Fitz Kreiner. Twenty years after VE day and I was still afraid to use my own name. Because people still remembered.' Fitz looked at the Doctor. 'These people are afraid. You don't forget a war when it's over and you don't forget being invaded.'

'Go on.'

Fitz held up his jacket. 'This is a nice suit, but it reminded me of something the moment I saw it. Those big square shoulders? We look like G-men.'

The Doctor smiled to himself. Fitz had it.

'It's Reds under the bed, isn't it?'

'A good analogy,' the Doctor said. 'After Pearl Harbor, America woke from an isolationist slumber. When they won the war, people looked to the next danger. It's a similar thing here. As you say, people remember.'

'And that's why you're trying to keep your head down?'

'The major cultural indicators – the clothing and architecture, even the literature – are built around themes of unity and strength. Listen to the news reports. The key adjectives are variants on a theme:

power, threat, strength. There are undercurrents of nerves and paranoia leaching across human society, the background noise to everyday activity.' He shifted in his chair. 'Humanity is preparing for the next war; they're just waiting to find the enemy.' He smiled. 'And I'd rather it wasn't me.'

'Fair point. The way McCray and his boys handled themselves, I can't blame you.'

'Why?' the Doctor frowned. 'What happened?'

Fitz explained what he'd seen in the docking bay. As he got to the end, the Doctor started playing with his computer terminal. A few seconds later a hologram appeared, hovering over the desk. It was a swirl of slowly dancing colours, vaguely spherical in shape. Streams of red and blue crisscrossed each other, white cubes revolved on their axes, golden spheres trailed each other around the exterior.

'AuDoc,' the Doctor smiled. Then he pointed to where a tiny black droplet was bleeding from one colour stream to be swallowed by another.

'It's an appropriation from the rescue and salvage funds, made by one of the science team.' He squinted. 'Dr Sara Mukabi. That must have been the woman you saw. Same name as the person Deschamps didn't want me talking to.' He frowned. 'Wrong sex, though.'

Fitz nodded at the hologram. 'This is all the money flowing in and out of the Station?'

'A representation of it, yes.'

'And you know what all these bits are?' Fitz peered sceptically at the mess of coloured shapes. He pointed to one at random, his fingertip sinking into a revolving sphere of yellow and black.

'What's that, then?'

The Doctor glanced at the sphere. 'Overtime on systems maintenance. The yellow and black indicates above average spending for the last quarter.'

'You're not making that up, are you?'

The Doctor handed him a colour key and said, 'Feel free to check for yourself.'

As the Doctor got back to work Fitz began to play with the hologram, zooming in and out. A few minutes later the Doctor turned to him and asked, 'Is there something in particular you're trying to achieve, Fitz?'

'Robertson said McCray's mob handle more than just salvage.' Fitz nodded at the hologram. 'There are some shipments the cargo crews are never allowed near. But those shipments will still have to be paid for, right?' He shrugged, checked his watch. 'It'll wait till tomorrow. Clocking-off time, and Robbie owes me a beer.'

'You go,' the Doctor said. 'I'll catch up with you later.'

When Fitz had gone, the Doctor returned his attention to AuDoc.

The personnel files of the military on board remained confidential. However, while he couldn't call up those records for the soldiers who'd attacked Anji, the files he did have access to could be useful. A simple request delivered the pair's time sheets, but no real answers.

The two man had been general workers, rotated around various departments – maintenance, shipping, communications – in the Station's outer rings. There was nothing linking them directly to any research projects.

Which left the Doctor back at square one, looking for leads. Fitz's mysterious cargo shipments were as good a place to start as any.

McCray's men belonged to the 101st Airborne. Calling up their time sheets generated a series of black cylinders. Wherever the 101st's duties coincided with other budgetary areas, AuDoc drew red lines to highlight the links. As the cylinders moved through the graphic the lines hung like ghosts behind them, gradually fading as they were absorbed into the budget. Several sets of lines showed interactions with fuel budgets and pilot hours. The figures suggested short hops; most likely research shuttles making trips into Jupiter's atmosphere.

Other connections were made with time sheets for the cargo and handling ledgers. Connections with inbound flights, the Doctor assumed, most likely picking up Fitz's shipments. But the pick-up wasn't the problem. It was where the cargo was deposited that was difficult. When the 101st delivered the cargo the black cylinders should have extended new lines to a new section of the accounts. Instead, when those lines were generated they simply faded into a grey haze.

The Doctor chewed on his thumb.

The grey area was AuDoc extrapolating. The AI could tell there was a funding program there because of the effect it had on the objects around it, but it couldn't define what that program was because the data was unavailable.

For all intents and purposes, the grey haze could have been a red sign flashing the words TOP SECRET at him.

The Doctor asked AuDoc to locate any similar anomalies, cross-referencing with other financial areas to see if there was any overlap. It proved to be a slow process, producing a handful of results. Almost all of them saw the grey area intersecting with the names Mukabi, S. or Mukabi, T., both civilian workers, which meant their records were on file and available.

Sara and Terrance Mukabi were one of the Station's few married couples. He could see their living allowance, their wages, the money spent on their food and their quarters. She was the Station's psychiatric therapist, while he was one of the computer-support team. Only their time sheets didn't match their income and outgoings, with no hint as to why that would be the case.

His frustration was only made worse by the fact that AuDoc appeared to be slowing down. He'd ring-fenced the AI's processing needs from the Station's computers, which meant the problem wasn't with the AI's thought processes, but with the lag time on the Station computers it was interacting with.

The Doctor accessed the comms system. 'Locate Commander Valletti, please.'

'Commander Valletti is currently off-network.'

He frowned. 'And when will she be back on network?'

'At 20:00 hours, Recreation Hall A.'

Fitz had dumped his sweaty suit and tie in the laundry, then taken a shower. Dressed in jeans, a T-shirt and dog-eared leather jacket, he was now ready for the evening. Robertson had said to meet him in the mess hall. The only trick, Fitz realised, was finding the mess hall.

He'd thought he was getting close: the right level, the right section, cigarette smoke and laughter on the air. Only somewhere he'd taken a wrong turn, because the corridor he was in was tighter and less well lit than the others. Approaching a junction, Fitz opted to make a U-turn; take the first right, then right again and keep going.

Rounding the corridor, he bumped into a maintenance man. 'Sorry,' Fitz said and, as he looked at him, he realised it was the same guy he'd bumped into in the cargo bay. Archer, he remembered. 'Oh,' he said, 'I really am sorry.'

Archer disconnected a lead from the open wall-panel, then tucked the computer pad into his pocket. 'Can I help you?' he said.

'Mess hall?' Fitz enquired.

'Back the way you came. When you reach the main drag, take the second right. It's signposted from there.'

Fitz turned back. He paused at the corner to offer his thanks, but Archer had already reconnected his dataslide and was fitting an earpiece around his left ear.

'Never mind,' Fitz said to himself.

His reception in the mess hall was friendlier. Robertson clapped an arm around him and grinned. 'You're late.'

Her hair was tied back in a crisp ponytail, exposing strong cheekbones and the hint of freckles on her skin. Her eyes were shut in concentration, her chin tucked against the violin. The black dress was sleeveless, and as Valletti worked the bow back and forth the Doctor could see muscles move beneath the skin. Her shoulders dipped, her body half-turning as she bent into the instrument and the music, back arching with each note, body alive with every stroke.

It was, the Doctor thought, an exceptional performance.

The other members of the quartet were good, but none of them delivered a performance like their commanding officer's.

As the other instruments sank away, Valletti was motionless save for the languid motion of her wrist, drawing out one last, long, mournful note. The room was still and then the audience began to applaud. As the clapping started Valletti opened her eyes. Almost, the Doctor thought, shocked to discover people there.

He rose from his chair, making eye contact with Valletti, the nod of his head making it clear this standing ovation was for her. She smiled in return, then stepped back into the quartet to take their bow.

Afterwards the Doctor approached her, taking her hand and bowing to plant a kiss on the back of it. 'Mozart,' he smiled. 'Exquisite.'

'You like our quartet?'

'The technical standard is very good,' he answered, pausing to find the right words. 'But some are more committed to the music than others.'

She laughed. 'I can't help it. It's how I play, how I've always played.'

'May I?' The Doctor nodded at her violin. There was a moment's pause, then she carefully passed it to him. He turned the instrument over in his hands, feeling the silky finish of the wood, carefully pressing a fingertip against the tensioned strings. 'Beautiful workmanship.' He frowned. 'Not antique, though?'

Valletti shook her head. 'My father made it. The last one he finished before the occupation.' She pointed to a small crest embossed in gold – an ornate 'V' with *Firenze - 2157* beneath it.

The Doctor smiled. 'It's a cliché, but Florence really is one of my favourite cities.' He paused, remembering. 'It was raining the first time I went there. Spent the entire day running from one museum to another, head under an umbrella. It wasn't until the following morning that I could look up. It's amazing how much the Duomo dominates the skyline, how I could have nearly missed it.'

'My father has a shop on the Ponte Vecchio, sandwiched between two jewellers.' Valletti smiled. 'I used to sit on the sill in the summer, dangling my feet over the water.'

The Doctor handed the violin back. 'The work of a craftsman.'

'You play?' Valletti asked.

The Doctor shook his head. 'I did. Until the monks started complaining about the noise.'

'If it's antiques you're interested in, you should talk to Terrance.' Valletti nodded at a thin man of African descent to their left, one hand on a cello leaning against a stand. 'That's a Stradivarius, the Lady Rose. Colourful history, so I'm told.'

The Doctor looked at the man. He hadn't consulted the programme he'd been handed as he walked in, had intended just to ask Valletti about the computer problems. But the quartet's performance was opening up possibilities for the evening.

He smiled. 'Could you introduce me?'

* * *

Even more than the cargo bay, the mess hall was the most untidy place Fitz had seen on the Station. But the coffee stains, cigarette burns and peeling posters signified one thing: life.

Some kind of jukebox was playing in the corner, a metallic console, shaped like an apple for what Robertson called historical reasons. Fitz just smiled and nodded. Notionally a place to eat, the mess hall had become the *de facto* nightspot for the people who worked in the outer rings. A couple of hours ago, the tables had been occupied by men and women eating. Now, food trays had been replaced by beer bottles; a surprising percentage of which had been emptied by Fitz and Robertson.

Robertson who was, as it turned out, in love.

The woman in question was crossing the mess hall – a latecomer, carrying a dinner tray – and Robertson couldn't keep his eyes off her. A couple of inches over five foot with mousy blonde hair; no honed military physique, but the natural frame of someone who needed neither diet nor exercise.

Fitz watched Robertson's eyes trace her across the floor, a hint of a smile on his lips.

It was increasingly obvious to him that his first impression of Robertson had been correct. He was indeed a bear of a man; only the bear in question was more teddy than grizzly.

Fitz laughed. 'I'll bet you haven't even spoken to her.'

'Spoken to whom?'

Fitz nodded at the woman. She was still looking for a seat. As she neared their table her eyes found Robertson, who smiled.

'I'm working my charm,' he whispered to Fitz.

And for a moment Fitz thought there might be something in that, then she turned right, to an empty space at another table.

'What's her name?' Fitz asked.

'Arquette,' Robertson replied. 'Caroline Arquette. Computer engineer, third grade, came by a couple of months back to fix a problem with the cargo scheduler.'

'And?'

'And look at her,' Robertson said.

'She's nice,' Fitz nodded.

'No,' Robertson laughed. 'You need to look at the way she moves, the way she thinks about things.' He smiled. 'You missed the best part; it's when she's in the queue studying the menu. It's the way she thinks about the food.'

'You,' Fitz said, 'are in love.'

'I am not.'

Fitz watched Caroline lean in to whisper and laugh with the women on her table. 'So,' Fitz said, 'how long have you been working your charm, then?'

'Like I said, a couple of months.'

'Does the charm go any further than just smiling?' Fitz asked. 'Have we had Caroline and Robbie sitting in a tree K-I-S-S-I –'

'If you finish that sentence, I will punch you.'

'In which case,' Fitz said, 'I will not finish it.' He picked up his beer, clinking its neck against Robertson's. 'Case closed.'

As Robertson put his bottle to his lips, Fitz darted sideways, slipping out of range before he could be caught. Robertson's eyes were wide in horror as Fitz grinned and slid on to the bench next to Caroline Arquette.

'Hi,' Fitz said, 'I was wondering what you were doing tonight.' He nodded at Robertson. 'Only my friend would really like to buy you a drink.'

The performance over, Recreation Hall A had become a dining room. The glass-domed ceiling that had been a perfect backdrop for music was now delivering the warm atmosphere of an outdoor restaurant. The Doctor and Valletti had joined Terrance and Sara Mukabi and another half-dozen staff at a long table.

'This used to be executive office space,' Valletti explained.

The Doctor looked up. Every minute or so, the Station's slow revolution would bring a slice of Jupiter into sight against the stars. 'A waste of a view,' the Doctor said. 'I approve of the change.'

'I'm glad,' Valletti said.

Further down the table someone laughed. 'Just don't complain about the cost.'

'Justified expenditure,' Valletti retorted.

The Doctor raised an eyebrow. Valletti smiled and got to her feet, crossing to select a bottle of wine from a nearby rack. Returning to the table, she showed the label to the Doctor. A Chilean Merlot, the red so dark it almost looked black as she filled his glass.

The Doctor swirled the wine around for a moment, inhaling deeply, then tipped the glass back. 'Perfect,' he judged. 'I'm amazed it keeps so well. South America to Jupiter is a long journey.'

'And that's why it's justified expenditure.' It was Terrance elaborating. 'It needed a bottle that would withstand the travel and replicate cellar conditions to keep the taste.'

'Quite a project,' the Doctor said.

'Earth Forces invest a lot of money in things like that,' Valletti said. 'Always with protesting accountants.'

'Couldn't it be better spent elsewhere?'

'There are lots of tricks like that.' It was Sara Mukabi speaking now. 'Like this ceiling and the windows on the Station and the transports. Space is black. Outside of an atmosphere, the stars are that much harder to see. Atmosphere makes them seem larger, makes them shine. And people missed the stars they knew. So, all the windows have a filter to replicate atmospheric haze.'

'Twinkle, twinkle little star,' the Doctor said.

Valletti nodded back down the table. 'Sara's field of expertise. The psychology of interstellar living. The theory is, and I'm sure she'll correct me if I'm wrong, but the theory is we're hard-wired for life on Earth?'

Sara nodded. 'The biggest problem with life in space is that we're separated from the things our bodies evolved around: gravity, daylight, the air we breathe.'

'But you can simulate gravity, day and night, even the seasons.' The Doctor gestured at the dimming light around them. 'Sunset? This late in the evening? Must be summer.'

Valletti smiled at him as Sara continued: 'But those things only take the brain so far. It's the small comforts that tip the balance: like seeing the stars and having wine that tastes like wine should.'

'And that,' Valletti explained, 'is why this is justified expenditure. We're a military outpost, but our goal is to facilitate the research of highly educated civilians. It's a difficult balance, so we make allowances. This isn't a front-line starship.' She shrugged. 'People deliver better results with home comforts available.'

Sara laughed. 'If front-line starships were like this, I'd probably still be married to Jonathan.'

'Jonathan did all right,' Valletti replied. 'He's got an Earth Forces' budget and an admiral's suite in Cape Town now, hasn't he?'

The Doctor studied his wine glass, then said, 'This doesn't always work, does it?' He looked up, staring at Sara. 'The pilot on the *Pegasus*, for example.'

Sara gave Valletti a quick glance, then said, 'We recovered the cockpit section this afternoon. The pilot will be shipped back to Mars on the next transport, but until then I'm trying to figure out what happened to him.' She took a sip of the wine. 'Space-related stress is my speciality, but he doesn't fit any of the usual protocols.'

'Can I ask,' the Doctor said, 'what a stress specialist is doing on a weapons-development station?'

'You can ask,' Valletti interrupted, 'but you won't get an answer. Your clearance is limited, I'm afraid.'

'Idle curiosity, nothing more.' He smiled at the Mukabis. 'Unless either of you is responsible for the excessive maintenance being logged, of course.'

Terrance laughed. 'Not my purview, thank God.'

'It's one of the difficulties of being this far from supply lines,' Valletti said. 'We have to be more self-sufficient than a lot of research posts. Things get repaired, not replaced.'

'Professor Deschamps mentioned that,' the Doctor said. 'He didn't understand the need to build the Station this far out.'

'Security,' Valletti smiled. 'Keep things away from prying eyes, it's as simple as that.' She drained her wine and smiled. 'Enough shop talk. Who wants to dance?'

The main lights were switched off, leaving glowing strips set into the walls to illuminate the room. The tables were moved back, the jukebox was turned up, and the room slowly filled with laughter and body heat. The past five minutes had seen more people come off shift, more pushing on to the impromptu dance floor.

At first Fitz had wondered if he'd done the right thing, dragging Caroline over for a drink. As she and Robertson had talked, Caroline had kept on giving quick glances back to her friends. But then a moment had come and she'd laughed a real rich laugh, and when she looked at Robbie again it was to meet his eyes full on. Now, Fitz was seated at one of the tables, a beer in hand, back against the wall, watching Robertson and Caroline dance.

You need to look at the way she moves, Robertson had said and Fitz understood now. It was a lack of guile or self-consciousness. You could see it in the easy way she laughed, but when she danced that attraction was turned all the way up to ten.

'Hey,' Fitz called, recognising the beer-drinking soldier passing in front of him.

McCray smiled as he saw Fitz. They clinked bottles and Fitz bellowed over the music, 'Nice moves in the docking bay.'

'All part of the service,' McCray answered.

'Your boys look pretty sharp. Were you down in the atmosphere in those suits?'

'Some of us.' McCray nodded at the dance floor. 'Think that's wild? Try riding the windstream down there. A man could lose himself in a place like that.' He snorted. 'Hell, you could hide a whole fleet down there and no one would ever see it.'

'I'm not sure I like the sound of that.'

'Don't worry,' McCray laughed. 'To get to you, it's got to get through me and that's not going to happen.'

'Hey.' It was Robertson approaching. 'You stealing my friends as well as my work, now?'

'Might take your girl too, if you're not careful.'

'You could try, but I wouldn't recommend it.'

For a brief moment Fitz was worried about a fight breaking out, then he caught the glint in Robertson's eye and knew he was being had. 'You two know each other?' he asked.

'We did basic training together,' McCray replied. 'Went our separate ways after that.'

Robertson nodded. 'I got into logistics and John ended up with the hard corps at Marineris.'

'Right until we both got assigned here and I started stealing his work. Six months and all I hear is how I'm stealing his work.'

'Or my girl,' Robertson reminded him.

'Or your girl,' McCray replied. Only, as he did so Fitz could see distraction sweep over him; McCray looked past Robertson, emotion draining away in the course of those three spoken words.

McCray blinked then said, 'Rain check.' He nodded across the room and Fitz could see the other members of his squad filtering in. 'I should spend time with my boys.'

'Oh, right,' Fitz said, and McCray was gone.

'Don't take it personally,' Robertson said. 'He does that a lot. Currahee.'

Fitz frowned. 'The Doctor said that, back on the *Pegasus*. Does it mean something?'

'It's their motto. Native American or something, means "alone together". We stand alone together.' Robertson wiped the sweat from his brow, watching as McCray was enveloped by his squad. 'The 101st, the Gurkhas, the Swiss Guard. There's only a handful of national units that made it through the last couple of centuries.'

'What do you mean?'

'The fundamentalist jihads, the occupation, even the two decades the wall was up, they all took their toll. The 101st used to have an eagle as their insignia.'

Robertson drained the last of his bottle then nodded at the floor. Caroline was waiting for him, the beat thumping, the walls vibrating. Robertson looked at Fitz and grinned: 'Let's dance.'

The black dress was cut low on Valletti's back and she could feel the warmth of his fingertips as they danced. Hands not really gripping her, just guiding, his skin barely brushing her spine. There had been a delay to their stepping out, a sensor glitch on the outer ring that needed her to sign off on a maintenance order. That done, the Doctor had taken her hand as a waltz played.

He was a nervous dancer; while his eyes never fell to his feet, you could see him working through the steps in his head. Each step was smooth enough, but there was a tension underneath for anyone watching to see.

There had been dances in her youth. On Victory Night, masses of people would fill the Uffizi Gallery and the squares in front of the Palazzo Vecchio. Women smiling as young men tried so hard to impress.

The Doctor didn't dance like that. It was the first time she'd seen him show any kind of nerves. Although he'd smiled all the way through dinner, there had been an edge to his conversation; the words sharp and probing. There was a phrase her father had used: an iron fist in a velvet glove. Smooth on the surface, hard underneath. That was so very nearly him.

He was a curiosity. There was toughness to him, but Valletti got no impression of malice. The distance in the eyes was a sadness. He could dance, but he'd never lose himself in it.

As if sensing her thoughts, he blinked. With a grin he stepped up the pressure against Valletti's back, taking a deep breath and spinning her away across the floor.

Sweat soaked the back of Fitz's shirt. The beat pounded in his ears, made the blood pump in his neck, his breathing ragged. As Arquette danced – arms above her head, lost in the music – he could hear Robertson's laughter amidst the thunderclap as he brought his hands together in time with the beat.

McCray and the 101st were positioned near the bar. In among the bodies around them Fitz could see some of Robertson's crew, the concentrated faces of the afternoon transformed by the promise of a long night.

He wished he'd brought his guitar. When the tempo started to ease, people would want something a little mellower to come down on. A few genuine Kreiner tunes would have been just the thing.

He looked again at Robertson and Arquette dancing and smiled.

The floor bucked beneath them and people staggered, grabbing for support as the Station juddered and then was still.

The Doctor was there before Valletti but only just.

The lifts were in shutdown, so they took the stairs. She ran barefoot, the hem of her dress in her hand. They made it to the docking bay in less than three minutes, approaching from the east.

The pristine walls were scorched black, equipment strewn across the corridor, the prongs of a forklift truck embedded in the wall. Beyond that, the docking bay was aflame. Some people staggered away from the blast area, clothing torn and bloody; others moved towards it, dragging fire extinguishers behind them.

Valletti grabbed one man. 'What happened?' she asked, but it was the Doctor who answered.

'The *Pegasus*,' he said.

Valletti looked. He was right; the main body of the ship was ripped apart, debris and flame spreading from that focal point.

Another fireball erupted, a wall of heat slamming into them. Valletti picked herself up, blood in her mouth where she'd caught her lip. The Doctor had removed his jacket, was smothering the flames on a man stumbling out of the docking bay.

'Fire suppression?' Valletti barked.

'Offline.' It was one of the docking managers, Alonso. 'Maintenance was on the way when it happened.'

'We're running out of time,' the Doctor shouted. 'If the flames reach the fuel lines, you could lose half the outer ring.'

Valletti looked into the fire, nodded at the main entrance to the docking bay: 'Everyone back. Seal the main doors, prepare to vent the atmosphere.'

'They're jammed,' the Doctor said, pointing. A chunk of engine was embedded in the floor, jamming one of the bay's doors.

'Then we'll evacuate this area too,' Valletti snapped. 'Everyone retreat to the next section. Both sides!'

She began ushering her crew up the corridor, glancing back to make sure they were doing the same on the other side of the docking-bay entrance. Another explosion roared and they ducked as flaming metal slammed into the nearby wall.

'I think that's everyone,' Alonso called.

Valletti took a long look at the chaos surrounding the main doors. Smoke was beginning to obscure the view. The Doctor was still at her side, looking intently into the flames. She grabbed his hand and pulled him back up the corridor to where the others were waiting. One last glance, then she smashed an elbow into a glass panel and a siren sounded as the pressure door slowly ground down out of the ceiling. She could see just enough through the smoke to spot a similar door descending on the other side of the entrance.

She turned to Alonso. 'Once these doors are shut, deactivate the atmospheric shield and open the exterior doors on the docking bay. No more than a half-metre, I want equipment losses at a bare minimum.'

Alonso prised open a panel and set to work. 'Fifty-centimetre gap. Might lose a few wrenches, but anything larger will sit up against the doors.'

'Commander,' the Doctor said, 'I thought I saw something.'

Valletti followed his eyes, peering below the descending door into the docking bay. Flames were roaring now and the smoke was dragging back down the corridor as the fire ate the oxygen.

'Whatever it is,' she said, 'it's going to have to wait.'

'There!' The Doctor pointed.

And as the smoke cleared, for a moment it was clearly visible: an arm and a shoulder pushing out from underneath loose plating. A body trying to work itself free.

Valletti shook her head. 'Too late. Once this is down, I can't reopen it until –'

'I understand. Don't wait for me.' The Doctor broke free of her grasp, dropping to the floor and rolling through the narrowing gap.

'By the way,' he said, 'I hate dancing, I'm not very good at it.' And then she lost sight of him as the door sunk home.

'Dammit!' Valletti swore, smashing her fist against the wall. 'Of all the idiotic –' She turned to Alonso. 'Is it done?'

'What?'

She nodded at the control panel. 'The sequence for the docking-bay doors. Is it finished?'

'Yes, but –'

'Then run it.'

'What about –'

'He knew what we were doing. Now run the damn sequence!'

Valletti could still taste copper where she'd bitten her lip. She wiped the back of her hand across her mouth, a thin smear of red across her pale skin. Beside her Alonso pressed a button on the control panel.

The sound didn't penetrate the pressure door, but beyond it the air would be screaming.

* * *

Fitz was late on the scene. The shock wave from the initial explosion had tripped something in the mess-hall doors and it had taken a minute to free them.

Running down Greenwich West, all he and Robertson found was a sealed pressure door and a group of confused and smoky personnel. Robertson glanced at a nearby screen: 'Fire suppression's offline. Someone's running a sequence from the other side of the docking bay; venting the atmosphere to put out the fire.'

'What's that?' Fitz asked. A thin trace of green liquid was running down the wall.

'Hydraulics have ruptured,' Robertson said. 'Getting that door up isn't going to be as easy as getting it down was.'

Fitz nodded at the screen. 'Any idea what happened?'

'Nope,' Robertson said, surveying the workers who'd been caught in the fire. 'I'm just hoping none of my people got hurt.'

The whole corridor groaned with the sound of aching metal. Robertson looked at the readings on-screen. 'The docking bay is oxygen-free,' Robertson said, 'and the fire...' He paused. 'The fire is out.'

A nearby intercom hissed. Valletti's voice: *'We're repressurising the docking bay.'*

'Understood,' Robertson replied.

There was a pause, then Valletti said, *'Robertson? Is that you?'*

'Ma'am.'

'Is Kreiner with you?'

'How did you know?' Fitz asked.

There was a silence, then Valletti said, *'We're releasing our door now.'* And the intercom went dead.

Fitz looked at Robertson. Valletti could only know he would be with Robbie if the Doctor had told her. Which meant he was probably with Valletti when the explosion happened. And suddenly she didn't want to speak to Fitz.

'Get the door open,' Fitz whispered.

'Fitz, I –'

'Get the bloody door open!' he snapped.

Robertson hit the switch, but there was no response. 'There's not enough pressure in the hydraulics to –'

'Here.' It was Caroline, pushing through the crowd. She took

Robertson's hand, moved it away from the panel and slipped past him to get to work. 'I can divert some power to the motors. Without the hydraulics it won't open all the way, but –'

There was grinding noise and a gap, just a little over a foot wide, appeared at the bottom of the door. The control panel exploded in a shower of sparks. Caroline yelped in surprise, bumping up against Robertson, then nodded at Fitz. 'That's all you're going to get,' she said. 'Go.'

Fitz dropped to the floor. It was a tight fit and there was no way Robertson's broad frame was going to squeeze through. There was a brief moment of claustrophobia as Fitz thought he was going to get stuck, then he was out the other side, picking himself up.

The pressure door on to Greenwich East was wide open and people were streaming through into the bay, some carrying salvage gear, others medical bags. Fitz saw Valletti, her face smeared with blood and soot, her dress torn down the thigh. She didn't have any shoes on.

The floor of the docking bay was completely clear. Large swathes of it were black or pockmarked, and at points the decking had broken away revealing the infrastructure below. But beyond that, everything – every box, tool, step and trolley – was haphazardly piled up against the exterior doors. Even the shuttlecraft had been dragged across the floor by the sudden loss of atmosphere.

When Valletti saw him she just shook her head. 'I'm sorry. He was your –'

But Fitz wasn't listening. He was looking at the pile of debris crushed against the doors. 'Over there!' he said.

'What?'

And then Fitz was past her, running across the floor, pushing through the rescue crews.

Nestled near the base of the debris, bolted into the junction of the floor and the wall, was a large metal box, the words CUTTING GEAR – EMERGENCIES ONLY stencilled on the side. A trolley was pressing down on the box, but there was just enough room beneath it for some movement.

And the lid of the box was pressing up from the inside.

Fitz grabbed the edge of the trolley, braced himself and pulled.

It came away with a crash, the lid on the box springing free. As he got to his feet, he was joined by Valletti who was shaking her head: 'I don't believe it.'

The Doctor pulled himself up out of the box, a young man held across his shoulders.

'Medic!' Valletti called, looking around, snapping her fingers at a green-suited man: 'Easter! Over here now!'

The Doctor laid the man down on the floor, then stepped back to let the medic in. 'He'll be fine. Some cracked ribs and a nasty burn on his back, but he'll be fine.'

He nodded at the box he'd just climbed out of: 'Even holding the lid down it wasn't completely airtight,' he panted, 'but who cares about completely? It was airtight enough, that's what matters.' He looked at Valletti. 'As it turns out, I'm both lucky and adaptable.'

Valletti knelt down by the young man. She squeezed his hand as his eyes turned towards her. 'Jason,' she asked, smiling, 'how are you feeling?'

The man said nothing, just nodded as the medic pushed an injection into his forearm, the needle piercing the thick blue lines of a tattoo. Then Fitz's attention shifted as the Doctor tapped him on the shoulder.

'Let's get out of here,' the Doctor said quietly. His eyes were tired and his face was pale and sweaty. Fitz frowned –

Behind them Valletti said, 'Someone tell McCray to meet us in sickbay.'

– and then the Doctor opened the flap of his jacket. Blood was staining the point where the harpoon had hit home. 'I may have overexerted myself.'

Fitz slipped an arm around his friend and they began to move back through the rescuers and out of the docking bay.

The Station's lighting had dimmed, signifying the end of the day. A quarter to one and it was dark as Fitz walked its corridors.

When they'd got back to their quarters, the Doctor had slumped on to his bunk and gone to sleep with barely a word of explanation. Fitz had dug out the contemporary equivalent of a newspaper – a holographic slide, constantly updated – and sat down in a chair, reading and occasionally glancing over to the sleeping Doctor. As he read, he slowly drained a jug of iced water. Adrenalin had delivered an immediately sobering effect in the docking bay, but now that it was wearing off the evening's beer was creeping back into his consciousness. The water was there to take the edge off the hangover he was due to have and make sure he was sober enough if the Doctor did anything unexpected.

The downside to this strategy was Fitz's need to take a leak on a regular basis. Every trip down the corridor to the toilet was creating a level of anxiety. Would the Doctor be there when he got back? Eyes shut, asleep, chest rising and falling with each healing breath? Or would he be up and about, manically working on some lead or another? Or, worse, lying half-out of his bunk, eyes open but unseeing, blood trailing on to the floor, one hand reaching out to the chair where Fitz should have been?

The door whispered open and Fitz stepped back into their room.

The Doctor was where he'd left him. The only change was the soft red light blinking across the room. An icon, shaped like an envelope, was flashing on the communications screen. It unfolded as Fitz touched it; the message was headlined GENERAL MEMO - ALL STAFF.

Early signs were that the explosion had been caused by a catastrophic systems failure on board the *Pegasus*; probably the result of its traumatic inward flight. Until investigations were complete, though, Station security was raised to Defence Condition Four.

Fitz closed the message, sat back down in his chair.

The headline on the slide had changed. There were riots on one of the system colonies, sparked by rumours of alien infiltrators. Seventy dead, troops dispatched to quell the uprising.

Fitz shook his head. He had his own problems.

Looking across the room to the Doctor, his voice little more than a whisper, he asked: 'Did you know?'

Had the Doctor known what he was doing when he ran into those flames? A few months ago, Fitz wouldn't have doubted it. His friend was a hero. But a lot had happened in the past few months.

'Did you know?' Fitz repeated.

The Doctor could have seen the box when they'd disembarked

from the *Pegasus*. When he knew what Valletti was planning and had seen the man trapped in the flames, had he immediately thought of that emergency locker? When he jumped into the fray had he had any idea what he was going to do? Fitz had checked the Station's logs. The Doctor had had less than thirty seconds to cross the docking bay, rescue the man and throw them both into the locker; hoping it would hold enough air, hoping it would be strong enough to protect them from the debris.

Before, Fitz wouldn't have worried. But now he realised it wasn't just the Doctor's loss of memory that worried him. He knew his own recollection of what the Doctor had done, how he had been stranded on Earth, wasn't what it should be. Something had happened; he had to fight to recall the details now, worried that the events themselves might fade away. But he could still remember his life, who he was.

The Doctor couldn't.

And without knowing who he was and what he'd done, could he still do this? Could he still be the hero?

When Fitz had heard Valletti's voice go dead over the intercom, when he had understood the Doctor was trapped in the docking bay, it had felt like his heart stopped. Because in that moment, he'd had no idea whether the Doctor was dead or alive.

So Fitz looked at him in the dark, at the face he had come to trust so well, and he wondered: when you did all that, when you rescued that man and saved yourself, when you put yourself in harm's way for the sake of others, did you know what it was you were doing and what you were doing it for?

'Did you know?'

'I hear your boss is a hero,' Robertson said.

Fitz shrugged non-committally, something that made Robertson pause. Yesterday's Fitz had been easy-going, half-truth, half-bravado; today's man, picking his way through the mess of the docking bay, looked nothing but tired.

Fitz forced a smile, gesturing to the overalls he was wearing. 'I brought my working clothes.'

When Robertson frowned, Fitz added, 'The hero is still sleeping things off. And if the boss is asleep, I have to find ways of amusing myself.' He nodded at the pile of debris stacked up behind them. 'I figured you could probably use a hand?'

'Sure.' Robertson tossed Fitz a pair of work gloves. 'Anything completely trashed goes in the container on the left. Anything that might be salvageable, you hand to the technicals. We don't do maintenance.'

Against the wall on Greenwich West a dozen workers stood at a hastily erected table, sorting through equipment. In the middle of them was a sight that had made Robertson's day when he'd walked in an hour earlier.

'Did you request Caroline for the job specially?' Fitz said.

'She volunteered.' Robertson grinned. 'Still working my charm.' He offered Fitz a hand up on to the debris next to him: 'You all right, Fitz?'

'Long night.' Fitz nodded along the line of workers. 'How come you can't sort the machinery yourself?'

Robertson looked. Fitz was staring at where Archer and Garcia were lifting scrap. He shook his head. 'We leave the smart stuff to the people with the know-how and the rank.' Fitz pursed his lips, like he was about to say something, then just nodded and got to work.

It was about five minutes later that Fitz asked, 'What should I do with this?' He was kneeling on a compressor which had lost its main cover.

Robertson shrugged. 'Looks pretty much OK.'

'Not the... the –' Fitz gestured at the compressor '– thing. I mean this.'

Robertson stepped across to take a closer look. Trapped between two compressor hoses was a book: dog-eared leather cover, a dark stain across one side. Robertson pulled it clear, then freed the loop of string holding the covers shut. Its pages held the occasional sketch – faces he recognised – but, for the most part, the book comprised poetry; line upon line of awkward longhand. On the first page there were three lines:

Stars climb high at night
The strongest hands cannot hold
Only hope breaks a chain.

Robertson checked the cover. 'No name on it.' He handed the book to Fitz. 'Finders keepers. Anyone asks, I'll tell them you're the man to see.'

At lunch, Caroline made her way over to join them. Seeing her approach Fitz just smiled and wandered off, chewing on his sandwich crust.

'Is he OK?' Caroline asked.

'He had a strange night,' Robertson answered, looking over to where Fitz was studying the locker where, rumour had it, his boss had rode out the decompression. 'I think we all had a strange night. Me more than most.' He smiled. 'Never got to say thank you for dancing.'

'You're welcome,' she said, her fingers struggling with the vacuum seal on her packet salad.

'Here,' Robertson said. 'Let me.'

'I can never get those things open.'

'I wanted to ask you...' he paused. 'I was going to ask you, last night, before everything... Well, I was –'

She looked at him and smiled, full of humour and life. 'Yes,' she said.

'"Yes" what?'

'Yes, I'll have dinner with you. You wanted to ask me to dinner, but you're shy.' She took the opened salad from his hands. 'It's very endearing.'

'You think I'm being shy?' Robertson smiled. 'This is charm.' She laughed then, clear and free of malice, and with that sound Robertson knew Fitz was right. He was in love.

They were interrupted then, as Fitz wandered back turning something over in his hand.

'What have you found?' Caroline asked.

Fitz handed it over; curled plastic, a face fading in and out beneath the charred surface. 'Security pass. It was in the locker over there, must belong to the bloke the Doctor saved.' Fitz shook his head. 'I didn't recognise him last night, but that's the guy, isn't it? The janitor round here?'

'That's Jason,' Robertson nodded.

'The name on the pass is McCray. It's Jason McCray. I hadn't noticed the resemblance before, but –'

'They're brothers,' Robertson said. He remembered a long night, doing basic in Guantanamo, a group of them drinking iced water and talking about their ambitions. He had always wanted logistics, but John McCray had talked about his older brother. He'd heard the stories, he knew what he wanted. First in, last out.

'Jason was a paratrooper too,' Robertson mused. 'Must have had an accident or something.'

'You never asked McCray?'

'Never knew to ask him.' Robertson shrugged. 'Jason's only ever been called Jason, and like I said McCray and me haven't talked much.'

He looked at the face on the card. He could see it now. The eyes were the same as McCray's, but devoid of expression. The signature caught his eye though.

'You still got that book?'

'Sure.'

'I think the handwriting matches.'

'Does it matter?' Fitz asked.

'Have you tried talking to Jason?' Robertson said. 'He can't talk, can barely process language at all. Not spoken, not written.'

Fitz opened the book, flicking through it, pages upon pages of verse.

MARS

'Happy anniversary,' Michael said.

'Happy anniversary,' Anji answered and they clinked glasses.

The champagne was from one of the bubble vineyards, up past Jacksonville. Good, but somehow the taste never matched what Anji remembered from Earth. She'd asked a wine waiter about it once; he'd replied it was the way grapes responded to the ammonia in the regenerated Martian soil. Which explained the why, but not what it was that was wrong with the taste itself.

The restaurant was full; a queue outside when Anji arrived. Inside, Michael had been wearing his nervous look. Not nervous like he'd been in the five minutes before he proposed, but she could easily guess the conversation he'd been having with the *maître'd* just before she entered.

As they drank Michael glanced at her. 'No regrets?'

'About married life?' Anji said. 'None whatsoever.'

'I was wondering,' Michael said. 'Given that the table was reserved for eight o'clock.'

'I know, I know,' Anji smiled. 'I never used to be late. And I'm very, very sorry.'

And it was true. She could remember when, a lifetime ago, she'd run from one building to another in the square mile, mobile under her chin, palmtop bleeping reminders, and she'd made every single meeting. The past couple of years, she'd lost that ability. It had bothered her for a while, but then she'd rationalised it as her body reacting to another world. The Martian day was thirty-seven minutes too long; close enough to Earth standard to be jarringly disconcerting. She rationalised those extra minutes as something that was always at the back of her mind, leaving her daydreaming more than she thought possible, and running late instead of on time.

'You were working,' Michael said.

'Yes,' Anji replied, hurriedly studying her menu. She could feel Michael's eyes narrowing, interrogation eyes that got results only because she couldn't help laughing at them.

'Not at the network.'

Anji looked up.

'I called there looking for you. Maggie said you filed the piece on the dollar collapse at midday.'

Anji paused, then reached across the table, taking hold of his hand. 'I should have said. I took the bullet train down to Nicosia. I was meeting someone there.'

'But not something for work.'

Anji broke a breadstick, chewing on one end. 'Military,' she said.

Michael nodded. 'Thought I heard one of your widows on the phone the other night.'

Anji looked at the window. There was a dust storm brewing on the horizon, the sunset a haze behind it. There had been a sand storm a year ago, turning day to night and hissing against the registrar's windows as they exchanged vows.

'Kathleen found someone who'd talk,' Anji said. 'She's come a long way since the memorial. I never expected to hear from her again, but there's a lot of us out there. Wives and husbands. People who want the truth.'

'Is that what you want?'

Anji found his eyes. Not criticising or carping, just inquisitive. Her past, Anji thought, was the part of her he'd never figured out.

'I don't know. I'm happy here, I really am.'

'But?'

'Whenever I hear about it, or pass the memorial, or see a picture of Jupiter...' Anji paused. 'It feels like I'm missing something. It's the only way I can explain it.'

'You might never know,' Michael said. 'It's important you realise that. I'm not trying to discourage you, Anji. But it's over two years ago and we might never find out what happened. This could be another dead-end; like that corporate ship that was in the area when the Station was destroyed.'

'I got a name today,' Anji said. 'The name. The guy who cordoned off Jupiter space after the disaster? He works here, he's stationed on Mars.'

'What's the name?'

'McNamara,' Anji said. 'I was checking the Earth Forces registry. My source says he's here, but there's no listing for him. But it fits, Mike, it all fits.'

'I don't recognise the name. Is he brass?'

'Do you remember the memorial service?' Anji asked. 'The uniform who just sat there, the one the protestor was screaming at. I never matched his picture to any name on file. That must be McNamara.' She paused. 'He's black-money funded, which suggests weapons research. And Farside was weapons research.'

'So?'

'So if the Station were destroyed by a test gone wrong, he's the man who'd know. If there are answers, he's got them.'

JUPITER SPACE
Now

Anji is back with the Wounded.

One in the morning on the Station clock and most people have withdrawn to their makeshift beds. Beyond the keening from the Wounded, the only human sound is dull conversation from the sentries.

Working slowly, Anji and the Professional have managed to ease the cargo-bay door back without provoking a rusty cry. As they move it one last time, Anji notices GREENWICH HOSPITAL daubed in red on its surface. The paint is flaking. Anji wonders who was responsible for the sign, and whether they're now one of its patients.

The Professional thinks the Station structure may be weakened here, incapable of supporting their magnetic grapples. So, they're going to use the cages as ladders, and climb up and make their way into the superstructure. According to him, they don't need to go far: a few metres to clear the sentries, barricades and automated weapons, then drop back down into the main corridor.

Four years to get here; now the Professional is going to drag her away after less than twenty-four hours on board.

He switches his suit's flashlight to its lowest candlelight setting, then passes it over the cages. The stale smell that had threatened to overwhelm Anji earlier remains, but she's prepared for it now. The Wounded are mostly asleep, but some still press against the wire.

There's one pair, though, reaching through the bars to brush each other's skin and sink fingers into unkempt hair. Anji's been trying to think of the Wounded as less than human. Since her talk with the Professional, she's been trying to see all of the survivors in that light. Mad, insane, beyond reason. But this sight makes her wonder about his hypothesis.

Such a basic human moment among these damaged people.

Anji has to stop herself thinking about it. The Professional's right: she can't allow herself to get caught up in this situation, with these people, their lives and emotions.

Not if she's going to get the answers she came for.

Kapoor's suit was returned to her shortly before the Station's crew retired; the physician, Easter, handed it over with an apology. Not, the Professional thinks, that Kapoor has a real understanding of the protection it offers.

Jupiter's atmosphere carries enough radioactivity to be deadly. The Station's EM shield is fluctuating: solid around the central hub, uneven over these outer rings. Another pressure that has contributed to these people's instability. Step off those safe paths and the Liebig cage of the Station's structure offers only limited protection.

Kapoor's suit, like the Professional's, is interwoven with tiny Dortmunium threads that will keep the radiation at sub-lethal levels for up to three weeks. Her behaviour suggests she is looking at it in psychological terms, barrier protection, keeping the outside at bay. But whether she realises it or not, she moves far more comfortably now than when dressed in just her own skin. There's still a problem, though. For all their micromotors and automatic systems, the armour can still be awkward. A combat suit like the one Kapoor has procured takes months to master, learning to interpret the sensor feedback that makes its surface a second skin and not iron plating.

As they climb the exterior of the cages, the Professional can feel the wire beneath his fingers and adjust his grip to compensate. Kapoor doesn't have that kind of control, is relying on eyesight to guide her.

Reaching the third tier, the Professional realises Kapoor is falling behind. He secures a hold on the nearest cage, swings around, flashing his light below to check on her progress. The beam catches her face and the shine from the reflective helmet is enough to catch her fingers closing around their latest handhold.

The cages have been constructed hastily to cope with human pressures. The suit's enhanced strength and the inexperienced grip of Anji Kapoor are enough to tear a lock from its housing. The

Professional can only watch as her handhold comes free and she tumbles back towards the floor.

Her landing wakes the survivors in the cages, filling the room with screeching and bodies crashing against bars. Worse, the cage door, suddenly shorn of its lock, is swinging open. Initially hesitant, its occupant gains confidence in moments, charging, leaping down to the floor below. Kapoor rolls out of its path and the creature – a woman – pushes at the main door, screaming and crying as it runs free into the compound.

Kapoor looks to the door: 'We should stay. We've got to stop that woman harming –'

'They can stop her,' the Professional answers. 'We need to leave now.' He turns and continues climbing. There's a moment of silence, then the cages rattle as Kapoor starts after him once more.

Two minutes later and they are into the ceiling, crawling through the infrastructure above the corridor. The Professional is running a scan of the area below, pinpointing their position in relation to the barricades.

A sudden spike on one of the readings gives him pause. A sound, too low for the human ear to pick up, easily registered by the suit. He raises a hand, signalling a halt.

Her voice whispers over their intercom: 'What?'

The Professional doesn't reply. The network of girders behind them is a hard, narrow space; in front, larger gaps accommodate the Station's workings. He recalibrates the sensor array and resurveys that area. The dark latticework comes into sharp resolution: beams and pipework covered in the rust that is endemic outside the docking bay, tangles of electrics and conduit.

And moving through it, a mess of shapes: grey and indistinct even with the suit's enhanced resolution. But he can see them in the paths they create, pushing wires aside, limbs and torsos connecting with each other and the metal stud work.

A half-dozen of them, closing from the front.

Indistinct shapes, clearly inhuman. Hostiles.

The girders are too narrow for the hostiles to fit through, but they are already fanning out, one pair moving round to close off that escape route.

The Professional takes aim, releases five rounds in quick succession.

The sensor that spiked with the sound of the hostiles' movement goes wild as the crawl space is filled with unearthly screaming.

The Professional stamps on the ceiling plate beneath them. 'Get behind me,' he tells Kapoor. As she moves he can feel the plate weakening; the bolts are rusted like everything else. He stamps again and, as he does so, he picks a single target, aims and fires, all the while trying to increase the targeting resolution.

'Loosen those bolts,' he tells Kapoor.

The hostiles are within ten metres and closing.

The plating creaks again.

His shots are striking home but dissipate across the hostile's skin.

Six metres.

The Professional abandons precision fire, switching to fully automatic, sweeping the plasma rifle back and forth over the target area. This slows the advance, but does not stop it.

Five metres.

There's a clang as Kapoor finally works one of the bolts free.

He brings his foot down hard. The remaining bolts snap and the Professional and Kapoor tumble backwards as the ceiling plate collapses into the corridor below. The Professional rolls with the landing, twisting away and coming up with the rifle aimed back into the superstructure.

There's stillness for a brief moment.

They're past the majority of the barricades, but a few of the electrified stanchions remain. The grind of motors signals the automated weapons focusing on them. The Professional hopes they are programmed to recognise only non-human targets.

Voices call down the corridor to them, the sentries, drawn by the gunfire and the ceiling's collapse. The Professional doesn't turn, keeps his eyes locked on the space above them.

'Get up,' he tells Kapoor. 'Get behind me and start moving.' He grabs her hand as she starts to head back to the compound, thrusts her back up the corridor, firing as one of the hostiles drops through the opening on to the floor between them and the compound; where Kapoor had stood a moment earlier.

The hostile swings at him and he ducks under its arm, raising his rifle.

The creature is tall, that's Anji's first impression. Almost seven feet high, it hunches over, filling the corridor. It flinches and screams, unable to avoid touching the awkward electrified shapes of the barricades. Double-jointed limbs covered in a hard dark carapace, the feet hooked and clawing at the floor. A bullet-shaped head sits on a multijointed neck, gliding back and forth; parallel rows of round black eyes, unblinking; teeth showing through two separate mouths positioned on either side of the head, jaws slowly opening and closing.

The Professional gets a dozen shots in before the corridor fills with noise and flame as the automated weapons on the barricade open fire. The guns are aiming at the creature, but in the tight space of the corridor they're all too close together. And the automated gunfire is getting very near to both Anji and the Professional as the creature advances, every jolt from the barricades making it angrier.

They back up the corridor as two more creatures drop through the ceiling behind the first. The guns readjust their aim, but the shots barely impact on them. For a moment their heads flick back and forth between the humans in one direction, the compound in the other. Then they settle on Anji and the Professional and begin to follow their compatriot, marching towards them, forcing them back into the open corridor beyond the fortifications.

The Professional keeps firing. He's walking backwards at an unflinching pace, not looking where he's going, the rifle at his shoulder, taking aim and firing every couple of seconds. As she retreats, Anji grasps the purpose of this painstaking accuracy: concentrating his fire, trying to pick out one spot on the carapace again and again. But the creature is still pressing forward, getting closer.

'Don't let them touch you,' she shouts. 'That's the law.'

The creature swings for the Professional and he parries the blow with the butt of his rifle.

Reaching a junction in the corridor, Anji darts left, moving deeper into the Station. Firing once more, the Professional takes a step after her, then shouts, 'Not that way.'

But he's forced to take another step back as the creature attacks again, and it's too late as the junction is filled with more of the aliens.

As Anji backs up the corridor, the Professional drops and rolls in closer to the lead creature, springing up within reach of its arms, planting the tip of the rifle next to one of its mouths. He can't get the angle to strike back through its head, but he's found the vulnerable point he was looking for and the plasma bolt tears the creature's jaw apart.

The Professional springs back as it writhes in pain, limbs thrashing against both sides of the corridor, blocking the path for the ones behind. He grabs Anji's arm and they're running now, the Professional not glancing back but focusing in front all the time, looking anxiously at the long curve ahead. Behind them, the sounds of alien movement.

'You shouldn't have come this way,' the Professional says.

And Anji sees why as they skid to a halt.

The corridor is blocked off. An undulating black field fills the space from wall to wall; a glossy black that shimmers and sparks.

'Energy barrier,' Anji says. 'The hub's cut off an energy barrier.'

The Professional opens the kit store on the thigh of his suit, throws a pair of pulse mines back down the corridor. There's a clunk as they attach, then the space is filled with a fusillade of blinding light.

'We're trapped,' Anji says.

The Professional ignores her, sinking to one knee by the barrier. He opens a small access hatch and plugs a lead from his suit into it.

The creatures are inching towards the mines, forcing their way through the lasers. The Professional ignores them, continues working. Anji's initial thought is that he's trying to take the barrier down, but that's not it at all. The screen on his wrist shows him downloading information.

There's a ping as a pincer shatters one of the mines, leaving just the other operational. The creatures' rate of advance increases.

'We need to get out of here,' Anji says.

The Professional detaches himself from the junction point, turning as the first creature makes it past the mine. Anji ducks as it charges, swinging its limbs wildly, one hooked claw digging into a wall panel, another stabbing at the Professional. He sidesteps, but then the creature is on him, throwing him up against the barrier.

And Anji hears a sound she could never have imagined: the Professional screams.

She can see his face contorting beneath the visor. Then he gathers strength, actually braces himself on the unyielding surface of the energy barrier and pushes back against the creature. He gains just enough room to slip the last of the pulse mines from its pouch, attaching it to the inner edge of the creature's hook.

Anji presses against the wall as the laser beams activate.

The creature releases its hold on the Professional, backing up to deal with the mine. As it does so, the Professional pulls himself clear of the energy barrier. His suit back is blackened and smoking, and he drops to his knees – the only moment of real weakness Anji's seen so far – then recovers himself. He picks up his rifle, starts firing, and, in conjunction with the efforts of the pulse mine, drives the creature back.

Anji's not sure how much more he's going to be able to achieve. The other creatures are past the remaining mine on the floor and the corridor is a mass of twisted limbs, screaming double mouths and hard, armoured skin. The Professional is struggling to contain one of the creatures and there are another five behind it.

Then, when he has the first creature backed up, the Professional switches his aim, raking fire across the far wall. Steam gouts from a ruptured conduit. The Professional aims once more and the corridor is filled with a wall of fire.

They still sleep together. Just sleep.

Robertson's body lies on the cot behind hers, arms around her, tight against each other and the world. Robertson remembers a time, years ago, when Caroline's body wasn't this hard shell. He remembers soft skin, softer scents, the give of her flesh beneath his hand. That person is gone now.

Sometimes he is awake when she dreams, can feel the muscles beneath her skin pushing against the images in her head. Robertson whispers to her in those moments. Only hope breaks a chain, he tells her. He wonders if Caroline has a face of her own, one that haunts her sleep like the one that haunts his. When he's asleep and she's awake, does he twist and struggle like this?

Robertson is dimly aware of distant gunfire. The enemy press the barricades on a routine basis, never making it inside the perimeter. He doesn't suppose it's going to be different this time. Caroline is normally less tolerant of such noises, awake at the first sign of trouble, but not tonight.

It's only when the Station bucks, throwing them from the cot, that trouble finally registers.

Without a word, they stumble from their compartment in the gutted shuttle, heading for the Meridian. Easter is there, holding on to David's body, directing others, shouting instructions. Archer is at the main computer terminal, but gives way as Robertson and Caroline approach.

'We've lost the feed from the hydrogen collector to the starboard array,' he shouts. 'We're falling.'

As Caroline settles at the terminal Robertson looks at the on-screen graphic. Keeping the Station steady in Jupiter's atmosphere requires a constant balancing of the positioning thrusters, often seeing them running at 110 per cent capacity for half the time. If anything disrupts those thrusters, the Station falls.

'Can you fix it?' he asks Caroline. She ignores him.

The exterior doors that have been jammed shut for four years are groaning behind them. Everyone knows the Station is operating at the limits of its structural integrity; the decay that's rampant across its surfaces speaks for that. If they drop much deeper those doors will buckle, bulkheads will crack and the Station will split open, casting them out into Jupiter's poisonous winds.

It's how they're all expecting to die.

But not now, Robertson thinks. Not with rescue so close.

Caroline says nothing for another ten minutes. She's working the systems they spent months jury-rigging, crawling through conduits and splicing wires, cannibalising any system they could get their hands on, turning them to purposes they were never designed for. Over the past four years Robertson has learnt a lot about engineering. He's one of the people who has made this Station their own and he knows how bad tonight is. So he stays silent, watching Caroline cut systems, reroute power and reignite the thrusters.

And ten minutes after he asked, the floor steadies beneath them and she says, 'It's done.'

Easter nods appreciation, but Robertson shakes his head: 'That was too close. We couldn't handle another failure like that.'

Caroline has already forgotten, is looking around. 'Where are they?' she asks.

Robertson looks too, immediately knowing who she's talking about. The Professional and Anji Kapoor are nowhere to be seen.

'They slipped out somehow.' Easter shrugs. 'Rebecca had got free and Jones and Garcia were helping get her back under control. When they got back to the barricade the two of them were in the corridor.'

Robertson remembers the gunfire. 'Enemy?'

Easter nods. 'They drew them away from the compound.' He checks David's readings. 'Apparently his weapon wasn't as effective on them as it was on one of our own.'

There's a bang as a deck plate flies free of its housing, crashing back down.

Robertson knows Greenwich Village inside out now. Underneath that deck plate is the primary hydrogen feed for the failed thruster array. He's expecting feedback, an explosion caused by a build-up of pressure from some blockage.

He's not expecting a smoking and charred hand to reach out from the hole in the floor.

The gloved hand of an armoured spacesuit.

The Professional's visor has a crack down its front: a silver line across smoky darkness. They just stand there as he climbs free of the fuel line, reaching back into the pipe to haul Anji up after him.

Their suits had been sleek curves and crisp lines, with occasional patches of heavy technology, even free fall through Jupiter's atmosphere failing to dull their appearance. Now they're matt black, patches of the exteriors flaking away as smoke rises from the joints.

More shocking than this, the Professional's panther-like movement has gone. He looks tired. He looks, for the first time, like he belongs among the survivors.

'You detonated the fuel line,' Robertson says.

The Professional releases the catches on his helmet. 'We were trapped by the energy barrier,' he says. 'These suits can withstand the temperatures of a burning fuel line. Your enemy can't.'

Easter looks confused, but Caroline has caught up. 'You shot open the fuel line, crawled inside while it was on fire. Too tight and hot for them to follow.' She nods, laughs. 'The only way out of a dead-end.'

It's months since Robertson has heard Caroline laugh. In all those nights, he's sometimes thought of her laughter as her dreams press against him. Dancing in the mess hall, hair slipping loose, laughing in pleasure. He wanted to hear her laugh again. But this isn't the sound of memory. It's short and ugly, punctuating her admiration for the Professional's actions.

And it makes Robertson angrier than he thought possible.

'You nearly killed us all,' he says.

'You rerouted the hydrogen, what was left in the pipe burned off. There was no danger when we opened that hatch.' The Professional nods to the computer terminal. 'You compensated for the power loss. It was well within your capabilities.'

Robertson shakes his head. 'You didn't know that. You were guessing. You could have killed everyone!'

There's a hiss as Anji removes her helmet. She brushes her hair back, fixing Robertson with a stare. 'Let it go,' she says. 'Even if you're right, there are more important things to do.'

'Like what?' Robertson snaps.

'Like getting everyone off this station,' Anji replies.

They crawled through the pipe in darkness, visors blanked to the fire burning outside, their voices the only sensation.

- This is insane.

- It gets us back to the docking bay. You should have stayed on the main corridor.

- I forgot about the energy barrier. A pause. *What were you doing back there?*

- It was one of the emergency datacores. That energy barrier has cut access to the main computers. A handful of back-up storage areas are positioned around the Station. I downloaded a snapshot of the Station's computers from before the attack happened.

- They're not insane, are they? You got it wrong, they really were attacked.

– They've rationalised their experience, extrapolating from the few facts they possessed. Creating a war, a blockade. Supposition to define their lives, giving them role and purpose.
– Those things back there. The enemy. They're real.
– Yes.
– Do we tell them the truth? That there's no war?
– No.
– Why not?
– They need to believe. Focus that belief and we can use them. They've been here four years, Miss Kapoor, they're tired and very close to the psychosis I'd assumed. Break their belief, you break them. We say nothing.

And nothing is what they continue to say as Easter presses for answers. 'What were you doing out there in the first place?'

Unashamed and unfeeling, the Professional has no interpersonal skills Anji recognises. Except one. He can lie. His cold face is the perfect vessel for lying and he knows how to weave fiction close to the truth.

Stripping the blackened suit from his body, he explains: 'Reconnaissance.' When Easter raises an eyebrow in response, the Professional continues, making Easter appear slow for not immediately understanding: 'Reconnaissance for the evacuation. This Station is beyond salvage. Even if they penetrated the blockade, bulk ships can't dock this deep in the atmosphere.'

It's an impatient tone that immediately puts Anji on edge, certain its use is not accidental.

Focus that belief and we can use them.

Anji had let that phrase slip by, but now she wonders just what the Professional meant.

'So how do we get out of here?' Easter demands.

'Escape pods,' the Professional replies. 'They won't make escape velocity, but they should reach high enough for a safe intercept by a smaller vessel.'

Anji watches as he scans the surrounding personnel, focusing on Arquette. 'Once the evacuation is complete, we destroy this Station from orbit, taking the enemy with it.'

And any doubts Anji had about his ulterior motives are dispelled by the look on Arquette's face. The Professional is playing to the crowd now.

We can use them.

There's silence. Anji has this one opportunity to break the Professional's hold on the survivors, to stop whatever he's planning to do. But if she tells them the truth now, the truth the Professional wants hidden, she can't be sure of the outcome.

She begins to open her mouth but is cut off by Robertson.

'Look around you.' He points. 'Over there, that trunking is from the inertial response systems from the pod on level three. The generator running the computer terminal right here, stripped from life support on the pod two sections across.' He shakes his head. 'What kind of life do you think we've been living here?'

'Robbie,' Arquette says.

'No,' Robertson snaps. 'No.' He fixes on the Professional, 'When the Station fell, the EM shield started fluctuating. Nearly 150 people spent six months crammed in those research shuttles behind you, because it was the only guaranteed protection from the radiation.'

Anji says nothing as Robertson continues.

'We took it in relays, five-minute spells to put together shields, lay safe paths, find anything from anywhere that might keep us alive!' He points to one of the crowd. 'That man has a tumour the size of your fist on his lungs. He's not alone. This place has taken years off all our lives. Escape pods?' he barks. 'You stupid sonofabitch, take a look at the life we lead. There are no escape pods left intact on this Station.'

As silence falls, Anji starts thinking that Robertson has done her job for her. A glance at the Professional dispels the idea. His face remains neutral, unconcerned by Robertson's broadside. It should call into question his competence and ability to control the situation.

When he answers, the Professional's face remains flat, his voice level. But somehow Anji can feel the smile beneath it. Like Robertson's outburst was exactly what he was looking for.

'Maybe you should look at that life you lead.'

'What?' Robertson says.

'How did you get here? Who brought you to this?'

'The enemy,' Easter says.

'There's more than one kind of enemy,' the Professional says.

Easter's a good man, Anji thinks. More suited to command than he realises, but cautious. Someone who examines the way ahead and acts only on certainty; a man unfazed by the Professional and unlikely to be taken in by him.

Suddenly Anji knows what the Professional is doing.

'There's the enemy at the door,' the Professional says, 'and the one that lives inside. Who keeps your head down. Who stops you from fighting.'

'What are you talking about?' Easter asks.

'Fear,' the Professional says. 'And you stink of it.'

Easter sees the jaws of the trap opening up to swallow him whole. And he blinks in the face of it. Blinks for everyone to see and in that instant he's finished.

'You all smell of it,' the Professional says. He turns round to Arquette. 'Everyone except you.'

Anji sees Robertson shaking his head. Like her, he's realised what's happening. His mouth is moving in silent prayer. *Don't do this*, he whispers, but the Professional pays no heed.

'Only strength can give hope.'

Robertson tries to take Arquette's hand, but she snaps it back. At that point, he turns and walks away.

Anji sees the hurt in his eyes and understands it. He's been party to the Professional's trick. The way he can't stand and watch Arquette follow Easter into the trap speaks volumes about how much he cares for her.

'You want this job?' Easter tells Arquette, pulling a set of threadbare stripes from his pocket. 'You can have it.'

The cloth lands on the ground by Arquette's feet.

It's Easter's last stand. To his credit he looks at Arquette, right until she finally breaks contact and sinks to her haunches, picking up the stripes. With that done, he silently turns back to David's cot, checking on his patient's condition.

Anji looks around. The others are accepting the change without hesitation, some nodding positively, momentum swinging behind the Professional. Except she knows the truth. She can't trust him and, on current form, he could dispense with her as easily as he did Easter. If she's going to achieve anything here, she needs allies.

* * *

A couple of hours later and Robertson is at the barricades. Shadows twist further down the corridor, throwing themselves at the electrified barriers; the automated weapons are conserving power, only firing once or twice a minute.

When he hears footsteps his first thought is that it's Caroline, but the tread is too crisp. Only one woman on this station has boots that aren't falling apart.

'I'm sorry,' Anji says.

'Joshua Easter's a good man,' Robertson says. 'He didn't deserve that.'

Anji settles on a crate next to him, stripped of her suit, uneasy in the thin clothing underneath it. She holds up a slender card. 'It's a download. From the emergency datacore.'

'Then he wants my wife, not me. She's the computer technician.'

Anji pauses, uncomfortable. 'She said you could do it. She's busy, helping with the repairs to our suits.'

Robertson snorts. He knows his wife. The frustration she's felt at Easter's caution has suddenly found an outlet. 'They're planning something? Some strategy?'

'I'm not sure.' Anji hesitates, then says, 'I'd like to see it too. The last readings from the main computer? There could be all sorts of data.'

'Fitz,' Robertson says, looking at the datacard. 'You want to know what happened to Fitz and his friend.'

'Yes,' Anji says quietly.

They sit in silence for a long while, listening to the noise of the barricade. Robertson tries not to look at her.

'How long have you been married?' she asks.

'Three years,' he answers.

A gunshot punches the air.

'You seem lonely,' she says.

That's too raw to answer. 'What about you?' Robertson says. 'Your friends are four years gone. You still came for them. Why?'

She smiles a little. 'Maybe I'm lonely, too.'

Robertson shakes his head. 'Maybe.'

There's a pause, then Anji says, 'I'm married too. His name's Michael; he's a journalist too.'

Another pause. Robertson is about to speak when she cuts him off. 'I had another life. Before I met Michael, before this station fell.' She smiles. 'And when it fell, I started again. And it's been good. I've seen things and done things, but...' She looks at him. 'My family weren't there when I married. When I lost the Doctor and Fitz, I lost any chance of keeping in touch with them and... I missed them. I still miss them. Talking with my dad, fighting with my brother. And Michael... I'd love for them to have met Michael.' She pauses. 'My dad was a good man. He'd have liked Michael.'

Robertson nods, eyes fixed on the floor.

'When I was a kid,' Anji says, 'he used to take me to the football, to see Leeds play.'

Robertson is confused for a moment, then catches up. Anji's British, like Fitz. When she says football, she means soccer.

Her voice is clear with memory. 'Rezaul wasn't old enough to go and my dad thought maybe I'd like it. And it was fine, you know. Cold, but the terraces were just getting friendly again. None of that trigger, trigger, trigger crap. And it'd be a cold day and he'd pull me through the crowd and I was fifteen and so grown up, but... His hand felt so big, so warm.'

Robertson looks at her. There are no tears, but there's a faraway look in her eyes. 'Did you like it?' He asks. 'The football?'

Anji smiles. 'Enough to keep checking the scores every Saturday. Did that for a good few years.'

'But not now?'

She laughs. 'Where I come from Manchester United are still a football team, not a junk-bonds clearing house.'

Robertson frowns. He never followed soccer much, but he could swear Manchester United hadn't played football for nearly 150 years.

'It wouldn't matter if I'd shipped out to one of the system colonies, I'd still have missed my dad.' She looks at him. 'That's why I'm here. If there's a chance, I'd like to see them again, like them to meet my husband.'

There's another moment of silence, then Robertson takes the data-card from her hand. They walk back to the Meridian and the computer terminals. As Robertson settles down, he asks Anji: 'Is he for real?'

'The Professional?'

Robertson nods. 'You're normal enough; you've got that vibe, like Fitz had. Regular people, and I trust regular people. But him? I don't know him and I need to know: can we trust him?'

Anji stays quiet. Robertson plugs the datacard in, sifting through its contents. Finally, Anji answers: 'I don't think anyone really knows.'

'How come?'

'The Professionals are one of those fairy stories – imps and sprites doing dishes and tidying the house while everyone's asleep.'

'Imps and sprites don't put holes through people.'

Anji shakes her head. 'The point is, you only ever see their work, never the person.'

'So who are they?' Robertson asks. 'Who is he?'

'No one knows,' Anji says.

Robertson stops working, turns to make sure she's serious. She is.

'No one I've ever spoken to knows, anyway, and I've spoken to lots of military.' A pause. 'You spot Professionals by the bodies they leave behind. Beyond that, they're anonymous.'

'That's it?'

Anji shrugs, 'There're some urban legends. Robots; clones of famous warriors; aliens fighting for Earth; the dead brought back to life.' She looks at him. 'That's just the sensible stuff. They have voodoo-markings tattooed on their bodies; they're blessed by oriental magicks; they're the physical embodiment of the Earth's spirit.'

Robertson snorts, takes a long look past Anji back into the heart of Greenwich, where the Professional is talking to Caroline. When did Greenwich become Greenwich Village? When did this place become their home?

'You know what I think?' Robertson says. 'He's just a soldier.'

Anji follows Robertson's gaze. 'You love her, don't you?'

Robertson can feel something building inside of him. Something that threatens to overwhelm him.

Robertson saw a face once and it will haunt him for the rest of his days.

'I don't know,' he says softly. 'I don't know any more.'

The terminal beeps and Robertson breaks from Anji's stare. He checks the computer, shakes his head. 'I got nothing for you. Not yet, anyway.'

Anji peers over his shoulder. 'Problem?'

Robertson gestures at the screen: 'There's a lot of data. Video streams, status reports, that kind of thing. But' – he points to a stream of symbols crisscrossing the screen – 'there's corrupted material overlaying it.' He shrugs. 'It's not unusual in holographic storage, but the computers can't self-clean with half the system caught inside the energy barrier.' He nods at the two terminals. 'Caroline had to rebuild the programming from scratch. Ghosts in every machine.'

'Can you clean it up?'

'Sure,' Robertson says.

'And do me a copy?' Anji asks. 'Of the corruption, I mean.' She shrugs. 'He wants to see everything, I say we give him everything.'

'Even if it's a waste of time.'

'Especially if it's a waste of time.'

Robertson smiles, then hits a few keys and slots a datachip into the printer. 'The clean-up will take a few hours. Everything should be ready to view tomorrow.'

Anji lays a hand on his shoulder. Her fingers are cool. She smiles. 'Thank you.'

When she finds him, the Professional's meeting with Arquette is over. Anji doesn't ask what they talked about.

He's sitting near one of the greenhouses. The damp smell reminds her of Regent's Park on a spring Sunday, but the Professional doesn't look like anyone from that life. A small set of tools is in his hand, checking components on the armour stripped from his torso.

'I thought you said those things could withstand the burning fuel,' Anji says.

'They did.' He nods to where her suit is stacked. 'Yours is fine. This is damage from the energy barrier.'

'What did it do?'

'Some components have an organic base; neural interfaces on the suit's AI. All burnt out.'

'Irreparably?'

'I can bypass.'

As he gets to his feet, Anji sees the burns for the first time. Calloused patches of skin, puckered red and white across his shoulders.

'Is that the energy barrier too?'

'Yes.'

'You should get a dressing on that.'

'It's difficult to reach.'

'Then get someone else to do it. Easter would have been the perfect choice, only I don't think you're on speaking terms.' She picks up his medical kit. 'So that leaves me.'

A moment's pause, then the Professional sits down, offering her his back. Anji begins to spray analgesic on to the burns. He flinches as the chill vapour touches injured flesh. There's an odd mechanical hiss as he does this.

'That's a big scar,' Anji says, looking at the back of his neck. There's a two-inch strip of raised, hard flesh at the top of the Professional's spine. 'How did you get it?'

'I don't remember,' he says.

Anji sprays more salve and the hiss sounds again. This time she locates the source. The Professional hasn't removed every piece of his armour. A bulky strip of metal encircles his right biceps; tiny vials arranged are along its surface. Anji looks at it, then gently prods the Professional's back. He gasps with pain and Anji makes a show of apologising; but, as she does, she hears the hiss as one of the vials bubbles.

Automated pain relief.

But there's more to it than that, Anji realises.

Up until now the Professional's voice has been vague; quite unlike the crisp orders issued previously. Maybe he was distracted by the burns and the drugs now dulling the pain are all it takes, but suddenly that focus is back.

'What did you recover from the download?' he snaps.

Anji hands over the chip containing the record of the interference. 'A ghost in the machine,' she says.

As he turns the chip over, she seals his wounds with a layer of synthetic skin. 'The file was corrupted,' she explains, watching the coating stiffen then go supple over the burns. 'That's the pattern overlaying all the data.'

The Professional slots the chip into the gauntlet from his armour, checks the data on its small screen.

'It looks random,' Anji says.

'I can see how it looks,' the Professional replies.

There's a clear implication to this sentence that Anji isn't happy with. The possibility that she's missed something.

'Anything else?' she asks.

'No.'

As he continues to study the file Anji repacks the medical kit. As she does so, she finds a small rack of tiny vials; replacements for the ones his suit pumps in response to pain, the ones that sharpen his mind. Checking he is still focused on the file, Anji slips a vial from the clip, then closes the medical kit.

As she moves away, the Professional does not even acknowledge her departure.

The Professional studies the file for fifteen minutes.

There's no formula here, no trace of infiltration programs or sign of alien thinking. Just a random series of letters and numbers. Except something nags at him, telling him there is more to see.

Continued study reveals nothing and he closes the file down.

For all the night's activities – the escape and firefight, their return and the subsequent manoeuvring – it is not yet dawn. The survivors have drifted back to their beds or their duties. In this corner of the compound, he is alone.

The Professional has felt like this before. His primary role is as an analyst: studying the possibilities of tactics, attack and counter-attack. On occasion, he has trouble focusing. It surfaces like a headache, pressure building inside his skull; most times, the medication relieves the tension. Sometimes it doesn't work.

An image comes to him in these moments.

A raid on one of the system colonies, targeting a group of alien insurgents. Explosions flowering above marshland. One of the hostiles pushing through the water towards him, his back alive with flames that will never burn out.

The Professional reported this problem to the colonel.

The colonel explained how the brain forms patterns. When the Professional's mind is overwhelmed by detail, it finds a release valve. This image has become that release. What is required is a more efficient distraction.

The longer he stays on the Station, the more options and scenarios weigh upon the Professional's mind. The more he sees that hostile, sees the flames. This place feels uncomfortable. He feels dislocated from the people and the surroundings.

He opens the suit's dictation routine. His new release valve.

The Professional pauses, giving his thoughts a voice: 'It was the first lesson we learnt when we reached for the stars: for everything, there is a limit.'

Four years earlier

'I've got it,' the Doctor said.

Fitz looked over sulkily as the Doctor hit a control, letting the video play.

The docking bay, the previous night. Jason McCray, slowly passing a cleaner over the *Pegasus*'s surface, paying close attention to its blackened underside.

'Heat scars,' the Doctor said, 'from the suicide dive.'

'I still don't see what's so interesting,' Fitz commented.

'Wait.' The Doctor slowed the footage as Jason turned away. 'Here, he flicks his right hand, like it's wet.'

'He's been cleaning, it probably is wet.'

'Oh, I'm sure,' the Doctor said. 'Now look. He realises he's dropped the journal, goes to pick it up.' He froze the picture, with Jason's arm outstretched. 'With his right hand.'

'Great,' Fitz answered.

The Doctor sighed. 'The poetry isn't that interesting, Fitz.'

'Look,' Fitz said, 'I checked. The 101st used to have an eagle as their insignia, right? But that's changed to a sword and a scythe.'

'Representing the power impellers and chain swords used as weapons during the occupation,' the Doctor said.

'So Jason used to be one of them,' Fitz said. 'I saw that tattoo on him last night.' He swung his feet over the edge of his bunk, looking down at the Doctor. 'McCray's got a brother, who used to be part of his unit, but barely acknowledges him when his boys are around. A brother who can barely talk, but somehow manages to pull a Byron on the sly.'

'And,' the Doctor said, 'that kind of discrepancy isn't unheard of. Autistic children can have phenomenal recall of shapes and numbers, for example.' He held the journal up. 'Now, does that look like a thumbprint to you?'

'I don't understand the fuss,' Fitz said.

The Doctor returned the comms panel to its default, the screen still showing Defcon 4. 'I'm concerned about the *Pegasus* exploding.'

'I thought that was a malfunction?'

'Or sabotage. People shouldn't just snap, ships shouldn't just blow up. It's another piece of random violence.'

'Ships aren't people, though, are they?' Fitz said. 'Ships don't commit suicide, they get blown up.'

The Doctor smiled. 'Exactly. Which brings us to this.' He tapped the stained cover of Jason's journal. 'Trace evidence.'

Fitz sighed. 'Go on, then.'

'Water shouldn't stain leather like this. Jason touched something on that ship, something he transferred to this book when he picked it up.'

'Bleach?' Fitz suggested.

'The cleaning agents here don't work like that, I checked.' He looked up at Fitz. 'Could your friend in the cargo bay spare some supplies for a day or two?'

'What do you want?'

'Some lab equipment.' He sniffed the book cover. 'I want to run an analysis of this. Traces of explosive, that kind of thing.'

Fitz shrugged. 'I'll see what I can do.'

As the Doctor continued to examine the book, Fitz read the newspaper headlines, following up on the riots. After quelling the protests, the shock troops had investigated the colonists' claims. To everyone's surprise, they'd found alien artefacts.

Fitz put the paper down, sighed. 'Are we getting a bit sidetracked? We came here for Anji, now we're looking at exploding ships.'

'Patterns of violent behaviour,' the Doctor repeated.

'Yeah, but detectives look for motive, don't they? And we don't have any, or any suspects, come to that. That stuff you mentioned, nerve gas, that kind of –'

'Dead-ends.' The Doctor handed Fitz a dataslide. 'The latest from AuDoc. The only research like that is designed for alien neurologies; it's completely harmless to humans.'

'So?'

'We look at other projects, other people. I want to know about those shipments for the Mukabis, what they're working on that's so classified. And I want to know why someone would destroy the

Pegasus. Something's going wrong on this station and there's got to be a trail somewhere.' The Doctor tapped the journal again. 'Lab equipment, please.'

'All right,' Fitz said, trying to think things through. 'This Mukabi pair. What about them?'

'Ah.' The Doctor smiled. 'I've had AuDoc joining some dots. A quick round of six degrees of separation, in fact.'

'Excuse me?'

'The first thing Commander Valletti did after explaining why the Station was built here was swallow all her wine. She sips wine; she'd been sipping all through dinner.'

'She was lying to you.'

The Doctor called up a graphic. 'This dot is Jupiter, this dot is Farside Station. I asked AuDoc to find the six people linking them. It only needed one.'

Fitz could guess. 'Sara Mukabi?'

'This dot' – the Doctor pointed – 'is an Earth Forces science mission to Jupiter fifteen years ago. A number of the crew suffered severe psychological trauma; the on-board psychologist was Sara Mukabi.'

'OK,' Fitz said, 'psychos then, psychos now, both connected to Jupiter, both connected by Sara Mukabi. What's the next step?'

The Doctor called up AuDoc's graphics program, focusing on the black cylinders of the 101st. There was no pattern to their interactions with the cargo-bay time sheets, the shipments appearing at random.

'Did your friend give any idea what these shipments are?'

'Not really. Big, long drums.'

The Doctor nodded, stared out of the window. Jupiter was coming into view.

He was hiding it well, but Fitz could see frustration beneath the surface. If he thought they were chasing their tails, the Doctor must have seen it a mile off.

Getting down from his bunk, Fitz knocked the newspaper on to the floor, jogging its controls. When he picked it up, the slide held an image from the system colonies: a trooper, holding a weapon designed for alien hands. The blue liquid on his hands and the gun could only be blood.

When Fitz looked up, he saw the Doctor's reflection in the window staring at him.

'Of course,' the Doctor said, 'there is another possibility. This is the cutting edge of Earth's defence research, and a prime target for any hostile force. AuDoc showed a lot of flights down into Jupiter's atmosphere recently. They might be searching for something.'

'This might have nothing to do with the Station personnel? There really could be Reds under the bed?'

The Doctor smiled. 'Sometimes when you're paranoid –'

'They are out to get you.'

'The only problem with that scenario,' the Doctor said, 'is that kind of hunt should be co-ordinated by Commander Valletti. And it's the Mukabis who are responsible for those flights.'

The sickbay was a large circular room: beds around the exterior, a bank of monitors positioned in the centre. When the Doctor arrived Jason McCray was the sole occupant.

The Doctor found the screen for Jason's bed. Burns under control, ribs healing, release imminent. He paused, then called up more detailed information.

'No evidence of nerve damage or deliberate toxicity,' he muttered. 'But... Hello. What's that?'

A hand reached across, clicked the monitor off. The Doctor turned to find John McCray behind him. 'Patient records are confidential.'

'Professional curiosity,' the Doctor smiled. 'I'm not just a doctor of economics.'

McCray looked at him, then his stone face relaxed and he sighed. 'I know Commander Valletti looks easy-going, but... We run a tight ship. Don't go sticking your nose where it doesn't belong.' He held his palms up. 'Honest advice, OK?'

'Appreciated,' the Doctor said.

There were footsteps, Valletti approaching. 'Is everything all right?'

'Fine, thank you,' the Doctor said. 'I was just returning this.' He held up the journal; there were scratch marks where he'd taken samples of the cover. 'It was recovered this morning; I understand it belongs to Captain McCray's brother.'

'I see.' Valletti looked at the control bank then slipped between them, reactivating the monitor. The cranial scan the Doctor had been examining was still there: a bright silver silhouette penetrating Jason's skull.

For the first time, the Doctor saw anger flash on Valletti's face.

'You shouldn't have seen that. And Captain McCray should know better than to cover up for you.'

'It's not his fault,' the Doctor said. 'I have this insatiable curiosity.'

'Lucky, adaptable and now curious,' she snapped. 'Anything else I should know about, Doctor?'

'Those three are probably enough to be going on with.'

Valletti looked at him for a long moment. 'Captain McCray, you're here to see to the discharge of your brother?'

'Yes, ma'am.'

'The Doctor can help you. He doesn't leave your sight. When you're done report as scheduled, bringing the Doctor with you.' She reached in, pulled the Doctor's pass from his jacket. 'Are we clear?'

'Yes, ma'am.'

The Doctor had left Fitz with a shopping list of equipment. Some Fitz borrowed from the cargo bay, but most of the items weren't the kind of thing you left hanging around.

Returning to their office, Fitz pondered how to proceed. He swung his feet up on to the desk, then jumped as a mass of colour exploded in his vision.

'Bloody hell,' he said, calming himself as he realised what had happened; his heel had hit the computer control pad, launching AuDoc. He was looking for the off switch when he remembered what the Doctor had said.

It's capable of adaptive thought, so if I ask AuDoc to locate black-money projects, it'll figure out how to do that itself.

Fitz nodded to himself and reached for the controls.

A little experimentation showed that asking the AI to do something was a simple matter of typing your question; with the hologram active, the answers drifted across the space over the desk.

'Right.' Fitz cracked his knuckles, leaning over the keypad. 'Let's see how you handle an initiative test.'

LOCATE UNUSUAL ACTIVITY ON THIS STATION.

– HIGH LEVEL OF MAINTENANCE OVERTIME, AuDoc replied.

'AuDoc, one; Kreiner, nil,' Fitz muttered and tried again, awkwardly tapping instructions with two fingers.

SCAN ALL STATION RECORDS FOR UNUSUAL PATTERNS AND ACTIVITY. He paused, thinking about how the Doctor had studied the video footage from the docking bay. INCLUDE ALL SURVEILLANCE.

Fitz thought about the Reds under the bed, added, PAY SPECIAL ATTENTION TO ANY SUSPECTED ALIEN ACTIVITY.

– ESTIMATED RUN TIME: THIRTY-TWO HOURS AND FORTY-SEVEN MINUTES.

USE YOUR INITIATIVE. JOIN THE DOTS.

– ESTIMATED RUN TIME: FORTY-FIVE HOURS AND TWELVE MINUTES.

Fitz sighed. 'No chance of you getting me this equipment, then?' he said, waving the Doctor's list.

The desk printer whirred into life, a completed requisition form gliding out.

'Oh,' Fitz said, 'you could have mentioned voice recognition.'

The Doctor felt no real surprise when McCray reported for duty. Level six. The one drawing the power from the reactor, the one Valletti hadn't mentioned. The lift doors opened on to a long corridor, so self-consciously devoid of features it probably contained more security systems than he knew what to do with.

Valletti was waiting.

'Don't move,' she said, reaching into the lift to pin the pass back on his lapel. 'I needed to upgrade your clearance. For this level, I have to authorise the pass personally.'

The Doctor stepped cautiously out into the scope of the invisible security systems. Nothing happened.

'You look surprised,' Valletti said. 'What did you think was happening? That you were going to be tortured?'

The Doctor smiled. 'Of course not.'

Valletti turned and led them down the corridor. 'I'm sure you've noticed some irregularities during your audit. You're smart enough to have realised there are black-money projects on this station, even before last night's dinner.'

'I couldn't –'

'It never made sense to me to have an audit that couldn't account for funds. There'd be no way for you to know whether or not it was going on legitimate projects.'

'And that's what this is?' the Doctor asked. 'A legitimate project?'

Valletti laughed. 'The singularity bomb is a legitimate project. This' – she nodded down the hall – 'is less conventional.'

They'd reached another security door now.

'Like a titanium implant sunk six inches into Jason McCray's cerebellum?'

Valletti shook her head. 'Not just Jason.'

McCray pulled down his uniform collar. Metal glinted at the base of his skull. 'Every member of the 101st has one.'

'Why?' the Doctor asked. 'What does it do?'

'Hurry up and we'll show you.' It was Terrance Mukabi, standing in the opening doorway. 'I don't want to tie up the network longer than necessary.'

The chamber was similar to the medical bay: circular with couches slung against its outside edge, a small platform occupying the otherwise empty centre. Another door was set in the wall on the far side: heavily plated, with yellow and black stripes, and a large keypad.

As the Doctor and Valletti entered, McCray removed his uniform jacket and rolled up his shirt sleeves. He settled down on one of the couches, the rest of the 101st seated around him. Valletti ushered the Doctor up a set of steps on to a catwalk above. From this new vantage point, the Doctor could see diamond lenses glittering on the central platform. A low whine was building, and he could taste ozone on his tongue.

Terrance was working on a console on one side of the catwalk, while Sara Mukabi was positioned behind a similar control bank opposite. They gave each other quick glances, then Terrance nodded.

Almost immediately the whine increased in pitch, and a small white spot appeared in mid-air above the platform. A moment's pause, then it expanded into a dull grey sphere.

'Holographic projector,' the Doctor said. 'I'm not sure I'm impressed.'

Instruments unfolded from the arms of the couches, ice-thin needles sliding into the muscle tissues of McCray's squad. Clamps followed, holding their heads in place as probes drilled into the implants they carried.

'The holograms aren't the clever bit,' Valletti said. 'It's the data that's projected.'

The Doctor looked down at the twelve men below, musing. 'Because they generate it?' He frowned. 'I don't see the benefit. The human mind is a wonderful thing, but even a dozen of them, linked together at their fullest potential, still wouldn't come close to this station's processing power.'

'That isn't the point, though.' It was Terrance speaking now. 'They're human, and the avatars they generate in there' – he pointed at the holographic sphere – 'believe themselves to be human.'

'A simulation programme,' the Doctor said. 'High-tech training. But why bother with the simulacra? Surely it's more efficient just to walk into an imaging chamber?'

Terrance was about to answer, but Valletti raised her hand to silence him. 'I want to see if the Doctor has the intellect to match his curiosity.'

The Doctor frowned at her, but it was a genuine challenge, devoid of underlying threat. He turned away, resting his hands on the catwalk railing, his fingers drumming as he surveyed the room's equipment. It was only when he spotted Sara Mukabi opposite that he smiled.

'This isn't about technology, is it? It's psychology.'

'Go on.'

'Military training is predicated around repetition and reduction. Everything becomes a series of small tasks. Repeat those tasks until they're as automatic as breathing and you can perform them in any circumstance. Reload, strip your gun, bind a wound, whatever. And for all the advances in weapons technology, that's how it's worked for hundreds of years. But it's all just training. You could use the most advanced holographic procedures and your soldiers would still know they were just in training. And training is no substitute for combat experience.' He brought his hand down on the rail in triumph, grinning. 'That's it, isn't it? This is like your wine bottle or the atmosphere filters on the windows. Something to trick the mind.'

'The implants link them to the computers,' Valletti said, 'then a pharmaceutical cocktail enhances the sensation and integrates the memories into the hippocampus.' She gestured at the holographic field. 'What's generated in there is, to all intents and purposes, real. If they're hit, it hurts. You feel mud under your boots, taste blood in your mouth, smell the fires burning.'

The holographic field began to flicker, shapes coming into focus.

'They believe it's real. And when the session is complete,' the Doctor said, 'they retain those memories, those experiences.'

'In this room,' Valletti said, 'we can create combat veterans without the soldiers ever once stepping into the field. It's the most important thing we do here.'

'Because a weapon is only ever as good as the soldier wielding it,' the Doctor agreed.

AuDoc had provided a remarkably simple solution to the problem of purloining the Doctor's equipment: walk into the labs and take it. Most of the scientists glanced wearily at the requisition form and handed the stuff over. It was all going well until Fitz turned a corner and ran into the thin man he'd seen leaving their office in a temper. Professor Deschamps.

The professor's eyes narrowed, then recognition dawned and he nodded. 'The accountant.' He pointed to the trolley Fitz was pushing. 'Leave that here. Come with me. Now.'

The holographic sphere had coalesced; the 101st crouched in a muddy field. The bio-readouts on the couches below jumped as this happened. The Doctor could see a black liquid being pumped into the men's arms.

'This is a classic training scenario,' Valletti explained. 'An actual mission and a West Point textbook example for almost 250 years. We re-create the landscape, equipment, opposition, even the weather, all down to the smallest detail.'

The Doctor looked at the sphere. 'Normandy, I'd guess. A German machine-gun emplacement, circa 1944. The sixth of June, perhaps? Near Brécourt Manor?'

Valletti smiled. 'You know your history.'

'So do you. The paratroopers who stormed those guns back then were also members of the 101st Airborne.'

The Doctor studied the holographic sphere. The dew on the grass; the dirt and shrapnel accompanying each explosion; the crease and movement of the uniforms; the awkward weight of the weaponry.

All down to the smallest detail.

And, the Doctor thought, the experience would be different for each soldier. Different perspective, sounds and textures.

Deschamps guided a reluctant Fitz into one of the sealed chambers on the lab floor.

Equations that hurt Fitz's eyes just when he looked at them scrolled across screens on the wall, a handful of staff keeping track of their progress. Behind them a cage of rats sat on a worktop, close to a set of generators producing an unsettling whine.

'I thought you were moving on to deep-space testing,' Fitz said, glancing uneasily at the machinery.

'Weeks away, boy,' Deschamps snapped. 'And we still need to work on the theory.' He pointed to one of the screens. 'There. Look at that.'

Fitz did. The symbols that glided elsewhere were stuttering here. 'Yes?' he said nervously.

Deschamps sighed in frustration. Fitz could see the man's temper building. 'It's not good enough,' Deschamps said. 'I'm underfunded and supplied with faulty equipment.'

Fitz smiled, edging back towards the door. 'It really is Commander Valletti you need to sp–'

Deschamps grabbed his arm, wheeled him over to the generators. Each one had a tiny screen set into its top. 'Look,' Deschamps ordered.

Fitz looked. The nearest screen was white, punctuated by tiny pinpricks of black snapping in and out of existence. 'What am I supposed to be looking at?' he asked.

'Singularities,' Deschamps said.

'Hang on,' Fitz said. 'Aren't singularities like black holes or something?'

Deschamps waved his hand dismissively. 'On this level, they're nothing like them and exactly the same.'

'How big are they?' Fitz asked.

Deschamps gave him an irritated look, pointing to the bottom of the generator's screen: 'Can't you read?'

All Fitz could see was a long mathematical formula. 'Oh, right.'

Deschamps tapped the generator. 'They last less than a billionth of a second. It's only the computer that lets you see them at all.'

'I'm really not the man for –'

'The screen, boy,' Deschamps said, slamming his hand down on the generator. 'You can understand the screen, can't you?'

'It doesn't seem to be working,' Fitz said.

'Precisely,' Deschamps said. 'And who is responsible for the upkeep of the theoretical-intelligence computers?'

Fitz took a guess. 'Terrance Mukabi?'

The generator behind them suddenly stepped up in pitch.

'Who is never anywhere to be found!'

Fitz glanced at the generator screen. The black dots were flashing with a greater frequency and getting larger. 'Is that supposed to be –'

An alarm sounded and the generator screen went black. Deschamps reached over, cutting the power, studying the readings. 'Bloody continuum imbalance,' he muttered.

Fitz watched him for a moment, then realised the scientist had already forgotten he was even in the room.

'Never look a gift horse,' Fitz murmured, edging towards the door. As he passed the cage the rats suddenly screamed at his presence, clawing at the bars and each other.

'Before your recital, you were off-network,' the Doctor said. 'In here? Running a training scenario?'

'Yes,' Valletti answered, 'How did you – ?'

'Time lag on the Station computers. I imagine this level of detail ties up an awful lot of processing power.'

'We're having some difficulty,' Terrance admitted. 'But we're hoping to extend the system's uses to justify the processing time. Pure research applications, for example.'

The holosphere filled with flame and mud as one of the emplacements was destroyed. McCray, crouched low, led his squad on through another trench, rolling grenades around a blind corner.

'What kind of research?' the Doctor asked.

'Whatever you like. We've duplicated Jupiter's atmosphere, for example, trying to understand its weather systems. Modelled ten thousand years of activity in just under five minutes.'

One of the men at McCray's side snapped back, a bullet exploding through his shoulder. The Doctor located the man on the couches below: he hadn't moved.

'You integrate these virtual memories with their real ones, yes?'

'It's tricky,' Valletti said. 'At present, it requires a regular drug regime to ensure the synapses don't reject the input, but yes, they'll remember all this.'

The lights were dimming as they walked back to their quarters. The Doctor had found Fitz as he was leaving their office. Fitz hurriedly told the Doctor about Deschamps and his schizophrenic rats; in return, the Doctor filled him in on his day's discoveries.

'Well,' Fitz said, 'I thought I'd had a good day on the investigation front. Deschamps is a complete nutcase, but I didn't need to bother you with that: you've got it sussed.'

'Have I?' the Doctor replied.

'Oh, come on,' Fitz said. 'Brain implants. The Mukabis are using them to control those soldiers. It's why they're so secretive about it.'

'They're secretive,' the Doctor explained, 'because that kind of work is highly illegal. During the occupation, the aliens kept a lot of Earth's population subjugated with neurological implants. Technology like that has been banned since 2171. That's why it's black money, that's why no one here knows about it. Besides,' the Doctor said, 'what would the Mukabis gain from that kind of mind control?'

'Whatever they want,' Fitz replied. 'Think about it. What couldn't you do with your own private army?'

'It's an interesting theory,' the Doctor said. 'But I have a few questions.'

'Yes?' Fitz said.

'The soldiers on Mars may not have had implants.'

'We didn't know to look,' Fitz said.

'True,' the Doctor replied. 'But the pilot definitely didn't. There was no implant and no scarring to suggest he'd ever had one.'

'Ah,' Fitz answered.

'Plus, there are those restricted cargo shipments. And there's another room on the far side of the Avatar chamber. One they didn't show me.'

'Do I sense breaking and entering coming on?'

'Possibly,' the Doctor said. 'The Avatar chamber couldn't account for all the power drawn to that level.'

He opened the door to their quarters. Almost half the room was filled with crates, test tubes, piping and gas canisters.

'Everything you asked for,' Fitz said. He smiled at the mess. 'Best of luck with it.'

'Why? Where are you going?'

'Dinner and a beer or two,' Fitz answered. 'Try not to get yourself killed while I'm gone this time.'

The Doctor settled down, the news channel running in the background.

Fitz's comments about the stability of Deschamps' experiments worried him. It wasn't the behaviour of the rats, as such; a scan of Deschamps' published notes suggested they might be able to detect the subspace friction his work caused, like birds fleeing a thunderstorm. Even if the soldiers on Mars had been in contact with the project, it was difficult to see how it could have affected them billions of miles away.

The concern was the instability Deschamps seemed unwilling to address: if one of his singularities began spiralling out of control, would he be able to contain it?

As the Doctor sorted through the equipment, he started wondering exactly how Fitz had got it all. Which sparked another thought. The power used by the Mukabis wasn't registering on the Station records, which presumably meant that any equipment requisitions wouldn't show up either.

But the Avatar lab indicated a large-scale project, with more rooms he had yet to see. And there was no way the shipments the 101st handled could account for all the equipment involved.

He picked up a slide holding the inventory AuDoc had drawn up, and began highlighting discrepancies between equipment ordered and equipment used. If he could identify components the Mukabis had siphoned off, he might be able to reverse-engineer some of their equipment.

Try not to get yourself killed while I'm gone this time.

That thought stayed with Fitz as he headed for the mess hall.

The Doctor hadn't mentioned his wound the entire day. The Doctor of old would have shrugged off that injury in an afternoon. When he'd lost his memories, had he lost that ability too? Fitz didn't know but was increasingly coming round to the idea that he should find out.

'We really need to talk,' he muttered.

He pushed open the door to the mess hall.

While a lot of the faces were the same, the mood was different. The cargo crews had been working hard to clear Greenwich of debris. Fitz hadn't been expecting a party, but he'd thought there'd be a rewarding beverage or two at the end of the day. There were drinks, but people weren't roaming the tables. They were clustered together, talking and whispering, casting glances between them. There was no music, no hustle, no life.

Robertson and Arquette were huddled in a group like any of the others. 'What's happening?' Fitz asked.

Robertson said nothing, but Arquette slid a newspaper over. A passenger ship on the edge of the solar system had come under attack; there were unconfirmed reports of vessels in the area that didn't match any known silhouette.

Fitz looked at a comms screen; the Defcon symbol had moved up another notch.

'It doesn't mean anything,' Fitz said. 'This is newspaper talk, like those missiles in Cuba. Nothing happened in the end.'

Robertson shook his head, 'They don't change the Defcon for newspaper talk. There's solid info backing this up. What it means is the one word they take real care not to use in that article.'

Fitz noticed Arquette's hand had slipped inside Robertson's, their fingers locked, holding tight on to each other.

'War,' Robertson said. 'It means there's a war coming.'

MARS

Anji ran, feet kicking up red dust, breath rasping against the filter.

Terra-forming efforts were slowly clawing the planet's atmosphere back, increasing the oxygen, thickening cloud cover and raising the ambient temperature. It meant her exposed skin still felt ice cold, sweat freezing like diamonds. But she could run without a cumbersome spacesuit, her arms and legs pumping freely. There were other benefits too. The atmosphere wasn't great – it was a long way from the Earth standard of the tent cities – but, in an emergency, you could breathe it.

Which was good. Because as Anji sprinted across the roof of the escarpment, her pursuers were closing and the alarm on her filter unit was sounding.

She glanced behind, found black-clad figures in her dust wake.

The filter was weighing her down, its mix stale and probably no better than the raw atmosphere. Anji fixed on the ridge where her pack was stowed, just a minute away, and unclipped the filter.

The unit tumbled clear and Anji Kapoor filled her lungs with chill Martian air. Maybe the breather's mix had been that bad, maybe she just felt freed by its removal. But where Anji should have been gasping for air, with legs like lead and her vision blurred, she was suddenly unchained. As if life beneath tent walls was an aberration.

She could imagine the look on the faces chasing her. Seeing her filter gone, thinking they finally had her, only for her stride to stretch, legs working harder, pushing up the ridge. To see her widen the gap.

At the top there was a sheer drop, empty sky the only thing beyond. Anji didn't even break stride. Leaning forward, one hand trailing to grab the shoulder straps on her pack, hauling it behind her as a foot planted on the very cliff edge drove her onwards into thin air. Back on Earth, the thick air would have pulled at the pack as she dragged it over her shoulders, the wind trying to tear it from her grasp, send her tumbling. But it didn't happen like that on Mars. The air offered some resistance but nothing that mattered.

The last buckle secured, Anji stretched out, turning her body into an arrow and pointing it down towards the plain seven kilometres below. She was falling, screaming through sky, alien wind on her face, eyes streaming with tears.

The pack's safety margin was set to engage at one thousand metres, but Anji hit the override. Anyone who'd jumped within thirty seconds of her could still catch up if she deployed at the margin. And she'd worked too hard – lungs bursting, legs burning – for that to happen.

The plain below gained focus. She could make out the contours of the land; dust clouds where vehicles circled, waiting for her; portable atmosphere tents and people moving amidst them.

Anji hit the button on her shoulder strap. There was a moment of heart-stopping terror as it felt like the pack wasn't going to engage. Then she felt the crack as it broke open, the tips of specially designed glider wings catching the Martian wind, the airstream dragging them open and locking them in place. She leant back into the pack, pushing against the currents.

There were cheers as her feet touched down. People crowded around her, a thermal blanket was thrown over her shoulders. Someone tried to push a breather towards her face, but Anji shook it off, releasing the glider wings, sinking to her knees. The red dust clouded, collecting on the sheer black of her sports suit.

She took a deep breath of Martian air, and turned it into a laugh, grinning as she looked into the air, the competition spread out against the cliff face, coming in to land. It didn't matter: the best any of them could do now was come second.

And then Michael was there. Pushing through the crowd, he dropped to the ground beside her. He too offered a breather, but Anji just grinned, one hand pulling him close as the other dragged his filter away, her mouth closing on his.

'Anji Kapoor,' Michael said, 'financial commentator, vanquisher of professional athletes and winner of the inaugural Olympus Mons triathlon. You're famous. How does it feel?'

Anji lifted her head from his chest, a sly smile on her face. 'I think I should feel knackered,' she said.

He laughed, the sound bouncing off the walls of the atmosphere tent. 'Somehow, I don't think that's the case.' He nodded to where the gold cup lay by the zip door, its shine dusted with Martian red. 'You should take better care of that.'

Anji laughed, kissed his chin. 'I had better things to do.'

'Bruno put himself in hospital trying to beat you to that cup.'

'Just because Bruno thought up the event, doesn't mean he had any right to win it.'

'True,' Michael answered. 'But I think the fact that it was you who beat him isn't going to sit well.'

'A girl's allowed to enjoy herself, isn't she?'

'I just didn't have you down for this kind of thing, that's all. I don't think Bruno did, either.'

Anji shrugged, sitting up on the mattress to tie her hair back. 'I used to do this back home. Kind of.'

'What does that mean?'

'Mountain biking at the weekend,' she laughed. 'A parachute jump for a kids' charity my mum was involved with.' She paused. 'Oh, and some rock climbing on an Outward Bound trip once.'

He laughed. 'A long way from that to a triathlon.'

'Almost as far as Earth to Mars.' Anji lay back down against him. 'I feel different here,' she explained as Michael ran a finger down her spine. 'This isn't the life I ever expected to be living. But you have to adapt to survive. And if jumping from mile-high volcanoes is what people are going to be doing for fun on Mars' – she smiled mischievously, reaching for her husband – 'well, I'm all for work hard and play hard.'

JUPITER SPACE
Now

They should be trying to get back some of the sleep they've lost. But Caroline can't rest and all Robertson can do is sit, watching her pace the floor: more energised, more alive than she's been in years.

'I don't trust him.'

'But I do,' Caroline says.

'Five hours ago, you were both ready to go toe-to-toe. Are you really bought that easily? A few stripes on a piece of cloth?' Robertson shakes his head. 'You should listen to Anji, the rumours she's heard.' He tries to impress the words on Caroline. 'Just think about it.'

She's not interested. He knows it from the body language before she even speaks.

'I have thought about it,' she says, looking at Robertson with a hard smile. 'I know what he reminds you of. He moves like one of the 101st, like a soldier.'

'And you'd follow him anywhere. Just like that.'

Caroline stops pacing then, turns to Robertson, shaking her head. 'You're jealous.'

Robertson can only blink at that. It takes him a moment to realise that his wife is actually serious, that this isn't some sick joke. Jealous. That's how far they've fallen.

'It's late,' he whispers. 'We both need some sleep.'

'You're jealous,' she repeats.

'He shot David!' Robertson yells. 'He aimed, he fired. Just like that, he put a hole through his chest.'

'You think he's replacing you.'

'Is that what I think? Because it's not what I feel.'

There's a silence, then Robertson looks at Caroline, getting some control back in his voice.

'Those stripes. You don't want them, Caroline. You don't.'

And he knows he has her then, because she turns her back, crossing to the corner of their compartment, strapping on battered pieces of armour.

'He's dangerous,' Robertson says. 'He doesn't care what happens here.'

'Maybe we could use some of that,' Caroline says. 'We could try fighting instead of scrabbling around this hole, just to survive another day.'

'We take it a day at a time because it's all there is,' Robertson says. He gets to his feet. Almost all the plating is on now, Caroline tightening the buckles around her chest. There's one patch of bare flesh remaining and he lays his hand on her left shoulder, feeling the chill of her skin.

'Is that really all you want?' he asks. 'To fight? Because I want better. I want some clean air and sky and fresh water and food that tastes of something again. I want out of here. I want back everything we lost.'

Caroline is still for a long moment, head bowed. Then she shrugs his hand free, fixes the last armoured plate into place and turns. Her eyes are locked in the past.

'I can never get back what we've lost,' she says.

Robertson's head drops, and he lets her walk away.

Anji waits until the Village has settled down again. Something she saw earlier has piqued her curiosity. She keeps an eye on the red-headed man, Archer, waiting until he is asleep.

Then she creeps round to the edge of one of the habitats, the spot where she saw him crouching earlier. There's a desperation to his behaviour that isn't typical of the others. Anji begins prodding the wall panels, finding one that's loose.

Tucked inside is what Archer was checking on.

It's an old data-storage unit: a silver cylinder, covered in dust, untouched in years. A long crack down its side reveals the crystalline cells inside.

Anji leaves it untouched, pushes the panel back. Whatever data the device held is unrecoverable now and it's of value only to Archer. Just more obsessive-compulsive behaviour from people driven too hard for too long.

* * *

When morning comes, Arquette calls them to the Meridian.

The Professional, so distracted last night, is resolutely focused now. And with his escape route unusable, Anji thinks, he'll need that focus.

As he speaks, though, there's compassion in his voice. Anji doesn't believe it for a moment; she can see her look reflected in Easter's and Robertson's faces. Like his provocations of the day before, it's just another manipulation.

'I've reviewed your reports,' he says. 'You've done well, done your duty, but that duty isn't over. Rescue here is a precarious option. We need an escape route. The enemy must have had a way to travel through the atmosphere to penetrate this station after the Fall. So our objective is simple. We find that transportation and take it for ourselves.'

Robertson looks at Anji for support. When she says nothing, he speaks up.

'We're supposed to find their ship, then run the blockade with it?'

'No,' the Professional says. 'No ship was docked on my approach to the Station. Something Miss Kapoor can confirm if you wish.'

Using them, Anji realises, and not afraid to use her either. Her situation is more awkward, because he's right: there was no ship. She can only counter his argument with a lie and, unlike the Professional toying with the survivors' belief in a non-existent war, it would be an easily proven lie. All he would have to do is give someone his suit and tell them to take a walk.

'So no ship,' someone calls from the crowd. 'What then?'

'An interstix,' Robertson says. 'You're talking about interstitial transport.'

'Interstitial vortexes have been banned for decades,' Archer snaps.

'Banned?' the Professional replies. 'You think the enemy know or care about the Brasilia rulings? If we locate their vortex generators, we can use them. Correctly focused, everyone would be past the blockade and free in a matter of hours.'

There's a murmur through the crowd, scepticism and hope.

The Professional tells a good lie, Anji realises. One people want to believe in.

Arquette speaks then: 'It's worth taking the chance for.'

The words are good, but Anji only has to look at Robertson's face to see how hollow the sentiment is when Arquette says: 'It's hope.'

'We know the enemy maintain a presence near the barricades,' the Professional says. 'We lure them in, then launch a counter-attack.' He holds up a small device taken from his kit store. 'We attach this tracker as they retreat. Find their base on this station, seize their transport.'

'They could be anywhere,' Easter says. 'What if the base is behind the energy barrier? We would have expended time and resources on a wild-goose chase –'

'Then we vote,' Arquette says, cutting him off before he can build up steam. 'We see who wants to believe in hope and who doesn't.'

Easter leaves before the show of hands: he knows what the result is going to be. If he were anyone else, he'd probably be making the same choice as they are.

Cut off in their own desperate world, he'd been able to contain Arquette. Everyone knew what had happened, everyone saw through the mask. But the Professional has given Arquette's anger an outlet. Worse, it's irrevocably changed the survivors' dynamic.

Assured and powerful, the Professional fills the others with a confidence they'd lost long ago. He and Anji are reminders of life before the Fall. That new-found memory makes the survivors bold. It's why Arquette is no longer an isolated voice; it's why Easter suddenly is.

He crosses towards the hospital.

Toby is near by; fifteen years too young for any meeting, he's created a small den, pushing loose plating up against the wall. As Easter approaches he's just emerging from one end.

'It's all right, Toby,' Easter tells him. 'You carry on.'

Toby gives him a suspicious look, retreats. Easter squats down. This section of the Village is dark – to avoid disturbing the Wounded – making it even darker inside Toby's den.

The boy glances at Easter, then returns his attention to an old computer pad. It's one of the few toys they've been able to provide. A yo-yo; a threadbare teddy; crudely fashioned charcoal sticks. The computer pad is a luxury. An argument had raged over it six months earlier: give it to Toby or break it down for spares? Until yesterday, that argument had seen Arquette's only victory. With no family, they were all responsible for Toby's upbringing, she'd said, and the pad would improve his hand-eye co-ordination. It was important.

Now Toby is playing with a crude program Arquette created, joining the dots to produce simple pictures. A house. A dog. A flower. Things he may never see.

'Hey.'

Easter turns, finds Anji behind him. 'Hello,' he answers.

Toby peeks out to see Anji, then retreats, emerging from the den's far end to run back into the Village.

'He doesn't like strangers.' Easter pauses, corrects himself. 'No, he just doesn't understand what a stranger is: he's never seen one.'

'His parents?'

'Toby's dad was trapped behind the energy barrier. His mother...' Easter pauses. 'She didn't know she was pregnant till after the Fall. And then...'

Anji nods, surmises. 'She was Wounded.'

'A couple of months after he was born.' Easter rests a hand against the hospital's door. 'She didn't name him. She wanted his father to see him, to decide together.'

'Who picked Toby, then?'

'Tobias,' Easter smiles. 'My father's name. My vanity, I suppose.'

Anji shrugs. 'It's hard, so far from home. I understand that.'

'I was two weeks away,' Easter whispers. 'An Earth Forces scholarship put me through medical school; I was two weeks from clearing it when the Station fell.'

'How did you end up out here?'

'Someone had broken an arm or something, I don't remember now. I was sent out to do triage.'

'You would have been stuck behind the barrier otherwise.'

'Yes,' Easter laughs, hard and bitter. 'But I wouldn't have had to do this, would I? The ranking officers were called back to the hub; when the Station fell there was one officer here outranking me.'

'Stokes,' Anji says.

'Who ended up in there. Too brave, too bloody stupid to not take the enemy on.' Easter sinks back against the door. He comes here when it's quiet, because no one else ever does. 'I can't do anything for them. I spent the best part of three years trying. I've isolated the infection, can identify when it's passed on.'

'But no cure,' Anji says.

'No resources,' Easter answers. He looks through the crack in the door, takes in the cages, the noise, the smell. 'They're getting worse. The first ones infected? Their minds are gone. They don't want to eat or drink; two of them are on IV fluids, but we can't keep that going long.'

'No resources.'

Easter smiles, wonders how much it shows on his face. Four years of doing everything he can to keep them all alive. Making sure no one took the misstep that would kill them or anyone else. How much do four years like that show?

He shakes his head. 'They're good as dead now. All of them.' Easter looks at Anji. 'But you know that, don't you?'

'What do you mean?'

Easter nods towards the Meridian. 'His grand plan. Most of them haven't figured it out and those that have don't care. Capturing this interstix? We'd have to fight them, fight every step of the way out. Even Toby.' He pauses. Cages rattle, low keening sounds. 'There's no place for the Wounded in that fight. They'll be left behind.'

'You could sedate them,' Anji says.

'Nothing we have works.'

'What about something new, to help fight pain, maybe focus the mind.'

'I thought you didn't bring any supplies.'

'I didn't,' Anji says, holding up a yellow vial. 'But he did.'

Robertson watches as Easter checks on David. The colour is slowly draining from the young man; the dressings on his wound are black and sticky. Easter doesn't say anything but it doesn't take a doctor to know: David's going to die soon.

Anji stands near by; like Easter, she left before the vote. She didn't get to see Robertson's wife complete her transformation into a wartime leader.

Caroline is standing by the forge with the Professional, talking Ross and Weir through the canisters they want machined, more smoke grenades to mask the deployment of the Professional's tracker.

Robertson doesn't like the plan.

The enemy could spot the tracker; they might not lead them back to their base; the base might be inaccessible; if they do find that base, they might not be able to take it. Even then, supposing everything goes right, there's no guarantee interstix generators will be waiting for them.

Robertson's a practical man: all his life he's worked with his hands. He likes solid and tangible, something he can feel beneath his fingers or taste on his tongue. This plan is less substantial than the tents strung against the east wall.

The computer terminal sounds. Robertson calls to Anji: 'Done.'

The housekeeping program has cleaned the computer download. Anji and Easter join him at the terminal as he constructs a menu to navigate the material. Robertson studies their reflections on-screen, sees them exchanging glances. When Anji looks to check on the Professional and Caroline, Robertson loses patience.

'If you're going to ask me something, get on and ask me.'

Another glance, then Easter says, 'Now the clean-up's finished, is there any spare capacity on the system?'

'You know there is.'

'Enough for a composition analysis?'

Easter unfolds his hand, revealing a small glass tube containing a poisonous-looking fluid. 'He uses this. To kill pain, stay focused.'

'So?'

'I want to know if it could work on the Wounded.'

Easter isn't explaining himself well, but Robertson understands anyway. The theory is the Wounded have lost all control of their actions. If this stuff can focus their minds, they might gain enough control to make it to the interstix.

There's a flurry of sparks from the forge, Caroline barking orders and curses. His wife and the Professional are going to be busy for a while yet.

'You shouldn't have this, should you?' he says.

'No,' Anji replies. 'But if it makes a difference –'

'I'm already sold, OK?'

He enters a few commands and the second computer chatters into life.

Robertson nods at Easter. 'You know what to do.'

As Easter prepares a slide, Robertson looks to the forge. He gets up, guiding Anji towards his seat.

'You wanted to see the download,' he says. 'And I want every-thing to look normal. All our friends will see is Easter working on David and you checking the download.' He taps the screen. 'So check. Open the security folders and you'll have the last video images on file.'

Over the next few minutes, Robertson keeps glancing between Caroline's progress and Anji's and Easter's.

He doesn't understand what Easter's doing; he can see the proteins and molecular chains or whatever the hell they are circling on Easter's screen, but they mean nothing to him.

Anji's progress is a different matter. The images take a long time to call up but they chill Robertson. The corridors are bright and white and clean; smartly dressed personnel frozen in mid-step. Everything tidy, everything ordered. No burnt-out cables, exposed bulkheads, or rust coating every surface.

It's the past brought to life and it frightens him.

'Dammit,' Easter whispers.

Robertson looks over as Easter removes the slide, closing down the analysis program. 'No good?'

Easter shakes his head. 'It's tailored to a specific neurology. Give me six months and I might be able to rebuild it, adapt it somehow.' He slips the vial into his pocket, starts checking David's wound again. 'As it is, it's useless to anyone other than the Professional.'

Robertson exchanges a glance with Anji: Easter's holding some-thing back.

'What is it?' Anji asks. 'What's bothering you?'

'The way that stuff works,' Easter explains. 'The synaptic inhibitors aren't just targeting pain, but affecting how the brain processes thought.' He glances nervously towards the forge. 'It'd need more study to figure it out, but –'

'But?'

'To get that kind of neurology would take some very invasive procedures. Whoever they are, your Professionals have had bad things done to them.'

Robertson absorbs this and follows Easter's gaze. Sparks spiral up from the forge. Caroline is standing next to the Professional, for all the world looking like that's where she belongs.

Four years earlier

The night before Fitz hadn't seen what the Doctor had done with the lab equipment. Whether by accident or design, there'd been a path cleared from door to bunk, so Fitz had just followed it and gone to sleep.

When he woke, he thought the bubbling sound must be coffee brewing, but the smell persuaded him otherwise. 'Bloody hell,' he coughed. 'What is that?'

'Sorry,' the Doctor said. 'My fault.'

Test tubes sat in racks, coloured liquids boiled, a centrifuge whizzed in one corner and some kind of Bunsen burner was positioned next to Fitz's shaving kit. The Doctor was seated in the middle of it all, peering down the lens of a microscope.

'When I brought all that kit in...' Fitz said.

'Yes?'

'I was expecting you to pick the bits you wanted and return the rest.'

The Doctor paused, lifted his head from the microscope to look around. Then he just said: 'Ah.'

'Still,' Fitz said, 'I'm sure you're putting it all to good use and absolutely none of it is here for show.'

The Doctor smiled, hurriedly refocusing on the microscope. 'You slept well. I was worried I might disturb you.'

'I always sleep well.' Fitz rubbed his eyes. 'Remember that time on Bathesda when I slept right through the entire revolu-' He stopped himself then, suddenly realising what he was saying. 'Sorry,' he said, 'I didn't mean to -'

'No, no,' the Doctor replied. There was a pause, then he looked up again. 'It must be difficult for you.'

Fitz smiled. 'Forget it.'

He climbed down from his bunk as the Doctor went back to work.

Fitz ran some hot water, and as he worked soap into his bristles the mirror slowly steamed up. He was about to wipe away the fog when he heard the Doctor's voice.

'More than a hundred years and I never felt at home there. From the moment I woke on that train, I didn't need memories to tell me I didn't belong. It took me a long time, decades, to figure out just why that was. To understand. The only hope I had was a note. A promise that if I endured, someone would be waiting for me. A friend. All of this, the ships, the planets, the TARDIS, all feels familiar. The ghost of memories.' He paused. 'But they're not what makes me sure this is my life.'

The voice faded into silence and Fitz wiped his hand across the mirror. The Doctor was revealed in the reflection, his eye on the microscope.

'We should talk,' Fitz murmured as he picked up his razor.

As he washed and dressed, Fitz watched the Doctor work. The samples from the journal were lined up in a row, each one floating in a test tube. 'Found anything?'

'No trace of explosive I can locate,' the Doctor answered. 'Not yet.'

'So, if you're doing this, does that mean there's no need to go into the office today?'

The Doctor waved at the comms terminal. 'You can run AuDoc from over there if you need to.'

'Ha,' Fitz said, rubbing his hands together. 'Let's see how it's getting on with the initiative test.'

As he called up AuDoc he could feel the Doctor's eyes on him: 'What exactly do you mean by "initiative test"?'

'I asked AuDoc to scan the Station records, look for odd patterns. Y'know, alien infiltrators, mad scientists.'

The Doctor leapt from his seat, pushing past Fitz to get to the comms panel, hands flying across the controls. Fitz's instructions blinked on the screen.

SCAN ALL STATION RECORDS FOR UNUSUAL PATTERNS AND ACTIVITY. INCLUDE ALL SURVEILLANCE. PAY SPECIAL ATTENTION TO ANY SUSPECTED ALIEN ACTIVITY. USE YOUR INITIATIVE. JOIN THE DOTS.

The Doctor sighed. 'I really wish you hadn't done that.'

Fitz blinked. 'What's the problem?'

'AuDoc learns and evolves, but it's still very literal in its interpretations.' The Doctor tapped the screen. 'Ask it to search all records and it will try to do exactly that. Including the confidential ones.'

'So?'

'So AuDoc isn't as good at breaking and entering as I am. It's likely to get caught.'

Fitz was getting a sick feeling in his stomach. 'Can't you stop it?'

'I have. The question is: how far it's got and whether anyone noticed it looking.' The Doctor was starting to calm down now, studying the screen. 'No system alerts. I think you got away with it.'

'Did it find anything?' Fitz asked.

The Doctor frowned. 'Video footage from the cargo bay.'

'We've seen that.'

'Different video footage.' He tapped the screen, peering at the grainy picture. 'Now, what is it AuDoc thinks we should be seeing?'

'The time code,' Fitz said. 'That's one of the shipments for the Mukabis.'

'Yes, but only the cameras with safety requirements were kept on during those deliveries; the ones governing the bay doors. There wouldn't be anything to –' The Doctor stopped, staring hard at the screen, whispered, 'Good work, AuDoc.'

Fitz looked. It was a side angle on the bay doors, very little of the interior visible. Then, in one corner, the flash of movement. The Doctor froze the video, zoomed in. Someone's shoulder, the corner of a drum. The drum was mostly covered by a tarpaulin, but a symbol was visible. Sharp black curves against a yellow background.

'Bio-hazard,' the Doctor said. 'Now, why would a computer simulation require dangerous biological material?'

'Did it find anything else?'

'Some station bureaucracy.' The Doctor scanned the results. 'The usual comment about maintenance overtime.'

'You can take the program out of accountancy –'

'But you can't take accountancy out of the program,' the Doctor finished.

The words trailed away as something else caught his eye. He looked accusingly at Fitz: 'You haven't been in touch with Anji, have you?'

'Not guilty, honest.'

'C&C are monitoring commercial wavelengths, looking for piggy-backed transmissions. Looking and finding. Someone's sending secret messages.'

Fitz was about to nod dumbly when something occurred to him. Something Robbie had said while they were clearing the debris. *We don't do maintenance.* If he wasn't conducting repairs, what had Archer been doing in that corridor when Fitz stumbled across him?

'I can't believe I was complaining about the lack of good suspects,' Fitz said. 'We've got at least three now. If we count our first lot of mad scientists –'

'The Mukabis.'

'As one. Our other mad scientist –'

'Deschamps.'

'Makes two,' Fitz said.

'And the third?'

Fitz looked at the Doctor. 'I think we might have a Red under the bed. Or in the cargo bay, anyhow.'

'If they start looking too hard for infiltrators, we could be in trouble.' The Doctor pursed his lips. 'It might be time to come up with an escape plan, just in case.'

'Doctor,' Fitz said, 'we're on a military space station, days from anywhere. What kind of escape plan is going to work?'

'A desperate one.'

A chime rang out from the comms unit. The Doctor closed AuDoc, checked the message board. 'It's a note from one of our mad scientists.'

'Oh, no,' Fitz said. 'I couldn't stand another inquisition from Deschamps.'

'It's Sara Mukabi,' the Doctor said. 'With an invitation.'

Sara Mukabi's office was a calm, white space with comforting furniture and soft lines. As Fitz and the Doctor settled in front of her desk she smiled.

'Don't worry. This is standard procedure; something I get to do with all new personnel. The only difference being, your security clearance means you know the context for what I'm doing.'

'Really?' the Doctor said.

'I help devise the speculative scenarios for the Avatar chamber,' Sara said. 'The challenge is to create something as realistic as possible.'

'And?'

'And fear is the key,' Sara responded, tapping at a glass slide. 'We need home comforts –'

'Like the wine.'

'Like the wine,' she nodded. 'But that need makes us vulnerable. My job is to identify those vulnerabilities and construct scenarios around them.'

'No wine,' Fitz assured her, 'would scare me.'

Sara ignored him. 'The key to this is a database, charting responses to a basic survey I designed.' She held up the slide; it showed an array of ever-changing ink-blot patterns. 'You're here to contribute.'

The test lasted about fifteen minutes, and as far as Fitz could tell didn't really get into his fears at all. Ink blots, word association, some hypotheticals, queries about their personal history. Fitz tried to keep his responses simple and give away as little as possible. Too often that meant he was left stumbling over his choice of words.

Contrastingly, the Doctor would consider the blot or query for a second, then smile with a concise answer. All the time, Fitz noticed, keeping his eyes on Sara Mukabi, even when she wasn't addressing him.

'Last question,' she smiled. 'If you were an animal, what animal would you be?'

Fitz considered, then said: 'A dog. Probably a golden retriever?'

Sara nodded. 'And you, Doctor?'

'Any animal?' he asked.

'Whatever you feel like being.'

There was a pause, then a smile fluttered on his lips. 'A unicorn, I think. Tomorrow, it would probably be a goldfish, but today…'

Sara nodded. 'Today is a unicorn kind of day.'

'Exactly.'

It took her a few minutes to finish recording their answers, logging dates and times. Then she just nodded. 'That's it. All done.'

'Most interesting,' the Doctor said pleasantly. So pleasantly Fitz knew something else was coming. 'Now, would you like to tell me about your interest in Jupiter's atmosphere?'

There was a silence, then Sara Mukabi gave a slow smile. 'Commander Valletti said you were clever.'

'The evidence is all over the accounts,' the Doctor said dismissively. 'The pilot hours logged and all the equipment you've siphoned off. Plus, I don't buy either you or your husband as amateur meteorologists, so what would be the point of re-creating Jupiter's weather in the Avatar chamber?'

Her smile tightened, then she nodded, impressed. 'You already know what my interest is. You saw it in action yesterday.'

The Doctor clicked his fingers, 'The pharmaceutical cocktail. You're distilling something from the atmosphere.'

'The holographic chamber only does half the work. The trick is convincing them it's real. The trick,' she said, 'is making them scared.'

'That's a bit cruel, isn't it?' Fitz said.

Sara shook her head. 'New frontiers, new challenges. We saw it during the occupation and now more and more on the system colonies. The biggest threat isn't sonic cannon or disruptor beams.' She paused. 'It's the unknown. More specifically, our fear of the unknown. Those soldiers have to learn to manage fear, and to do that they need to feel it.'

The Doctor let her words fade away into silence. He sat there for a long moment, staring at nothing, then smiled and nodded.

'You found something in Jupiter's atmosphere, didn't you? Something that helps with that? That research vessel you were on, the one that had the hull breach in Jupiter's atmosphere. The crew exposed to the atmosphere developed extreme post-traumatic stress disorders. Only they weren't psychological traumas, but neurological ones. Something in the atmosphere, some gas or particle they'd inhaled caused it.'

Sara said nothing, just looked at him.

He got to his feet, began to pace the room. 'Whatever it is, it plays havoc with the chemical transmitters in the brain. The very things that govern memory. And what we fear is governed by what we know. By memory.'

'You really are clever,' Sara Mukabi said.

'Overly analytical thinking,' the Doctor replied. 'Standard accountancy job hazard.'

'Is there anything else you over analysed?'

He shrugged. 'I was bothered by that simulation of Jupiter's weather, but it makes sense now. An attempt to identify new caches of this substance?'

'Gas,' Sara sighed. 'It's a gas. When a distilled and modified version is combined with the data from these psychological screenings, we can generate absolute fear.' She paused, then crossed to a security locker and entered a code. The door swung open to reveal vials of black liquid. 'We call the stimulant Nightmare.'

The Doctor looked at the vials. 'That's what you give the 101st when they're training.'

'There are a number of variations.' She shrugged. 'One induces fear, another helps facilitate the integration of the simulations into their memories.'

They spent the rest of the day in their office.

The Doctor kept busy, covering AuDoc's tracks as well as looking for something they could use if they needed to make a getaway.

Fitz was reluctantly collating AuDoc's accountancy findings into a standardised report, a necessary evil if they were going to maintain their cover.

All the time, the Doctor found his mind distracted.

He was certain Jason McCray's condition was the result of exposure to an earlier, experimental version of Nightmare.

The human memory was governed by activity in the synapses – the junctions between neuron cells in the brain – and how they responded to the release of chemical transmitters. When absorbed into the system, Nightmare would disrupt those chemical transmitters, causing an imbalance. Accessing any memory would then generate a fear reaction.

In Jason McCray's case, that imbalance was probably permanent.

Could someone have got hold of a dose of Nightmare and tailored it to provoke violence instead of fear? It was possible, but the Doctor could see no motivation. Plus, from what he had witnessed – the bio-readouts jumping as the 101st were injected – Nightmare delivered an instantaneous reaction; something that didn't fit with the circumstances on Mars or the *Pegasus*.

There were still too many unanswered questions. The cargo the 101st handled was too big to be atmospheric samples. Then there was the issue of what was behind the other door in the Avatar chamber.

Maybe Fitz had the right idea in setting AuDoc loose. Maybe it was time to get a bit more proactive in gathering data.

He set AuDoc to monitor the real-time payroll and notify him as soon as Terrance and Sara were both logged on in their official roles.

The Doctor's upgraded security clearance got him through the automated checks and on to the sixth level. He showed his dataslide to the waiting guard, smiled: 'Inventory.' There was a moment of indecision, then the guard nodded and let him pass.

Entering the Avatar chamber, the Doctor glanced back. The guard was speaking into his comms unit. Despite his new credentials, the Doctor somehow doubted his presence here would be tolerated. It all depended on who the guard was calling. But whoever it was, he had very little time.

When the entrance closed he crossed the chamber to the other door. It would take too long to break the algorithms generating the locking code; better to prise open a wall panel and circumvent the lock entirely, just like he'd done on the *Pegasus*. Except it proved far less easy than that. The wall was thick with electronics. Worse, the access he'd been able to create only allowed room for his arm, so he was working blind.

Working blind in more ways than one. Too many suspects, too many leads, not enough motives, and still no chain of evidence to link the troops who'd attacked Anji to any of them.

And he was out of time. A distant hum echoed through the open panel: the lift arriving down the corridor.

He gave the lock one last, bitter look, then withdrew his arm.

When the main entrance opened twenty seconds later, the panel was back in place, the Doctor working on his inventory. Expecting to see the Mukabis flanked by the 101st, he saw Jennifer Valletti.

Nothing was said as they looked at each other.

Then she took a step into the room, keeping her eyes on his. The Doctor smiled. 'I was just –'

'Don't.' Valletti shook her head. 'Don't lie to me. Curious, adaptable and lucky, isn't it? How far does that curiosity take you?'

'I'm not –'

She slammed her hand down on a console. 'I'm trying to help you, damn it! You've got the access you need to do your job, now leave it at that.'

'Is that an order?'

'Yes, it's an order,' Valletti snapped. 'Are you as smart as you are curious? Do you know when to stop?' She took a deep breath, eyes closed, some of the rage bleeding away before she said, 'This place is illegal. You know that.'

'Yes.'

'Hard copies of your credentials are being sent to Earth Forces' headquarters in Cape Town. They'll be delivered in person to Vice-Admiral Carter, who will add your and your assistant's names to a very short list: staff who are immune from prosecution should this project ever become public.'

'Immunity?' the Doctor said.

'I insisted on it before I took this command. Acquiescing to Admiral Carter's request to host the research was my decision, it's my responsibility.'

He looked at her, suddenly understanding the tension she felt. 'You don't like this place, do you? You're risking everything for it, but it makes you uneasy.'

Valletti said nothing.

'Something more than the stimulant Sara Mukabi's created. Those implants,' he said, 'they look very advanced. They wouldn't be alien technology, would they?'

Valletti laughed then, shaking her head. 'Alien resources are the responsibility of Colonel McNamara back on Mars.' She looked at him. 'You don't understand at all, do you? Do I like the Avatar project? No. But bad as this is, it's better than the alternative.' Her mouth tightened. 'The Professional programme is monstrous – a dangerous abomination.'

The Doctor looked around him, suddenly gaining insight. 'An arms race. Between the Mukabis and this McNamara.'

'Something you have no part in.' Valletti's voice turned hard. 'You're smart, you're inquisitive, I like you and I don't want to see you hurt.

Go back to your ledgers and leave the fighting to the people who are trained for it.'

'So,' Fitz said, 'what does all that mean?'

'It means when those hard copies get to Earth our cover's blown.' The Doctor was looking hard at Fitz. Presumably, Fitz thought, checking he understood the implications.

'How long?'

'A week,' the Doctor said, toying with the lab equipment. 'Maybe less.'

'I hate a deadline,' Fitz said. 'Especially the dead part of it.'

'Tomorrow I'll get to work on the escape plan. I think there's a project I can adapt to give us a head start, at least.' The Doctor was playing with one of his test-tube samples. 'Hand me that oxygen bottle, will you? The small one?'

Fitz passed it over and the Doctor began filtering oxygen through one of the test tubes.

'Can I ask what you're doing?' Fitz said.

'That stain on the journal might be organic. The computer analysis couldn't identify it, but if I can cultivate a proper –'

'It's boring then,' Fitz said.

'Very,' the Doctor answered.

Fitz looked at him for a moment, then said, 'Don't worry. We'll figure it out. We always do.' He patted the Doctor on the shoulder. 'I'm going to go eat. Do you want to come see the mess hall?'

The Doctor nodded at his experiment. 'I need to finish this.' As Fitz reached the door, he added, 'When you see your friend Robertson, find out some more about that crewman.'

'Archer.' Fitz nodded. He pressed the door release but nothing happened. Another press, still nothing. 'Did you lock this?' he asked.

The Doctor frowned. 'No.'

Fitz stepped aside as the Doctor knelt by the lock. 'Nothing wrong here.' He put his hand against the door frame, then snatched it back. 'That's hot. The mechanism's fused solid.'

'Shall I call maintenance?' Fitz said.

'That depends how hungry you are.'

'Very.' Fitz activated the comms panel: the usual menu was overlaid with static. 'Looks like my mum's old telly.'

The Doctor glanced over at the unit to see what Fitz was talking about and his face darkened. His shout of 'Get down!' came just seconds before the explosion.

Valletti was in her quarters when the alarm sounded. Every threat had a distinct tone. Intruder alert, power surge, fire. And this one: hull breach.

Running for C&C, Valletti was taking constant updates *en route*: crew quarters in the outer ring, something had sealed the breach, no indication of how long that would last.

It was only when she reached C&C that she discovered the quarters affected.

'Oh, no,' she whispered, then snapped. 'Have the rescue crews got in there yet?'

'The door's jammed.' It was Graves, one hand at his ear, taking reports from his engineers on site. 'They could cut through, but if whatever's holding the breach fails –'

'Evacuate the surrounding area and depressurise, then get some suits in there with cutting gear and survival equipment,' Valletti ordered, struggling to keep her voice level. 'I want them out alive.'

'That's going to take time.'

'Then get started!' she barked.

'Too late,' Graves said. 'The seal's failing.'

Valletti looked at the faltering gauge. Lucky and adaptable, she thought. 'Is there any other way out? Air ducts? Anything.'

Thomasson looked up from his position at the security station and shook his head. 'All too small.'

'It's going!' Graves shouted.

Valletti looked at the screen: the red line plummeted, oxygen levels dropping to zero. Sensors showed small objects cascading in the station's vicinity; debris sucked through the hole. Her voice tightened as she asked, 'Anything?'

'The internal security net's running again.' The screen flickered, showing a hazy image. The cabin walls were pockmarked, panels black where the power had overloaded. An empty hole lead directly on to the vacuum. Anyone inside had been sucked out when the seal had gone.

Valletti turned from the picture. She closed her eyes, bowed her head, fingers rising to cross over her chest when –

'Commander.'

'What?' she whispered.

'Strange readings; hull sensors registering multiple hits.'

'Debris,' she said, 'bouncing back.'

'Commander,' Thomasson insisted. 'Look at the pattern.'

Valletti looked. Regular impacts, marking an almost straight line.

'Exterior cameras,' she said. 'Section Twelve. Now.'

The screens flickered, showing the long curve of the Station's hull, silver against the black of Jupiter space. The image faltered for a moment, then zoomed in, tracking movement.

There was a long silence in the control room. Finally someone said, 'I don't believe it.'

Lucky and adaptable.

'I do,' Valletti said. She activated the comms panel: 'I want the 101st suited up in airlock nine in the next two minutes. Emergency rescue procedures.'

She turned back to the screen. He was there. Eyes screwed tight against the vacuum, hair splayed by weightlessness, fingers stiff with cold, pulling himself hand over hand across the Station's exterior. His lips were clamped tight around a thin rubber tube, a tiny oxygen bottle attached to its other end.

Something was wrapped around his waist. Strips of bed sheet, knotted into a makeshift line, stretching out behind him. Tied on to the far end, bouncing lifelessly against the hull, was the body of Fitz Kreiner.

Fitz's face was black against the white pillow; his skin a mass of bruises and burst capillaries. An IV pumped drugs to clear the radiation he'd absorbed; another machine fed oxygen into his blood as more equipment repaired his lungs. The medics called it a ReGene process; it would take a day or so to repair the core damage.

'Another few days and we'd have had him fixed quicker,' the medical officer had commented. 'There's a more advanced unit stuck in the backlog in the cargo bays. Then again, another minute or two and there'd have been nothing we could have done anyway.'

The Doctor had just nodded; swallowed the anti-radiation pills he'd been given. While the medics had worked on Fitz he'd spent an anxious half-hour plugged into a ReGene device himself.

The damage wasn't so severe for him: his lungs had stayed inflated, blood had kept pumping. The few exploded veins he had were fading. Once he was happy the device had done its work the Doctor had unplugged himself and wiped its memory.

Now there was nothing to do but wait.

The room filled with light. Sound vanished. Fitz flailed for a handhold. Something flashed past on the left. Then sound returned and he dropped to the floor.

The Doctor was pressed up against the exterior wall, holding the long metal slab of his lab bench. Their room had been hit by a hurricane.

Fitz touched his cheek, bleeding where a bottle had smashed against it.

'We're in trouble,' the Doctor said.

'What happened?'

'An overload, taking a chunk of the hull with it.' The Doctor stepped cautiously back from the bench, which stayed attached to the wall. Fitz was aware of a high-pitched whistling sound, air getting cold, his ears starting to hurt.

'Bugger,' he coughed.

The bench creaked, a thin crease forming down its middle.

Fitz tried the door again.

'That won't work,' the Doctor said, sorting through the chaos, turning the debris over. 'And that bench isn't going to hold.'

Fitz began studying the walls, checking off escape routes. It didn't take long. 'No way out.'

The Doctor kicked through the remaining equipment. 'There's nothing here to shore up that bench.'

'They'll come for us.'

'They'll need to cut through and there's no time.'

Fitz watched him then, looking around the room, studying everything. So focused, springing into life, reaching down to pull the Bunsen burner free along with a length of rubber hose. He lit the flame, told Fitz, 'Find the oxygen bottle.' The bench gave another creak, began to buckle. 'Quickly.'

'What's the plan?'

The Doctor was heating the end of the hose, plunging his fingers into the flame to manipulate its shape. 'When the seal goes, you're going to have to use the oxygen to breathe.'

Fitz handed the bottle over, and the Doctor began to mould the pipe on to it with one hand, adjusting its valve with the other. 'This is undiluted, you want to sip at it, not take full breaths.' Fitz nodded.

'Start ripping up that sheet.' Fitz did as he was told. 'What's this for?'

'There's an airlock three hundred metres to the left on the Station hull.'

Fitz paused, something creeping upwards in his mind. 'There's only one bottle.'

The Doctor said nothing.

'What happens to you?' Fitz insisted.

'You tie yourself on to me, pull me to the airlock.'

'You'll die,' Fitz said.

'There's no other way.'

Fitz looked at the bottle then the creaking lab bench. His breath was steaming in the air, his lungs cold, his ears throbbing. 'Yes, there is,' Fitz said. 'You take me.'

'No,' the Doctor answered.

'You're stronger, your constitution's better, you don't smoke thirty a day. If I take you, we'll both die. The other way round and we're in with a chance.'

Fitz lashed a sheet around his wrist, knotting it to another, throwing the free end across to the Doctor. The bench screamed, wind from nowhere tearing through the room.

'When we get out of here,' Fitz shouted, 'we need to talk.'

There was a pause, then the Doctor nodded, tying the sheet around his waist.

They stood there for a moment, fixed against the maelstrom around them. The Doctor spoke, but Fitz couldn't hear the words. It didn't matter: he could read the Doctor's lips well enough.

In the docking bay, the Doctor was saying, I knew what I was doing.

Fitz nodded: 'I know.'
The bench screamed, folding in on itself as the vacuum claimed them.

There were burns on Fitz's chest where McCray had used the defibrillator. The Doctor had been crouched on the airlock floor when that happened: exhausted, aching, trying to shift the chill from his lungs, regain feeling in his hands.

Unable to help as someone else forced life back into Fitz's body.

He thought of Anji's forehead, split open by the trooper's bloody knuckles.

As the Doctor looked down at Fitz, he promised, 'Whatever's happening, this is the second time it's hurt one of my friends. There won't be a third.'

He checked Fitz's vitals, then turned away, dispensing with his hospital gown, collecting the suit that had been left near his bed.

'Computer,' he ordered, 'locate Commander Valletti.'

She was playing the violin, casually dressed, hair down, a look of concentration on her face. The recreation suite's soundproofing absorbed the music, but this clearly wasn't the elegant freneticism of her recital. It was less studied, as if she was feeling her way though the piece.

The Doctor studied her through the window a moment longer. Calm and considered when in command; losing herself in a moment outside of it. A strong personality, but governed by circumstance and the mood of others.

For a hundred years, he'd passed for one of them. Spoken their language, eaten their food, looked like them, moved among them. But however close he'd come to them, however much he had laughed and talked and smiled with them, there had always been an unknown corner inside. Something he'd learnt never to show. The part that was alien and cold and beyond them.

Anji had been hurt, Fitz had nearly died, countless others might be at risk. It was time to let the façade drop a little, to let the darkness show.

He opened the door, letting music fill the corridor.

The bow stopped moving and Valletti looked up.

'I'm not an expert on music, so I forget,' the Doctor said, slamming the door behind him, 'does that tune signal surprise or disappointment?'

Valletti shook her head. 'No.'

'Why do I think that's an answer to a question I haven't asked yet?'

He could see the strain within her. On her face, the way she held the violin, the grip on the bow. She'd trusted him, had thought he trusted her. If this was going to work he needed to break that trust. He needed her angry.

'Did you do it?' he snapped. 'That overload was no accident.'

'No.' She turned her head, the violin back under her chin, starting to play once more.

The Doctor paced around the room, reached out as he passed the selection of instruments and snatched up a violin.

She looked at him, uncertain, unsure, as he glared at her.

His thumb found a resting place on the underside of the instrument's neck, fingertips picking out the individual strings. His right hand grasped a bow. The aim, he remembered, was always to keep the bow as upright as possible, maintaining a right angle to the vibrating string. His mouth tightened and he angled the bow down on the strings, dragging it sharp across them, a first discordant note cutting into Valletti's melody.

She flinched at the sound but played on.

'Jason McCray,' he said. 'What happened to him?'

He took a step closer, swivelled the bow again, pressing down on the fingerboard with his other hand, feeling the tension and give and contrast of the strings.

The noise was sharper this time, still she played.

He drew again and again, a hard rhythm breaking against Valletti's long, graceful movement.

She turned away, bending into the music. The Doctor stepped after her, twisting his wrist, dragging the note out. He watched Valletti's elbow, judging the pace, trying to predict where it was going.

'His lobotomy. Terrance's work or Sara's?'

Still no answer. He stepped closer, finally working the bow into a steady figure-of-eight movement, delivering not one note, but several. A counterpoint to her melody.

'Is it worth the price?'

A tune of his own. Hard and cold.

Alien.

And Valletti dropped the violin, span round. 'Yes, it's worth it.'

'Why?' he said. 'What's so important? What's so special?'

The heartbeat he'd generated dropped, pitching low, running beneath the conversation, slowly picking up the pace as Valletti spoke, drawing her in.

'The Avatar project is our best option for –'

He cut her off with a final savage twist, then let the bow drop.

Silence dwarfed them.

He could see it in her face, the set of her shoulders. He'd pushed her far enough. She stepped up, close enough for him to feel her breath on his face, then she snatched the violin up, drew a sharp note of her own.

'The best defence,' she said. 'No alternatives. No options. This is it. They are our best defence, our only choice.'

The Doctor stroked the bow over the strings again.

'Really?' he said.

Slowly at first, starting low, he began drawing the figure of eight. The dark corner revealed in music.

'That's the best Earth can do?'

She was still, but he could see it building inside her.

'War games with no value.'

Faster still. Stepping closer to Valletti, unflinching.

It just needed one more push.

'The right opposition would show that project up for the façade it is.'

And finally she broke, snapping, 'What opposition? You? You wouldn't last five minutes.'

The Doctor twisted his arm, one last note cutting the air, signalling full stop. And said: 'Challenge accepted.'

MARS

It had taken a while for Anji to understand, but the Martians were like the homeless two centuries ago. When you first arrived in London, you would see them: sleeping on the Embankment or drinking by Hungerford footbridge. But they would slowly become background, until one day all you noticed was the book fair by the National Film Theatre or the sun shining on the Thames.

The Martians were like that. A small handful had jobs as bodyguards; the rest just looked sad and alone in the human tent-cities. After six months, they slipped from your sight, lost in what their world had become.

They proved harder to forget when they stepped out of the background and into her office, taking Anji and her colleagues hostage.

The siege had been going on for five days.

The Martians' bulk only exaggerated the fragile nature of the prefabricated office. A punch from one of them was enough to put a hole in the plasti-board partitions; one burst from a sonic weapon levelled a wall.

They were demanding the return of their planet. The usual aim of the militant clans. The only question was whether the answer involved the deaths of the hostages as well as their captors.

Michael was off-planet, on assignment. Anji wasn't sure whether that made it better or worse. The past couple of months had been difficult; something she couldn't pin down. They hadn't argued or stopped talking, but their marriage felt increasingly distant, like it was one step removed from her life.

'Anji,' Michelle hissed.

Anji looked up. The Martians were talking in clusters, taking up different positions. The background noise that had filtered into the building – sirens, engines in hover mode – had faded. It meant only one thing: the police had cleared out, Earth Forces had been called in and the end was very close indeed.

Anji nodded to where the bureau's desks had been overturned. 'Get everyone back,' she said softly. 'Find some cover.'

Michelle looked confused for a moment, then realisation dawned. 'Oh, no,' she whispered, and turned to tell someone else.

Then it was too late.

The building jumped, air filled with dust and debris as detonations thudded in every direction. Anji was thrown back on the floor, and when she lifted her head she could see Michelle screaming but heard nothing. The fingertip she touched to her ear came away bloody.

There were flashes of light through the smoke and the dust.

The Martian closest to her had raised its hand towards the dust storm, but the hand and the sonic weapon lodged in the forearm were obliterated before it could fire. It staggered backwards, silent holes punched in its chest armour, green blood spitting across the carpet.

The floor shook as the dead Martian landed next to Anji.

She pushed herself back, eyes fixed on the corpse, only dimly aware of the other gun flashes around them. Then she bumped into Michelle and turned to see what she was looking at.

The smoke billowed in strange patterns around the Martians' sonic blasts. But through the clouds you could see tall figures calmly advancing through the debris. The Martians were hitting their targets but nothing was happening. As the figures came closer the dust seemed to part before them, revealing smooth, armoured lines and the mirror sheen of their helmets. A dull ache in Anji's jaw brought understanding. Each set of armour had a shield or something, emitting its own sonic bursts; enough to dissipate the blasts from the Martians' weaponry.

One of the Martians had realised this, pulling a sword from the harness on its back and charging the attackers. Its target dropped as the Martian swung the blade and kicked out one leg in a wide arc, connecting with the weak point at the back of the Martian's knees; as the Martian buckled the attacker plunged a short knife into the neck joint of its armour.

The smoke was clearing.

Anji watched the armoured soldier get to his feet and look around. In the time it had taken to dispatch his opponent, the other Martians had all suffered similar fates. The last of them, retreating towards the lifts, took a direct hit, tumbling back into the empty shaft.

As the hostages climbed from the wreckage not one of their rescuers moved to help. Instead, they stood almost immobile, their heads alone sweeping back and forth. Checking for any further danger.

The Martian with the knife in its throat was still alive. It struggled to find purchase on the floor, one hand reaching up to pull out the knife. Only when it had pulled the blade clear did the soldier kick it from its hand. The Martian didn't move as the soldier raised his rifle and put one shot through its head.

An hour later Anji was in Sheffield Memorial Hospital, a temporary implant in her ear until her hearing recovered. The news channels were all covering the same event, a follow-up to the end of the siege. Journalists milled around a blank room, jostling for position in front of a podium. They were all working from the same press release, every channel using the same words.

The soldiers who had broken the siege were part of the Professional Unit, a special-ops squad. Today's operation was the first sanctioned appearance of a project years in the making.

Anji's interest was piqued long before the press conference started. But when the man with salt-and-pepper hair took the podium, her hand tightened on the bed sheet. She'd seen him before, knew his name before the press officer announced him: *'Ladies and gentlemen, questions will now be taken by Colonel McNamara, commanding officer of the Professionals.'*

JUPITER SPACE
Now

Forty-eight hours since he kicked it from her hand, the Professional returns Anji's gun to her. The reason is simple: he wants her on the mission with them, helping trace the enemy. She's not combat trained, she hasn't got the experience the survivors have accrued, but in contrast to most of them she's fully fit and alert.

When he hands the gun over Anji looks at him, wondering if this indicates some kind of recognition. But there's nothing in his eyes or tone; just the same dispassionate evaluation.

She takes the weapon and the job.

An hour later, she is in the middle of chaos.

It was Arquette who lured the enemy towards the Village. Masked by smoke bombs, the Professional planted his tracking device. The crossfire laid down – a hard five minutes and the closest thing they could muster to all-out assault – was enough to put the enemy into retreat, hissing and flailing. The survivors took a few minutes to regroup, then followed.

Robertson is in front of Anji now, tracing the signal. He's struggling to filter the background noise Jupiter is putting out, but the signal is just distinctive enough.

Only they are not sure they should follow where the enemy have gone. Because the corridor in front of them looks like hell.

Robertson consults the tracker, shakes his head. 'This is it.'

Anji checks the Station map on her visor. Before they left Robertson updated it, marking the points where the EM shielding is weak. For the most part, their journey has kept to the safe routes, and radiation exposure has been minimal. Not now. They're at the very edge of the survivors' territory. On the map Robertson provided it's marked with the legend *Here Be Dragons*.

Did he have any idea, Anji wonders, how accurate that was?

It doesn't need a map to explain why the survivors haven't ventured further, though. At some point this section has borne the worst of a meteorite hit. Flooring is buckled, bulkheads twisted, the mangled Station infrastructure all too visible in places. Steam vents from cracked pipes, short-circuits flare. The background noise of the Station's struggle against Jupiter's gravity and air pressure is to the fore here. The looks the survivors exchange tell the story: the corridor is a death trap, waiting to close its jaws around them.

Robertson saw a face once and it will haunt him for the rest of his days.

'That's it,' he says. 'This little expedition is over.'

'No,' Caroline says.

Robertson looks at her in disbelief. 'Even forgetting that corridor isn't stable, there's no EM field and the shielding is shot through with meteor rock. Twenty minutes, we take on enough radiation to kill in six months. Twenty-five and that's down to six weeks. Five after that, we're talking hours.' He points to the Professional and Anji, safe in their armour. 'They've got protection. We haven't.'

And he can see confusion and desperation on her face now. She knows he's right but wants to carry on anyway. Whatever the cost. Unable to see a future, unable to see beyond this Station.

That's when Robertson finally understands. He's lost her to this place and she's not coming back. He remembers her dancing and the way she looked as she studied the menu. He can still feel the cool touch of her hand in his as war drew close.

Only hope breaks a chain.

He sees the confusion in her face, sees her looking at the Professional. And Robertson's heart is stretched to breaking. He's breathing hard, screwing his eyes shut, trying to do anything to keep from remembering. When he opens his eyes again Anji is looking at him, but she's the only one.

Because the others are looking at the Professional.

He's on the edge of the safe zone. Without a word, he reaches up and uncouples the helmet. Piece by piece, in less than a minute, he removes the hard shell of armour. The medication dispenser Anji described is all that survives. With no protection save a cotton undersuit, he slings his rifle over his shoulder and steps into the hot zone.

Robertson knows what's coming. Easter lost to the Professional's grandstanding, just like Robertson's losing now. He's worked with Weir and Garcia and Alonso and Bluth and all of them for years. But they're all tired and desperate, and they hold faith with the Professional now. Lost to the same place as Caroline. Robertson breathes hard, white-hot flame in his lungs, scouring his veins.

He screams, raises his weapon and charges, past Anji, past Caroline, pushing by the Professional, on into the hot zone, deck vibrating beneath his feet, steam in his face, sparks burning his back. There are shouts and footsteps behind him, the walls and floors beating with their footsteps. Movement flashes to Robertson's left, the junction of another corridor, and he screams, swivels, his rifle connecting with a carapaced hook, pivoting, thrusting the barrel back, under the joint of the creature's arm and firing.

There are tears on his face.

The air is filled with white light and noise; the others yelling, firing, twisting, charging. Everything is lost to the hammer of his pulse in his ears and the screaming ache of his muscles and the roar of breath in his lungs.

It's the same for all of them. As the creatures press forward against them, they fight.

Robertson doesn't know how long they fight for. It feels like hours but it can't be. And as the enemy finally fall back he feels the rage seep from his body, and as they disappear into the dark the fire burns itself out and he drops to his knees.

He flinches at a touch on his arm.

He thinks it must be Caroline but it isn't. It's Anji, blinking tears, mouth trying desperately to form words. Robertson wipes his own eyes and looks at her. Like the Professional, she's stripped her suit off in a show of solidarity. Only now there's a ragged tear across her right shoulder. It's not a deep cut, but Robertson can see the tiny hairs embedded in it: the signature of the enemy's touch.

'How long?' Anji asks.

Robertson shakes his head, pushing up on to his feet. 'It varies. Easter can run tests. He'll tell you.'

Flashlights stab the darkness around them. Like everywhere outside the Village, the wall and floors are coated by the rust of Jupiter. Beyond that, the corridor has few similarities to the rest of the Station. It's one of the handful of points where the outer rings meet the Station's towers; power lines and computer systems run through here. It's not a room as such, but this nexus point of corridors has become the enemy's base.

To that extent, the plan is a success.

Machinery is crudely wired into the surroundings, tapping those energy cables. But there's no sign of an interstix or a teleport or anything like it. Everyone can see this, everyone knows the mistake they've made.

Weir turns to the Professional: 'You stupid son of a –'

'Hold it,' Robertson says, pointing across the hallway.

A large chunk of machinery is built into the walls; battered and scarred, but familiar. 'ReGene.' Robertson pulls at the memory. 'Davis was hauling a new ReGene unit to sickbay just before the –'

'It's not a transport,' Caroline snaps, 'it's not a weapon, it's no –'

'It'll keep you alive!' Robertson shouts, striding towards his wife. He is still a big man, still towers over Caroline, his body clenched, trying desperately to keep control: 'We've all taken too much radiation. Get that machine back to Greenwich, we flush it from our systems.' He glares at the Professional. 'If we're quick enough, we might give David a chance.'

Neither Caroline nor the Professional responds. Robertson breathes deep, points to where the ReGene unit is wedged into the walls. 'Marcus, Susan, get that thing free.'

It's only as they set to work that Robertson realises how easily he won this particular victory. His wife, he can see, is stunned into silence by the plan's failure or his own show of temper. But not the Professional.

Robertson glances at Anji. She nods to where the Professional is standing, looking into the darkness where the enemy fled. And Robertson finally notices how the Professional is standing: one hand holding his biceps, amber liquid trailing between his fingers. At some point, the medication dispenser has been shattered.

* * *

'Hold still,' Easter tells Anji. He slips the needle into her arm, drawing a vial of blood. As he pulls it clear, Easter presses her thumb up against the puncture mark. 'Push down, it'll stop you bruising.'

'You don't want me to bruise,' Anji says flatly, 'but going insane will have to wait?'

Easter places the vial in a rack. 'There's nothing to worry about just yet.' He peels back her T-shirt, begins to clean the wound. 'The cut isn't that deep. Infection is governed by the level of penetration, plus your general fitness and good health should help.' He presses a dirty bandage on to the wound, tries to offer a reassuring smile as Anji rearranges her clothes. 'You're the fittest patient I've seen in years. It'll be a week or two before you start showing any symptoms: forgetfulness, bad temper, that kind of thing.' He nods to where Robertson is wiring the ReGene unit into their computer terminals. 'When I get a chance, I'll run the test, give you a timetable. As it is –'

'You need the computers for the ReGene unit.' Anji nods. 'I understand.'

'Priorities,' Easter says. 'The sooner we get David into the unit, the better his chances.'

Anji nods and Easter crosses to supervise Robertson's work.

Since they returned Robertson has seemed quieter than Easter's ever seen him.

Even in the beginning, during the long months spent in close quarters on the shuttles, Robertson never gave up. Even when his face said otherwise, something in him signified strength. Whether he realised it or not, Robertson was always the one who stood for hope. That's gone now; eyes and mouth flat, his movements mechanical.

Nobody has given Easter a report on what happened, but snippets of conversation are enough to know what Robertson did. If the ReGene unit doesn't work, Robertson has killed everyone who followed him down that corridor and he knows it.

Robertson ties off the last connection. 'Try it now.'

Easter powers up the terminal. There's a moment of uncertainty between the two machines, jury-rigged processor meeting standardised equipment, then the ReGene unit recognises the connection and uploads its software. The DNA protocols look to have survived the past four years intact. It's not surprising. It looks as if the enemy have been using the machine themselves, repairing the handful of wounds the survivors manage to inflict.

The unit has a number of different configurations but it's years since Easter worked equipment this advanced. So he chooses the default: analyse the patient's genetic structure, extrapolate the necessary sequences to fill any gaps, then advance tissue repair.

'We're ready,' Easter says. 'Load him in.'

Robertson and Marcus lift David from the cot. The young man's face is pale; he doesn't even stir as they lay him inside the ReGene unit. Easter connects the different probes and instruments, makes one last check on the readings. With everything registering normal he slides the glass cover down over the unit. The machine hums and the glass frosts over, and all that's visible of David is a backlit silhouette.

It is, Easter realises, like glimpsing someone through the lid of a coffin.

The Professional approaches then. At first Easter assumes he's checking on the ReGene unit, but it's given no more than a cursory glance. Instead, he steps up to Robertson and says: 'Come with me.'

Robertson thought the Professional was going to berate him for his suicide charge but the raid goes largely unmentioned. It's only referred to as the source of the damage to the Professional's suit. Or rather, Robertson realises, the medication dispenser.

'Arquette said you repaired the microhydraulics on the automated weapons,' the Professional explains. 'This is similar.'

They're sitting in the quiet corner near the greenhouses that's become the Professional's territory. The armour once again covers his body, restoring the implacable image. Except, Robertson thinks, there's a sliver of vulnerability where he has removed the medication dispenser. Robertson is holding it, poking its shattered innards with a tiny screwdriver. A thin trail of wire marks an umbilical cord between the device and the Professional's suit.

Robertson shakes his head. 'This isn't microhydraulics.'

'Close enough.' The Professional blinks rapidly, then his eyes snap open, focusing on Robertson: 'Keep working.'

'This is Easter's job,' Robertson says, 'I'm not medical.' He lifts the dispenser. 'And this is medical, right?'

'Standard issue,' the Professional answers.

Robertson probes further into the mass of split wiring. 'For what?'

And as Robertson looks at him, the Professional frowns again. 'For operational duties.'

'Look,' Robertson says, 'if I know what it is that it does, it might help me fix it.'

He wonders how much he can reasonably have figured out on his own, makes a show of turning the dispenser over in his hand. 'It's medicine, right? Some kind of pain relief?'

'Yes,' the Professional says. 'It responds to feedback from this suit's neural monitors.'

'I'm not registering any input from your suit here.' Robertson purses his lips. 'If I can fix the link, could you run diagnostics?'

His thinking is simple: if the suit can tell him what the problem is, he has a better chance of fixing it. Simple enough, but it takes the Professional for ever to catch up and nod agreement.

Robertson hunts through his tool box for a circuit to splice into the wiring between the suit and dispenser. The Professional repaired his suit earlier, so should be capable of doing this himself. Only the Professional is a different man now. Distracted.

Robertson tries to remember the fight.

Was the Professional touched by the enemy? Robertson's memories are confused snapshots but he recalls glimpses of him. Smooth and swift movements, fluid and controlled. Stepping and twisting, taking aim, firing. Robertson can't believe that a man who fought like that would get caught by the enemy.

It's only as he leans close, connecting the fault-locator circuit, that he sees it. The tendons standing out on the back of the Professional's hand, the fingers stretching, clenching, doing anything to stop themselves shaking.

Feedback erupts from the fault locator; static beneath a tinny voice.

– It was the first lesson we learnt when we reached for the stars: for everything, there is a limit. No matter how far we had come, no matter how hard we had struggled –

The Professional snatches the circuit free of the wiring. His hand opens and closes around it, over and again. They sit there for almost a minute, Robertson trapped in the Professional's stony gaze. Then the

Professional reaches out, lifts the dispenser from Robertson's palm.

The Professional smiles very thinly, shaking his head slowly, chastising a child. Robertson holds his hands up in surrender, climbs to his feet. When the Professional makes no further response, he collects his tools, turns to leave. As he does so, he says, 'It was just an honest mistake, OK?'

The Professional says nothing and Robertson walks away.

Before he turns the corner he glances back. The Professional is trying to force the dispenser around his biceps. Whether it's the shake in his hand or the fact that something no longer fits, he is left trying to close the circle again and again and again.

It was the first lesson we learnt when we reached for the stars.

As he walks, tool box banging against his thigh, Robertson remembers. That tinny voice was thick with the past.

He finds Easter easily enough; still hovering by the ReGene unit, waiting for it somehow to go wrong. It's a good hour before Robertson can take the medic aside and speak to him privately. It's not a useless hour, though; it gives Robertson time to pull at his memories, collating his thoughts.

In the end, they come down to one question: 'Was Jason dead?'

The shadows under Easter's eyes are deeper than ever; he blinks slowly in response to the query. 'Sorry?' he says, 'I don't think I –'

'Jason. When we found Jason, he was dead. There was no mistake?'

The tiredness is replaced by annoyance and confusion; a look that says *You pulled me away for this?*

'Yes,' Easter answers. 'Yes, I'm sure. You should be too; you were there.'

'I know, but…' Robertson stops, checks over his shoulder. 'He keeps a journal. The Professional. A diary or something, recorded on his suit.'

And now annoyance and confusion are replaced by simple curiosity. Easter tries to hides it: 'There's nothing unusual about that.' But he doesn't hide it well; the words say one thing, the way he says them another.

'Not for one of us, maybe. But him? For that man?' Robertson shakes his head. 'And the words. They weren't the words of the guy who snaps orders and puts holes in people.' He pauses, because he knows how this is going to sound. 'It sounded like Jason.'

Easter laughs. 'Jason never spoke.'

'He kept a journal,' Robertson says. 'There was a poem.' He still remembers reading the words, remembers speaking them, his breath on Caroline's neck:

Stars climb high at night
The strongest hands cannot hold
Only hope breaks a chain.

Easter shakes his head. 'So?'

'The Professional's journal entry had the same meaning.'

'Jason was dead. You saw the state the body was in.'

Robertson nods at David's silhouette, clear in the ReGene unit. 'What about one of those?'

'There are limitations on the technology, Robbie. You can't bring back the dead.'

'But you could rebuild someone, right? If they were still alive? Make it so you didn't recognise them?'

'Rewriting the DNA like that would generate mutations,' Easter says. 'You'd never be able to re-create the original pattern in its entirety.' In the end, it all comes back to that first question. And Easter's answer remains unchanged: 'Jason was dead.'

Robertson says nothing in reply. What worries him more is his own attitude. Desperate theories from second-hand myths and a handful of words years apart. It only tells him how lost he is, how lost they all are.

'We're not going to make it,' he whispers.

'The ReGene unit –' Easter begins, but Robertson cuts him off.

'Buys us time from the radiation. Beyond that, how long before we start dying?' He looks around, looks at the Greenwich Village he helped to build. He knows the stitches holding it together are starting to show. 'We had a good run, Joshua. God knows we tried, but this place has six months, maybe a year. Then the shields reach capacity, water recycling goes, oxygen scrubbers start to fail.'

'The Professional –'

'Isn't going to save us,' Robertson says. 'He can fool them, fool Caroline, but we know better.' He pauses, then says: 'We're done, aren't we?'

* * *

Before Robertson dragged him away, Easter freed capacity for Anji on the second terminal. He said it would help her to stay busy.

She thinks she could probably find other things to occupy herself with, but there's little harm in keeping Easter happy. So she sits at the terminal, slowly working through the snapshots from the Professional's download. It's hard to identify the decayed panels and tarnished surfaces outside with the pristine corridors on the screen. They are a fiction that has no relation to this dirty, hard life.

At some point Arquette walks up behind her. Robertson's wife has been subdued since the raid; startled, maybe, by her husband's ferocity. She tries to ignore the screen, but Anji sees her reflection drawn to it; in the end Arquette stands at her shoulder, watching her flick onwards.

It's not just empty corridors, of course. There are people too, frozen in action: reaching for controls, bracing themselves, holding each other. Even in still frame, fear and excitement are writ large on their faces. This was what these people trained for. The opportunities they waited on, the moments they dreaded.

Anji flicks forward and stops.

She doesn't say anything, neither does Arquette.

There are footsteps behind them; Anji is all too aware it could be the Professional. If it is, what will he make of the chaos on the screen?

It isn't the Professional, though. It's Easter, checking on David's progress. He taps at the adjacent terminal for a minute before noticing Anji and Arquette motionless beside him.

'Something wrong?'

Anji is expecting Arquette to answer, but she stays silent. Anji nods at the monitor.

Like the rest of the pictures, it shows a stark, white interior. A tall room, maybe three or four storeys high; the camera set up high, too. It's easy to place this as ground zero for the madness that's overtaken the Station. The walls of the room are vaulted, filled with the remains of tall glass cylinders. The picture isn't clear, but while some of the cylinders look empty others seem to hold blurred forms, slumped and disfigured bodies.

'I don't recognise that,' Easter says. 'Where is it?'

Anji checks the reference. 'Level six.'

Fire rages, caught in one corner, smoke thick over one-half of the screen. It's still possible to make out other figures behind it. Anji zooms in. The computer doesn't have image enhancement. As they close on the faces the resolution drops, but it's still good enough to see expressions of pain and fear. It's good enough for recognition.

'That's Commander Valletti.' Easter points to a tall woman with one hand on a communications panel, head tilted, looking back into the room. He tracks across the screen. A thin man reaching for a woman, her arm in a sling. 'That's...' He pauses, trying to remember. 'African name. Husband and wife.'

'Mukabi,' Anji says flatly.

She sees Easter's puzzled reflection.

'It's been four years,' Anji answers. 'I know the 228 off by heart. Commander Valletti? Her first name is Jennifer. Her brother works in Toronto. Her father still prays every day at the Santa Croce, hoping his daughter will be found alive.'

'What about those two?' Easter says, frowning. 'I don't think I –'

'That's Fitz.' It's Arquette, speaking for the first time. She points to the man with scruffy hair, crouched on the floor, looking across the room in horror. There's another man lying next to him; Fitz pressing a jacket down over his body. The man's blackened sleeve tells the story: Fitz is smothering flames.

'Is that him?' Easter asks.

Anji looks at the two bodies on-screen, one wrapping the other in a McCartney fashion four years out of date. Fitz staring out of the past and right at her.

'Yes,' Anji says, 'that's the Doctor.' Her eyes drop as she whispers, 'It feels like another life.'

'It was another life.' Arquette's voice is as flat as Anji's, but somehow the pain is more evident because of it. 'I don't know if I remember life before this.' A pause. 'I'm not sure I can ever be that person again.'

And with that, she turns and walks away.

Anji looks at Easter. 'What the hell was that about?'

'It's complicated. Her and Robertson,' Easter says, then stops, shakes his head. 'Doesn't matter.'

As he starts to leave Anji catches his wrist. 'I wanted to ask you something. These pictures. They're from just before the energy barrier went up, right?'

Easter frowns. 'I think so, yes.'

'I've been looking through them and there's nothing that could be creating it. No force-field generators, no projectors.' She nods at the screen. 'Nothing like that visible in the corridors.'

'Alien technology,' Easter shrugs. 'In four years, we've never got a proper reading on the barrier; it barely registers anything's wrong.'

'It's just...' Anji pauses, thinking about how to phrase this. 'There were inquiries, after the Station fell. Every project came under scrutiny.'

'So?'

'They all got a clean bill of health. All but one. Singularity weapons.'

'I'm a doctor,' Easter says.

'Not a rocket scientist, I know,' Anji smiles. 'Neither am I. The inquiry used lots of long words and physics stuff I didn't understand.'

'There's a "but" coming, isn't there?'

'If a singularity isn't properly regulated, it could do serious damage.' Anji takes a deep breath. 'Like destroying space-time.'

Easter's confused expression finally manifests itself in a laugh. 'I really don't –'

Anji taps the screen. 'What if it isn't the work of the enemy?'

Easter is silent, then slowly says, 'You mean something already on board.'

Anji smiles. Like a slow fish, Easter has finally seen the bait in what she's saying.

'If one of those singularities got out of control,' Anji says, 'it could have disrupted everything and we'd never know.'

'Quantum uncertainty,' Easter says. 'The energy barrier's the border of a state of quantum uncertainty. We're trapped on the outside, where everything's fixed, and the inside is just a mess of possibilities...'

'Or,' Anji prompts, 'the inverse.' She looks to the exit. Somewhere beyond is a shimmering black field. 'No one knows what one of those things might do.'

Easter looks away but the line of his shoulders tells Anji he's not dismissive, is thinking about what's been said. And slowly he turns back to her. From the excitement on his face, Anji worries she's said too much.

'"It was another life." We say it all the time.' Easter is flushed with energy. 'You said it could be the inverse. What if everything inside the barrier is stable and everything outside is uncertain?'

'I was just thinking aloud,' Anji says.

But Easter doesn't listen. He's caught on the hook of the idea.

'Think about it,' he says, 'everything that's happened since the barrier went up could all just be one of an infinite number of possibilities.' Something comes to him and he smiles. 'If we could break through, we might be able to change everything.' He taps the screen. 'The past might still be there, waiting for us to find it, to resolve the uncertainty.' He looks around them, at their desperate ghost of a life. 'We could stop all this from ever happening.'

Across the Village, Robertson catches sight of the Professional.

At first, Robertson doesn't think he's moved since he last saw him; still seated in the same spot, offering the same silhouette. He knows there's no reasonable connection between a body four years dead and this man. But so much in recent days has brought back the past that he wants to be sure.

So he circles closer, studying the Professional, trying to remember Jason. Height, weight, hair colour, profile. Robertson tries to find any trace of the man he remembers. But there's nothing there.

Jason died and he hasn't come back.

Robertson is close enough to see what the Professional is doing. The medication dispenser is disconnected on the floor near by; a familiar computer pad is in his hand.

It's the corrupted data from the security download. The ghost in the machine. There's a schematic of the Station on the pad too. As Robertson watches the graphic swivels on its axis, glowing dots overlaid on to it. It takes him a minute to realise what the Professional is doing. He's translating the pattern in the Ghost file as co-ordinates, seeing how and where they might intersect with the Station.

The Professional's head suddenly snaps around, fixing on Robertson. 'There's no scale,' he says.

And Robertson is scared. Up until the past hour, the Professional has moved like a hunter, but that power and assurance are gone.

There's an urgency that doesn't seem to fit his character, like a caged animal, desperate to escape.

'There's no scale, no starting point.' The Professional turns back to the screen. 'I can see the pattern. I just don't recognise it.' He looks at Robertson again, his eyes wide. 'If I can find the scale and the starting point, I'll understand what it means.'

Robertson knows the file is a nonsense. He's filtered that kind of thing from their systems enough to know the pattern's random. There's nothing to be found.

But the Professional believes. So Robertson nods his head in quiet reassurance, says: 'I'm sure you'll get there.'

Four years earlier

Their new quarters were the same design as their old. With very little left in the way of belongings, it only took the Doctor a few minutes to settle in. Then he got to work.

The leads AuDoc had identified before the hull breach still needed checking. The bureaucratic documents it had identified didn't immediately mean anything to him: details of the voting on the committee that had decided where to locate the Station. The same name featuring on the proposals and delivering the casting vote: Admiral Jonathan Ferguson.

He wanted to ask AuDoc what dots it had joined to make that information relevant, but he'd already set the AI another task.

Fitz woke on a pristine white bed. The sight on the nearby monitor was like the Doctor's schematic of the *Pegasus* only with his own body in place of the spaceship. Similarity came in the way vital sections seemed to be covered in red warning signs.

It was only when he shifted to get a better look that Fitz realised just how much pain he was in.

A hand loomed at the periphery of his vision, something cold hissed against his neck. Pain receded and movement became easier. Fitz tracked the nurse as she disappeared, passing Robertson and Caroline on the way in.

Robertson looked at him, then turned to Caroline. 'Now that's ugly.'

She gave him a dig in the ribs, but Robertson continued, leaning over the bed. 'I mean, there's frostbite, radiation exposure, a whole load of burst capillaries and talk about bloodshot, those eyes are going to be red for weeks.'

'The eyes are open,' Fitz said, 'and there's nothing wrong with the hearing.'

Robertson turned to Caroline again: 'He's alive! It's a miracle!'

She smiled at Fitz. 'How are you feeling?'

'Glad there's no mirror near by,' Fitz managed. As he pushed himself up in the bed, the fog of how he'd got there lifted. 'The Doctor,' he said, 'is he OK?'

'Improvised space walk to drag his friend to safety?' Robertson shook his head. 'No one's sure if accountants qualify for medals, but there's talk.'

Caroline squeezed Fitz's hand. 'Do you remember what happened?'

Pressure in his ears. Cold on his eyes. Blood thumping in his neck. Fighting for air, breathing ice.

Fitz shook his head. 'Not a thing.'

They stayed for almost an hour, Fitz's body getting stronger as they talked. Looking at Robbie and Caroline he felt like Rip van Winkle, waking from a lifetime of sleep. A couple of days ago they'd barely known each other; now, the way they spoke and acted made it look like they'd been together for years.

Robertson's hand was resting on the arm of his chair. Without missing a beat, without either of them noticing, Caroline's fingers wrapped around his. Two days ago Fitz had seen them do this for the first time, self-conscious and unsure as the news reports left the future looking so bleak.

A moment of simple comfort, now as easy as breathing.

Neither of them mentioned those reports today. Fitz could guess what people would think had caused the hull breach, though. The popular theory would be sabotage. Alien sabotage.

He looked again at their hands.

Fitz's earliest memories were of wartime London. The father who towered over young Fitz – a figure of trust and warmth – making himself look small as he walked the streets, fearful of being recognised. The looks his father received had left Fitz confused, but had also brought them closer. Because Fitz had understood what his dad needed, and he had held on to his father's hand on those walks. Not for himself, but to comfort his dad.

It would have been easy to see Robertson taking Caroline's hand as a thing of the moment. Passion in the face of war. Fitz didn't believe that, though.

* * *

As soon as her temper receded Valletti knew the Doctor had goaded her into the challenge. For all she'd thought about it in the hours since, she still couldn't see why he had.

There was a large market for industrial espionage on the system colonies, but the Doctor's current level of access provided enough information to retire on. There was no need for him to enter the Avatar system. Similarly, if sabotage were his goal he already had the necessary privileges.

Either way, it didn't seem to matter to the Mukabis.

Valletti had mentioned the Doctor's proposal to Terrance as they rode the elevator together, making idle conversation. She'd focused on the ludicrous nature of the idea, stressed that she was going to withdraw the challenge.

Five minutes later Terrance had come to her office.

'It's an opportunity,' he said. 'We can test out the non-invasive interface. It's good, but it's not as good as the implants. We're restricted on who can help refine the process.' He'd shrugged. 'He's interested, let's take advantage.'

As he said it, Valletti knew he was right.

Their ability to develop the system was limited by the number of test subjects available. If any other member of her staff had the security access and was willing to volunteer, she wouldn't have hesitated. Why make an exception for the Doctor? She knew the answer, of course. The whisper of his feet on the dance floor, the light in his eyes as he laughed, the cool touch of his fingertips against her back.

Terrance was still waiting, but her eyes were fixed unseeing on paperwork.

'Commander?' he prompted.

'All right,' she said reluctantly, 'but nothing too advanced. Earth standard conditions, basic training. That's it.'

When Fitz woke the next time the Doctor was waiting.

'You should be up and about in a few hours,' the Doctor said, nodding at the equipment surrounding him. 'Very impressive stuff. They had me plugged into one for a bit.'

'I thought you didn't want any medical attention,' Fitz said.

The Doctor smiled. 'They had a patient who required attention far more than I did. A bit of concentration and I was able to regulate my body to the human median; enough to fool the diagnostics until I could wipe their memory, anyway.' He paused. 'Which gave me a bit of an idea.'

'Why,' Fitz said, 'am I suddenly worried that "up and about in a few hours" is code for "you're putting me in danger again"?'

'Nonsense.' The Doctor held up a computer chip. 'You won't need to move from this bed. You simply plug this into your terminal at the right time.'

'The right time being?'

'Three in the afternoon.'

Fitz raised a painful eyebrow.

'Which is when I'll be joining McCray and the others in an Avatar training programme. At Commander Valletti's invitation.'

'This invitation,' Fitz said. 'She wouldn't have been provoked into making it, would she?'

The Doctor shifted uncomfortably. 'She may have. But there's little danger. If I can fool the medical diagnostics, I should be able to trick the Mukabis' systems into creating a human avatar of myself.'

'The point being?' Fitz asked.

'It's very simple,' the Doctor said. 'Creating the avatars uses up vast chunks of computer-processing power.'

'Which makes getting into a fight with the 101st useful how?'

Power crept into the Doctor's voice as he spoke. 'Because it won't be an easy fight. My avatar should register as human, but with my anticipation and reaction times. Commander Valletti thinks her troops can't be beaten. I'm going to show her otherwise and I'm going to push the Avatar system to its limits.' And then that steel vanished, replaced by a disarming smile. 'That's the aim. If I can just increase the drain on the Station computers by a few per cent, gaps should start appearing in more vital systems.'

Fitz shook his head. 'Still lost.'

'It's a distraction, Fitz. Slow the computers enough and we should be able to break through the firewall programs.'

'And if we can do that –'

'Then we find out everything we need to know about the Mukabis, Deschamps, singularity bombs and the hunt for alien infiltrators.'

'And this,' Fitz said, taking the datachip from the Doctor, 'is going to get that information?'

'I told AuDoc to redesign itself to operate under minimal conditions.'

'So it won't be affected by what you do to the computers.'

The Doctor nodded. 'And it is under orders. Search all Station records, use your initiative, that kind of thing.'

'And all I have to do is plug this into the bedside computer here?'

'At the right time, yes,' the Doctor said.

Fitz looked at his friend. So much just the same: the energy, the smile, the easy way with people. Superficially, all a hundred years on Earth had done was add the odd grey hair and deepen the lines around his mouth. But there was something else underlying this. Initially Fitz had thought it was a lack of confidence, that the Doctor was bluffing it. Maybe he was, but that wasn't the difference.

There was something harder below the surface.

Whether it was years spent alone, or whether on some level he remembered the events that had stranded him on Earth, Fitz could see a steel in his friend that hadn't been there before.

That steeliness was catching Fitz off guard and it was leading the Doctor to risks he might not have taken before. But it had also dragged Fitz across the exterior of a space station, it had brought them here to stop anyone else being attacked like Anji had been. It brooked no room for interference, but the focus – the need to help – was still there.

They would talk, soon, and maybe that talk would give the Doctor enough answers to allow him some peace. But for now, Fitz looked at his friend and saw the things that remained the same. The man he had long ago chosen to trust with his life.

He turned the chip over in his hand and glanced at the bedside terminal. 'This better not be dangerous,' he said. 'That thing about not dying as an accountant? That still stands.'

The Doctor hung his jacket over the back of the couch, and began rolling up his sleeves.

'Cooler in here today,' he said, lying down.

Terrance massaged gel on to the Doctor's temples before attaching a series of pads. 'The lower temperature helps the conductivity on the interface. Better conductivity means more input for the computers and a better avatar.'

'I'll have no awareness I'm an avatar?' the Doctor said. 'It'll all seem real?'

Terrance smiled. 'That's the theory.'

'Excellent,' the Doctor replied. 'I love putting theory to the test.'

He looked up to where Valletti was standing next to Sara Mukabi. The pyschologist had barely paid him any attention at all. Valletti, though, had watched his every move. It was only now, when he turned to look at her, that she broke away.

The Doctor felt a pang of regret at how he'd had broken her trust, then pushed the feeling to the back of his mind. Terrance attached sensors to his forearms, carefully inserted a needle into one wrist. The Doctor breathed deeply, focusing on his body's reactions, making sure it mimicked human normal as closely as possible.

It was a gamble and if it didn't pay off, he'd be trapped inside the Station's most secure area with little hope of a getaway.

'The swelling seems to be doing nicely,' the nurse smiled.

There were, Fitz thought, too many replies he could make to that. In the end, he took his medication and watched her walk away.

It was almost three o'clock. He was just reaching out to slip the datachip into the bedside terminal when a trolley was wheeled in. Fitz recognised the patient immediately. Archer, his hands blistered and burnt.

Fitz lay back in his bed, trying to look casual as one of the medics fussed at Archer's hands. Archer looked anxious and, as the doctor turned to a trolley for some spray, pulled something from his overalls and tucked it under his bed.

His grimace as he did it told Fitz everything he needed to know about the object's importance.

When he closed his eyes: the air in the lab was cold, his breath steaming; Valletti had stopped pacing the gantry; the 101st were settling into their couches; an icy sensation pushed down the needle and into his veins.

When he opened his eyes: the lab was gone.

He blinked rapidly. There was a man standing before him: medium height and build, waiting like an animal on the hunt. Captain McCray, dressed in a grey-green sweatsuit. There were trees all around, and beyond McCray a path, leading on to cargo nets and tyres, trenches and water tunnels. An assault course.

McCray held up a stopwatch: 'On my mark.'

There was a sheen of sweat on his forehead. Other men were already negotiating monkey bars, stripped to their sweat-soaked vests and bare arms. Sunlight fell through the branches of tall trees. Humid Georgian weather. In the distance, he could see Mount Currahee, rising above Camp Toccoa.

'Mark.' McCray clicked the stopwatch.

A chill on his skin didn't seem right. Like he was caught outside on a frosty morning. He didn't move.

'Don't stand there,' McCray barked. 'You're losing time. Run!'

He heard voices in the distance, issuing from mouths nowhere to be seen.

– *level of disorientation* –

– *not handling the transition. There's resistance to the environment* –

– *bring him out of there. I'm giving you* –

And he remembered. 'Of course,' he said, moving off.

As he ran – stretching his calf muscles, slowly pushing into a longer stride – the awareness came back to him. Twigs snapped beneath his feet, there was a damp taste to the air.

The Avatar system used one form of Nightmare to subdue the conscious mind, routing sensory input via the subconscious. The participant's mind filled in some of the details from its own experiences, he guessed, drawing on real-life memory to help cement the virtual experience in the hippocampus.

He ran, jumped, came down in knee-high water, its resistance dragging at him as he pushed onwards.

His body had mimicked human reactions too well; for his first few moments, he had responded to the Avatar system like a human would.

There were footsteps: McCray keeping pace with him. Except the McCray following behind would have no idea this was fake and, if Valletti was right, even when withdrawn from the system the imprint on his memory would be indistinguishable from the real thing. Specific medication, the Doctor mused, would be needed to help the soldiers' neurology deal with that contradiction.

'Move! Move!' McCray shouted at him.

The Doctor took one last look, breathing deeply in the sticky Georgia air, admiring the beauty of the simulacrum.

Then he stopped sightseeing and got to work.

The space walk had left a crack across the face of Fitz's watch. The second hand ticked around to the top of the dial, drawing the minute hand after it.

Archer was resting in the bed opposite, unattended, but wide awake with a venomous look on his face. And he was looking straight at Fitz.

A glance at the watch told Fitz he couldn't wait any longer. For all the times he had pulled these stunts, he still had the urge to whistle nonchalantly whenever he was doing something people weren't meant to see. His lips were too swollen for that, so he settled for smiling at Archer as he inserted the datachip.

'*War and Peace*,' Fitz said, nodding at the screen. 'Have you read it?'

Valletti turned from the holographic sphere. She'd been the only one watching it; Terrance and Sara no longer needed the visuals to know what was happening.

Terrance studied the code tracing across his console. 'He's picked up the pace,' he nodded. 'Quite impressive.'

Valletti glanced back at the hologram.

The Doctor's face was coated in mud as he wriggled under barbed wire, but there was no obvious discomfort. Despite his initial hesitation, he'd made up the thirty-second gap with the soldier in front, leaving McCray some metres behind.

A strand of Valletti's hair had worked its way loose. Keeping her eyes fixed on the holosphere, she began tying it back.

'Medical readouts all within normal,' Sara said. 'I'd like to see how he responds to a more interactive environment.'

Done with her hair, Valletti laid her hands on the railing, leaning out to look down on the room below. As their bodies pushed on through the Georgia summer, the 101st and the Doctor slept soundly on their couches. The rail was cold against her palms.

'What did you have in mind?' she asked.

'Does he have any combat training?' Terrance queried.

'His file says nothing beyond Earth Forces basic.'

'Something historical, then,' Terrance mused, 'but not too far back. Thousand Day War, maybe?' He consulted the on-screen menu. 'Ambush in Achebe Gorge?'

Valletti considered, then nodded: 'Make it a smooth transition. If he gets shot because he's disoriented it's not really a good test, is it?'

Approaching the finishing line only open ground remained.

The Doctor pushed on, passing through the 101st, arms and legs settled into a long rhythm. As he rounded the last corner he could see the leader in front of him; a hundred metres further on, a sergeant stood with another stopwatch. The Doctor breathed deep and kicked.

He was taking a risk. Coming from behind like this could raise suspicion, but he had to balance this against the pride of Valletti and the Mukabis. If he was going to create gaps in the security systems, things had to get more complex than an assault course. And they'd only do that if he could demonstrate that everything so far had been a walk in the park.

He needed to challenge the soldiers on their own terms. But it wasn't an idea he was completely comfortable with.

He remembered the first time he'd killed. The man had been trapped in immovable arms, a lunatic whose obsession had caused massive destruction, and the Doctor had aided his demise, kicking him back into raging flood waters. He'd felt so alone back then, so cold and divorced from the people around him. He hadn't understood the good things that they were capable of.

He didn't feel that cold any more. But he needed that ruthless streak now, and just as he'd provoked Valletti before, he needed to provoke the 101st and the Mukabis. He passed the soldier at the line, and as the sergeant snapped at the stopwatch he felt the ground get harder beneath his feet, his limbs growing heavier as battle armour and a breathing unit coalesced around him. His mind filled with the detail of the campaign against the Martian aggressors.

Georgia was gone and a red Martian storm raged down canyon walls towards him and the 101st. The clouds rippled from a sonic discharge and one of his comrades was thrown backwards, armour rupturing, oxygen exploding into the cold.

The Doctor threw himself forward, shielding the body with his own and shouted: 'Medic!'

Fitz frowned.

He knew this was a slimmed-down AuDoc, but even so it was surprising when all he was presented with was an on-screen button that read GO. A world away from the layered hologram he'd been prodding a few days earlier.

Fitz glanced at Archer, then pressed the button. It winked, then folded in on itself and disappeared from sight.

'Well?' Valletti asked.

'No disorientation, but...'

'What?'

'He's supposed to be a member of the Third Tactical, only he's not following the mission specs or rules of engagement.' Terrance pointed to the hologram. 'Look. Pinned down by snipers, they should be retreating under cover of the storm. It's what the Zens did when it happened for real, it's what he should be doing now.'

Valletti activated the head-up display on the hologram, coloured letters bobbing above the silhouettes visible through the storm. One was moving forward, drawing fire, percussive blasts tearing at his shadow. And then, just as they appeared to be closing on him, he darted left. As Valletti watched he sprinted along the far edge of the gorge, close to the canyon walls, drawing fire after him.

The image stuttered for a moment until Terrance flicked a couple of switches. He shook his head, bemused. 'A simple firefight shouldn't need that much extra processing to –'

'Yes, it should,' Valletti said. 'It always does when dealing with major changes to the environment.'

'What do you –' As Terrance saw what Valletti was referring to the words died on his lips.

The Doctor had dived for shelter below an overhang, the cliff behind him shaking. Weakened by millennia of bitter winds and dust storms, the sonic blasts had sheared its support. The image juddered again as the Station computers struggled to keep up with the falling rocks; the canyon wall buckling and blistering, outcrops exploding into thousands of fragments under suddenly changed pressures.

Valletti pulled the image back and the scale of the change was easy to see. Snipers on one side were attempting to flee as the ground disappeared beneath them. A handful made it, but most were dragged to their deaths in the rockfall. Amidst all this the 101st had regrouped, taking aim at the Martians on the opposite ridge. The range was too great and they were scoring only a handful of hits. But it didn't matter. The enemy were beaten.

Valletti had seen the 101st tackle the scenario a handful of times; victory rated as keeping the casualty rate below 80 per cent.

A low chime issued from the comms pad on Valletti's wrist. She shook her head in irritation. 'I'm needed in C&C,' she said. She checked the hologram. 'He's still alive under that outcrop?'

'That's compacted silicon,' Terrance said. 'Combined with the armour, he's at no risk.'

'Let the scenario run; see if he gets out from under that rockfall by himself.' Valletti nodded. 'Someone gets lucky like that, you wonder if it's luck at all.'

Deschamps stood in his laboratory, working on the generators. One glance told him the system was struggling to keep the containment algorithms balanced. The black dots of the singularities were flaring across the observation screen.

'Bloody Mukabi,' he muttered, shaking his head.

Terrance watched Commander Valletti leave; his eyes on her until the door slid closed. There was a pause – to be sure Valletti wasn't suddenly about to return – then Terrance looked at his wife: 'Well?'

'Too good an opportunity to miss,' Sara said. 'When was the last time we had a new test subject?'

'Valletti'll have our bloody hides if she finds out.'

'Only if something goes wrong,' Sara answered. She tapped her fingers against the console. 'Hide and seek,' she said. 'A bug hunt.'

Terrance nodded. 'Asteroid belt?'

'No mission specs, in at the deep end.' And as Terrance began to enter the commands, Sara continued, 'With one added ingredient.' She leant over her console, ordered: 'Nightmare.'

Below them the IV pumping fluid into the Doctor's arm billowed as the liquid turned jet black.

'Drop the room temperature again,' Sara said. 'I want that connection to sing.'

The Doctor could feel the shift coming this time and prepared himself. As the red planet faded away, the weight vanished from his limbs and he found himself tumbling over and over. Arms and legs flailed against nothing, his head snapping around to make sense of his surroundings. The visor and armoured suit were much the same, but the dust was gone, replaced by the distant glare of the sun. Light and shadow flared dizzyingly as he fell through space.

More than that, the Doctor realised, his heart was pumping too fast. His eyes twitched one way and another and he realised he was panicking, lost again, forgetting this wasn't his body.

Shadow loomed over him and as his breathing accelerated he threw out a hand, fingertips scrabbling against the rock slowly spinning past. His glove scraped soundlessly across the surface, finding no purchase, and he bounced terrifyingly into free space again before finally taking hold of a thin ridge. He held tight and let the asteroid's motion swing him around in its wake, bringing his feet down on to its surface.

The relief was only temporary. The rock itself provided a firm horizon, but its movement meant the rest of the world was now tumbling around him. As he struggled to find his feet, nausea threatened to overcome him. It was only when his stomach began to clench that he remembered where he was.

'Fitz,' he said, finding memories to anchor on. 'Fitz and Anji.'

And with that, his focus returned. Even so, he was having trouble lowering his heart rate and keeping his breathing under control. The entire environment now seemed that much more real.

As he took stock of his surroundings, he realised something else. There'd been no mission briefing or illusory history to provide any context.

It didn't really matter. The laser bolts that tore at the surface a few moments later made the scenario perfectly clear. Using military-grade EVA suits, the 101st were closing from all sides and he was their target.

The Doctor turned, checking the positions of the approaching troopers, then crouched down on the asteroid's surface, waiting for the optimum moment to push off and out into the fray.

'Bloody hell,' Terrance swore. The Avatar projection juddered, losing resolution at the edge as he increased the system's draw on the Station computers.

'What is it?' Sara asked.

'He's taken down one of the troopers,' Terrance replied, 'and got control of an EVA.'

'That's allowed for within the scenario: what's the problem?'

The image came back into resolution. Flame guttered along the edge of one of the asteroids, sending it spinning off in a different direction.

'Same as Achebe Gorge, using the environment against the opposition. That cannon fire's setting off a chain reaction.'

Asteroids began to tumble into each other, rebounding again, hurtling towards the circling troops as their target manoeuvred his EVA unit through the chaos.

'Only this time it's not one cliff face, but hundreds of moving objects affected.' He looked at Sara. 'We're already exceeding our allocated processing by 35 per cent. Any more of this and –'

His words were cut off as the floor shook, a deep throb resonating through the Station's structure. The lights in the lab came on full for a moment, then flashed red as an alarm sounded. The bass noise and movement echoed again.

Terrance looked at Sara in shock. 'That's the defence batteries opening up,' he said, starting emergency-shutdown procedures. 'We're under attack.'

The asteroid field faded. Gravity pulled at his limbs, a chill settled on his skin and unfamiliar sounds echoed in his ears. He opened his eyes, finding the Avatar chamber around him.

'Home sweet home,' the Doctor breathed.

As he pulled himself up he could see McCray and the 101st disconnecting themselves. Sara Mukabi was snapping orders: 'Take your meds, report to your duty stations immediately.'

As the Doctor peeled sensors from his arms and forehead, the troops filed out of the room; each one stopping to self-administer an injection of golden fluid. The Doctor nodded at them: 'Do I need a shot of that?'

'Not for one session,' Sara said, approaching. 'It helps integrate the simulations with real memory, but it's only necessary after prolonged exposure.' She drew the needle from his wrist. 'Your mind should cope with a one-off; give it a day or two and it'll feel like a very vivid dream.'

The Doctor looked at his wrist. There was a faint smear of black around the puncture wound.

Helping him to his feet, Sara wrapped an arm around his waist, the movement taking him by surprise. He winced, but Sara didn't notice.

'Get to your quarters,' she said. 'We're on alert.'

He slipped his jacket on, quickly buttoning the front; he couldn't look to check, but he was fairly sure there would be fresh blood on his shirt.

In the sickbay, Fitz was suddenly surrounded by a mad rush of activity: doctors pulling out carts of instruments, preparing beds, getting ready for casualties. All undercut by klaxons and that deep vibration running through the Station.

And then it all stopped. Moments later, Valletti's voice came over the intercom: 'This has been an emergency response drill. The drill is now over, debriefing scheduled for 09:00 tomorrow.'

Fitz could see the relief on the faces around him. They'd thought it was real, they'd thought this was war.

He returned his attention to the bedside terminal. There was a message waiting for him. He frowned, pressed the icon. It was from AuDoc, a data file attached to the message: DANGER. TIME TO RUN.

'What the bloody hell does that mean?' Fitz said. He tapped the icon again, but nothing happened. 'AuDoc?' When there was no response, he opened the file. The data looked incomprehensible, and not just because it was all high-powered scientific stuff.

'Arse,' Fitz said.

As he settled back in his bed he looked over at Archer, wondering how long he'd be in for, and, more importantly, how deep a sleeper he was.

The Doctor had strapped a new bandage around his waist.

When the technology had become available, he'd taken the opportunity to test his own DNA. The gene pattern was broadly similar to the human norm, but had a stronger regenerative capability. This had explained a lot: his constitution usually cleared cuts in days, a broken bone in a week.

But this wound was taking an unusually long time to heal, most likely because he wasn't getting an opportunity to rest up; an impromptu space walk wasn't exactly the best recuperative experience.

There was a message waiting; a copy of the report on the hull breach. He scanned it, then called up the Station schematics. The power vents running along that part of the Station exterior had been closed, the feedback enough to disrupt electronics in the outer wall and blow out a small section of the hull.

A malfunction in a low-level environment system. The conclusion being, as Valletti had claimed, that the breach was an accident.

Except while the Doctor could accept the cause of the breach, he couldn't believe it was an accident. And, he thought, if he and Fitz were someone's target then he needed to organise that escape plan.

Fitz glanced over at the nurse's bay. The shift had changed, and it was a bloke now: occupied, watching some war movie. Providing he was careful, Fitz was free to roam.

Archer was a deep sleeper and a snorer.

Giving his fellow patient a quick glance, Fitz started prodding the nearby screen. He was familiar enough with the Station computers now, but it still took a few attempts to find Archer's records.

There was a break in the snoring. Fitz looked up. Archer was still asleep, his breathing reverberating again a second later.

The medical stuff looked normal to Fitz's eyes – Archer had burnt his hands in an overload in the docking bay – but he saved it to disk for the Doctor anyway.

There was another break in the snoring, but still no movement as Fitz crept closer to Archer's bed. He wanted a look at the object Archer had slipped under his mattress. He waited for the snoring to begin again, then dropped on to one knee and carefully began to slip his hand along the edge of the bed. He found it almost straight away: a slender, metallic cylinder, cold to the touch. There was writing on the side, but Fitz couldn't easily make it out. He was peering more closely when he realised the snoring had stopped again.

There was dim light at the periphery of his vision, Archer's voice whispering: 'Put it back, or I'll put this laser scalpel through your throat.'

Fitz swallowed. 'There are security cameras here. You wouldn't get away with it.'

'Put it back and I won't have to try.'

The light edged closer to Fitz's skin and he pushed the device back under the mattress.

'Good boy,' Archer said. 'Now keep your mouth shut for another day or so, or I'll put you in a grave you can't come back from.'

It took him a few hours to put the finishing touches to the escape plan: a subroutine added to the Station's communication systems. On his command an initial burst of sonic feedback would incapacitate anyone around him or Fitz; a subsequent wave would blanket all sound across the Station, making it that much more difficult to co-ordinate security responses.

It wouldn't be a huge advantage and Fitz probably wouldn't appreciate the bleeding eardrums, but if it came to it the Doctor was reasonably sure he could carry his friend out of harm's way. It would have to do.

As he worked on the program, though, his mind kept returning to other things. The Avatar chamber had stirred his subconscious and things were rising to the surface.

Chiefly, Sara Mukabi at the dinner table: *If front-line starships were like this, I'd probably still be married to Jonathan*.

Then there was the Avatar chamber itself. Something to do with how the 101st reacted when those asteroids had started hurtling around.

He paused, thinking about the implants in the back of their heads. The first time he'd seen one had been in the sickbay, on Jason McCray's scan. A couple of hours later, Valletti had introduced him to the Mukabis and the Avatar chamber.

He hadn't thought anything about it at the time, but now this seemed odd. As far as Valletti was concerned, he was an accountant. Was keeping him apprised of where the money was going really a reason for allowing access to the most secretive project on the Station?

He'd told Fitz that Valletti was nervous because implants were illegal. But he'd only known that because Valletti had told him. He'd abused her kindness – to get close to the Mukabis, to get himself into an Avatar simulation – but had she been manipulating him in return? And, if so, what exactly had she been trying to hide?

The Doctor finished inputting the escape program, then accessed the Station's legal database.

Valletti had only been in the bath for a couple of minutes, but she was almost asleep when the door chime sounded. Everything she'd been trying to forget – the defence bays, the security reports – snapped back into focus.

'Dammit,' she whispered. The chime rang again.

Wrapping a towelling robe around her, she left the bathroom. In the three years she'd been running this station no one had ever come calling this late. Which meant she had a good idea who was at the door.

'This isn't appropriate,' Valletti told the Doctor.

'I'm sorry,' he replied, 'but something occurred to me.'

She glanced down the corridor. 'All right,' she sighed, standing aside to let him in.

Valletti could see him taking in the room: her violin on its stand on the dresser, steam drifting though the bathroom door. He sniffed the air. 'Coconut?'

'This had better be something more than a discussion of my bath oils.'

He swivelled, fixing her with a stare. 'The 101st.'

Valletti kept her face like stone, but something inside her was breaking. He was too smart. She'd worried about that the moment he started talking to the Mukabis in the recreation hall.

'What about them?' she said.

'They don't react the way they should.'

She didn't reply.

He crossed to the dresser, slowly running a fingertip along the neck of the violin. 'If I'd been paying attention, I would have seen it before. As it was, it wasn't until I started thinking about that asteroid-belt scenario.' He drew a fingertip along one of the strings, producing a long low note. 'They don't feel fear, do they?'

Valletti said nothing. He was trying to draw answers from her; if she kept quiet he'd have to show his full hand. Reveal just how much he'd figured out.

'Those implants,' he said, 'they're not really necessary for accessing the Avatar simulations. I don't have one and that session felt real enough to me.'

'They help the –'

'Once I'd seen the implant in Jason's head, you needed to tell me something. Telling me they were there to facilitate a training programme was obviously far more palatable than the truth. Technically illegal, but not irresponsible.' He paused, then fixed his eyes on her. 'They do something else, yes? Not a hive mind, because the 101st act like individuals. But something similar; linking the subconscious, maybe.'

She realised then that when he'd come to her door he hadn't had it all worked out. Even when he'd started talking, he hadn't quite known where it would lead him. There was an energy in his voice as pieces began to fall into place.

'Something,' he said, 'that allows each squad member to feed off the strength of his colleagues.'

Which was close enough.

'You're just theorising,' Valletti said, trying to end the conversation before he got any further, 'and I'm not discussing that with you.'

'I can see why. It's stupid and dangerous,' he snapped. 'A collective strength sounds like a brilliant idea. Brought together in times of stress people are inspired to acts of the greatest courage. Only you can't create bravery the same way you simulate gravity or replicate the seasons.'

She shook her head again. 'There's nothing to discuss.'

'Then let me fill in the blanks,' he said. 'The Avatar project is illegal because of those implants.'

She said nothing.

'And the law you're being ordered to break, that's the Riley Act of 2171? Which outlaws cerebral implants for what reason?'

'I won't –'

'Let me remind you. Implants are dangerous, because they leave the recipient open to outside control –'

'We have safety protocols to –' She stopped herself.

He glanced at her, smiled briefly, then continued. 'And because they are a fundamental infringement of human rights. Most specifically, the right to privacy. Recalibration of those implants would strip those men of that, laying bare their innermost thoughts.'

It was getting harder and harder to maintain her stone face. 'You're a legal expert now, are you?'

'I don't need to be. Even supposing you kept that kind of abuse from happening, even supposing those implants work as they're meant to, there are other reasons why this is a bad idea. Reasons Riley never thought to include in his Act, like what the long-term effects might be on those men's personalities.'

Valletti opened the door, pointed. 'You need to leave. Now.'

The Doctor looked at her, then exited. As she started to close the door he caught her wrist, looking straight into her eyes. 'Please,' he said, 'think about what that confidence you're creating might mean. For every act of collective bravery, there's one of insanity. History is littered with people feeding off each other's beliefs and doing so to justify the most heinous acts against their fellow men.'

She said nothing, just looked pointedly at his hand. He let go of her wrist and she closed the door behind him.

Steam still curled in the air, but Valletti no longer wanted the bath.

Sitting at her desk, she accessed the reports from C&C that she'd been studying. The defence batteries hadn't opened up as part of any drill; it had been yet another malfunction. The experts assured her there hadn't been any more attempted security breaches in the last couple of days. Which left the latest theory: that there was a previously unseen flaw in the computers' operating system.

'Techno-speak,' Valletti muttered, closing the report.

Secret messages piggybacked on the commercial frequencies, system glitches, malfunctions, firewall breaches, whatever. All techno-speak. What mattered was that somehow, someone was taking a hammer to her station. She wanted to know who and she wanted to know why.

And whoever it was, was being very smart about it.

Valletti sent a message to the computer-security team, telling them to recheck the system records. Then she put in a call to the Mukabis.

Fitz was discharged in the morning. Puffy and discoloured, his face was, at least, recognisably vintage Kreiner again.

Archer had just smiled at him as he left.

It took Fitz a few minutes to locate their new quarters, but on entering he was greeted by a now familiar sight: the Doctor strapping a bandage over his stomach.

'You have got to be kidding me,' Fitz said.

'I tensed up during the simulation,' the Doctor replied. 'Plus there were a couple of knocks from panicked crew members during the defence drill.'

Fitz nodded.

'Except it wasn't a drill,' the Doctor said. 'Maintenance logged overtime yesterday afternoon and on into the night. A malfunction which left a dozen cannon firing blindly into Jupiter's atmosphere.' He shook his head. 'I don't like it, Fitz. We're missing something here and I don't know what it is.'

'Do you want the bad news, then?' Fitz held up the datachip.

The Doctor's eyes closed. 'AuDoc couldn't penetrate the security systems?'

'Not quite.' Fitz handed the chip over. 'But it all looks really garbled.'

The Doctor inserted the chip in the comms panel, tapped the top corner of the screen. 'That's a security code, so AuDoc got through the firewall programs. Except...'

And as his voice trailed away, Fitz could see life returning to his friend's eyes. 'It was attacked,' the Doctor said. 'AuDoc was attacked.'

'AuDoc's not the only one.' Fitz described his encounter with Archer.

The Doctor listened and then nodded. 'I wonder,' he said, 'if that might not be the same cause and effect.'

'What do you mean?'

'What do we know? Someone on this station has been sending secret messages; Archer threatened you; AuDoc was attacked by something else behind the security screens. If Archer threatened you in order to keep his secrets, then whatever attacked AuDoc was probably doing the same.' The Doctor peered at the mess of numbers and letters on the screen. 'Something triggered this. AuDoc spotted something in the computer system and that set it off.'

'Archer,' Fitz said, 'was doing something with a computer link, just before the *Pegasus* blew up.'

The Doctor nodded. 'I've been thinking about that. The kind of problem that caused our hull breach could also have destroyed the *Pegasus*. A vent closed that should have been open, catastrophic overload of the cooling systems.'

'Boom,' Fitz said.

'Boom, indeed,' the Doctor replied. 'The kind of thing that would be easy to orchestrate from anywhere on the Station, provided the *Pegasus* was linked to Farside's systems.' He clicked his fingers. 'Which it would have been while in dock for repair and analysis.'

'All roads lead to Archer,' Fitz said.

The Doctor sighed. 'All except the one we came here for. He could be responsible for all the chaos we've seen on this station but not for those soldiers on Mars.'

Fitz thought about this. 'This thing that attacked AuDoc, it'd be like a computer virus or something, right?'

'Yes?'

'Well, if those two squaddies did have those implants, aren't they like computer chips stuck in your head?'

'I see where you're going, but there's no motive, Fitz.'

'Maybe that's it, maybe that is his motive. Chaos. Disrupt life as much as possible. Leave the Station open to attack.'

'Then what's on that cylinder he was hiding? Why tell you to keep quiet just another day?'

'Because whatever it is he's planning, it's going to happen soon?'

The comms system chimed. Fitz recognised the tone now: message waiting.

The Doctor read the memo, pursing his lips. 'Another invitation from Sara Mukabi. How opportune.'

* * *

Although he'd heard the Doctor's description, Fitz hadn't actually seen this part of the Station himself. When the lift doors opened on to the long sterile corridor he said, 'I don't like this.'

'Why not?'

Fitz nodded down the hall, 'Last walk of the condemned man, isn't it?'

The Doctor sighed. 'We can't just ignore the message, Fitz.'

'And I'm glad you haven't.' It was Sara Mukabi, emerging from the guard's station, waving a dataslide. 'The analysis of your performance. Quite impressive.' She moved off down the corridor. 'If you'd care to follow me.'

As they followed her, Fitz couldn't help but notice the lights switch themselves off as they passed; like the corridor was closing down in their wake. He tugged on the Doctor's sleeve, nodded at the darkness.

The Doctor winked slowly at him, a thin smile on his lips.

Fitz felt a sudden chill of anxiety and anticipation. If Sara Mukabi was leading them into a trap, the Doctor was ready for it.

The room matched the Doctor's description except for one thing. The door that had resisted his attempts at breaking and entering was wide open. As Sara disappeared through it, the Doctor gave Fitz a shrug and walked after her.

'Bloody hell,' Fitz muttered, following on behind.

The room was almost five storeys high, vaulted gantries spiralling up its walls, metal cylinders lining them. In its centre there was a pair of operating tables, surrounded by gleaming, multijointed arms. The lower level was flanked by a succession of video screens.

Terrance Mukabi was working at a console and just nodded a greeting when they entered. As the Doctor circled, taking in their surroundings, Fitz glanced nervously around.

There was no immediate sign of danger.

Sara had connected the slide to a video screen that filled with shots of the Doctor, dressed in running gear, clambering over a high wall in a forest.

'Very impressive,' Sara explained. 'It's rare for someone to adapt that well to the dislocation first time out. Rarer still for them to perform like you did.'

'I'm adaptable,' the Doctor said.

It was the phrase Valletti had used to describe the Doctor in C&C, Fitz realised. Only then it had been a joke, delivered with a smile and offhand sincerity. This time the steel he'd heard in the Doctor's voice in the sickbay was back. As Fitz looked, he realised that the Doctor's eyes were moving over the video screens, absorbing the information, flicking from them to the gantries in the room to the operating tables.

Whatever this place was, whatever secrets it held, the Doctor had just figured them out.

And he was angry.

'It occurs to me,' he said, 'that I've only seen a fraction of what the Avatar chamber can do. Georgia, Achebe Gorge, hide and seek in the asteroid belt. Very nice, but missing one vital component for combat training.' He prowled the room, his hand trailing over the controls as he gave Sara Mukabi a hard smile: 'Alien opposition.'

His hand came down on a switch and the screens surrounding the cylinders lining the walls drew back with a hiss.

Fitz yelped. The cylinders were full of an electric-pink liquid and floating in that liquid were corpses. Alien corpses to be precise. Each cylinder marked with a yellow and black emblem.

'Dangerous biological material,' the Doctor said, 'to be handled only by the 101st. You wouldn't want everyone knowing what you were bringing on board.'

'Very good, Doctor,' Sara said.

'I'm ashamed it took me so long to work it out. I was focusing on those fear-suppressing implants of yours. That is what they do, isn't it?'

She nodded. 'Commander Valletti mentioned your chat.'

'I'd forgotten about the rest of your system. The part that relies on biological input to create the avatars.'

Fitz looked at the corpses. 'I don't see how.'

'They're not dead, Fitz. None of them is.'

The shapes varied – humanoid, or amorphous, or reptilian – but you could work out the biology easily enough. You could see the injuries they carried, the holes punched, the limbs missing.

'Front-line enemy casualties from the past five years,' Sara said. 'Placed into stasis before they expired.'

'These are sentient beings,' the Doctor snapped. 'They're prisoners of war.'

'No,' Sara barked in return. 'They're dead bodies that just aren't dead yet. Not one of them would survive more than two minutes outside those capsules.'

Fitz saw his friend's shoulders tighten, his jaw clench firm. Then the Doctor took a deep, shuddering breath and turned away from the cylinders. As he studied one of the computer screens, Fitz could see him struggling to keep his revulsion in check.

The Doctor tapped a chemical formula visible on one of the screens: 'This is your stasis fluid?'

'Yes.'

'That's a volatile mixture. Very invasive.'

'It completely halts cellular decay. Correctly applied, that could freeze the electrical impulses driving a computer.'

The Doctor nodded. 'You use these facilities to re-create them in the Avatar chamber. As and when required, you poke the bodies with an electrical stick and produce enough base input to create functioning alien avatars. Very crude and, with a stasis mixture like this, very dangerous.'

'The fluid's volatile,' Sara responded, 'but the avatars need to be as real as reality itself.'

'Because,' the Doctor said, 'you think that if you can understand how we react to a fight, then you can master that fear.'

'Via the implants,' Fitz said.

'And Nightmare,' Sara added.

The Doctor smiled. 'I wanted to talk to you about that.' He nodded to a mess of equipment in one corner. 'That's what you use to distil Nightmare from this gas you discovered, yes? Strip-mining the properties that disrupt the chemicals of the brain?'

She looked at him impatiently. 'You know all this.'

'"If front-line starships were like this, I'd probably still be married to Jonathan". That's what you said. Not Admiral Jonathan Ferguson? The man who conveniently located this station right next to the only supply of the material needed for your project?'

And suddenly Sara Mukabi looked nervous. 'What if he did?'

'You pulled strings to get this up and running. I'm wondering about any other short cuts you might have taken. What is it in that gas that you use?'

'Nightmare works fine, Doctor.'

'Oh, I can testify to its effect,' the Doctor said. 'You used it on me, didn't you?'

'We give it to anyone entering a combat simulation. The 101st have been subjected to all the terrors we can throw at them; every one enhanced by a dose of Nightmare. And they've survived it all, thanks to those implants.' Sara paused, pointing to the results from the Doctor's session. 'All of which got me thinking,' she said, 'about how you survived the Avatar chamber.' She drew a silver pistol from her coat: 'Your psychological profile was very interesting, Doctor.'

'Oh, balls,' Fitz said.

'For one thing, it has the hallmarks of a man with a reconstructed living context, typically symptomatic of amnesia. Only there's nothing on your record to indicate such an event.'

'Ah.' The Doctor smiled.

'Then there are other underlying traits. Things no one would normally notice, but that the trained eye can spot if looking for them.' She cocked the pistol. 'Like whether you think of yourself in human terms, or whether you really are a unicorn.'

Fitz's first instinct was to follow plan A and run for the door. But the Doctor said nothing, just looked at Sara, a faint smile on his face.

'You see,' Sara said, 'it occurred to me that if you are an alien, you might be smart enough to fool the Avatar system into thinking you were human.'

There was a bustle of noise around them. Figures stepped out on to the galleries, filled the exits. Fitz couldn't remember the names, but he knew the faces: the dozen members of the 101st. Stepping into the room behind them were McCray and Valletti.

The commander looked tired, but there was no mistaking the anger and disappointment as she looked at the Doctor.

'You might be able to fool the Avatar system' – Sara nodded to the operating tables – 'but you won't be able to fool a dissection.'

The Doctor smiled at Valletti. 'I really am sorry.' And then said: 'Jericho.'

There was a moment of silence.

Fitz got the impression that something impressive should have happened. The Doctor opened his mouth to repeat the phrase.

Valletti struck him across the face, the slap echoing around the galleries.

Hell hath no fury, Fitz thought, as Valletti stared the Doctor down.

'The trumpets sounded and brought the walls of Jericho down. Prosaic name for a sonic weapon.' She shook her head. 'You're good, Doctor, but you're not as good as you think you are. You underestimated this station's staff. That first attempt to breach the firewalls was ham-fisted.'

Fitz winced and looked apologetically at the Doctor.

'It was enough,' Valletti said, 'to make us track every shred of computer activity on the Station.'

'This isn't what you think,' the Doctor said.

Valletti ignored him. 'But there's so much activity on this station it was impossible to trace the culprit, even when we found an anomaly. But last night, you finally overplayed your hand by adding that subroutine to the comms protocols. It was easy to disable it.' She turned to Fitz. 'They also uncovered Mr Kreiner's activities yesterday. You have one chance: what did you do with the files you stole?'

'Your security programs rendered them useless,' the Doctor answered.

'Security,' she snapped, 'didn't know you were there till after the event. The truth, Doctor.'

'I'm sorry,' the Doctor said, 'but whatever's happening on this station, I am not responsible.'

There was a long pause.

Then Valletti shook her head. 'We'll find out, won't we?' she said, turning to McCray: 'Strap him down.'

MARS

- Anji, it's Jenna at the network. Can you call me when you get -
- This is your husband calling. My shuttle lands at five, so I should clear customs by -
- Miss Kapoor, this is a message from the Bradbury Pharmacy. You wanted to be informed when we received this year's cold vaccine. Surgeries will be open from nine each morning, or you can purchase a self-administered -
- It's Kaylie from the Families Association. Anji, please call me when you get this message, there's been a development. A big one and you need to -

Anji hit the erase button. The terminal had been bleeping through her dreams all afternoon, but checking it hadn't been worth getting out of her sickbed. Now she'd made the effort, she wished she hadn't. The network could wait, the cold vaccine was two days too late, the war widows never had any real news.

And then there was Michael.

'And what am I going to do about you?' she whispered.

It was approaching the fourth anniversary of Anji's new life. In that time she'd found a job, made a home and married. An interesting life to live.

She'd realised during her hospital stay four years ago that medicine had moved on since 2001. It stood to reason diseases had too, and Anji had no idea what she was immune to any more. As soon as finances had allowed, she'd signed on at a local doctor's and got every vaccination going. It was the kind of scrupulous behaviour that Michael laughed at, but she'd not had a sick day in four years.

Except the latest cold vaccine had shipped late and five days ago Anji had been stuck on a bullet train to Jacksonville with an offworlder with a hacking cough. Now she had a temperature, and her forehead was caked in sweat, her body shivering.

And Michael was back in town.

Their first couple of years seemed like a dream now. They didn't row or fight, he wasn't violent and she didn't sleep around or anything like that. They were just drifting apart. Anji's job kept her tied to the Sheffield conurbation, while Michael had progressed to war correspondent, spending months at a time on the system colonies. A distance between them that was hard to overcome.

Anji sat down on the sofa, dressing-gown tight around her, cradling a cup of cocoa. Almost seven o'clock in the evening; Michael would have cleared customs and decontamination, was probably hauling his dusty cases across town, could be walking through the door any minute.

Anji turned the holoscreen on; the default was set to the news channel. Six-fifty-seven, the shipping forecast. A dust storm brewing in Mars' southern hemisphere; possibly the global event mathematicians said was now overdue. Hurricanes sweeping the gulf coast on Earth, disrupting the operation of the Yucatan space elevator. Unusual weather activity on Jupiter closing the surrounding area to civilian traffic; transport ships bound for outposts around Neptune needed to allow extra fuel for the diversion.

'Freeze broadcast.' Anji picked up the remote control, zooming in on the pictures from Jupiter. The change was clear to see. The storms that passed for the planet's atmosphere usually circled in bands around it, faster around the equator; the infamous red spot the eye of an ever present hurricane.

It wouldn't be obvious to a casual observer, but Anji had seen enough pictures of Jupiter to recognise the difference.

There'd been no news about Farside Station for almost eighteen months now; Anji's contacts had all met a stone wall. Either the information was so closely guarded only the top brass had access, or it genuinely wasn't there and all the conspiracy theories really were just theories. Jupiter, Farside Station, the Doctor and Fitz had all faded from Anji's mind and, without really making the decision, she had simply got on with her life.

Now, curled on a sofa, her body wracked with spasms from a virus she wasn't equipped to fight, her eyes losing focus and the cup increasingly distant in her hand, Anji Kapoor looked at the picture of Jupiter and remembered what she had tried so hard to forget.

For all her efforts, she had never moved past that day in the New Jupiter Café and the Doctor's and Fitz's attempt to solve the mystery of her attackers.

JUPITER SPACE
Now

Robertson is asleep when the screaming starts.

Unable to face his bed, he's slumped back against one of the habitats; knees tucked up against his chest, arms wrapped around them. The comforting position of a scared and tired boy. His dreams are filled with the Professional, imprinting his face on to the past; faces from years ago appearing in the present.

Breaking glass and a scream snap him awake. He's on his feet in moments, running towards the noise.

His first thought is that the enemy have breached the barricades. Because there's a monster loose in the compound: a tall silhouette, with hunched shoulders and distorted physique. The head tilts back, the creature howls.

The Meridian is chaos.

A computer terminal lies sparking and smoking, irreparably damaged. The ReGene unit is twisted, the misted glass-front in pieces on the floor. Easter's medical supplies are spilt among the shards. Carvacchio, Gould and Fletcher are there, backing slowly away from the creature.

Caroline's near by. Like the rest of them, she's had no time to don armour or pick up arms, but she's not retreating. She's just waiting, balanced on the balls of her feet, hand resting on the hilt of her knife.

Robertson knows if the creature attacks, she won't stand a chance.

'Run!' he screams, but she doesn't listen.

Then the creature moves, away from Caroline, towards the main entrance, everyone parting in front of it.

Robertson looks around: 'Where's the Professional?'

'He's coming.' It's Easter, stumbling out of the chaos. 'What is that?'

'I don't know,' Robertson answers.

Caroline is on the move now. 'Fetch the guns,' she tells Weir, as she starts jogging after the creature. Robertson pushes through after her.

'How did one of them get in here?' she barks at him.

The creature is studying the barricades in front of it. The rusty metal forms blocking the corridor are completely intact, no sign of it having fought its way in. As it moves, light from the forge catches its back, revealing a circle of hard puckered flesh.

Caroline yanks at Robertson's arm: 'How did it get past the defences?'

Robertson watches the creature as it reaches the edge of the Village, shakes his head, whispers, 'It didn't.'

The creature reaches out to tear at the first barricades, ignoring the electricity sparking from the metal stanchions. Only when its oversized hand closes on the rusted metal does it snatch it back. The creature howls again, striking the obstacle, snapping the bolts securing it to the wall. It steps forward to charge once more, but as it does so it begins to howl again. Anger and pain.

Someone pushes Robertson aside. The Professional, plasma rifle at his shoulder, blinking down its sights. Just like he did with David in the corridor. Only this time, he doesn't take the shot instantaneously. He looks at the creature, blinks, raises his head and refocuses.

A moment of hesitation in which the creature turns from the barricades, back towards the Village.

'Shoot it!' Caroline screams, but it's too late.

It catches the Professional with a vicious backhand and he tumbles across the floor, rifle skittering away in another direction. There's a moment when everyone is frozen, stunned by the ease with which the Professional has been dispatched. Then the creature charges back into the compound.

Weir has found a projectile weapon, fires, the shot going wild. The flash is enough for Robertson to see the survivors are fleeing.

The only one left in the creature's path is the tiny figure of Toby.

Awakened by the noise he sits, quiet and confused, by an overturned camp bed. The computer pad Caroline fought so long for him to have is in his hand.

Robertson saw a face once.

He begins to run.

'Get out the way!' It's Caroline's voice.

Robertson ignores her. He can guess what's happening. She's behind him, holding the Professional's rifle, one hand struggling with its awkward weight, the other firmly wrapped around the grip, finger on the trigger.

'Move!' she cries.

He's in her line of fire, but Robertson runs straight, watching the creature close on Toby. Its stride is longer than his, but he moves more quickly, more smoothly, and is closing the gap.

'Robbie!' Caroline screams desperately.

Robertson reaches down as he passes the ReGene unit and as the creature reaches out for Toby, and Caroline screams one last time, he throws himself forward, sinking one of Easter's syringes deep into the creature's neck.

The world spins as the creature throws Robertson off and he lands hard among the wreckage, lungs burning as the wind is knocked from his body; as he coughs and claws his way to his feet he sees Caroline closing, aiming the rifle again. He tries to yell at her to stop, but his voice has no volume.

The creature is swaying, one hand pawing at its neck. Then it keels forward, crashing to the floor before Caroline can shoot.

As she advances, holding the rifle in trembling hands, Robertson finally finds the air to wheeze: 'It's David.'

The words are barely a whisper but they carry in the sudden quiet. Caroline pauses in her advance and slowly turns to Robertson.

He meets her eyes and repeats, 'It's David.'

There should be screaming when a marriage ends. Love is meant to grow and evolve, to last a lifetime and its loss should hurt. There should be screaming and crying for what is gone and can never be recovered.

Robertson would have died for Caroline Arquette.

In those first moments, when he watched her dance and saw her face fill with life, when they joked and laughed, when she entwined her fingers with his, he knew. He wanted to spend his life with her and wanted her to be safe and loved for the rest of her days. He still does.

'We've not lost a single man,' Robertson says. 'I wasn't going to start.'

Caroline nods, swallowing hard. 'I understand.'

'We've come so far. It just feels like if we lose one person now, then that's it, that's the sign.' His eyes drop. 'It would all be over.'

'I understand.' She lays her hand across his and squeezes. Robertson looks up to find tears in his wife's eyes. 'It's not your fault, Robbie. None of this is your fault. You can't make it better.'

'I should give up,' Robertson says. 'I know I should give up.' The words swell in his throat and he can barely get them out. He shakes his head. 'But I had to take the risk. I can't give up yet. I just can't –'

'Toby could have died,' Caroline says softly.

'I couldn't give up,' Robertson whispers. 'I won't stop hoping. Not yet. I can't.'

There's a pause then and Caroline's hand slips free from his. Robertson knows what's coming. Their marriage ends not with screaming, but with simple acceptance and three soft words: 'Hope died, Robbie.'

The only time Robertson encountered an actual Rorschach test was on his arrival at Farside Station; some psychological screening one of the coats was running. Everyone knew the principle, though; like lying on your back in the long grass, looking up and seeing shapes in the clouds. The coat had been at great pains to explain how it was impossible to fail a Rorschach test.

A couple of years later, Robertson proved her wrong.

The face appeared from a cloud of static. Never really there, but so clear Robertson could reach out and touch it.

Eighteen months after the Fall and they had been married a year. It had been a couple of months before they were certain, but Caroline was pregnant.

With Greenwich Village still in its infancy, equipment was scarce and life was hard. Neither of them had spoken much about the baby, had made sure the news wasn't common knowledge.

They'd told Easter, though. He managed to rig up a scanner. It wouldn't provide anything like the foetal monitoring that was now standard but, he assured them, it would give some idea of how things were progressing. Robertson had watched as Easter started the scan. He told them there wouldn't be much to see. No more than a heartbeat. But looking into the screen, Robertson found it.

The face appeared in a cloud of static. Small and delicate, eyes closed, cheeks rounded, mouth closed tight in sleep.

Robertson is a practical man, not a man of words. He still doesn't know how to describe what he felt in that moment when their tight, tawdry world fell away and he saw the face.

It was the future and it was hope.

But even before Easter started speaking Robertson remembered: too small to register more than a heartbeat. And in the blink of Robertson's eye the face vanished, lost to the static. Robertson almost cried out, to tell Easter to go back, that he'd had it.

No more than a heartbeat.

He doesn't remember exactly what Easter said to them – something about radiation and malnutrition, chromosomes failing to match, whispered regret – but he remembers Caroline's hand tightening on his.

Robertson remembers the face.

He remembers hope dying.

As Caroline leaves, Robertson has no strength left to follow. He never told her. Never told her that he saw a face once and it will haunt him for the rest of his days.

'They must have transport. They have to have it.'

Easter watches the Professional circle the Meridian. Holding court before, he has been measured in word and movement. Not this morning, though.

David is chained up in one of the stronger cages in the hospital, someone on constant watch with a tranquilliser. Easter wants to get back to work, salvage something from the ReGene unit, understand what happened to David's physiognomy. Except he needs help to get their remaining computer terminal back online and there's none on offer.

Robertson sits mute, alone among the other survivors; Arquette stands, anxious, supposedly chairing the meeting but really just watching the Professional pace. Of the rest, some – Bluth, Alonso, Marcus – are nursing minor injuries from David's rampage, while Garcia and Weir are heading a party to secure the barricades, and others are trying to catch up on their sleep.

There's a bruise on the Professional's cheek where David struck him. Easter knows that's not where the real damage lies.

'They must have supplies, support from somewhere.' The Professional turns to look directly at Easter. 'A ship,' he says. 'An interstix would be the logical answer. But they're alien, their technology would be different. An Earth vessel could never hold position in this atmosphere, but they might be able to. They could be keeping a ship near by. Something to run supplies.'

Easter looks at Arquette, hoping, but there's a distant look in her eyes and she says nothing. It's left to Easter: 'That's supposition.'

'We'll prove it,' the Professional says. 'The external sensors are intact, they just need power. Route the signal through your terminal here and locate their vessel.'

'You'd need to go outside to connect the –'

'My armour can cope with the pressure of Jupiter's atmos –'

'And,' Easter emphasizes, 'even if you did come back in one piece, it's still pointless.'

The Professional blinks.

'Supposing you locate a ship, you can't reach or attack it, can't even trace it for more than a minute or two.'

'The external sensors –'

'Need power.' Easter points to the wreckage around them. 'We can maybe use the one terminal we have left to monitor the signal. But if we divert power to the sensors we have to drop the supply to the barricades.'

The Professional says nothing. On the periphery of his vision, Easter can see Arquette slowly shaking her head. The others are stirring, perhaps listening to him for the first time in years.

'Have you heard them?' Easter says. 'Because there's always one of the enemy out there, testing, waiting for an opportunity. Go and stand at that entrance and listen. There's one of them there, waiting for you to drop the power.'

Among the crowd, Easter finds Anji's face.

She's been quiet since last night; the sight of her friends frozen in time unsettling her. But even Anji, with the promise of madness awaiting her, is nodding encouragement.

'Your plan,' Easter says, 'gains nothing and risks everything. I think –'

'"I think"?' the Professional snaps. '"I think"? You're not in charge here, Easter.'

'No,' Easter answers. 'I let you take that away from me. But that mistake doesn't allow you to –'

The Professional snaps a hand out, grabbing Easter's throat, kicking his feet from under him. Easter lands on the floor, the Professional pinning him down, fingers tightening on his windpipe. He fights, tries to claw at the Professional's arm, but he's too slow, too weak, caught by the speed and ferocity of the attack. The Professional is going to kill him. People are screaming, pulling at the Professional's arm, but he's stronger than all of them and the motors in his armour make the hand an immovable vice.

There's a sharp crack and the Professional's head snaps forward, blood trickling down one temple as his eyes flutter and close. He is hauled off Easter, revealing Robertson, a length of pipe in his hand.

'Strip that armour and lock him up,' Robertson says.

There's a moment's silence, then Bluth and Jones take an arm each and begin dragging the Professional away. It's only now that Arquette finds her voice: 'Stop. I'm telling you to stop. He's our only link to Earth Forces. If we're going to help in the –'

'There is no war.'

Everyone stops then.

It's Anji's voice. Heads turn towards her, but she can't meet their eyes. 'He lied,' she says. 'I shouldn't have gone along with it, but...' The words die on her lips. Under the weight of everyone's stare, all she says is: 'There is no war. There never has been. I'm sorry.'

Her head lifts and Easter can see the shame as she absorbs the look on all their faces.

'I'm sorry,' she repeats. And then she turns and walks away.

It's an hour since the meeting. An hour since the Professional was confined to the hospital. An hour since Anji Kapoor revealed his deceit.

Robertson shrugs off Easter's gratitude, gets to work mending the barricades.

Easter tries to piece together the ReGene unit.

* * *

Caroline Arquette sits at the remaining terminal, flicking through the security download.

It was another life. I don't know if I remember life before this. I'm not sure I can ever be that person again.

Arquette looks across the Village to where her husband works, power and life drained from him.

I'm not sure I can ever be that person again.

She has her answer now. Arquette switches the monitor off and walks away. When Joshua Easter looks up, he sees a scrap of cloth left by the terminal.

Nearing her habitat, Arquette's eye is caught by a flash of silver. Light catching on the fishbowl of Kapoor's helmet, the rest of her suit piled near by. Arquette pauses, looks around, but Kapoor is nowhere to be seen.

The Professional recognises the smell as he wakes: he's with the Wounded. A cautious hand finds tender skin and dried blood on his skull. More worrying than pain, though, everything feels distant, like he is living a dream.

He scratches at his bare biceps. He's been stripped of his armour, of course, and has limited hope of breaking free. This cage is solid. Without some kind of tool, there's little he can achieve against welded metal.

As he tests the bars, he realises he is not alone. Sitting near to the door Caroline Arquette watches him, gun in hand. Only when he's done testing does she speak.

'Who are you?'

The Professional frowns. 'I don't understand.'

Arquette's voice is quiet and thin. 'You lied about the war. You used me, made a fool of me. What happened? Who are you?'

The Professional looks at her. The light is dim, but he can see tears on her cheeks.

'Where's my equipment?' he asks. 'My armour, the datafiles.'

'The armour's safe. The pad they gave to Toby.' She laughs, hoarse and cold. 'David damaged his. He thinks yours is a lot better.'

There's a pause, then she gets to her feet, crosses to stand in front of his cage. They look at each other, neither moving, then Arquette reaches out a hand, slipping it between the bars to touch his face. Her fingertips are cold.

'You're feverish,' she says.

'Training is based on routine. We adapt in combat situations. I made an error removing the armour.' He pulls away from her touch. 'It's this place. How did you survive down here? It's small, stifling, so dark.' He looks at her. 'Don't you miss the sun?'

'Why was it a mistake to remove the armour?' Arquette asks. 'When we were hunting the enemy, yes? Was that the mistake?'

'Never remove the protection around the physical control unit. It's one of the basic instructions.' He pauses, blinks, shaking his head, trying to clear his thoughts. 'We're told to adapt in combat. It was a qualified risk.'

'That's why you attacked Easter?' Arquette says. 'Because you'd lost your medication?'

His head snaps towards her: 'We have to reactivate the sensors. The external sensors. It's the only thing that matters.'

He still has flashes of lucidity amidst the dream. He has one now, looking at Arquette's face. Reluctant, but she still wants to believe. *You used me, made a fool of me.* So he tells her the truth. 'Look out that door. Look at your fellows. Look at what truth has done. Tell me I was wrong to lie.'

'I don't care,' Arquette says, her voice slowly breaking. 'It doesn't matter.'

It's what she doesn't say that the Professional hears.

He once ran OpTech to an Earth Forces unit out on the rim. The look on Arquette's face is the same as the way those soldiers looked. Orders and objectives were irrelevant. They were damaged, all they wanted was to fight back. It no longer mattered what the fight was.

She has it all prepared, he is suddenly sure. Before she snuck in here, she worked out what they needed. She's carrying his gun, probably has his suit near by. Any guard is dismissed or unconscious. Arquette's prepared. All she needs is to hear the words.

The Professional reaches out between the bars, taking her hand as he makes the only promise that will buy his freedom: 'Find their ship and I'll kill them all.'

Easter is buried in the ReGene unit when his name is called. Garcia and Carvacchio, shepherding Anji towards the Meridian; stripped of her armour, feet unsteady, a drowsy angle to her head.

'What happened?' he asks. He's worried about the enemy's infection. The answer he gets is not even close.

'Found her by the airlock,' Garcia answers. 'She said Arquette and the Professional attacked her, took her suit.'

Easter lies Anji down on a nearby cot. As he checks her pupils, he asks, 'What are you talking about?'

'The airlock by the exterior doors cycled five minutes ago. Carvacchio and I went to check, to make sure there wasn't a malfunction or something.'

'You're sure it was –'

'The Professional's gone, his suit is gone.' Garcia points to where Anji lies in her underwear. 'Hers is gone too.'

'Damn it,' Easter snaps. 'If he's free with a willing accomplice –'

'We know,' Carvacchio answers. 'But no one was expecting him to be a fake, no one expected Arquette to still be on his side.'

Easter attaches Anji to the terminal's triage diagnostic, then turns to Garcia and Carvacchio: 'Set a guard by the airlock. They've got to come back some time; hopefully, it'll be there.'

'And if they do?'

'Short the exterior door, keep them confined until they tell us what they've been up to.' Easter glances towards the barricades. 'You'd better get Robertson; she might still listen to him.'

When they're gone, Easter draws some blood from Anji and starts the analysis program.

Repairing the ReGene unit is going to be weeks of work, making this as good a time as any to check the status of Anji's infection. The system already has a copy of the blood work he ran when she was brought into the Village two days ago. A basic compare and contrast with the new sample is all that's required.

With her blood work clear and the DNA analysis confirming she was human, Easter hadn't looked too hard at Anji's original results: fit and well, clearly in better shape than anyone else on this station. There simply hadn't been the need. But as he sets up the test on the new sample, Easter checks that data over, just to be sure there's nothing to confuse the analysis program.

A small red icon is flashing next to the gene pairs governing Anji's immune system.

Easter leans forward, his face reflected in the screen as he traces a finger across the code. The distortion has its centre in the immune system, but there are traces of it throughout her body, specifically the parts governing chemical activity in her brain. Easter is reassured in one way: he's seen the enemy's infection often enough to know that this isn't it. But that's small comfort. Whatever the infection is, it's taken years to rewrite Anji's DNA.

Something else flashes on-screen. The results from the triage diagnostic: no concussion, no fracture, no injury at all. Easter checks for a bug in the program. Because if Anji wasn't attacked, then she's given up her suit willingly, which makes no sense.

As he leans back in his chair, Easter's reflection no longer fills the monitor. Instead, he can see Anji unfolding from the cot behind him in one fluid movement, reaching down to pick up a piece of debris.

As Easter turns, he's already far too late.

Robertson reaches the airlock just in time: the exterior door is creeping open.

He feels sick as he looks through the glass.

When Garcia found him, he didn't need to be told; he could guess what Caroline had done. The wife he loves is lost, all he's left with is what others expect of him. As he looks through the airlock door, his face reflected in the visor of Caroline's stolen spacesuit, he knows she feels the same.

The Professional just paces the airlock, tapping instructions into his suit, drumming his fingers against the walls.

Robertson activates the speaker: 'What did you do to Anji?'

Caroline's voice hisses with static: 'What are you talking about?'

'You're wearing her suit,' Robertson snaps. 'What did you do to get it off her?'

Caroline's face is invisible behind the mirrored helmet. 'Nothing,' she answers.

Robertson shakes his head. 'I don't believe you.'

'Atmosphere reaching normal,' Garcia says.

'Hold it there,' Robertson answers. 'Lock the interior door. Any trouble, start venting –'

The alarm blares, weapons fire sounding from the entrance.

'Enemy,' Carvacchio says.

Robertson's first instinct is that Carvacchio's right. Except that the enemy constantly test the barricades. Only no one ever sounds the alarm for that and the weapons fire isn't stopping.

Robertson runs, Garcia and Carvacchio behind him. As they clear the greenhouses, the main entrance is illuminated by flashes of light: the yellow of gunfire, electric-blue from the barricades.

It should be over by now, the enemy should be retreating, but Robertson knows that isn't going to happen. Not this time. He grabs a weapon from the rack, pumping rounds into the chamber, the very last reserves of his energy gathering inside of him.

It's not just one or two of the enemy. They fill the east and west corridors, pushing against the barriers, gunfire ricocheting off carapaces. Weir and Alonso are already there; Marcus marshalling others; Archer holding a gun in trembling hands. Garcia and Carvacchio step up next to Robertson, finding places in the line.

'Concentrate your fire,' Weir shouts. 'Front targets! West corridor!'

And they raise their weapons, joining the fusillade.

As he breathes cordite, Robertson hopes the airlock door will be enough to hold the Professional.

Arquette watches as the Professional hauls Easter's body from the terminal and drops him to the floor. She kneels down, presses her fingertips against his neck. There's blood on his face, but the pulse is strong enough.

There's no sign the enemy have breached the defences. 'Who did this?' Arquette asks.

'It doesn't matter,' the Professional answers.

And only then does Arquette realise what he's doing: accessing the energy supply grid. It only took him thirty seconds to crack the code

Four years earlier

'Only hope breaks a chain.'

Robertson whispered the words, his lips brushing her ear, his hand warm on her shoulder. Caroline smiled, rolled towards him. 'What is that?'

'One of Jason's poems,' Robertson answered. 'My kind of poetry. Short.'

Caroline sat up on the bed, looking around his quarters. 'What time is it?'

'Almost ten. I'm due on shift in fifteen minutes. New equipment for the medical bays, supplies for hydroponics.' He grinned. 'All exciting stuff. What about you?'

'Same shift, same location.' She gave him a hard stare. 'Still trying to sort out the mess your guy made with the electronics yesterday.'

'Archer should know better than to mess about with a comms panel.'

Caroline rescued her uniform blouse from the top of a nearby chair. She gave Robertson a smile. 'Means I can meet you for lunch, though.'

He smiled. 'Every cloud…'

The Doctor lay back on the operating table, wrists and ankles fixed down. The automated arm of the surgical computer swivelled above him, a thin beam slicing his shirt open.

It was Valletti who raised her hand, calling a temporary halt. 'Interesting wound, Doctor.' She nodded to his abdomen. 'How did you get it?'

'Saving the *Pegasus* from one of your men.' He tested the restraints, but there was no give. Looking directly at Valletti, he implored: 'This isn't the Earth you believe in.'

Valletti just turned to Sara Mukabi. 'Start with the blood work around this wound; nothing invasive until we have some answers.'

'Those creatures lining the walls are not resources,' the Doctor said. 'They're people, with cultures, beliefs and families of their own. Everyone has something they want to protect.'

'They're all as good as dead, anyway,' Sara snapped. She manipulated the controls and a clear probe extended, burying itself in his wound.

The Doctor gasped, then clenched his teeth, glaring at Sara. 'I wish I could say the only inhuman thing was the way you're denying them the release they deserve. But your little project to overcome the flight-or-fight impulse is equally insane. You pulled strings to get this station located here. What other short cuts have you taken? Are there any medical bodies that validate illegal research?'

'You're not helping yourself, Doctor.' Blood bubbled in the probe. 'Analysis under way,' Sara said to Valletti.

A video screen came to life: an image of the Doctor's blood, slowly increasing in magnification.

'Unusual iron levels, unique structure to the white blood cells. Indicative of quite impressive recuperative powers.' Sara turned towards Valletti. 'Some basic similarities, but that blood is not –'

The restraints on the table clicked open as the probe withdrew.

McCray sprang forward, but the Doctor swivelled, lashing out and catching him with the heel of his boot. The paratrooper fell back, blood streaming from his broken nose.

Sara reached for the controls, only to cry out as light flared and a pinpoint scorch mark blistered her sleeve. Everyone looked at her, then after a moment's pause the blinding light returned.

Pulses flashed from laser tracks around the room. The Mukabis and the 101st dived for cover. Valletti reached for the Doctor, only for him to drag her down behind the operating table as a blast struck the point where she'd stood a moment earlier. A paratrooper levelled his weapon, only to have it shot from his hand as the laser fire intensified.

'I really am sorry,' the Doctor told Valletti. Then he chopped at her neck and she collapsed on the floor.

The Doctor waited a moment, studying the firing pattern, then broke cover, racing towards the door. He grabbed Fitz's hand, pulling on the airlock door. The external sensors will be powered up in half that time.

'Stop it,' she says. There's a scream from the entrance. 'We'll lose the barricades.'

'Acceptable risk,' the Professional snaps. 'We have to find their ship.'

'Not now!' Arquette says, reaching out to grab him. 'You have to wait until –'

But he swings around, punches her full in the face. Arquette tumbles over Easter's body, blood in her mouth. By the time she's back on her knees, the Professional is already executing the sensor sweep.

There's a click as the defences switch off, and everyone hears the hum of the electrical charge vanish.

Someone shouts: 'Hold steady!'

There's a moment of caution as the first of the enemy touches the barricade. Then, with no flash of electricity, they swarm forward, clawing at each other and the walls and hacking at obstacles; automated weapons are torn from their posts.

People begin to creep backwards.

There's a panic Robertson has never seen in the survivors before. Deep down, they know: this is the end. The collective will that's kept them alive breaks and they push past him to escape, every one forgetting the Village is a closed environment. There's nowhere to escape to.

Robertson thinks of the face that haunts him. All the hopes he had in that single moment, the sights he wanted to show his child, the things he wanted to teach, the way he wanted to be a better man as a result.

He thinks of the face and knows there's nowhere left to hide.

So Robertson stops moving and he turns, raising his gun. And as the enemy break through the barricades and rush into the compound, he starts firing.

The survivors push through the compound, their flight tearing it apart. Colliding with each other, tables overturned, barrels falling, the forge tumbling in a blaze of flame. Amidst it all, the Professional is unmoving at the computer terminal, trying to block out the chaos around him. There's a coldness within him. He wants to scream and fight until there is silence and he can think and do what needs to be done. An impulse that's been building for days, since the control unit was destroyed, since before then.

The Station is too close, too hot. Ragged and unpleasant, surfaces coated in rust, the air warm and damp and stale. It is impossible to breathe here.

He needs to escape this place.

To his right Arquette throws herself forward, wrapping the child in her arms, stumbling away as the enemy close in. There is a clatter as the pad the boy was holding falls to the ground.

None of this matters.

The sensor sweep scrolls over the screen: a hazy outline of the Station, scrolling information about windspeed, radiation levels, magnetics. The image shrinks as the sensor wave pushes out, covering a greater and greater area. And then, finally, the screen blinks, reforming as the sweep begins again.

There is no spaceship within 100,000 kilometres of the Station.

The Professional feels the pulse in his throat crushing the air from his body, the energy from his limbs. He squeezes his eyes shut.

The screaming and the chaos are all too familiar.

His knees give way and he falls backwards. In the distance there is the whoosh of a small explosion and he can feel its heat on his skin. There is a sweat on his brow and he wants to tear at his armour, to break it away so that his chest can expand and he can breathe once more. He needs to breathe.

There are footsteps near by.

The Professional's eyes flutter shut, opening to see...

The computer pad the child was playing with is lying on the floor. The image blinking at him shows the co-ordinates he entered from the Ghost file. No longer mapped on to the Station architecture or swivelling and rotating around three dimensions in search of the correct fit.

They are laid out across two plain axes.

And the boy has simply joined the dots the co-ordinates represent to produce a simple and elegant picture.

him out from behind a console, shielding him with his body and throwing him forward.

Fitz tumbled through the lab door. He took one last glance back into the tall chamber, filled with laser beams, then the door slid shut. The Doctor examined it for a moment, then shrugged and drove his elbow into the keypad, smashing the lock.

Fitz could still smell smoke. 'What the hell was that?'

'These labs are fitted with very sophisticated intruder-alert capabilities,' the Doctor said.

'That just go haywire and shoot everybody?'

'No,' the Doctor snapped. 'That shoot anybody who isn't me.'

'Is that your escape plan?' Fitz started towards the exit. 'This Jericho thing?'

'No, Jericho was a subroutine in the comms system. The one Valletti found and disabled.' The Doctor frowned at Fitz. 'What are you doing?'

Fitz paused. 'Escaping?'

The Doctor shook his head, climbing the gantry towards one of the control consoles. 'Not yet. Those lasers were nothing to do with me.'

Fitz started after him. 'So now what?'

The Doctor was working the console, casting quick glances at the door to the other chamber. 'We've been asking the wrong questions, looking for a "who?" the entire time. We should have been looking at the evidence and asking "why?" and "what?"' He tapped the console, emphasising the words. 'Something activated that security net to protect me just now. Why? Sara Mukabi's distilling something from the atmosphere. What? The pilot of the *Pegasus* was trying to destroy the ship in Jupiter's atmosphere. Why? The defence grid opened up and targeted Jupiter's atmosphere. Why?'

'McCray said something, how you could hide an alien fleet down –'

The Doctor shook his head. 'It wouldn't explain why this wound hasn't healed.'

And finally Fitz caught on, the way the Doctor had been studying the screen as he hectored Sara Mukabi. 'You saw something, didn't you? On her scan.'

'Valletti said AuDoc wasn't attacked by the security systems. Something else was responsible. And you'd need a very smart and adaptive computer virus to get the better of AuDoc.' The Doctor nodded. 'Curiously, the thing I saw on the scan of my blood was an infection. Something probably carried by the pilot's blood on the harpoon. A very smart and adaptive infection.'

'How the hell could that get into the computers?'

'It all depends on how smart and adaptive it is.' The Doctor punched a control and a hologram appeared in the centre of the room. 'This is a simulation of Jupiter's weather systems, probably using a sample of the atmosphere to create an accurate template.'

'So?'

'There are patterns of activity I want to look for.' The Doctor zoomed in through weather fronts and clouds, getting closer and closer in, his hands working the controls.

A glass of water had been left by the console. As Fitz leant over to watch what the Doctor was doing, he knocked it over. The glass rolled off the edge of the console, tumbling away to smash on the floor below.

'The two that attacked Anji,' Fitz said. 'They worked in the cargo bay, didn't they?'

'Yes,' the Doctor murmured, 'but only for a couple of days.'

The image zeroed in: clouds swallowed the room, dust particles exploded to the size of planets, zooming in on nothing at all. Fitz guessed they were at some kind of microscopic resolution now. Then a chain of spheres appeared, twisting and turning.

'Got you,' the Doctor whispered.

Something else caught Fitz's eye. A screen had come to life on an adjacent console, information flashing at tremendous speed. He pointed. 'What's that?'

The Doctor frowned. 'I don't know.'

He overlaid the screen's contents on the hologram. It was moving too fast for him to make sense of it; brief flashes showed the Station and equations, personnel files streaming across the edge of the hologram. A repeating sequence, playing over and over again.

Then there was a crash, sparks flying as the door burst open. The hologram folded in on itself and they were plunged into the red of emergency lighting.

The 101st advanced into the lab, weapons levelled at the Doctor and Fitz.

* * *

Valletti explained that no finger of suspicion pointed at them. Robertson suspected this was true, but the fact that the commander was conducting the interview with him and Caroline told him something was seriously wrong.

Fitz and his friend had travelled using good forgeries, Valletti said, and – whatever their motives – were highly skilled at infiltration techniques.

'I don't care,' Robertson said. 'I never met the other guy, but Fitz is solid.'

Valletti rubbed the back of her neck. 'There's no –'

'I hear what you're saying, Commander; I just can't square it with what I saw. They saved the *Pegasus*, this Doctor guy saved Jason, they were both nearly killed in that hull breach.'

Caroline laid a hand on his arm. 'Robbie.'

'No.' He shook his head. 'I'm sorry, I'm not security, but I'm good with people. And Fitz is a good man. I'd bet my life on that.'

'The evidence says otherwise.'

Robertson shrugged. 'I can't help the evidence. You're asking my opinion, Commander. I'm giving it to you.'

Valletti turned to Caroline. 'What about you?'

There was a pause, Caroline looking between Valletti and Robertson. He could see the light in her eyes, like they were still dancing.

'I trust Robbie's judgement,' Caroline said.

Valletti sighed. 'You're not making life any easier.' Her communicator chimed and she got to her feet. 'Wait here.'

As she left, Robertson and Caroline looked at each other. 'Thank you,' Robertson said.

'Do you really believe what you said?' Caroline asked.

Robertson's replies had been front to an extent, the result of being taken by surprise. Now that Caroline was asking, he considered his answer and found it the same. 'Yes,' he said. 'Yes, I do.'

Caroline nodded. 'Good,' she said.

As she did so, Robertson looked past her. Valletti had left via the main door, but behind the desk was an entrance to the brig. The light on its keypad was green.

* * *

Fitz had been given a first-aid kit to patch the Doctor's wounds with. It was something he had gotten used to in the past week. With the Doctor propped up against the cell wall, Fitz was securing another layer of bandage when there was a tap at the door.

Fitz peered through the glass panel in the door. 'It's Robbie.'

The voice was muffled, but Robertson's baritone was still audible enough. 'How you guys doing?'

'We've had better days.'

A pause, then: 'What's going on, Fitz?'

As Fitz opened his mouth to speak, the Doctor slowly shook his head. And Fitz understood. Even if Robbie could get them out of the cell there was nowhere to run.

'Long story,' Fitz answered. 'We came here because a friend of ours had been hurt.'

'Anyone I know?'

'I don't know,' Fitz smiled. 'Ever heard of Anji Kapoor?'

'No,' Robertson answered.

'Best you don't get involved, then.'

Robertson nodded and smiled through the glass.

'Robbie,' Fitz said, 'when we first met, you told me something. You said anyone who breaks things on your team doesn't stay on your team. Did you mean it?'

The Doctor glanced at him then, a smile of admiration creeping across his face. Fitz grinned in return as Robbie said, 'It's the rule I work to.'

'I've got a question,' the Doctor called out.

Robertson frowned at the new voice. He craned his head, unable to make out the Doctor through the small window. 'That your friend?' Robertson asked. Fitz nodded.

'The 101st deal with the restricted cargo. What about atmosphere samples?'

'No,' Robertson answered. 'That's our job.'

'A couple of men were transferred out of cargo six weeks ago. Was that because they broke something?'

Robertson nodded. 'A capsule from a research shuttle. The pilot released it too early, they failed to hold it.'

The Doctor smiled, leaning back against the wall. 'What happened to the pilot?'

Robertson glanced back down the cell bay. 'Relegated to passenger duty.' Another glance, then he said, 'I've got to go,' and vanished.

Fitz looked at the Doctor. 'Three people break the capsule. Two end up on shore leave, one on a passenger transport.'

The Doctor nodded. 'And we've met all three. Good work, Fitz.'

'What about all the others? Deschamps?'

'Our mad scientist,' the Doctor said, 'is just a bad-tempered scientist.'

'And Archer?'

'The source of those unauthorised transmissions and in possession of those stolen files Valletti mentioned. And nothing to do with any of this.'

The call that had summoned Valletti was from the security team in C&C.

The AI the Doctor had used to penetrate the secure files was still in the systems. Security's bloodhound programs had achieved some success, deleting parts of its core programming before it escaped into the maintenance systems on the outer rings.

Like an old submariner, the AI was running silent and deep.

Like old warriors, the security team were brandishing the limbs they'd managed to cut off before it escaped. In this case, the AI's language centres.

Which, Valletti supposed, wasn't a bad thing. Although security hadn't been able to trace its path, they were assuming it was the AI that had taken control of the Avatar lab's defence screen. If the AI didn't have direct language centres any more, it would have trouble obeying any vocal commands from the Doctor.

Caroline was casting nervous glances at the door when Robertson returned. He smiled quickly, sitting down just as Valletti returned; she shook her head. 'There are cameras in the cell bay.'

'They didn't ask me to help,' Robertson answered. 'They had the opportunity, they didn't ask the question.'

His stare met hers. There was a brief silence, then Robertson finally broke away.

Valletti shook her head again, said quietly, 'You're dismissed, both of you. Get back to work.'

The Doctor and Fitz were being frogmarched from the brig. Fitz kept on tugging at his handcuffs, but there was no sign of any give. The Doctor, he noticed, wasn't even doing that.

'What you said last night,' Valletti commented, 'about the reasons why implants were made illegal? It has interesting implications.'

'Such as?' the Doctor said.

'The loss of privacy. And how the Riley Act makes no provision for loss of privacy among alien life forms.'

'Allow me to let you into a secret,' the Doctor replied. 'I'm not concerned about your project or the arms race with Earth Forces on Mars. They're a side issue. A misguided and dangerous side issue, but they're not the problem.'

'And what is?' Valletti sighed, stopping as they reached the lift.

The Doctor stepped forward. It didn't matter that he was the one in chains or that Valletti had the men with guns backing her up. In that moment, the Doctor towered over her.

'There's a contagion loose on this station,' he said.

Valletti just stared at him.

The Doctor shook his head. Fitz could hear the frustration in his voice. 'Two hundred years into the future and you're all still the same. You've done so much and come so far. But underneath it all, the same bitterness, the same anxieties, the same baseless fears.'

'I've been charmed by you, Doctor,' Valletti said. 'Do you really think I'm going to be any more impressed by your slurs?'

'The evidence is all around,' he snapped. 'You only have to look.'

The lift doors opened and Fitz and the Doctor were pushed inside. As the lift rose the Doctor looked at Valletti again. 'The thing that Sara Mukabi is distilling from Jupiter's atmosphere, the thing that lets her create Nightmare, is an organism, a virus that's probably been there thousands of years.'

'I'm well aware of what Sara Mukabi is doing,' Valletti said.

'And neutered as Nightmare that virus is largely harmless. Its raw form is another matter. The Mukabis ran a simulation of Jupiter's weather systems to locate stockpiles of the gas the virus lives in, yes?'

Valletti said nothing.

'When they did that,' the Doctor continued, 'they created a virtual version of the virus itself. And viruses evolve, Commander. So when the simulation pushed forward ten thousand years that virus got very smart, very quickly. It became aware of its environment.'

'It escaped,' Fitz said.

'The security protocols around the Avatar system are very efficient at stopping intruders getting in, not stopping things getting out.' The Doctor paused. 'The malfunctions, system failures, even the excessive maintenance are the result of this virus exploring its surroundings.'

Valletti turned to him, impatient. 'And how does this explain your escape from the lab?'

'When my AI breached the secure files the virus followed it back in. That gave it access to the defence systems. It's the virus that fired the gun batteries yesterday, the same virus that activated the security systems in the lab.' He paused. 'It recognised a threat to its biological counterpart, the one in my blood.'

Valletti was silent and Fitz could see the Doctor's shoulders tensing. His voice grew harsh: 'The one that infected the pilot and those soldiers when they broke that research capsule.'

Still no reply.

'One that could have infected a friend of mine, that could be loose on Mars.' He slammed his fists into the side of the lift. 'You have a responsibility here!'

And finally Valletti turned to him. 'My responsibility is to Earth.'

The doors opened, revealing the interior of the Mukabis' lab. There was still an acrid smell in the air and the players, Fitz thought, remained largely the same. Sara Mukabi now had her arm in a sling, the 101st looked impassively on. The only difference was the figure laid out on the second operating table: Jason McCray.

'What's going on here?' the Doctor snapped.

'We're testing your hypothesis about the dangers of the implants,' Valletti said. 'You're not allergic to titanium, I hope.'

'What do you need Jason for?'

'You fooled the Avatar program once.'

'You're using Jason as a filter to screen out any duplicity on my part.' The Doctor's anger was spent now, replaced by an overwhelming sadness. 'This is foolishness, Jennifer.'

'No one's coming to help you, Doctor. Your AI is crippled, the security systems in this lab have been isolated. Your only option is to explain what you're doing here, what your species is planning.'

'I can't.'

'Then I can do nothing for you.'

The Doctor gave Fitz what he hoped was a reassuring smile, then slipped his jacket off and handed it over to his friend.

This time he didn't protest as he was secured to the table.

The important thing was to deal with the virus, both real and virtual, before the situation got out of hand. Except he couldn't do that until he was shown to be innocent. Unpalatable though it was, the implant was the best opportunity to prove his word. It wasn't an easy option, though. If the link became unbalanced there was a real danger he'd lose himself in the mix.

Then there was the virus itself fighting his system.

It had clearly learnt from its initial attacks on human hosts. He suspected it was trying to use his DNA's recuperative abilities to its advantage somehow. If Anji was infected, he hoped it was taking the same approach. Otherwise, by the time they got back to Mars she'd have been driven mad by the virus, like those troopers had been.

The immediate trouble was he'd never been certain how much control he had over his body's systems. The prospect of the virus gaining a hold on him while he was distracted by the mind-link worried him. As cocktails went, it was as volatile as the stasis fluid that held the alien bodies.

The table swivelled, leaving him face down and looking at the floor, the back of his head exposed. Sara Mukabi's voice sounded, something cold pressed against his spine. 'This may sting a bit.'

'I can't believe this is happening.' Fitz turned to Valletti. 'I can't believe you're doing this.'

'I wish I weren't,' Valletti snapped. The icy tone had an undercurrent of regret now. She didn't want to do it, but she didn't have any choice.

'He doesn't remember anything,' Fitz said. 'There's no information for you to find.'

Sara Mukabi studied her console. 'Good readings on the link; signal strong and clear.' She turned to Valletti. 'We're ready whenever you give the order.'

Valletti glanced at Fitz, then nodded. 'Proceed.'

Sara called over to her husband, 'Bring the Avatar system online. It'll take a minute or two to calibrate the system.'

'And after that?' Valletti asked.

'Anything we retrieve should be displayed in Avatar form.'

'Good.' Valletti nodded. 'I want this done with.'

Fitz looked at the video screens. Most had been blank as Sara inserted the probe into the Doctor's skull, only a handful showing schematics of the procedure. Now that the Mukabis' contraption was starting up, more and more screens flicked into life. As Sara manipulated the controls Fitz caught flashes of familiar images: the blue of a police box; Anji smiling; one of the princesses from Earthworld. Then things he didn't recognise: a blonde teenager; a city consumed by flame; a statue falling into a river.

And then he noticed something else that was familiar.

One corner of one of the screens was filled with the same mess of data they'd seen in the Avatar room a couple of hours earlier. Only, as he looked Fitz noticed something he hadn't seen earlier: a counter in the bottom corner of the screen, ticking away towards 100 per cent.

'Now 99.5,' Fitz read, frowning. 'Up to 99.6.'

Valletti looked at him. 'What are you talking about?'

'That screen.' Fitz pointed. 'What's it for?'

But as Valletti turned to look, the counter hit 100 and the screen went dark.

Valletti turned to one of the 101st. 'Restrain him.'

Except there was no response from the paratrooper. 'Lieutenant,' Valletti said, 'I ordered you to –'

She was cut off as the Doctor screamed.

Eyes shut a moment before snapped open, his back arched against the table, jaw wide in pain. Then he collapsed, head slumping to one side.

'What happened?' Valletti demanded.

'I don't know,' Sara answered. 'An upsurge in computer activity caused an imbalance. Terrance?'

Her husband was studying the nearby screens. 'All nonsense. Personnel orders, power surges, security programs going crazy. I need to compensate.'

Fitz was looking at the Doctor. His eyes had shut again but his lips were moving.

'What's he saying?' Fitz asked.

Valletti knelt down by the table. 'It sounds like... It sounds like some kind of poem.'

There was a moment of silence as the Doctor's voice filled the laboratory. Then a pneumatic hiss sounded as every door slid open.

'What the hell?' Valletti murmured.

She was crossing to a comms panel when she was shoved aside by McCray. Without a word, the 101st were striding towards the exits. By the time Valletti had picked herself up they had vanished.

'Something's happening,' Terrance said urgently. 'Environmental controls have been hacked, air pressure's increasing in the outer rings. Every door and hatch is open for a dozen floors.' One of the screens flared. 'That power surge is building again.'

Fitz saw Terrance's eyes go wide as he studied the console.

'Get them out of there,' Terrance shouted, punching a control. The restraints holding the Doctor and Jason clicked open. 'Get them out!'

The Doctor knew something had gone wrong.

The link was painful at first, but he'd been able to relax his mind in the end. It was cruder than the machine on Earthworld, but the principles remained similar. Jason McCray was a shadow across his mind, echoes of old passions and fears and feelings, but no more than that. Then searing heat had lanced through his thoughts and the shadow had gained substance, had weight and form, and was thrashing around inside his head.

He was going into shock.

Something was happening inside his body. His system was already traumatised by the infection; this new pain was suddenly more than he could bear. Then the link closed down. He could feel it click off and to draw him in. As he tumbled and twisted in the air, he could see it then, a cloud racing after him, trying to swallow him whole.

Even in his shattered state he recognised it. The cloud was the pink of the stasis fluid.

He was slowing, the wind roaring in his ears. The bottom was close now. He screamed at the fire on his back, the broken bones from his fall, the voice inside his mind.

He screamed.

And then the fall ended, the cloud solidifying, catching him on its outer edge. There was just enough momentum left to pull him free of its grip. And he fell the last two metres to the base of the lift shaft.

Glancing up, he could see the cloud filling the shaft. With an electric shimmer, it was gas no longer, growing solid. Steam to water to ice in a second.

And there it was, a glistening black wall suspended above him.

The Doctor's body screamed with the movement as he turned, reaching out to grasp the lip of the shaft, to pull himself up and out through the open doorway. He got halfway before the pain became too much. Every cell in his body on fire, as though it were fighting itself. He raised his head to look down the corridor in front of him.

And then his strength deserted him and his head fell forward, and his eyes fluttered shut, before opening to see...

THE SYSTEM COLONIES

McNamara looked at the squad. The helmets left them anonymous, but occasional flashes of light across the visors told him they were reviewing orders. All except one: Nine.

Garvin had seen it too, nodded towards Nine. McNamara just waved him away.

The engines deepened as the dropship hit atmosphere.

As one, the Professionals formed a line down the centre of the hold. The rear door dropped. A purple sky lay beyond. They stepped forward, activating thruster packs. Nine was second to last. Like the others, no hesitation as he jumped.

As the door closed, Garvin shook his head. 'Too soon.'

'He's been imprinted more than three years. He's been in-field before.'

'On support missions,' Garvin replied. 'And it's not the time that counts, you know that.' He shook his head. 'The personality imprint registers normal, but he's not ready. I'm not sure he'll ever be ready. OpTech? Analysis? Yes. Not combat.'

McNamara studied the tactical board as he answered. 'He's fast. Faster than all the others. Not physically, but the way he thinks. It's what makes him the best of them.'

'In training. He only goes along with it because he knows they're simulations.'

'That's just your theory.'

McNamara thumbed a nearby control pad. Images from the remote drones materialised over the board. He focused in on Nine, who was holding the rear as the squad closed on the insurgents' camp. An idea was forming in his mind. Putting Garvin's theory to the test.

'Patch me in. Closed comms with One, Five, Six and Eight.'

* * *

wondered what was happening. It should have been a relief, but it wasn't. He could still feel Jason McCray inside his head. And what the Doctor had suspected before he now knew for certain.

Jason McCray had been the leader of the 101st before his brother. The first to undergo Sara Mukabi's rigorous testing procedures, his implant had worked fine. It was an experimental version of Nightmare that had crippled him.

He had overdosed on fear.

Jason would remember the man he had been and wonder, afraid, what had happened to him. He would try to take solace in writing, but the inability to verbalise the words he wrote confounded him. He would see his brother and comrades, and the knowledge that he no longer belonged made him shake. Every step, every glance, every touch, taste and sensation in every waking moment provoked only one reaction.

Fear.

The Doctor could feel all of this now. And he screamed.

Electricity flared across the Mukabis' equipment. The computer banks overloaded, raining sparks.

Before Fitz or Valletti could reach the operating tables the massive surgical arm exploded, the fireball swallowing Jason and the Doctor. By the time Fitz picked himself up, the centre of the lab was lost to smoke and flame.

'Doctor!' Fitz shouted.

He saw a silhouette, its back aflame, and ran, launching himself forward, bringing the man down, rolling him over and over and smothering the flames with the Doctor's jacket.

It wasn't the Doctor, though.

The body flinched and stirred against him, and Fitz pressed the jacket down against the smouldering torso. 'It's all right, Jason,' he said, 'you're going to be all right.'

As Sara Mukabi moved in to help, Fitz glanced back into the pillar of flame. 'Doctor!' he shouted again.

'Oh, no,' Sara said beside him. 'The stasis capsules.'

Fitz looked up and the clear glass cylinders lining the walls were suddenly broiling, the pink liquid churning as the energy surge that had swept through the lab equipment was poured into the stasis fluid.

'We're losing stability on the fluid. Volume and pressure increasing exponentially.'

'Shut it down!' Valletti screamed at Terrance. 'Close the doors and shut everything down!'

'I can't!' He pounded the computer bank. 'The environmental systems have gone haywire!'

Movement caught Fitz's eyes and then he saw him, a man of fire, freeing himself from a blazing backdrop, clothing alight, skin blistering and burning. Stumbling across the laboratory for some kind of safety. He fell, rolling across the floor, trying to put the fire out, mostly succeeding. Another explosion puckered the floor between them and Fitz couldn't reach him, could only watch as he pulled himself away from the flames, began to stumble to his feet, to run.

Fitz heard Valletti cry out, 'No!'

Only then did he see the danger. The Doctor was stumbling towards one of the doors that had opened as the 101st fled the room. One that opened onto an empty lift shaft.

'Stop him!' Fitz cried. An ache was building in his ears, his breathing was getting heavy. It felt like he was drowning. He could see Valletti, stranded in no man's land, halfway between the Doctor and the comms panel. She turned, activated the intercom: 'Defcon 1! Repeat: Defcon 1!'

The Doctor reached the lift door, teetered on the edge as the flames licked his back, then pitched forward into darkness.

'No!' Fitz screamed.

As he screamed, there were explosions all around him, glass cracking.

And then Fitz knew nothing at all.

The Doctor fell, trailing smoke and flame, body twisting, careening off the lift shaft, light strobing through open doorways all the way down. There was wind on his face, building stronger and stronger. An acid taste filled the air. He saw but did not really comprehend the bottom of the shaft racing towards him. The air pressure increased, as if it were as thick as water, slowing his fall, pushing him back.

And then he could feel it. The speed was draining away, something else was taking hold of him, clawing at the flames on his back, trying

The sky was purple above, the silhouette of the dropship visible against one of the moons. The kind of error that could disrupt the mission profile.

The Professional returned his attention to the camp. The valley rose around it, the other squad members taking position along the ridges. He was back-up, sited in the marshland at the valley's exit. The others would deliver magnesium charges into the camp, destroying the hostiles in one strike.

That strike wasn't due for another minute when the first explosion sounded.

Consulting the head-up display, the Professional could see half the squad hadn't been in place. As a result, the strike was far from clinical.

The squad opened fire from the ridges as the insurgents fled.

The suit registered the sound of the aliens approaching. Cold-blooded, they were difficult to detect on the heat sensors. All save one.

A young man, charging forward, arms and shoulders on fire. The flames cast enough light for the Professional now to see the others. Over two dozen, ploughing through the marshes.

The Professional raised the rifle to his shoulder. Minimal offensive capabilities, already weak and tired, stunned by the attack. Simple targets.

He scanned back and forth across the advancing line.

He did not fire.

He blinked. The suit hissed, a chill in his arm.

The young man was closer now. The Professional could see the magnesium flames. A fire that would burn for days; a long, slow death.

Something was itching inside his head. The suit hissed. He swung the rifle across the group again. A chill in his arm.

He fired.

The young man twisted with the impact, fell back into the marsh, flames still burning beneath the water. A clean shot, an immediately fatal wound.

The rifle motionless at his shoulder, the Professional locked on to the body illuminated beneath the water.

He saw a different face on the body.

The Professional raised his visor, looking at the boy with his own eyes. One of the hostiles screamed, swung a fist, connecting hard with his face. As he rocked backwards, blood streaming from his nose, the insurgents moved past him, wading through the marshland.

The dropship's engines screamed as it circled around, belly guns raking the waters behind him.

The *Aviator* was a state-of-the-art ship, six months out from the lunar dockyards. As its engines fired, driving it back into the system, back towards Mars, the deck in McNamara's cabin shook.

There was a light pen on his desk; all the holoslide required was his signature.

They'd put theory to the test. Twenty-six hostiles; one kill, the target already good as dead.

McNamara picked up the pen.

There was a knock at the door and Garvin entered. He held a holoslide of his own, the black and red lettering marking it EYES ONLY. He nodded at the termination order in McNamara's hand. 'You might want to delay that.'

'You should be pleased. You were right.'

Garvin handed him the slide. 'There's been a development. It's the *Charing Cross*.'

'Captain Southon's ship,' McNamara said, 'stationed in-system, surveying…'

He remembered then, the recollection showing on his face because Garvin nodded.

'They've found it. Deep in the atmosphere, but intact.'

There was a pause, then McNamara activated a comms channel: 'Bridge, this is McNamara. I want a secure signal to Cape Town as soon as we're in range.' He turned to Garvin. 'I want control of that rescue mission.'

Garvin smiled. 'I thought you'd be interested.'

'It's the perfect test for his personality implant.'

'It'll need work. An increased level of sublimator in the medication,' Garvin mused. 'Maybe some other psychological tricks to reinforce it. It's the core personality held in the subconscious that's the problem. If we could give that some kind of outlet…'

'Details,' McNamara snapped. 'Just details to be worked out.' He sat back in his chair, picking up the tumbler of whiskey that had sat untouched since he poured it. 'If he succeeds, we get copies of all the research conducted at Farside. If he rescues any survivors, that's our funding secured for the next decade.' He picked up the termination order, smashed it against the edge of the desk. 'And if he fails, he dies a hero and it's no reflection on the project.'

JUPITER SPACE
Now

... that the boy has simply joined the dots the co-ordinates represent to produce a simple and elegant picture. One hoof raised, its head turning towards him, a unicorn looks out from the pad's screen.

Buried memories surface, the tension in his body unwinds and clenches over and over. The man known as the Professional runs a hand over his face, taking in the changes: the removal of the Mukabis' implant has left a ridge of scar tissue at the back of his skull, his hair is cut back close to the scalp, there's a break in his nose.

His eyes stay fixed on the picture. Then a shadow falls across him and he looks up, blinking.

Unlike him, her appearance hasn't changed in the slightest.

In the four years since they left her in a Martian hospital she hasn't changed one bit. The hair hasn't grown, there's no change in body weight, no new lines on her face.

He's had a bad haircut and hasn't been acting like himself. But there's nothing so changed that she wouldn't have recognised him the moment she laid eyes on him in the airlock of Farside Station.

'Anji?' he says.

She tucks a strand of hair behind her ear, smiles. Not a warm smile. 'Well, well, if it isn't the real Slim Shady.'

She pivots, twists, one leg arcing around, heel connecting with his jaw.

His head snaps back. By the time he's regained his senses Anji is levelling one of the survivors' weapons at his head. She's learnt from the airlock too, taking a step back, out of reach so he can't disarm her. She doesn't say anything, just tightens her finger on the trigger.

His eyes flick left, tracing movement. Anji thinks it's a trick and ignores it. It's her one mistake, because a second later she's bowled over as a bear of a man brings her to the ground. Anji and her assailant roll apart, get to their feet. The gun is lying on the floor between them. They look at each other, then Anji gives the man a last glance and shakes her head.

Without a word, she turns and walks away; not back into the safety of the compound, but straight into the enemy lines and on towards the exit.

Fires and smoke fill the compound, screams of pain and fear drifting across the air. The hulking shadows of the enemy pause, then begin to retreat. It's a slow movement at first; they have no confidence in what they're doing. Then, almost as one, this caution is gone and they march towards the entrance where Anji Kapoor is waiting.

The lights are out and the hallway beyond is impossible to see.

One by one the enemy slip past Anji and on into the dark. Across the wreckage of the compound, Anji locks eyes with him once more. Then she takes a step back and is lost to shadow.

There's a cut on his shoulder and his sleeve is wet with blood, but Robertson doesn't really feel the pain. His head is spinning, his pulse thumping.

The attack is over.

When his gun was empty he'd used it as a club, and only when the club was broken had he fallen back. He'd reached the Meridian just in time to see Anji getting ready to blow the Professional's head off. If he'd given it any thought, he wouldn't have stopped her. But he'd carried on running, catching her before she could fire.

And now, it's over.

There's something different, though.

The Professional looks the same, but he moves like a different man. There's a weariness to him and the clipped military movement has gone. He's looking at his hands and his armour like he's never seen them before. And there's a freedom to his face that wasn't there before.

The Professional looks at him and frowns, like he's trying to remember: 'Robertson?'

Robertson's eyes narrow. 'Who are you?'

'A pity you didn't ask that days ago,' the Professional answers.

'Anji said –'

'Anji isn't quite herself at the moment,' the Professional whispers. 'There's been a lot of that going around.'

'Who are you?' Robertson demands.

'We've met before,' the Professional says. 'You spoke to me through a cell door. I asked you about research capsules and breakages.'

The face that's been so cold breaks then, filling with life. The smile isn't in his mouth, but in his eyes, because as he speaks it seems to Robertson that they shine. 'I'm the Doctor.'

Anji moves through the corridors of the Station, fast but assured. The enemy follow, oversized bodies and awkward limbs crowding the space behind her.

All the way through her preparations on Mars and the journey here, looking for the Doctor and Fitz had been a good cover story. It fitted her background, offered a plausible motivation. The only problem was she'd never expected to find either of them alive. They were four years dead.

Which had made that first encounter in the airlock interesting.

She'd known straight away there was something wrong with the Professional's face. The face of a dead man. There'd been no emotion in that face, no life or soul. Set flat against the world, its lines spoke of hardship not joy.

Fortunately, although she likes to plan for the future, Anji's always been able to improvise. It was obvious very quickly that he had no recollection of her, subsumed in his role as a Professional. Obvious too which urban myth the Professionals really were. The question had been how to use that knowledge to her advantage.

Achieving this has pushed Anji to her limits in the past few days. She's had goals of her own: understanding what happened on the Station, what it's being used for, how she can help facilitate that process. But in trying to find those answers, she's had to keep the Doctor off the scent. She didn't know him well, but she saw enough to know what he was capable of. Even buried under Earth Forces' armour with his mind locked behind a face of stone, he was a threat.

* * *

The Doctor slips the cable home and the defences hum back into life. He doesn't think the enemy will be coming back, but it's best to be prepared. There are things that need to be done and he doesn't want interruptions.

The survivors are clustered together, the Meridian a makeshift triage unit. He looks at them working for each other: washing wounds, tightening bandages, comforting the injured. There are still no dead, but half of them are injured, and a half-dozen of those have life-threatening wounds. And everyone touched by the enemy has the threat of madness looming over them.

He glances at the blood work on the computer screen.

Everyone except Anji, it appears.

Easter approaches, wiping his hands. There's a bandage wrapped around his head. The Doctor guesses he has a mild concussion and really shouldn't be practising medicine, but there's no opportunity for bed rest.

'It was Anji,' Easter says. 'There's something wrong with her, isn't there?'

'Yes,' the Doctor replies. 'One small mistake can lead to the gravest of situations. And there's been more than one mistake made here.'

'What is that thing?' Easter nods at the screen.

'A virus. Something from Jupiter's atmosphere, something that escaped on to the Station just before the Fall.'

'It doesn't look like any virus I've ever seen.'

The Doctor looks at the screen, trying hard to put the pieces from the past few days together with ones from four years earlier. To join the dots.

'I don't think it's a natural phenomenon,' he says. 'There's a pattern to the behaviour, a level of resourcefulness that suggests this virus was built rather than evolved.'

Anji can imagine the Doctor right now, sitting down, trying to figure things out.

How long, she wonders, will it take him to know what she knows?

It took years for the virus to work its way into her mind. Beyond defining her goals, the virus hasn't delivered any level of awareness. You can feel a cold's impact, but would never know what it's thinking.

Her theory goes like this. Whatever the virus encounters, it attempts to take over. Those first humans it encountered – the squaddies who attacked her in the New Jupiter Café – it tried to overwhelm with brute force. Only they were more resistant than expected. The resulting neurological conflict drove them mad.

'Just like it drove the pilot of *Pegasus* mad,' the Doctor says.

'I still don't see how any of this connects to Anji,' Easter says.

'She received a nasty cut in that fight, the virus was passed on.'

'So why isn't she insane?'

The Doctor points at the screen. 'What are the defining characteristics of this virus?'

'Resourceful, adaptable.'

'Exactly,' the Doctor says. 'Trying to force control over a human didn't work, so it developed a softly-softly approach.'

It's only in retrospect that Anji is able to see how the virus worked its way into her system. She hasn't aged, which suggests it operated in sympathy with her body, boosting its immune system, stealthily working its way into her genes.

And as it did that, Anji's perceptions of the world changed.

It took four years, but the virus got its way in the end. Anji's never been able to forget Jupiter, it's part of the virus and so it's part of her, and over the past few weeks that memory has become a need. The virus generates instincts, not ideas, and she's felt compelled to get to Jupiter, that there's something here she's missing, some purpose she's supposed to fill.

The discovery of the Station's continued existence crystallised that instinct in her head and provided her with the vehicle to interpret the virus's goals. Looking for answers about the Doctor and Fitz allowed her to look for the answers to her own questions.

What is it that's drawn her here? What links the virus to this place?

'What does it want?' It's Robertson approaching, a bandage on his shoulder.

'Good question,' the Doctor says. 'One I couldn't answer four years ago, one Anji's been trying to stop us from asking. Why? There's a purpose to its actions, so what does it want?' He smiles. 'I didn't have all the evidence. Not until now.'

'What evidence?'

Walking the Station corridors, being with the survivors, searching the files. All these things have prompted more of those instinctive responses from the virus. Combine those feelings and senses with Anji's own deductions, and she's finally got a good idea of what's happening, what it is that drives the virus and has, as a consequence, been driving her.

Anji imagines David's transformation is the clue the Doctor needs to work it out.

Without the virus riding his system, he wouldn't have recognised what she had realised about the substance covering the Station's surfaces. He would have needed to see it in action before guessing its purpose.

'When David touched the rust on the barricades, his hand burnt. That's the evidence.'

'You're still talking in riddles,' Robertson snaps. 'And I've had enough of this.'

'The rust,' the Doctor says. 'The rust that's prevalent everywhere on this station except here. It's a weapon.'

The virus has one goal, Anji knows. Something that's written into its being and, as such, it's the motivation she's been working under.

Destruction.

Not random carnage, though. This aggression is targeted.

'We'll call our virus Fear,' the Doctor says. 'And you need to understand its purpose to understand its actions. Like any suspect in a crime, you look for motive, means and opportunity. Its access to the computers four years ago provided opportunity. The rust and this station are the means. Which just leaves motive.'

'You said it was built,' Easter replies. 'That suggests it doesn't have a motive of its own. It would be something it was programmed with.'

'A weapon,' Robertson says. 'A biological weapon.'

'Yes.' The Doctor nods. 'But what would the purpose of such a weapon be?'

There's a pause, then Easter says, 'To destroy its enemy.'

'And that,' the Doctor breathes, 'is what I was missing four years ago.'

When Anji came to Jupiter she didn't really know why. She recognised the trigger – those pictures of its weather patterns stirring recognition – but didn't understand it. It took time in Greenwich Village to appreciate the virus's goal, to figure out what it was that had made her skin crawl from the moment she woke in that cage.

The virus controlling her has an opposite.

'If our virus is called Fear,' the Doctor says, 'we'll call its opponent Loathing.'

'Another virus,' Easter says. 'In Jupiter's atmosphere?'

The Doctor nods.

Easter shakes his head. 'Too big a coincidence.'

'It isn't coincidence,' the Doctor barks. He glares at Easter. 'Humans. Too self-important and obsessed with your own history to think beyond it. You're not the first race to walk among the stars.' He slams the palm of his hand against the terminal. 'Why conduct weapons research in space? Why not Brasilia or Munich?'

'There's a danger to civilian populations if –'

'Exactly,' the Doctor snaps. 'You're not the first species that ever wanted to protect itself. Not the first that needed a safe place for research. The scientists here were in an arms race. Racing time, unknown enemies, each other.' He breathes deeply, calming himself. 'Think about Mars: one virus released in retaliation for another. Something similar happened on Jupiter thousands of years ago. Only here it was two weapons, both with very similar aims and abilities.'

'Jupiter was a testing ground in an arms race.'

'Or a last battlefield,' the Doctor says. 'We'll probably never know which. Either way, Fear and Loathing have been locked in a stalemate for millennia, just waiting for something to break the deadlock.'

'Us,' Easter says.

The Doctor nods. 'A virtual replica of Fear got loose on the Station, using everything it could find to destroy Loathing. And it kept on looking and testing until it found a way to win.'

The rust, Anji knows, is a weapon. An advanced biological weapon whose reassuring touch can mean only one thing: it's been engineered to kill off the opposite once and for all.

The virus that's controlling her likes to use things. To bend them to its purpose. Wherever they've come from, somehow the creatures behind her are in the same thrall as Anji herself. They all serve the same master: the virus. And so they all have the same enemy: the virus's opposite.

Anji is guessing these creatures, the survivors' enemy, were responsible for sowing the seeds for the new biological attack against the opposite. That for the past four years the body of the Station has acted like a giant Petri dish, slowly being transformed into this weapon.

'Fear used the Station computers to leapfrog the limits of its evolution. It worked out a formula for a new weapon that was advanced enough to eradicate Loathing. You only have to look at how the rust burnt David's hand to see how effective it's been.'

Easter shakes his head. 'No, that doesn't make sense. How would David be vulnerable to –'

'He's been infected by Loathing.' The Doctor looks at Robertson and Easter. 'Every one of your group has.' He gives them a moment to absorb this, then asks: 'Do you remember the *Pegasus*?'

Robertson nods.

'On some level, when the pilot tried to destroy the ship in Jupiter's atmosphere he was attempting to carry out the virus's mission. He'd dived into a pocket of Loathing, some of which attached itself to the ship.'

The Doctor pauses; remembers Valletti being called away from dinner for a sensor glitch in the docking bay, remembers Jason McCray washing down the ship's hull, remembers the stain on Jason's journal, his tests, feeding the results into the computer for analysis.

'Fear detected Loathing on board. It blew the *Pegasus* up in an effort to destroy it, tried the same again when it found it in my quarters. It didn't matter; enough survived the *Pegasus*'s destruction to infest this docking bay.' The Doctor looks at them both. 'Over the past four years, you've all been touched by it. The ReGene unit simply rebuilt David according to his mutated biology.'

The Station, Anji has worked out, is a bomb.

The changing weather patterns around them will deliver its yield all over Jupiter, decimating the opposite. The only thing that isn't immediately evident is what constitutes the detonator.

However, the presence of the enemy, their ReGene unit, and the way they recognise and react to the virus she carries suggests a plan. The virus has no substantive physical presence; it can only use and influence what is around it. As it has with the rust, the survivors and the enemy.

The detonator must be on board the Station. And there's only one place it can be. With the enemy still following, Anji rounds a corner. The energy barrier shimmers in front of her.

The Doctor shakes his head. 'I'm sorry,' he says, 'You're not fighting a war. You never have been. You're just caught in the crossfire from someone else's battle.'

There's a pause, then Easter says, 'One thing. I understand, at least, I think I understand what you're saying about this virus.'

'Yes?' the Doctor prompts.

'The body, the one we found before the Fall, the one we thought was Jason. That was you?'

'I'd been badly hurt,' the Doctor nods. 'My DNA was in flux; a cursory scan would have found just enough to make a match.'

'How is that possible?'

There's a long answer to that, the Doctor knows. One that involves his body's regenerative qualities. When he'd been hurt, he'd felt something pushing through his blood. A chemical release that had finally purged Fear from his system. It felt like a precursor to a bigger event, like a caterpillar wrapping itself in a chrysalis. As if some physical change was coming.

If his body were capable of that it would be a natural version of a ReGene unit, reaching out across the link, trying to find a pattern to base the repairs on. But as soon as he'd noticed it happening, as soon as he'd thought about it, it had stopped. As if a shutter had come down across that part of his mind.

This is the long answer. It's not the one Easter is pushing him for.

He looks at them, unflinching, and says, 'Because I'm not human.' There's a pause. 'You need to decide whom you trust.'

Anji has a plan. For now, all it involves is waiting.

As she waits, the enemy cluster around her. They seem confused. At some level they recognise the virus within her; probably from when they tasted her blood during the fight. It's what drew them to mass against Greenwich Village, it's why they've been following her like pets ever since. They seem uneasy just waiting.

Anji wonders if they understand her. Says, 'Sit down.'

There's a moment's hesitation, then they follow the instruction.

Anji smiles.

Easter and Robertson have gone, leaving the Doctor alone.

It felt good to put the pieces together. It distracted him from the memories.

One hundred years ago he'd woken on a train, the sound of the engine in his ears, smoke and steam in his mouth. He had a name – Doctor – and a note leading him to a rendezvous a century distant, and that was all.

He'd thought not knowing was the worst thing that could happen to a person. To be cut adrift from your past and left to find your own way.

Robertson and Easter have left him alone and he knows now there are worse things than not knowing. Because he remembers.

He remembers talking to Fitz Kreiner four years ago. *This ball bit is where the important people live*, Fitz had said. *Whereas out here is where you find your minions. And never the twain shall meet.* The Doctor had been impressed, but had somehow barely ventured out of the central hub, spending his time with command and the researchers. He'd barely been glimpsed by the people out here. One face in a crowd, seen for a moment in moments of chaos. Four years later it was no surprise they hadn't recognised him.

'There are worse things than not knowing,' he whispers.

The Professional is a construct, a personality implanted in his head by Earth Forces, his own mind buried by conditioning and drug therapy. The Professional, he knows, is not him. But everything the Professional has done, he remembers.

His body learning unarmed combat at Marineris base. His hands stripping down a plasma rifle. His eyes absorbing mission briefings.

He remembers looking at a purple sky and three silver moons. Explosions echoing down the valley, the distant scream of a dropship's engines. The splash of movement as the insurgents wade through marshland towards him.

He remembers a young man among them, arms and shoulders on fire; the residue of magnesium charges that will never burn out. He remembers the sight resonating with something forgotten inside. He remembers the chill of medication pumping into his arm. And he remembers raising the plasma rifle as the young man nears.

Another mercy killing.

'This is not who I am,' he whispers.

It feels as if his whole body is sucked into those memories. His knees buckle and he stumbles, catching himself. And he stops then, breathing hard, looking at the thing he is holding on to. The crutch he has propped himself up against.

Has he come so far only to fall again?

'This is not who I am,' he says.

He is dimly aware of noise in the background. There are shouts and raised voices over a constant murmur of conversation. Robertson, Easter, the rest of them, wondering where to go from here.

The Doctor pushes up on the crutch. Slow steps, regaining his balance, turning to where the meeting is. He holds the crutch in one hand, looks down at it, then back to the survivors. The first step is hesitant, the second stronger, the one after that stronger again.

By the time they see him, those steps are a stride, infused with passion and purpose. His eyes are locked, unwavering, on the centre of their group and the survivors part before him, the noise and hubbub dropping away.

He pauses, turns, lets everyone see him.

They looked at him like this before, when he was the Professional.

The same mix of uncertainty and wonder. Only last time those looks also held hope for the future. Hope now replaced by fear.

This is not who I am.

He takes the crutch in both hands, raises it high above his head. And, in a sudden snatch of movement, brings it down as he snaps his right leg up. The plasma rifle breaks over his knee, links popping, components shattering, trigger falling away. His hands open and the two halves fall to the floor, sputtering, sparking. Dying.

'Everyone is getting out of here alive,' he says. '*Everyone.*'

The first thing he does is repair the ReGene unit. Robertson watches the Doctor tear it open, furiously rewiring the innards. When he's done, he mutters Sara Mukabi's name and says, 'Two can play at that game.' Then he starts running a sample of David's blood through the machine. Robertson can't follow what's happening. According to Easter, he's refining it somehow.

Robertson leaves them to it.

He finds Caroline on their bunk, a blanket around her shoulders, a blank look of defeat on her face as she smiles at him.

'I got it wrong, Robbie,' she whispers. 'I got it so wrong and it nearly cost us, it nearly cost us everyth–'

'Hush,' Robertson says as he sits down next to her. She fingers the cut across his shoulder. He smiles. 'It doesn't hurt too much.'

'This place.' Caroline shakes her head. 'It's this place. It isn't me, Robbie, it was never who I am.'

And Robertson laughs. 'I know. I know who you are, remember?' He turns her face towards him, gently kisses her forehead. 'I never forgot. Neither did you. This place? It's just a place, Caroline. It's just a place.'

Caroline says nothing, looking away as her lips tighten and her body stiffens. Robertson pulls her to him, wraps his arms around her as her head presses against his chest and her body shakes, shivering with cold and years of tiredness and exhaustion.

Her body shakes with tears.

They sit like that for a long time, holding on to each other, only breaking apart when they hear footsteps approaching.

The Doctor raps on the door frame. 'Sorry to intrude,' he says, 'but I need help. Someone to get the people here organised.'

'For what?' Robertson asks.

'Escape,' the Doctor answers. 'There's a lot to do and they need to be ready. Everyone needs to know the rendezvous point, everyone needs to take responsibility for getting at least one of the Wounded there.'

Caroline wipes her tears. 'The Wounded can't travel. We don't have the –'

'You'll have help. There'll be medical teams here within the hour.' He nods outside. 'Easter's going to be busy and –'

'I'll do it,' Robertson says.

The Doctor smiles. 'You're not the one I'm asking. It needs to be someone everyone knows and respects.' He pauses. 'Not that they don't respect you. It's just that you're coming with me.'

They're running down the corridors now. Robertson wears Anji's spacesuit: the joints and seals expand enough to make it adaptable to each wearer, but it's still a snug fit. He's taken enough radiation in the past couple of days so he doesn't see how wearing it makes a difference, but the Doctor's insistent.

And it's the Doctor who's in the lead, pausing at a junction to get his bearings, then turning left, off the safe paths, in towards the central hub.

'Anji's smart,' he explains. 'She's probably well aware of what's happened here. If we're going to make it out alive, we need to regain the initiative.'

'I don't understand.'

The Doctor runs his fingers along the wall, lifting some of the rust. 'This Station is a bomb waiting to be detonated. Fortunately the fuse hasn't burnt down yet.' He drops down through an open set of lift doors, beckoning Robertson after him.

'Primarily because it's safe behind that.'

The energy barrier shimmers above them. The Doctor examines the sensor readings from his suit, nodding to himself. 'Just as I thought. The power's dropped off a fraction over the past couple of days.'

'Am I here just to ask questions?' Robertson says.

'No,' the Doctor answers. 'I need your help.' He nods at the barrier.

'Your energy barrier is actually a suspension of stasis fluid. Very volatile and, given the right stimulation, the kind of liquid that will increase its volume exponentially. When Fear got the chance, it gave it just that stimulation.'

'Exponentially?' Robertson says. 'How come it didn't swallow the whole Station.'

'The air pressure was adjusted, slowing the expansion long enough to run an electrical charge through the cloud. At just the right frequency to solidify it. That charge is wearing off. In a few weeks' time the suspension would dissipate, releasing everyone and everything inside.' The Doctor leans over, begins adjusting controls on the suit Robertson is wearing. 'We need to get into the central hub before Anji does.'

'She's going to light this fuse?'

'That fuse has been burning down for four years; Anji just wants to stop me snuffing it out.'

The Doctor finishes his alterations and unravels a lead from the suit's wrist unit. He positions Robertson on one side of the lift shaft then crosses to the other and extends a lead of his own. 'When I say, all I need you to do is insert the probe into the suspension.'

'And what will that do?'

'We're releasing a countercurrent to the one holding the suspension in place. Ready? Now.'

Robertson plunges the probe into the energy barrier. Nothing happens. He glances across at the Doctor, who's studying the screen on his wrist.

'The Mukabis' lab is on level six,' the Doctor says. 'How far from there to the reactor controls?'

Robertson shrugs. 'Another half-dozen floors. Why?'

'We're not going to have much time.' The Doctor nods at the energy barrier. 'Get ready to take hold of my back.'

Robertson can't see it at first. Then a ripple flows across the black surface. And then the energy barrier shakes and begins to dissipate before his eyes, pockmarks appearing in its surface suddenly disguised by a gaseous haze. A suspension of stasis fluid, the Doctor said. Now dissipating, retreating back up the lift shaft.

* * *

Anji still can't guess what the energy barrier is, but she's sure the Doctor knows. And if he knows, he's likely to collapse it.

Because he'll have worked out what Anji's worked out. The best detonators for this biological weapon are the Station's fusion reactors. So Anji has placed herself at the ready on level twelve, as close as she can get to reactor control.

The enemy begin to shift uneasily. Anji looks over her shoulder.

The energy barrier is vanishing.

Noise echoes where there has only been silence, light filters down previously dark corridors. People, machinery, the hum of electrics. Whatever the plan to overload the reactors is, the Doctor's going to try to thwart it.

She looks at the enemy, tells them: 'The man I was with. Find him, kill him.'

Movement catches Fitz's eyes and then he sees him, a man of fire, freeing himself from a blazing backdrop, clothing alight, skin blistering and burning. Stumbling across the laboratory for some kind of safety. He falls, rolling across the floor, trying to put the fire out, mostly succeeding. Another explosion puckers the floor between them and Fitz can't reach him, can only watch as he pulls himself away from the flames, begins to stumble to his feet, to run.

Fitz hears Valletti cry out, 'No!'

Only then does he see the danger. The Doctor is stumbling towards one of the doors that had opened as the 101st fled the room. One that opens on to an empty lift shaft.

'Stop him!' Fitz cries. An ache is building in his ears, his breathing is getting heavy. It feels like he's drowning. He can see Valletti, stranded in no man's land, halfway between the Doctor and the comms panel. She turns, activates the intercom: 'Defcon 1! Repeat: Defcon 1!'

The Doctor reaches the lift door, teeters on the edge as the flames lick his back, then pitches forward into darkness.

'No!' Fitz screams.

As he screams, there are explosions all around him, glass cracking.

There's a moment of cold disorientation and Fitz shakes his head, blinking hard to clear a stinging from his eyes. Jason is flailing against him. Through blurred vision Fitz sees Valletti by the comms panel, coughing; Sara Mukabi trying to find a way through the flames to her husband.

Fitz should be looking for an escape route, but he can't help himself. He skirts the fire, edging towards the lift shaft. There's a whistle of air and a thump as something hits the wall near his head and he stumbles backwards, falling over.

'What the –'

There's an electric whine and two figures – one clinging on to the other – spring up over the lip of the shaft. There's a click as the lead figure disconnects the grappling line from his spacesuit.

Fitz blinks through the smoke at one of the figures. 'Robbie?' he says. Then he takes a good look at the other man, looks past the shaven head and broken nose, and sees –

'Isolate the reactors!' the Doctor shouts.

He walks through the flames towards Valletti. 'We're short on time, Jennifer. If you want your crew to live, use your command codes and isolate those reactors now!'

Valletti looks at him for a long moment, her mouth wide open. Then she sees something and a dark look crosses her face. Fitz thinks she's only just recognised the Doctor, that she's about to pull a gun or something. Instead, she turns and enters a code into the comms pad.

The Doctor nods, satisfied. 'Thank you.' He looks at Valletti. 'What made you trust me?'

'The insignia,' she says. 'On your armour. Marineris base.'

Robertson is working on a wall panel and seconds later sprinklers burst into life.

The Doctor reaches down, grasps Fitz's hand, hauls him to his feet. 'How are you, Fitz?' he asks.

Fitz's mouth opens silently as he studies the Doctor's face. Then he notes the damp residue over the nearby surfaces and his own clothes and skin. A faint trace of electric-pink, just like… He turns, sees the stasis capsules smashed behind them and finally answers: 'Suspended animation. You?'

'Burnt to the brink of death, ejected, rescued, restored, mind-wiped and drafted into Earth Forces' Special Ops.'

Fitz sucks his teeth, nods authoritatively: 'Same old, same old, then.'

'If it hadn't been for the last remnant of AuDoc trying to remind me who I am, I might still have been playing with guns.' The Doctor turns to Valletti, contempt flashing across his eyes. 'The Professional programme at work. Brainwashing alien prisoners into thinking they're human, press-ganging them into fighting for Earth. You strip away every trace of personality, culture, who they are.' He shakes his head. 'As you said, a monstrous abomination.'

Caroline Arquette feels the Station judder. Moments later the lights flicker. She's standing at the door of Greenwich Hospital, marshalling the rest of the survivors.

'Robbie,' she whispers. 'What are you doing out there?'

'Four years?' Sara Mukabi scoffs.

'He's not talking to you,' Fitz snaps. The Doctor smiles a 'thank you', then returns his attention to Valletti, who is taking damage reports from her staff.

'Tell them to check the computer systems for the reactors,' the Doctor says. 'There'll be an overload routine buried in there somewhere, something set to trigger as the stasis field collapsed.'

Valletti nods. 'They've already found it.' She looks at Terrance Mukabi. 'What do your systems say?'

'Same as C&C. We're several thousand kilometres down in Jupiter's atmosphere with a disparity between the chronometers in the central hub and the outer rings.' He looks at his wife. 'A four-year disparity.'

'Your stasis fluid, pervasive enough to stop cellular decay and halt computer systems in their tracks. Another triumph of misjudgement.' The Doctor looks at Valletti. 'I can't explain everything right now, but you have to trust me. If we're going to get everyone off this station I need your help.'

Valletti shakes her head. 'It's a lot to take in, Doctor. I can't forget –'

And then Fitz realises that the Doctor isn't even looking at her any more. The door to the lift shaft is still open and there's a sound echoing through it.

The Doctor pulls Valletti aside as something huge appears in the open doorway. Fitz sees a confused blur of motion as Robertson raises his gun and fires. The thing in the doorway leaps towards the Doctor, who takes hold of the creature as it flies at him, pivots and tumbles, flipping it over his head. He doesn't let go as it rolls, but holds on, riding the movement, and as the creature lands on its front the Doctor is somehow on its back, reaching up into the chaos of the wreckage and snatching a cable.

There's a burst of electrics, blue flashes strobe across the lab, then it's over.

Fitz looks over to the lift shaft, sees shadows moving. 'There's more of them.'

'Have you got control yet?' Valletti shouts at Terrance Mukabi.

He nods. 'I think so.'

'Then shut the damn doors and activate the security nets.'

As the Doctor pulls the fizzing cable away from the creature's head the lift doors slam shut. Beyond, Fitz can hear the familiar sound of pinpoint lasers.

The Doctor looks at Valletti. 'You wanted proof?' he says. 'Take a good look.' He points to the creature's limbs. 'Remind you of anything? A sword and a scythe, perhaps?' Then he reaches down and pushes the spider-like head forward, revealing the blackened patch where he plunged in the electric cable. There's a hint of silver in its centre. 'Or how about that?'

Jason McCray has been sitting curled up in a corner since Robertson treated his burns. He unfolds himself now and crosses to where the creature lies, frowning at it, reaching towards the metallic shape with one hand, touching the back of his head with the other.

Fitz blinks. 'That's one of those implants, isn't it?'

'Because this is one of the 101st.' The Doctor draws a lead from the wreckage, slides it home in the implant.

He glares at Sara Mukabi. 'I don't think much of your safeguards. Each one downloaded with a set of simple instructions. Go here, do this and continue until told otherwise.'

A computer screen flickers with information. Chemical equations; a map of the Station, certain areas highlighted; a half-dozen sentences of text.

'Design for the ReGene unit,' the Doctor mutters to himself. 'Formula for the rust and where to seed it. Indicators for the presence of the biological virus.' He pulls the lead clear of the implant and turns to

Valletti. 'Take a look. The eyes, the skin, the joints, the way they move. Those familiarities that Earth Forces have worked so hard to create? The atmosphere filters, the bottles of wine? These creatures are intended to create the opposite reaction.'

'Alienation,' Valletti says.

'I wonder whose files our virus got that idea from?'

Fitz realises Robertson has been looking at the enemy body, thinking something through. 'The ReGene unit,' Robertson says. 'The 101st used it to turn themselves into this?'

The Doctor nods. 'Fear needed you to keep the Station intact. It kept the reactors safe and the command staff neutralised behind the stasis field. It left the rest of you outside to make sure the Station survived long enough to complete its transformation.' He gestures to the prone creature. 'Those men lacked the knowledge to do that. But a few commands downloaded into their implants were enough. A design to program into the ReGene unit, then orders to keep you fighting for survival, stop you thinking too hard about what happened.' He pauses. 'You've done well, but it's no coincidence that all the people you needed were in the outer ring when the Station fell.'

As the Doctor speaks Fitz realises exactly what the rogue videoscreen he saw was. The Doctor's virus, running simulation after simulation, until it found the right combination of events and personnel to achieve the outcome it was after.

Valletti is staring impassively at the creature. Her eyes are fixed on the shining metal of the implant. 'Collective strength can be a terrible weakness,' she says.

'Yes.'

'You told me that.'

'Yes.'

'I didn't believe you. I should have.'

'There's still time,' the Doctor says. 'Please, do as I asked.'

Valletti looks up at him and nods. She activates the comms panel: 'This is Commander Valletti. I am ordering the evacuation of this facility. Medical staff report to the docking bay with supplies of sedatives, and follow the orders of Lieutenant Easter and Technician Arquette.' She glances at the Doctor, who nods. 'All other personnel assemble in Recreation Hall One in the North Tower immediately. Standard procedures are voided. All personnel report to the North Tower for evacuation.'

Valletti releases the switch, turns back to the Doctor. 'What now?'

'I need access to the Station's transmitter,' the Doctor says. 'Beyond that, it's up to you.'

Valletti nods and draws her side arm. She looks down at the creature, a sword and a scythe in place of hands.

'The best and the brightest.' She shakes her head bitterly. 'Now look at them.'

She raises the gun, turning towards the Mukabis. 'The Riley Act was passed for a reason. There's people and there's technology. And one's got no place dictating the feelings of another.'

Sara snarls, 'This isn't something you can –'

Valletti looks at Terrance. 'Get your wife out of here. Stop to collect any of your data and I'll shoot you myself.'

'You've no right to –'

'This is my station, my command,' Valletti barks. 'You operate here under my authority, in my name. And I never should have agreed to this project.'

She pushes Sara Mukabi out of the way and studies the console for a moment, one hand resting on the controls. Then she raises her weapon and fires into the heart of the computer banks. 'Project Avatar dies with this station.'

Corridors silent for years resound with noise. There's confusion – reports of alien creatures breaking from the lift shafts and a civilian pushing through the central hub – but purpose also.

Some areas are unsafe, others blocked. The shock as systems four years out of synch attempt to reintegrate with dilapidated and jury-rigged equipment produces fires and short-circuits. The network of controls and thrusters that the survivors have been using to control the Station's position begin to misfire.

The Station shakes and bucks beneath them as the exodus begins.

O'Connell is asleep at the shuttle's controls when the signal sounds. Dreaming of a bar he knew back in Marseilles, he jerks awake, an imaginary *pression* at his lips. Three days of extended orbit with old sports and older movies, waiting for a call that's never going to come. Except the signal he's receiving now shows a unique tag. The Professional.

O'Connell swears and opens the channel. The eyes are there, cold and unblinking.

'Prepare for intercept,' the Professional says.

'What?' O'Connell manages, then looks at the co-ordinates on the screen. He shakes his head, checks the reading from the *Charing Cross*'s subspace buoy, then says, 'There's nothing there. You're twenty clicks below that position. An escape capsule is never travelling that far in a straight line in this weather.'

'That's where I want your shuttle and I want it there in less than thirty minutes. On your way in, you're going to vent the auxiliary fuel tanks, then flush them and pump in clean air. You have your orders.'

'There's nothing there!' O'Connell answers.

There's a pause as O'Connell realises what he's just said. The Professional looks out of the screen at him. 'You know me, O'Connell. You know what I'm capable of. If you're not at that rendezvous point, you won't have to worry about Earth Forces discovering the bribe Kapoor gave you. You'll have to worry about me.'

The screen clicks off. For a moment O'Connell thinks about breaking orbit and burning the engines all the way back to Mars. He thinks about it.

You'll have to worry about me.

Then he tips the nose down for atmospheric entry and starts purging the fuel tanks.

Valletti insists on coming with them. This is how her people survived the past four years and she needs to know what happened. As they push on through the outer rings, she's amazed at the Station's condition beyond the central hub. As they close on the docking bay, they begin to pass survivors coming in the opposite direction.

Some are faces she recognises. But just like when she caught sight of Robertson in the Mukabis' lab, these are not the people she knew but phantom versions of them. It's hard to take in, difficult to meet their eyes. As they pass, she nods encouragement, tells them to keep moving.

Further on, and they meet a chain of people carrying stretchers, shepherding confused and half-naked men and women.

'Holy Mother,' Valletti whispers.

Caroline Arquette is there, directing the efforts as the medical teams subdue the insane and hand them over to those who are escorting them to the North Tower. It's a dark and dirty life they've lived, and Valletti wonders how on earth they managed to survive in this place. Then she feels a hand on her arm and finds the Doctor at her side.

'You trained them well,' he says. 'They survived this because you showed them how.'

Another ghost face appears before them. Joshua Easter, dark shadows beneath his eyes, lines on his face. He's pushing a trolley containing four glass canisters.

'This is as much as I could get,' he says to the Doctor. 'The repairs burnt out halfway through the –'

'This will be fine,' the Doctor assures him. He looks at Easter and then Robertson. 'Are you ready?'

They nod and he smiles at Valletti. 'The quickest way to the defence bays, please?'

Easter and the Doctor disappear around the corner, following Commander Valletti. Robertson knows the way, though, and can catch up. He pauses as he reaches the barricades. He knows what's coming and he knows that, whatever happens, he's never returning to this place.

He looks up above the doors, to the unevenly painted letters marking this Greenwich Village. His fiefdom once upon a time, the community he helped build. It feels like he's lived his entire life here.

Across the compound, past the showers he helped to rig and the computer terminals they built and the habitats they scraped together, he can see his wife. She's working hard, pointing and shouting at the orderlies, making sure everyone's accounted for. And then there's a moment when she suddenly finds herself with nothing to do and her head falls forward, a brief surrender to tiredness.

Robertson remembers a girl with a wicked smile who would dance all night.

The entrance to Greenwich Village is dark with shadow and he knows she can't see him. He looks at her as she picks herself up and starts pointing again, and he smiles.

'I love you,' he whispers, then turns and starts after the others.

The reactors throb, energy flaring up one enormous tower and down another.

Fitz is standing on the gantry that runs around the edge of the room. Passing the last remaining technicians on the way in, he'd smiled and told them to contact Commander Valletti if they were worried about what he was doing there. He suspects they were too busy running for their lives to follow his advice.

'Amateurs,' he mutters, then takes another drag on his cigarette.

The Doctor's instructions were clear and easy to follow. He'd left Fitz with four things to do. One he accomplished on his way; the second he completed two minutes ago. Since then, he's been standing there, leaning back against the reactor control console, waiting for the third thing on his list to turn up.

When he hears her footsteps Fitz flicks the cigarette away, watches it spiral into the darkness below. Then he looks up and smiles. 'Hi, Anji.'

'Oh, look,' Anji says. 'The comedy sidekick. No dumb blondes or beer down here.' She doesn't break stride, just continues walking around the gantry towards him. 'Get out of my way.'

According to the Doctor, both Anji and the 101st were infected by the same thing; only Anji got the real Fear virus while the 101st had its virtual version download itself into their heads. According to the Doctor, both Anji and the 101st have been working to destroy Fear's enemy, the other virus, the one the Doctor called Loathing. According to the Doctor, Fitz shouldn't worry about what he's got to do because it's not really Anji.

All of which is very easy for the Doctor to say because he's not the one who's going to have to stop her.

Fitz draws the pistol Valletti found for him. 'You don't need to do this,' he says.

'Because somewhere deep inside part of me is still fighting this? Deep down I just don't want to do this? Well, let me tell you something –'

'No,' Fitz says, nodding at the console. 'You don't need to do this, because I've already done it for you.' He sees her eyes flick to the controls, scanning the readouts. 'The reactors should blow in about twenty minutes.'

Anji continues walking towards him. A few more steps and she'll be within touching distance.

'And if you're worried about this gun,' Fitz says, 'don't be. It isn't for you.' He turns and fires three times into the console, wrecking the controls. 'I think you'll find that countdown is now pretty irreversible.'

Anji stops walking, looks at the console in confusion, then turns back to Fitz as he takes a step forward and punches her in the head. The butt of the gun connects with her temple and she crumples to the ground.

Fitz tucks the gun into his jacket, then bends over to hoist Anji up over his shoulder. With one hand holding her, he uses the other to place another cigarette in his mouth.

'Amateurs,' Fitz says, shaking his head.

O'Connell's shuttle closes on the rendezvous point. The weather's kicking him around the cockpit and he's worried about his fuel levels. The *Charing Cross* can rendezvous when they make open space. But while the auxiliary tanks are clean enough to host a dinner party, they're not going to help when the time comes to clear Jupiter's gravity well. He can hold position for maybe fifteen minutes, but that's it. After that, even if the Professional does make it, there's little chance of clearing Jupiter's atmosphere.

O'Connell checks his instruments. The Station is still twenty clicks below and there's no indication of any incoming vessel.

He shakes his head. 'I should have run.'

Robertson's keeping watch down the long corridor that leads into the defence bays. Behind him the Doctor and Valletti are slotting the third of Easter's glass canisters into a waiting torpedo. Robertson squints into the distance, then calls over his shoulder: 'I think they're coming.'

'I love a dog with a good sense of smell,' the Doctor says, snapping a cover into place. 'Detonators set, safeties disengaged.'

'Lock and load,' Valletti mutters, sliding the torpedo home in a launch tube.

The Doctor slams the cover behind it, raises his hand over the firing controls. He looks at Robertson. 'Ready?'

Robertson nods and the Doctor presses the fire button. The room shudders as the torpedoes launch.

The Doctor counts down on his fingers. 'Five. Four. Thr–'

'They're here!' Robertson shouts, backing across the room to the other exit.

None of them hears the torpedoes detonate. The room is suddenly filled with noise as the enemy sweep into the chamber.

Robertson stumbles, but the Doctor catches his arm, pulls him upright. Valletti is in front, reaches the exit first. A claw scythes the air behind the Doctor and Robertson, and they throw themselves through the doorway. Valletti activates the locking mechanism and the door slams down behind them, the enemy battering against it.

'Now!' the Doctor says. Further up the corridor Easter is crouched next to a conduit, feeding the last remaining canister into the environmental controls. The purple liquid drains away, reappearing as gas inside the defence bay. The hammering on the door gets more and more intense.

'What is that?' Valletti asks.

'A concentrated dose of Loathing,' the Doctor answers, 'extracted from David Verger's blood.' He peers through the glass window, watching dispassionately as the 101st thrash and fall. 'I only hope the torpedoes are having a similar effect on the Fear living in the atmosphere.'

O'Connell's own deadline is getting closer and he's still wondering what the hell the Professional's playing at. Then the shuttle kicks with hard turbulence. O'Connell looks out of the cockpit and sees what's happening. Jupiter is going crazy around him. He checks the sensor logs.

Something detonated in the atmosphere thirty seconds ago and whatever that something was, Jupiter really doesn't like it.

Beneath him an enormous storm is brewing up out of nowhere. A tremendous bubble of atmospheric pressure, building higher and higher; in five minutes' time it'll be enough to distort the planet's silhouette.

O'Connell is suddenly having to fight to keep his shuttle in position, but he has a reason to fight. Because the perimeter alarms are sounding now, as the turmoil raging below pushes the Station higher and higher in the atmosphere.

'There's only ten,' Valletti says. They're standing in the middle of the defence bay, the enemy unconscious around them. Along with Easter and Robertson she's been loading their bodies on to the mag-trolleys that normally carry munitions. The Doctor is crouched near the entrance, studying a gouge in the wall.

'One of them escaped,' he says. 'I think it's probably McCray.'

'How can you tell?' Easter asks.

The Doctor points across to the far wall and ceiling: there are scratches and gouges along both surfaces. 'The one that escaped climbed the wall and fled across the ceiling the moment the gas started, indicating a level of tactical awareness. It was also the first one in.'

'McCray,' Robertson nods.

The Doctor checks his wrist. 'Just over ten minutes.' He points to the trolleys. 'Get them to the North Tower, you'll find transport waiting. Count them in, Jennifer. Count every one. No one gets left behind.' He begins to move, trotting away into the dark of the corridor. 'I'm going after McCray.'

'There isn't time!' Valletti calls after him.

His answer echoes down the corridor: 'No one gets left behind.'

'Can you operate one of these?' Robertson asks, indicating the mag-trolley.

'Yes,' Valletti answers.

'Good.' Robertson pushes the trolley towards her. 'Get it up to the North Tower, Commander. Get your people home safe.'

'What are you doing?' Easter cries as Robertson heads towards the entrance.

'He's strong,' Robertson replies, 'but he'll never be able to carry one of them on his own.'

* * *

By the time he reaches the North Tower Fitz realises that the smoking-while-carrying-Anji combination has done little for his cardiovascular system. Gasping for breath, he lays Anji down, then pushes through the heaving mass of people, working his way into the centre of the recreation hall.

On the way, he glimpses someone he thinks is Caroline Arquette, her arm around one of the sedated women. There's a hardness to her body now, a knife strapped to her thigh and a lost expression on her face. She doesn't meet his eyes and Fitz doesn't have time to talk.

Reaching the middle of the hall, he pulls a metal object from his jacket pocket and, raising it above his head, thumbs the device into life.

When the Doctor detached it from his spacesuit he said it was some kind of beacon. Looking through the glass ceiling, into the chaos of Jupiter, Fitz wonders who on earth is meant to be receiving it.

And then a shape appears out of the haze.

A snub-nosed ship, battered by the winds, slowly drops towards them. There's a moment when it swings about, perilously close to the glass roof, and Fitz can see right into the cockpit. It's impossible to hear the pilot's words as he looks down and sees the Station personnel crowded in the hall, but there are certain phrases Fitz can lip-read a mile off. Sonofabitch is one of them.

The ship swings around again, and returns with more purpose. Landing feet emerge from the undercarriage, the joints contorting to match the shape of the roof. As the ship drops, Fitz realises how delicate this operation is. It looks incredibly stormy out there and one wrong move from the pilot is going to crack the ceiling and kill them all.

Instead, the ship's touch seems light as a feather and there's a hiss as the feet secure against the glass. A fat tunnel extends from the underside of the craft, a blue light shining where it touches the ceiling. Fitz is awestruck, and only just gets out of the way as a twenty-foot wide circle of glass falls away and shatters on the dance floor.

He finally gets a good look at the ship. The tunnel has formed a seal against the glass. In the centre of the circle it creates on the ship's hull, a set of doors are now sliding open.

'Right,' Fitz says, as a ramp unfolds through the hatch. 'All aboard that's coming aboard!'

The Doctor can hear Robertson's footsteps behind him.

McCray may not have been overcome by the dose of Loathing, but he's slowed down enough for the Doctor to be confident of catching him, speed-wise. Direction-wise is another matter.

Reaching a junction, he pauses.

'Which way?' Robertson asks.

'Good question,' the Doctor replies. He raises his hand, listens intently. Any sound is lost to the creaking of the Station's hull and the increasing throb from the reactors. 'Outer rings or the central hub?'

'He's still McCray?' Robertson asks. 'Underneath all that stuff, inside, he's still McCray?'

'With a few key instructions hard-wired into his cerebellum, yes.'

Robertson turns left. 'The central hub.'

'Why?' the Doctor asks, following on behind.

'Four years,' Robertson replies, 'and all everyone's wanted is to get back the life we knew.'

'Of course.' The Doctor nods. 'He'll be looking for a place where he feels in control. The Avatar room.'

Valletti watches as Easter pushes the second mag-trolley up the ramp and into the shuttle's interior. The survivors have been giving the trolleys a wide berth, unaware exactly who their enemy has been.

Fitz is standing with her at the base of the ramp. 'The pilot's opened the hatches into the empty fuel tanks. It's a bit of a squeeze and it doesn't smell that good –'

'But there's enough room for everyone,' Valletti says. She watches as the last of the Wounded is guided up the ramp. 'Exactly 226 accredited personnel, plus the half-dozen off the books, one child and your friend Anji.' Valletti looks anxiously at the Station interior; reactor noise is reverberating down the corridors. 'Come on, Doctor.'

'Robbie's with him.' Valletti turns. It's Caroline Arquette, standing at the top of the ramp. Jason McCray is hovering at her side, his clothing charred, one side of his face puckered with burnt skin. 'He's with him,' Arquette repeats, 'isn't he?'

Valletti nods.

The Station judders. There's an ominous creak from where the shuttle is perched on the ceiling and its engines rise in pitch. The pilot's voice crackles over the intercom: 'We can't wait. I'm burning too much fuel just holding position here.'

Valletti smacks her fist against the intercom. 'This is Commander Valletti. You hold as long as you have to, are we clear?'

'I play the percentages,' the pilot replies. 'You've got one minute, then we're leaving.'

Valletti raises her hand over the intercom to reply, but the energy drains from her face. And she nods her head. 'One more minute.'

The intercom goes silent and Valletti turns to Fitz. 'He's right,' she whispers. 'He has a responsibility to these people. So do I.'

Jason McCray is starting down the ramp towards them, brow furrowed with concentration, one hand reaching up to hold the back of his head.

'Don't worry,' Fitz says. 'They'll make it.'

The Station rocks and the ominous creak becomes a roar as the seal loses contact and Jupiter's fog breaks through to swallow the ramp. Fitz doubles over, grabbing Valletti's arm, and they blindly push back up the ramp towards the safety of the shuttle. Then the pilot makes an adjustment and the seal's good again, and the fog begins to dissipate.

Eyes blinking, Fitz looks around. He and Valletti are alone on the ramp.

The lights are flickering in the lab. The Doctor looks around at the chaos. The stasis tubes lie in pieces, the bodies they held scattered like discarded waste. He wanted to set them free. He knows he should stop, offer some words of remembrance and apology for not being able to help them, for not making their final release any more dignified.

He kneels next to one body.

A blue-skinned female, a hint of scales around the cheekbones, blown pupils in green eyes staring at nothing at all. The wound that consigned her to the stasis tube cuts across her chest. He looks at those eyes, then reaches down and draws the eyelids closed.

He would like to do the same for all of them, but there's simply no time.

'He's up in the cables,' Robertson says.

The Doctor looks up and a flash of electricity catches McCray, his body hunched over, wedged in the darkness between machinery and burnt conduit. The surging reactors are causing more and more overloads and the Station is shaking beneath them.

There may be a little leeway in the Doctor's countdown, but in around five minutes' time the reactors will buckle, and the Station will be scattered on Jupiter's winds. He doesn't want to hurt McCray, but he's running out of options.

O'Connell glances at the clock set in the shuttle's cockpit.

The extra minute he allowed has gone. When he reaches for the intercom his message is going to be simple: whoever's outside has ten seconds to get up the ramp or they're left behind, whatever their rank.

Except his hand never connects with the intercom. Because as O'Connell leans forward, an arm slips around from behind, something cold and sharp pressing the flesh of his neck.

'It's quite, quite easy,' the Knife whispers in his ear. 'My husband is still on that Station. You can put your hands –'

'The fuel levels,' O'Connell says. 'I'm carrying twice the maximum payload and it's already touch-and-go on getting –'

The blade twitches against O'Connell's neck and he falls silent.

'You can put your hands on the controls,' the Knife repeats, 'you can use them to keep this shuttle docked. But try and disengage before he is on board and I will slit your throat.' A pause. 'Nod if you understand me.'

O'Connell nods. His eyes are fixed on the fuel reading as the gauge drops into the red zone.

The grapple lodges in the pressure tank to McCray's right. The Doctor tests the line – a good hold – then activates the motor. There's a tug of gravity, then he's airborne, carried up through the lab's air.

A sharp twang and his momentum vanishes, and he tumbles backwards to land hard at Robertson's feet, the grappling line snaking down around him. The Doctor looks at the frayed end. 'He cut the line,' he says, looking up to where McCray is retreating back into cover.

'He doesn't want to be saved easily, does he?' Robertson says.

A power lead ruptures in the roof and sparks cascade around McCray who cries in pain and confusion.

'Three minutes,' the Doctor says.

'I'm sorry,' Robertson says, 'but we're out of options.' He raises his gun, training the sights on the ceiling. Sensing what's coming, McCray shrinks further back into the machinery.

'Wait!' the Doctor cries.

'I'm only going to wing him,' Robertson replies. He squints, begins to tighten his finger on the trigger.

Then he feels a hand close on his and he turns.

It isn't the Doctor who takes the gun from his hands and tosses it away. Jason McCray is standing next to him, looking into his eyes.

Jason smiles, shakes his head, then steps back into the centre of the room where his brother can see him clearly. He looks up to the rafters, holding out a hand. His voice is clear and true. 'Fighting's over, John. Time to go home.'

There's a long moment of stillness, the four of them motionless as steam billows and flames gutter and the Station aches around them.

Then a tiny piece of plating tumbles from the ceiling, clattering on the floor next to the Doctor, dislodged as John McCray climbs free of his hiding place. He skitters down over the first storey of machinery, then drops over the edge of a gantry to land on the floor next to his brother.

McCray carefully extends an arm, the edge of his scythed hand softly connecting with Jason's burnt cheek. His disfigured head, with its hard carapace and multifaceted eyes and distorted mouths, tilts to one side as Jason nods at him.

There's a hiss from deep inside the Station. The floor judders again and the hiss becomes a roar.

'That's the reactor containment wall,' the Doctor says. 'We need to run.'

It's been more than a minute, both Fitz and Valletti know that. They exchange glances, neither saying a word. If the pilot's giving them longer, so be it. But as the Station begins to tear itself apart they begin to wonder how much longer they can wait.

Power surges at impossible levels through the cabling, scorching the carpet at their feet, tracing long lines of flame over the wall. The room is filling with smoke and Fitz and Valletti retreat up the ramp towards safety. Then a violent movement throws them off their feet and there's an ominous creak.

Through the smoke Fitz can see a spidery crack spreading across the glass dome. 'Oh, no,' he whispers.

Valletti pushes him in the small of his back, forcing him up the ramp. 'Go!' she barks. 'We're out of time.'

Fitz pushes against her, turning to protest. As he does so, he sees them. Four shapes pushing through the smoke and flames. 'There!' he shouts.

Three men running; the twisted oversized form of McCray bounding forward.

'Go!' the Doctor shouts. 'Go!'

And as he nears, Fitz can see him mouthing something else: 'Anji?' And Fitz nods in reply: job done.

Valletti hits the controls to retract the ramp, shouts into the intercom: 'Get us out of here!'

Fitz ducks out of the way as McCray's monstrous form jumps, landing on the ramp and crowding the entranceway. The Doctor is next, the air hissing as the shuttle begins to lose its atmospheric seal. Fitz doesn't know what Jupiter tastes of, but it isn't pleasant. McCray reaches down with a claw, dragging Jason up on to the ramp.

Coming in last is Robertson.

Too big, too slow, too tired from four years of hell to keep pace.

O'Connell feels the Knife twitch at his throat as the big man comes into view through the cockpit window, and there's suddenly no doubt who his captor's husband is.

The one coming in last.

O'Connell's already started to disengage the landing struts and the Knife hasn't objected. Her husband is last but he's going to make it.

He switches the intercom to a view of the ramp. Jupiter is starting to creep in and fog the view. It's cramped, but they both see her husband make the jump and clamber up on to the ramp. As the ramp retracts O'Connell hits the switch that will close the hatch beneath it, and turns the ship's nose upwards, preparing for their one chance at getting out of here. Then something hits – hard wind shear or debris from the Station – and the shuttle jerks.

And they both see it. The big bear of a man, the Knife's husband, stumbles and falls, back between the closing hatch doors.

'Stop,' the Knife says.

O'Connell just clicks the viewscreen off.

'Stop,' the Knife says, but O'Connell carries on and activates the shuttle's thrusters, pushing them up away from the Station.

'I'm sorry,' he says, 'but it's too late.'

There's a moment of silence. Then a clatter of metal on the floor, followed by clumsy, broken footsteps as the woman stumbles away.

Then someone reaches down by the side of O'Connell's chair, picks up the knife and places it safely on top of one of the consoles. The Professional.

O'Connell wants to punch him. 'We don't have enough fuel to clear the gravity well.' His hand reaches for the control to the shuttle's main burn. 'But if you're going to go out, you may as well go out fighting.'

'Better not to "go out" at all.' And the Professional's hand closes over O'Connell's before he can fire the engines.

'Patience, Mr O'Connell,' he says. And then the Professional does something extraordinary. He smiles. 'If a plan works once,' he continues, reaching past O'Connell, manipulating the controls, tilting the shuttle's nose upwards, 'it'll work twice.'

'I don't –'

The shuttle rocks as the Station falls away beneath it, the bubble of pressure that's been holding it up finally breaking.

There's a long pause, then the sky in front of them flares a brilliant white. The flash of fusion reactors tearing themselves apart. Clouds billow and stream around them in the wake of the explosion and the shock wave catches the tail end of the shuttle, propelling it higher and higher. O'Connell just watches the Professional work the controls with one hand, balancing the shuttle, riding the wave, keeping the nose straight and true.

It's only as the momentum from the blast abates that the Professional releases his hold on O'Connell's hand, says: 'Punch it.'

O'Connell doesn't need telling twice. Everyone on board should feel the push of the engines and the pull of Jupiter's immense gravity trying to drag them back down. There are going to be nervous looks throughout the shuttlecraft, O'Connell knows, but there aren't any in the cockpit.

O'Connell's a seat-of-the-pants pilot. He knows his ship, knows what his controls tell him just by their touch; long before the canopy clears above and he can see the stars again, O'Connell knows.

They're going to make it.

The shuttle's interior is still cloudy, the ventilation systems still clearing Jupiter's atmosphere. Caroline Arquette breathes it deep, doesn't care, pushing past the Professional as she leaves the cockpit, heading back towards the hatch. She's going to be too late. By the time she reaches the hatch, the pilot will have fired the engines, and the Station and Robbie will be kilometres behind them.

She's going to be too late, but she can't give up.

Everyone's coughing, the atmosphere thick around the hatch. Caroline leans against a bulkhead for support, coughs hard to clear her lungs, then tries to get her bearings through the mist. She can make out Fitz, pulling Commander Valletti to her feet. Jason McCray is in one corner, the massive shape of one of the creatures crouched near by. A few of the Station personnel are crowded in the doorway opposite.

And then she sees him. There, in the centre of the hatch, lying across the join between the doors, breathing hard, trying to push himself up on to his knees.

'Robbie?' she whispers.

He rolls on to his back, reaches for his forearm to disconnect the line from the grapple that's embedded in the ceiling. He sees her, forces a smile. 'Neat trick,' he coughs. 'Doctor showed me.'

And Caroline Arquette sinks to her knees next to her husband.

His back arches as he coughs and he rolls over on the floor, looking straight down. And as he freezes, Caroline looks too. There's a glass panel in the hatch beneath them. The storm below is blowing itself out. As the shuttle tilts upwards they can see the Station, dropping away. As it falls back into the atmosphere, the pressures grow; the stresses of the past four years begin to show and pieces of hull plating fall clear, snatched by the wind.

The Station still retains an elegance that Caroline remembers from when she arrived years ago. The interlocking bridges and spires, the long curves that give it the echo of a spherical shape, and, in the central hub, lights still burning bright.

It's only when she looks away that she realises Robertson's eyes are still locked on to the sight.

She places her hand on his, intertwining their fingers.

'It's just a place,' she whispers.

His hand begins to shake beneath hers. Still he can't pull himself away.

Light shines through the glass panel, flares across his face. It only lasts a moment and as their eyes readjust, they can see it. The Station is being torn apart by fire. The explosions ripple out along its surface as it drops further and further away. Containment failure. Only moments are left.

Then the Station is gone from sight, swallowed by the planet below.

And suddenly the planet itself burns, the shock wave rippling out across the clouds. Caroline Arquette thinks of the rust that coated every inch of the Station's outer ring, infused by radiation, scattered on the winds.

Robertson's eyes are locked, hollow and unseeing, on the destruction.

Caroline pulls his face away from the panel, turning his head towards her. His whole body is shaking now, and as he looks around the shuttle it's in disbelief, tears welling in his eyes. She kisses him, tells him, 'It's only a place, Robbie. It's not who we are.'

He nods and sinks back against the wall, and Caroline sits there, holding his hand as he coughs and cries and looks at her. They can both feel the pull of G-forces as the shock wave hits and the engines burn. Jupiter flows over the outside of the window.

'We're going to be fine, Robbie,' Caroline says.

'I know.' He smiles, gasping and crying. 'But I never told you, and I should have, and I never told you.'

And Caroline can see it in his eyes, in the tears on his cheeks and the way his body can't stay still. She takes his hand, brings it up to her cheek, lets him feel the cool of her skin.

'Whatever it is, it's all right,' she says, 'I love you.'

'I know.' He pauses, then looks at her and explains: 'I saw a face once.'

HOME
Six weeks later

The lights are dim, but it doesn't matter. He knows the corridors of Marineris base too well.

It's like a dream in my head. It was me, but another me that I don't really remember. That's what Anji said, lying in a hospital bed.

What do you remember? he'd asked. A loaded question, so many different answers. *What's the last clear thing you remember?*

Anji had said nothing, but the Doctor saw it in her eyes. Dave Young incinerated by the planet hopper's engines. Running for her life on Earthworld. A mezzanine café on Mars.

We were going to have coffee, Anji answered. *There was some commotion. I looked around and then I was in a dream. This dream.*

The ReGene machines have been running a program he wrote on the journey back to Mars. They are slowly eroding every trace of the virus from Anji's systems.

He's been able to piece together most of Anji's past four years from public records. To her, those years are a dream fading fast. It's one that will echo through her life, but for ever remain on the edge of her consciousness.

If only it were that easy to rewrite the past.

He has spent six weeks slipping through the cracks in the sensor nets on Mars. Smiling at cameras, vanishing from view like a stage magician. McNamara is looking for him, has AI programs scouring the surveillance feeds for any trace. Unfortunately for McNamara, he trained his Professionals far too well. And the Doctor himself knows how to run silently.

He places his hand on the sensor pad. The light flashes green and the doors slide open. The chamber is dark, illuminated only by the screens surrounding the equipment. Although the sensor registered his handprint and allowed him access, the Doctor's willing to bet it also alerted McNamara. A chime sounding in his office, an urgent message flashed on to his desktop screen. Right now, the Doctor thinks, McNamara is probably signalling every Professional on the base, telling them to rendezvous with him in the conditioning chamber.

Being here leaves a sick taste in his mouth. His nose is thick with the scent of burning flesh. The machine in front of him is crude, but still sophisticated enough to capitalise on the fragile state of his mind after its link with Jason McCray.

He accesses the personnel records, finds the audio tracks from the chamber. Just over four years ago. He hits play. McNamara's voice fills the room, talking with one of the conditioning staff.

– *He's very resistant.*

– *You should have seen him. That body was burnt black. Unrecognisable. He's come a long way in a couple of months.* A cold laugh. *Almost looks human again. The imprint's always easier when they look human. Don't have to condition them to see a different face every time they look in a mirror.*

– *There's nothing human about these neural pathways.*

– *Can you break him?*

– *There's already plenty of holes to work from. Those butchers on Farside took care of that. We should be able to imprint the standard profile without too much trouble.*

– *There's a 'but' there.*

– *Almost all activity is being routed through the forebrain. The rest of it... It's like there's a part of his mind that's walled off.*

– *Break it down.*

– *I don't think we can. He can't access it. The pathways are closed. He might be able to reopen them himself, but it'd take hard surgery before we could even begin to –*

– *No, no. We don't want to risk losing him to some vegetative state. Run the imprint. We'll just have to keep an eye to make sure that nothing –*

The Doctor shuts the recording off, presses the delete key.

Then he looks at the machines around him. *The pathways are closed. He might be able to reopen them himself.* Could he do it?

If he used this equipment could he finish what they started on Earthworld? Could he remember?

Except he already remembers.

He remembers every minute of the last four years. Every step taken, every blow traded, every shot fired. He can smell burnt flesh, feel the calluses from his rifle still on his hand. Could he remember?

He shakes his head.

Don't even think about it.

There's a hiss as the door opens behind him. The Doctor doesn't turn. He knows what he would see. The squat form of a middle-aged man, flanked by mismatched shapes in armour.

'Good evening.' The Doctor smiles. 'I'm so glad everyone could join me. We all need to have a little chat.'

Anji has an awareness of what's happening.

The Doctor explained it to her.

The human memory is based around activity in the synapses, the junctions between neuron cells in the brain.

– Our most basic actions are governed by those synapses responding to the release of chemical transmitters, the Doctor told her. *Fear made itself one of those transmitters. Every time you accessed your memory, from the simplest of things like boiling a kettle, to deep-seated memory like childhood, the experience was filtered through the virus.*

– That was me, then? Playing those people off against each other?

– It was you, in the sense that it was your intellect, your instincts making the decisions. But it was a you whose priorities were generated through a filter. And in that sense, not you at all.

The ReGene program is clearing the infection from those chemical transmitters, flushing the dendritic spine of the affected synapses. The machines will go back before the infection, find the pattern of older memories, use them to fill in the gap. The Doctor has warned her that some memories and feelings will be more intense as a result, but it's the only sure way to eradicate the virus from her system.

There is only one other issue remaining. The repair process will be completed in a few more days. If she is going to see him, she needs to do it now.

* * *

In years to come, Anji Kapoor will remember him. Not directly, but in years to come Anji will be married. As her husband wipes the table or prepares dinner, she will think she sees in him someone she used to know. Someone she will never directly remember again, someone who will only ever be an echo to her.

'Hello,' Michael says.

Anji smiles. 'Hi.'

There's an awkward pause, then he gestures at the door. 'I had to sign so much stuff to get in here. If I even breathe where you're –'

'It doesn't matter,' Anji says.

Another pause, then he settles down in a chair at her bedside. There are documents in his hand.

'Are those the papers?' Anji asks.

He looks at them, suddenly remembering they're there. 'Two sets,' he says. 'One set like you asked for, giving me everything. The other's a standard decree nisi, splitting communal assets right down the –'

So like him, part of her thinks, to be so clever and reasonable about it. 'I don't want any of it,' she says.

He shakes his head. 'It wasn't that bad, Anji, was it? We were in love once, weren't we?'

The memories are dim, every day eroded bit by bit, but there's still enough there. Anji can still just remember.

Chestnut hair against the sunset the first time they met. The big case he was carrying across Boone Plaza when he recognised her. Taking the train to Jacksonville and dancing in a club built out of an old nest, bass beats running across her skin. The touch of his hand, fingers gripping tight on bare shoulders. Pasta boiling on a stove. Laughing with Jenna and Clair and Otto on the staff picnic. Champagne in a restaurant as a dust storm builds outside. Plunging from the Martian sky to wrap herself in his arms.

'Yes,' she says, 'we were in love.'

He holds out the papers, his signature already on them. As she goes to take them he pulls them back, looks her in the eyes. 'I don't know what's going on, Anji. I don't know why you're stuck in the middle of a bloody military hospital and I'm signing official secrets and everything. And I don't care.'

'Please don't,' Anji says.

'We could try again,' he says. 'Whatever's happened, we could try again.'

What could she tell him? Any hint of the truth and he will dig and keep on digging until he learns everything that happened. Even if she listened to the part of her that wants to say yes, what would happen tomorrow or the day after when she wakes up and the memory of him is gone?

He would be a stranger, the life they had shared less than a dream. And her father and mother and Rezaul and her sisters, everything that her life was, will only be weeks in the past. Dave will have been gone for less than a month.

'I'm sorry,' Anji whispers. 'This isn't my life.'

Earth's gravity tugs at Jennifer Valletti as the transport starts to break against the atmosphere. A blazing trail, miles long, chases them across the Atlantic and on towards Europe.

The seat next to her has been empty all the way from Mars.

Somehow it's no surprise when he appears out of nowhere in the aisle, dropping down beside her. His hair has grown out again, three times as far and as thick as it should have done in the weeks since Jupiter, while the nose has straightened itself out.

'I've got a few questions,' she says.

'I thought you might,' he replies.

'Jupiter's red spot. They tell me it's no longer quite so bright. That it might even vanish completely.'

'Oh, I doubt that,' he answers. 'It's just a side-effect of that particular war coming to a close.'

'The weather systems seem to be behaving like you thought they would. Orbital tracking suggests anything released into the atmosphere by the Station's destruction is scattered across half the planet by now.'

'The other half to be coated within the next six months. Fear did its sums well.'

'But that weather isn't a coincidence, is it?'

'No,' he replies. 'Fear was obviously able to communicate the needs of its plan to its biological counterpart in the atmosphere.'

'Orchestrating the weather required.'

'Over that four-year period,' he nods. 'There are two possibilities for that communication. Either the virus had some kind of residual telepathic ability…'

'Or?'

'Easter said warheads were fired just before the Fall. They could have contained a chemical payload with the message encoded.' He shrugs. 'We'll never know.' He hands her a slip of paper. 'You'll need a marker buoy to keep Jupiter off-limits until the Station's payload destroys Loathing. When that's done, a dose of this formula should clear Fear too.'

'Don't want it getting loose again.' Valletti nodded. She gives the paper a brief glance, then slips it into her jacket pocket. 'Your friends are on board?'

'Back in economy. And I've got some cargo in the hold.'

'The woman, Anji, she doesn't remember anything?'

'No. Fitz doesn't know the details of what happened, but I asked him not to say anything anyway.'

Valletti nods, thinking about the faces of the people she passed in the corridors. The people she guided into hospitals on Mars. Tired and broken, struggling to come to terms with their lives again. They're good people, though, and Valletti is sure they'll adjust. But it's going to be a struggle.

'There are going to be hearings,' she says. 'They caught Archer on the *Charing Cross*, trying to upload data from an old storage device. He was signalling a defunct IMC transmitter on Titan.'

'Your stolen files,' the Doctor nods. 'Industrial espionage, of course.'

'Meanwhile, the Mukabis want me court-martialled,' she says. 'Collusion with alien infiltrators, loss of research.'

'The project was illegal, the research negligent at best. They're not in a position to complain too hard. Besides,' he says, 'I was working for Earth Forces the whole time. And you've got the only surviving copy of their data on a chip in your jacket pocket. The chip no one else saw you take from their laboratory.'

'Is that what you came for?'

Acknowledgements

Thanks are due:

My wife, whose copy-editing skills I never give the attention that's owed.

My friends and family, for the many years they've put up with me.

Sarah Stokes, who showed me it could be done.

Lance Parkin, for an advance look inside *The Gallifrey Chronicles*.

Paul Cornell, for the first small break, and Justin Richards, for the second big one.

The cast and crew of TAPE (Consultancy) Ltd, the world's finest performance piece on the Internet, for all the lessons on story-telling and assorted rantings.

Terry Joynson, with whom this would have been a co-write once upon a time.

Ian Gregory, Matt Kimpton, Bradley McGrath and Chris Payne for their comments on the original proposal.

Simon A. Forward, Mags L. Halliday, Craig Hinton, Mark Michalowski, Kate Orman, Lloyd Rose and Paul Dale Smith for their comments on the manuscript and making me feel welcome.

And, finally, my very own rogues' gallery, whose criticism and advice have proven invaluable during the writing of this book: David Ball, Philip Craggs, Steven Kitson, John Seavey, and Geoffrey D. Wessel.

We only learn from the dissenting voices.

'No,' he says. 'Fitz and Anji thought a couple of hours' sightseeing in Florence might be fun. I just came to say goodbye. You're free to do whatever you want.' He smiles. 'I should have trusted your judgement more on the Station. So I'm trusting it now.'

Valletti pauses. 'If I ask you something, will you answer it?'

'If I can.'

She switches on the seatscreen, calls up the item she saved two days ago. The news from just before they left Mars orbit. A man with unkempt brown hair addresses the camera. Behind him, a building in flames.

– not known exactly what caused the explosion. However, it is widely believed this area of Marineris base was the operational headquarters of an élite special-operations group –

The picture changes to a shot of wild-eyed man in uniform being treated by paramedics.

– would seem to be confirmed by the presence of this man, Colonel Benjamin McNamara, head of the Professional response program. However, there are genuine concerns that the cause of this explosion may never be known –

The screen is filled with a close-up of McNamara's face, confused and terrified.

– Professionals themselves are notable by their absence from this scene, while Colonel McNamara claims to have no knowledge of what happened. According to sources, he is alleged to have no memory of any events prior to the explosion and cannot even remember his own name or –

Valletti switches the screen off. She doesn't ask the question. The answer is there in his eyes: steel, satisfaction and just a hint of sadness.

'If you check the archives for that date,' he says, 'you'll probably find reports of several unidentified aliens being sighted.'

'Most of them around the Sheffield space elevator.' Valletti nods. 'Yes, I saw.'

'The Professionals have been disbanded,' the Doctor says. 'Every member receiving an honourable discharge.' He reaches down into the aisle. 'I've got something for you.'

He lifts the case up on to the table between their seats. At first Valletti thinks it's a replacement for the violin lost in the Station's destruction. As she flips the catches and opens the case, she realises it's no replacement.

'I had Fitz make a detour *en route* to the reactors. One final spot of breaking and entering.' He smiles. 'I hope you don't mind.'

Valletti nods and quietly closes the case.

She removes the chip from her jacket, turns it over in her hand. Sunlight shines through the window, catching on its edge. Below them, the steel blue of the Atlantic has been replaced by the glare of snow-topped mountains. The Pyrenees rather than the Dolomites or the Alps, but it's not the cold of space or the swirling mass of Jupiter or the red dust of Mars.

She's that much closer to home.

It's cold in Florence, the sun obscured by a chill mist. Damp, early morning weather that seeps into your bones.

She sees Fitz and Anji briefly at the spaceport as the Doctor makes arrangements about where to meet them and where to deliver his cargo. Then his friends vanish into the subway and he returns to her side. With a smile, he picks up her case and they walk on into the city.

It takes a couple of hours to reach the centre. Which is fine; two hours makes the timing almost perfect. They walk through the Boboli Gardens, climbing the long hill up from the fountains as red squirrels jump between the trees on either side, then on through the courtyards of the Pitti Palace.

A few hundred yards down the street is the Ponte Vecchio.

'It's the only bridge to have survived the Second World War,' the Doctor explains. 'The Nazis mined all the others as they retreated.' He pauses, frowns. 'But you probably knew that already.'

She nods. The bridge's span is crowded, shops and homes hanging chaotically over its sides, but in the centre buildings give way to a trio of arches that look out over the river. The sun is climbing higher now and the mist is beginning to burn off. Another hour and this will be a beautiful day.

Valletti slows and stops, leaning against the railings. The computer chip is still in her jacket pocket.

Out on the waters, a rowing crew glides out of the mist. The movement of their arms is strong, slow and graceful as they pull towards the bridge.

Valletti thinks about the last thing she did before boarding the flight.

A visit to a military hospital, standing next to Jason McCray. In so many ways, the only good thing to come of the whole disaster. However much Jason had infected the Doctor's mind, the Doctor had infected him in return; still nervous and unsure, but there was a semblance of sanity and order in his mind again. The medics were confident some additional therapy would leave him capable of leading a normal existence.

He had his life back once more.

He hadn't said much though. They'd both simply stood at a window, looking into a long isolation ward where his brother and old comrades lay. In theory, everything that had been done to their bodies had been done by a ReGene unit. In theory, what Earth technology had created, Earth technology could undo.

The reality was human bodies weren't meant to undergo that kind of radical reinvention. The carapaces were softening, the joints were reknitting themselves. Even the glands that had been primed to create doses of Nightmare, the thing that had kept the survivors at bay for almost four years, were now dissipating back into soft tissue.

The Doctor is standing behind her, still holding her bag.

She smiles at him. 'Even if they can regain human form, the medics say they'll suffer from nerve damage, arthritis, early onset of osteoporosis. They can't even guess at what's going to happen to their minds.'

'John McCray recognised his own brother,' the Doctor says. 'He knew to trust him. There's still hope.'

'Yes,' she says, 'but that's all it's ever likely to be. Hope.'

He smiles. 'Only hope breaks a chain.'

Valletti slips the chip from her pocket and drops it over the side of the bridge. The splash is lost in the stroke of the rowers' oars. 'I never liked that project. I don't like turning men into machines. I won't be a party to it.'

As expected, the shop front is dark. Four years and her father hasn't changed the locks. She opens the door, drops her case inside, then closes up again.

They cross the bridge to the other side. Valletti would normally walk along the river bank, but at the Doctor's insistence they continue through the Uffizi Gallery and on past the Palazzo Vecchio; decades since the occupation and reconstruction work is still going on. Building dust mixes with the scent of freshly ground coffee from one of the cafés. Then it's a right turn and on through the narrow side streets – the Doctor talking about the city's history the entire time – to emerge in front of the Basilica of Santa Croce.

Only now does the Doctor pause. Valletti looks at him and realises this is as far as he's coming.

He takes her hand in his and bends down to plant a kiss on her wrist.

'Make them listen to you,' he says. 'Make them see with eyes that are open.'

And then he releases her hand and walks away, back towards the river. His friends are waiting in a doorway, a tall blue box planted near by.

Valletti doesn't watch him go. Instead she turns and climbs the steps up to the basilica. It's dark inside and it takes a few moments for her eyes to adjust.

He is small and alone, seated at the front, his head bowed down. There's a gallery of candles before him. One, she knows, will have been lit by him that very morning.

Michelangelo is buried here, so is Galileo and, though his bones rest elsewhere, on the wall there is a monument to Dante. Valletti ignores them all as she walks down the aisle.

He doesn't turn around as her footsteps echo on the floor. He doesn't lift his head as she slips on to the pew beside him. His eyes remain shut as he continues to mouth his prayers. Only when he has done this, does his head lift and turn towards her, the thin line of his mouth breaking into a smile years in the making.

Valletti smiles back, takes his hand and says, 'Hello, Papa. I'm home.'

The Doctor watches as Anji smiles and disappears into the TARDIS's interior. 'Off for a quick bath,' she says. 'I always feel grungy after a long flight.'

'Why we had to get on that ship, I'll never know,' Fitz murmurs.

The Doctor fixes him with a look. 'I explained that. My control of the TARDIS isn't what it should be. But we're back on Earth now, which means all we need to get Anji home is a temporal journey rather than a spatial one. It should make things a lot simpler.'

Fitz nods. 'Next stop the other side of the universe, then.'

The Doctor frowns, glances at the door Anji left through. 'How is she?' he asks.

'She doesn't remember me punching her in the face,' Fitz says. 'She doesn't remember much of it at all.' He pauses, then says, 'I hear there's a lot of that going around.'

The Doctor looks up from the controls. Fitz is staring at him and for a long time they say nothing at all. Then the Doctor looks away. 'Memories aren't all they're cracked up to be.'

'We were going to have a conversation,' Fitz says.

The Doctor stays still. His eyes are open, but he doesn't see Fitz. He remembers a purple sky and three silver moons. Explosions echoing down the valley, the distant scream of a dropship's engines. The splash of movement as the insurgents wade through marshland towards him.

He remembers a young man among them, arms and shoulders on fire; the residue of magnesium charges that will never burn out. The sight resonating with something forgotten inside. He remembers the chill of medication pumping into his arm. And he remembers raising the plasma rifle as the young man nears.

He remembers all this.

He remembers the hundred years before as well. Boarding a space shuttle. The smile on his daughter's face. Alan Turing, unsteady on a bicycle. Another body, falling back into flood waters. The rocking of a railway carriage and soot on his tongue. He remembers all this, but nothing before it.

It's like there's a part of his mind that's walled off.
Break it down.
I don't think we can. He can't access it. The pathways are closed.

He looks at Fitz. There's something about his friend's face, an urgency, as if he desperately needs to tell him whatever he knows. But there's something else there. An anxiety, that he's afraid of what needs to be said.

How bad could it be, the Doctor wonders.

He remembers raising the plasma rifle as the young man nears.
Don't even think about it.

'Another day, Fitz,' the Doctor whispers. 'It'll wait for another day.'

Fitz looks at him. The Doctor can feel his eyes on him, studying his tired head, the way his hands grip the edge of the console, the angle of his shoulders. And Fitz nods, reluctant. 'Don't leave it too long. Like I said, this forgetting-things lark?' He taps his own head. 'There's a lot of it going around.'

The Doctor hears Fitz's footsteps, then a click as the interior door closes behind him.

He doesn't remember anything from before that railway carriage. But there are things that he knows anyway. That Fitz is his friend and he can trust him with his life.

He also knows his ship.

It's as old as he is, possibly older. It knows him better than he knows himself. He felt that the moment he stepped through its doors. The long curve of the roundels set back into the walls. The dusty smell of the books on the shelves. The comforting hum of the engines. The texture of the console beneath his hands. The whispers of light that trace through the central column.

What does he remember?

He remembers this. He remembers the feel of those switches, the potential behind those controls, the ability to travel anywhere, to any time, to any place. The wide open space of possibility before him.

His hand closes on the dematerialisation switch.

Next stop the other side of the universe, then.

He looks up. The light of the central column plays across his face, unlimited power just waiting to be unleashed.

The Doctor smiles and says, 'Let's go.'

And he throws the switch.

About the author

Nick Wallace is either: (a) deep undercover, infiltrating Afghan terror cells. Look for an anonymous star on the walls at MI6 soon; (b) down and out on the South Bank (if you're accosted by a smelly man with a scruffy beard, give him a quid, cos he could use a drink); or (c) a happily married father of one, who has spent the past decade working for a company who offer analysis and advice on script development and programme acquisitions for broadcasters worldwide.

Not one of these options is necessarily more likely than any other.

New series adventures coming soon from BBC Books

The Deviant Strain

By Justin Richards
ISBN 0 563 48637 6
UK £6.99 US $11.99/$14.99 CDN

The Novrosk Peninsula: the Soviet naval base has been abandoned, the nuclear submarines are rusting and rotting. Cold, isolated, forgotten.

Until the Russian Special Forces arrive – and discover that the Doctor and his companions are here too. But there is something else in Novrosk. Something that predates even the stone circle on the cliff top. Something that is at last waking, hunting, killing...

Can the Doctor and his friends stay alive long enough to learn the truth? With time running out, they must discover who is really responsible for the Deviant Strain...

Featuring the Doctor, Rose and Captain Jack as played by Christopher Eccleston, Billie Piper and John Barrowman in the hit series from BBC Television.

Only Human
By Gareth Roberts
ISBN 0 563 48639 2
UK £6.99 US $11.99/$14.99 CDN

Somebody's interfering with time. The Doctor, Rose and Captain Jack arrive on modern-day Earth to find the culprit – and discover a Neanderthal Man, twenty-eight thousand years after his race became extinct. Only a trip back to the primeval dawn of humanity can solve the mystery.

Who are the mysterious humans from the distant future now living in that distant past? What hideous monsters are trying to escape from behind the Grey Door? Is Rose going to end up married to a caveman?

Caught between three very different types of human being – past, present and future – the Doctor, Rose and Captain Jack must learn the truth behind the Osterberg experiment before the monstrous Hy-Bractors escape to change humanity's history forever...

Featuring the Doctor, Rose and Captain Jack as played by Christopher Eccleston, Billie Piper and John Barrowman in the hit series from BBC Television.

The Stealers of Dreams
By Steve Lyons
ISBN 0 563 48638 4
UK £6.99 US $11.99/$14.99 CDN

In the far future, the Doctor, Rose and Captain Jack find a world on which fiction has been outlawed. A world where it's a crime to tell stories, a crime to lie, a crime to hope, and a crime to dream.

But now somebody is challenging the status quo. A pirate TV station urges people to fight back. And the Doctor wants to help – until he sees how easily dreams can turn into nightmares.

With one of his companions stalked by shadows and the other committed to an asylum, the Doctor is forced to admit that fiction can be dangerous after all. Though perhaps it is not as deadly as the truth...

Featuring the Doctor, Rose and Captain Jack as played by Christopher Eccleston, Billie Piper and John Barrowman in the hit series from BBC Television.

New series adventures also available from BBC Books

Featuring the Doctor and Rose as played by Christopher Eccleston and Billie Piper in the hit series from BBC Television.

The Clockwise Man
By Justin Richards
ISBN 0 563 48628 7
UK £6.99 US $11.99/$14.99 CDN

In 1920s London the Doctor and Rose find themselves caught up in the hunt for a mysterious murderer. But not everything is what it seems.

The Monsters Inside
By Stephen Cole
ISBN 0 563 48629 5
UK £6.99 US $11.99/$14.99 CDN

The TARDIS takes the Doctor and Rose to a destination in deep space – Justicia, a prison camp stretched over seven planets, where Earth colonies deal with their criminals.

Winner Takes All
By Jacqueline Rayner
ISBN 0 563 48627 9
UK £6.99 US $11.99/$14.99 CDN

Rose and the Doctor return to present-day Earth, and become intrigued by the latest craze – the video game *Death to Mantodeans*. Is it as harmless as it seems? And why are so many local people going on holiday and never returning?

Recently published by BBC Books

Monsters and Villains

By Justin Richards
ISBN 0 563 48632 5
UK £7.99 US $12.99/$15.99 CDN

For over forty years, the Doctor has battled against the monsters and villains of the universe. This book brings together the best – or rather the worst – of his enemies.

Discover why the Daleks are so deadly; how the Yeti invade London; the secret of the Loch Ness Monster; and how the Cybermen have survived. Learn who the Master is, and – above all – how the Doctor defeats them all.

Whether you read it on or behind the sofa, this book provides a wealth of information about the monsters and villains that have made *Doctor Who* the tremendous success it has been over the years, and the galactic phenomenon that it is today.